THE BIRDS
OF BACHELOR
LANE

THE BIRDS OF BACHELOR LANE

HANNAH McNIVEN

POOLBEG

Published 2021
by Poolbeg Press Ltd.
123 Grange Hill, Baldoyle,
Dublin 13, Ireland
Email: poolbeg@poolbeg.com

A catalogue record for this book is available from the British Library.

ISBN 978178199-418-4

www.poolbeg.com

About the Author

Hannah McNiven is an Irish-born writer of Scottish and Irish descent. She has been longlisted (2017) and shortlisted (2018) for the Colm Tóibín International Short Story Award. Her debut novel *The Loves of Mrs McAllister* was published in 2020.

Acknowledgements

Thanks again to all the team at Poolbeg. To Mam, Dad, Dale and especially Dee for all their notes and encouragement when reading earlier versions of the story. Thanks to Mam again for all her knowledge about farming and socialising in her parents' day. Thanks to my accountant because I forgot to thank you last time, Polly! And thanks to Kate because I forgot to mention you last time – and I know I still owe you lunch.

To everyone who has encouraged and helped me along the way – you know who you are – thank you.

Dedication

To my glorious friend, Barbara McCombe.

Chapter 1

Ewan Cameron was not a local. Aside from the name that marked him as an outsider in a rural Irish community, his physical bulk exposed a sense of otherness to anyone who cared to look. And look they did.

Ewan was not the sort of man who could go unnoticed even though he made an effort to do so. But it was always a challenge when those around you were so keen to know each other's business and so prepared to discover the minutiae of acquaintances' lives by whatever means necessary. Yet, with a degree of success, the native Scotsman managed to maintain some privacy and remain an anomaly. Locals – mostly women – lamented the fact that they knew nothing of him, which is to say that they, in fact, knew a great deal. The real man, however, was held tantalizingly out of their reach. Part of the women's problem was that there were relatively few opportunities for them to either observe or engage with Ewan. He had the avoidance of public and social occasions whittled down to a fine art. He entered society only out of necessity – always in a hurry, always coming to the point of a situation – though he always offered a few pleasantries which prevented folk from thinking him rude and aloof.

Indeed, the opposite was more likely to be thought of

Ewan. He was respected by many – even revered by some – for his ability as a farmer and his quiet, well-mannered behaviour. He was a newcomer who caused no trouble. The pride the community took in their land and produce was not diminished by the addition of an outsider. It was enhanced by the man's new knowledge and techniques. And Ewan was always willing to listen to the improvements of others without judgement.

Yet judgement on him was still rife.

Everyone had an opinion. Everyone had a tale, an encounter and a verdict, all of which added to the mythology of Ewan Cameron. But since knowledge of the man himself was limited, much of the discussions focused on his appearance which clearly delineated the difference between him and the natives. Firstly, he was tall. He stood a good six inches above almost every local man and, at the commanding height of six foot four inches, towered over their womenfolk. But height alone did not explain away the allure of his appearance. The simple fact was that Ewan Cameron was a handsome specimen. It was not the kind of handsomeness that a rare number of adolescent boys possessed in the eyes of equally adolescent girls, but the kind that everyone noticed, whether male or female. While his length of limb did, of course, lend itself to the attractiveness of this Scotsman, once this caught the observer's attention, they found it difficult to look away.

Neither youthful nor unworn, it was the lived-in nature of his features that lent him a rugged rather than pretty handsomeness of a man in his late thirties. His skin was tanned and lined from exposure to the elements, but it was also burnished to a lively glow instead of burnt to papery dryness. A wide, lined forehead and deep-set eyes gave a darkness to his gaze that people, no matter how well they knew him, sometimes found deeply disconcerting if they caught his expression when throwing him a casual glance.

Their speech would falter, laughter would be cut short or they would visibly balk at Ewan's look. It seemed that he was aware of this particular effect as he would blink benignly and look away with a small smile playing on his lips, breaking whatever moment of fear or tension he had unintentionally created. This awareness of the effect he had on others was another reason for his guardedness. He was conscious of the admiration of others, especially women and young girls, and was sensitive to the dangers of such appreciation. He was flattered but also deeply uncomfortable to know that women spoke and generally approved of his appearance.

Aside from these prominent brow-bones that hooded his eyes (which in themselves were an object of speculation as no one was quite sure what colour they were), his high, pointed cheekbones added to the mystery of the man. They curled around the corners of his eyes, hugging the outer edge with each point sporting an irregular pitted scar. And while this scarring suggested that Ewan might once have gone a few rounds in a boxing ring – or outside of one – his overlong nose was perfectly straight – though when viewed in profile the bridge protruded slightly. However, the lower half of his face was a little less knowable. This was down to the fact that at certain times of the year, Cameron's jaws and chin were masked by a thick growth of beard – though not because of his liking of facial hair. It was more a case of whether he would rather an extra five minutes' sleep or a cleanly shaved chin. One could tell when Ewan was working hard by the length of his beard or lack thereof. Often, there was at least a smattering of stubble along the line of his jaw which was generally agreed a favourable addition to the handsomeness and mystery of this quiet, confirmed bachelor. Or so the locals thought.

Cameron would have continued in the same carefully carved niche if it had not been for the prodigious growth of his beard. The tight curls that masked his sharp features and shapely mouth were the very thing that ripped a permanent hole in his neat little existence of activity and self-denial.

It was the spring of 1953 when Ewan Cameron's life changed irrevocably for the second time in his thirty-eight years. The winter of the previous few months had been terrible. Storms felled trees and flooded rivers washed away every scrap of flora and fauna in their wake. This made life exceedingly difficult for Ewan as this year, more than any other, he had to make a success of his farming. He had expanded his flock by thirty ewes in October of the previous year, meaning he had nearly eighty head of sheep to lamb in the new year. Ever the industrious man, he had believed himself capable of taking half as many sheep again as he had the previous year, surmising that while one ewe was lambing, he might well be able to keep an eye on another who was giving birth at the same time. However, he did not increase his numbers on such naivety alone. Ewan knew his limits. He had farmed within them for many years and turned a good profit. But while money had its charms for Ewan, the growth of his flock was more of a chance for him to test himself and his methods, to see if they could work on a larger scale. It was also another excuse for him to shut himself off from society and plead he was too busy to leave the farm. Alone with his animals, he was content.

His farm was located eight or ten miles from the town of Enniscorthy. The house and yard were down a long dirt and stone track with grass, rolled out like a stair carpet, growing along the centre. Ewan's farm stretched along almost the entirety of the right side of the laneway, with the farm buildings halfway down the track so that the rest of the land fanned out around them for ease of access. The lane was book-ended by two other farms – one at the top of the lane, the other standing guard over the entrance.

The Top Farm was run by an enthusiastic but quiet young man and his widowed mother. The Gate Farm at the entrance was the property of a late-middle-aged widow – one Mrs Evelyn Burnley who shared the farmhouse with her eldest daughter and her youngest (and only) son. Given her position as self-appointed gatekeeper to the lane, Mrs Burnley was perfectly placed to exercise her natural talent for observing and later recounting any and all of the goings-on at the other farms. And then there was also the delight she took in telling anyone and everyone about the excellence of her own son's ability to farm.

In the eyes of Mrs Burnley, Young Bertram, her darling and only boy, could do no wrong. The truth was that Bertram Burnley was a mediocre farmer at best and, being in his early twenties, could only just still claim enough youthfulness to maintain his title of Young Bertram. In fact, many of the locals had a number of much less flattering epithets with which they liked to describe the youngest Burnley. There was nothing definitively wrong with Bertram other than his belief in his own self-importance which was fuelled by his mother's unerring praise. Listening to her talk, one might have thought Bertram was her only child but she, in fact, had several more. Most evenings, Evelyn was found at her writing desk crafting missives to one of her four married daughters. These letters included recipes (or, as she called them, *receipts*) for various dishes, instructions on cleaning, the raising of children, their education, their religious studies and any local "strange" she had picked up that day. And at the top of each and every single one of her letters was the address: *The Gate House, Bachelor Lane*.

It was a thing of great irony for Evelyn to find her abode in such a place. Each time she wrote *"Bachelor Lane"* in her neat curlicue script, she felt a little thrill of defiance, a stab of female pride at the fact that she had infiltrated such an address. But there was also still, despite an almost forty-year residency on the lane, a twinge of embarrassment that her address should have such an overtly male association. To her sensitive ears, being known as Evelyn Burnley of Bachelor Lane made her sound smutty and unrefined. When she gave her address, there was always the hint of a challenge in her tone which, in her opinion, negated the place's connotations. But when someone else gave it, she cringed internally. What did not help Evelyn's sensitivities was the reality of her situation. Bachelor Lane was home to three unattached men, a widow, Evelyn's eldest daughter Lilian Burnley (also single) and Evelyn herself. In her eyes, Bachelor Lane was looking all too much like its name suggested. Her family were no longer in the majority and, having previously claimed sole responsibility for providing the lane with more female residents than male, she realised that it was through her own manoeuvrings to marry off her daughters that this was no longer the case. The other more pressing issue, however, was that men starved her of gossip. They were less inclined to tattle, less inclined to call – less inclined to talk in general. And there was also the problem of no relationships or marriages to observe, comment on or criticise.

Chapter 2

A dark evening in early March found Ewan Cameron in a sopping gabardine coat that had long since given up keeping out any water. A constant shiver ran through his body as he trudged down the lane to a lower field opposite the Burnleys' farmhouse. It had been raining all day, turning the track into a muddy river. The drains either side had backed up again, clogged with sods of earth, dead leaves and grass. Having nowhere to go, water had flooded the path yet again. On previous occasions, Ewan had done his part in clearing the blockages to ease the backlog of water but now he just didn't have the time.

As he passed the Burnleys' he cast an evil eye over the house and quietly cursed Young Bertram's idleness. The drains always clogged outside their farm but the young farmer did nothing about it. The water overflowed its confines and spilled across the lane and through his mother and sister's garden around the side of the house. Ewan could see the ripple of milky-brown water cutting a stream over a flower bed, exposing the roots of shrubs, washing out newly planted primroses and unearthing tulip bulbs. They were slowly being dragged away by the constant flow of water that flattened the grass and left a debris of uprooted plants strewn across the garden. Ewan felt a brief twinge of sympathy for the Burnley women saddled with such a useless lump as Bertram. But he quickly quashed it. He had more pressing things to worry about.

The ewes were lambing at much too quick a rate for his liking. He also had a far greater number of twins and triplets than he had anticipated and, given the state of the weather, he was struggling to keep the damned things alive. As he walked along the headland just inside the ditch of the first field, he struck out with his shepherd's crook, savagely whipping through freshly sprouted briars that hung from it.

"You and your damned-fool grand schemes, Cameron," he muttered.

He ploughed on through the mud and knotted grass to the sheep field where he kept the yeaning ewes. He had other fields closer to the house but what with the bad weather and flooded lane he had decided to leave the sheep where they were. Besides, the shelter available in their current pasture was much better than the coarse gorse hedge of the other field. The real inconvenience was his own as there was greater distance between the sheep and farmhouse. But if the sheep were contented and safe, he tolerated the extra bit of effort required.

However, the sheep looked far from content when he reached the field. There was a large woolly group huddled under two giant conifers at the far end with stragglers scattered across the open space in the middle. Scanning the flock and paying particular attention to the headland, Ewan spotted what he was looking for but had hoped not to see: ewes lambing. There were at least three. No, four. He barely broke his stride as he cast about making sure there were no others in a similar state. No, just those four.

One was well on her way with two lambs already at foot but as she spun around her new babies, nuzzling and bleating at them, she turned her backside to Ewan exposing another lamb protruding from underneath her tail, its head and front legs exposed to the icy rain. Ewan changed tack and strode over to the ewe. Just as he approached, her final baby slithered out, landing on the grass with a wet splat and a snort of protest. The ewe took no notice of this new addition at all. All her attention was focused on her first two offspring who were already pitching drunkenly onto their blunt little noses, attempting to stand. As they skittered about on the slippery grass, their mother followed them doggedly, nudging insistently and making soft plaintive bleats. But as she did so she moved away from her final baby, leaving it to shiver in a puddle of quickly cooling amniotic fluid.

A guttural noise of frustration escaped Ewan's throat as the ewe and her two lambs tottered away. He pulled a length of sackcloth from under his coat. Dragging the lamb out of the pool of birthing fluid, he quickly deposited the tiny creature in the centre of the fabric and began to rub its coat vigorously. The cloth was a little damp but the friction quickly began to warm both man and beast. It really was a wee thing. It was a female with a head from poll to nose that was barely three inches long. Its body flopped limply about throughout Ewan's ministrations, dwarfed by his big gnarled hands as he scrubbed the cloth over the tight little curls of wool. Ewan hissed through his teeth as he did so. His hands were chapped and cracked with wear and exposure to the elements. He'd had similar problems with his hands previously but this year, with its terrible weather, constant dampness and the extra workload, the skin across his knuckles and palms had split and refused to heal. Between the rough sackcloth and the damp amniotic fluid of the tiny animal, his hands stung as if he had plunged them into a patch of nettles. He finally wrapped the lamb up in the cloth and tucked it under his coat to keep it warm, hoping that some of the tiny creature's heat would spread to him.

As he looked about at the other lambing ewes, he saw two had completed the task themselves and produced two healthy-looking lambs apiece. However, before making his way to the remaining ewe further down the headland, he made a quick check of the six lambs that had just been born, including the two siblings of the baby wrapped beneath his coat. All seemed well so without further ado he made a beeline for the final ewe.

She had one lamb at foot already and in the fading light Ewan could see another pair of legs sticking straight out from her rear end. Squinting into the dimness, he tried to fathom why the lamb hadn't simply slithered out. He broke into a stiff trot as he realised the angle of the little legs was slightly off: it was a breech birth.

Reaching the ewe, he bent quickly and pulled the lamb free. Straightening his damp-addled joints with a grunt, he held onto the little sheep's back legs and hung it, head down, to allow the fluid it had inhaled during its birth to drain from its lungs. It hung limp and lifeless in Ewan's hand until he dealt it a sharp slap on the ribs, making the lamb wriggle, jerk and snort, purging itself of the thick, suffocating mucous. It was another small lamb and even though it had started to breathe its movements were lethargic and weak.

The ewe swung her head and bawled crossly over her shoulder at Ewan.

"Oh, give over, you wee fool!" he said crossly. "Without me the wee bugger would be dead." The ewe continued to stare with bulging eyes. "And you didn't exactly bust yourself with them, did you?" He threw a hand wide encompassing the two sorry little creatures. They really were small – too small. "Damn."

It was the most Ewan had spoken in over a week, but he

never noticed. He was too busy sizing up the ewe, trying to see through wool, flesh and bone and discover whether she had another lamb waiting to emerge. As he watched, he noticed the subtle subterranean rippling heave of fresh contractions.

"Well, I hope it's bigger than the other two," he muttered.

It wasn't long before the ewe had dropped the final lamb on the sodden grass. It was considerably larger than the other two. Unusually, the second lamb was still the smallest of the set. It was still flopping about as Ewan attempted to prop it up to stand and suckle its mother, but it was too dazed by its less than dignified arrival to even attempt to stay upright. The other two were making a better fist of their first few minutes of life while their mother fussed over them. She began to slowly sidle away from the smallest as if she didn't want Ewan to notice. Another one, he thought. Wearily, Ewan pulled the other triplet from under his coat, opened out the cloth and placed the breech lamb beside it. He rubbed the second lamb briefly with the corner of the material, careful of his aching hands, and gathered them both up in the damp fabric. He took one more look through the gathering gloom for more yeaning ewes but, seeing nothing imminent, turned about and began to traipse back to the lane with his two abandoned babies.

As he walked on with them, he fought down the flutter of panic as he remembered that he had used the last of his supply of beestings – the rich colostrum or first milk that was so important for the growth of healthy lambs. Rich in antibodies and high in protein, it was vital for the two undersized and weak animals cocooned under his coat. Not only could he not afford to lose them, he did not want to. As a farmer he was relatively detached. He could deal with the inevitability of death. But if it was within his power to keep an animal alive, he would sit nursing it all night rather than risk leaving it to its fate. Indeed, he was not above bringing smaller animals into the bedroom of the farmhouse or sleeping alongside them in front of the range downstairs.

Another night-time vigil awaited him tonight. First, he would have to milk one of the freshly lambed ewes. There was a lame ewe in the field close to the yard who had yeaned just before he had come down to the lower fields. She would have to do. If he had been a weaker man, at this point he might have wept. He would have to walk back up the flooded lane, leave the lambs in front of the range in the house, go back out into the dusk, catch the ewe who, despite her lameness would put up a decent fight and then, to cap it all, milk her udder with his already aching hands.

Frustrated and already completely exhausted as he climbed over the gate to the lane, Ewan muttered a string of curses under his breath.

"*Mr Cameron!*" The shrill chastisement came from somewhere to his left.

Shocked that he was not alone in the world, Ewan nearly dropped the two lambs he had been cradling under his coat. The voice made him jump – made his heart thunder in his ears which, in turn, made his head hurt. He did not have the patience to deal with the interference of Evelyn Burnley on a good day when he was composed and well-rested. This was most definitely not a good day.

The lady in question appeared from behind one of the larger garden bushes bearing a glowing Tilley lamp. Ewan glanced at the lamp with longing, imagining its warmth and the comfort of its light washing over him. Its soft illumination made even the dullest evening more bearable. He had left his Tilley in the house, perhaps in the hope that if he didn't bring it with him he would find no need to use it. So much for that hope. However, looking beyond his neighbour's lamp, the romanticism of it was lost as he saw her stout figure, red cheeks and beady black eyes – the woman looked very much like an overgrown toad. In that moment, he truly hated Evelyn Burnley.

"Mrs Burnley." He nodded tersely and began to walk on.

"Now, now, Mr Cameron, I won't have you running away on me like that, now!"

Ewan would have liked nothing better than to continue running off and beg temporary deafness later when Mrs Burnley would ask him why he had moved on in such haste. Alas, the woman made use of his brief hesitation to park herself in between him and his route home. And a formidable form it was too. Evelyn was tall by local standards, raw-boned and paunchy. In other words, she was large and fat which meant she looked rather like something that, if upended, would wobble precariously then right itself like the most excellent of children's roly-poly toys.

Nevertheless, Ewan made an attempt to evade her.

"I'm sorry, Mrs Burnley, but I have to get these wee lambs up to the house." He gestured at his coat.

He was momentarily blinded as Evelyn hoisted her light high to see the tiny nose of one of the lambs poking out of the top of his coat. But her roving eye did not rest and was drawn upwards to the heavily bearded face that squinted directly at her with watering, hooded eyes. Evelyn Burnley prided herself on being unflappable. She could face any person, any animal, any situation and know just how to handle it. Yet as her gaze raked up her neighbour, it stuttered to a halt as she craned her neck to see his face. Ewan's height, his bedraggled appearance and his burning eyes made him look nothing short of murderous in the pale light of the Tilley. He was like some vengeful apparition that haunted country lanes in search of aged housewives who snooped about the hedgerows.

An unflattering, frightened squawk burst through her

lips as she looked, transfixed by his face. But, as she felt the lamp slip from her grasp and her feet begin to involuntarily stutter backwards, she recollected who stood in front of her and, more importantly, who *she* was. She was Evelyn Rose Lucetta Burnley, respected – *revered* even – member of the local community, member of the parish council and head of the local Mothers' Union. She would not be fazed by the roughness of one of the local farmers.

Besides, Ewan had noticed her reaction. And, just as if all his malicious thoughts concerning this interfering old biddy had been doused in cold water, he lowered his gaze and took a step back, giving Evelyn time to recover.

She cleared her throat and swallowed.

"Well … Mr Cameron … I think …" She struggled to find something to say. She really hadn't thought it through. Staring at his chin instead of looking into his eyes again, she managed, "Misplaced your razor, is it? What a beard!" A small spark went off in her imagination and she latched onto the idea. "Yes! What a beard! You look absolutely wild, so you do," she finished triumphantly.

Ewan shuffled his feet uncomfortably and ducked his head in embarrassment. He hadn't looked in a mirror for days, avoiding his own reflection. But the day before, he had spotted a heavily bearded figure out of the corner of his eye in the kitchen window and, pausing, was quite shocked to find he was looking at himself. He had hoped that no one would see him in such a state. However, with a neighbour like Evelyn so close, he should have realised that such hope was futile.

"I – no, ma'am, I haven't lost my razor. I just haven't had a spare minute to think of using it," he answered with a shrug, acutely aware of the movement of the long coiling hair on his chin.

Evelyn grasped a handful of his coat sleeve and began

towing him forcibly towards the pathway to her home. "Well now, we can sort that for you in no time," she said as she cheerfully dragged him along behind her.

He was so tired and at a loss as to what to do that he simply stuttered out the word '*no*' in several different pitches.

"No, no! I won't have it, Mr Cameron. We're going to make you respectable and that's the end of it." Evelyn was positively bouncing up and down with the prospect of having Ewan in her house for a fixed period of time. Even though they had lived on one another's doorsteps for several years, Ewan had never been in her house and it was a fact that Evelyn genuinely lamented. Her deep-seated curiosity regarding him had very few outlets and now she was to have him sitting at her own fireside where, as her guest, he would be obliged to answer her questions out of courtesy.

The same thought seemed to come to Ewan halfway down the garden path. He dug his heels into the slippery gravel and after a moment of slithering over their wet surface, fighting for balance as he juggled the two lambs under his coat, he ground to a solid halt. Undeterred, the formidable Mrs Burnley leaned forward, using her own considerable weight to shift her prize. But, in this instance, Ewan had the upper hand. Just.

"Oh, would you come on, Mr Cameron, save the both of us getting wet!" His assailant looked at her boots. "I can feel the damp getting in around my feet already. Yours must be no different." She gave another tug. "Come in out of the wet now."

One of the lambs gave an audible bleat under Ewan's coat, saving his exhausted brain from coming up with an excuse. He gestured to the interior of his gabardine and the two little creatures that were becoming more and more restless. "I can't, ma'am. I must get up to the house and milk one of the ewes for these two poor wee things. I cannay leave them too long, see." He relaxed his taut body a little as he got to the end of his explanation, knowing that Mrs Burnley, who had lived her life around farms, would never deny him the chance to look after two that were so young and ailing, no matter how scruffy his appearance. But, as he relaxed, he felt a renewed strain as Evelyn once more began hauling him towards her back door, breathing heavily with the strain of moving such a sizable man.

Ewan felt a swift flame of anger rip through him at the obstinacy of the interfering old biddy and had to stop himself from wrenching his coat from her grasp – mostly because he didn't want to rip his coat.

"Mrs Burnley, really!" he protested angrily but got no further.

"No, no, no, Mr Cameron! That's no excuse at all!" Evelyn almost sang the words, she was in such a state of ecstasy. "Shur hasn't Lilian got fresh beestings just this evening that she never used. The poor little thing was dead before she got to feed it anything." She strained on Ewan's sleeve again. She had got him this far and wasn't about to let him go now. "Besides," she added, latching onto the fleeting thought that had skittered through her head, "you have the look of a criminal with your beard and you all draggled like a drownded rat."

She'd done it. She knew she had. Something she said in that last moment had struck a chord with Cameron. She saw the flash of it in his eyes by the light of the Tilley lamp. But then it was gone so fast that she wasn't sure she had seen it at all. Besides, it didn't matter. Ewan's shoulders slumped and in ill-graced silence he allowed himself to be dragged over the threshold of his neighbour's house.

The first thing he heard on entering was a small yelp. It took a moment for him to realise the sound had come from his own lips. It was as if he had entered a bejewelled, shining cave. A fire burned brightly in the open range, throwing its heat across the room. The flames flickered on the rich creamy-yellow-coloured walls and cast dancing shadows of furniture across the space. A large burnished-copper oil lamp hung from the ceiling, but it was turned down to only the softest of glows, giving its guest sufficient light to see the rest of the kitchen. Every surface was scrubbed clean, wood bleached white by salt and elbow grease. There was also the rich gravy smell of stewed meat making the air so thick with its scent that Ewan felt he was almost drinking it. His mouth watered and his stomach rumbled audibly. How long was it since he had eaten?

But more than the heat, the light and the smell, was the woman.

Ewan had not seen the figure buried in the depths of the large-winged chair by the fireside at first but the growling of his starved belly had been so thunderous that a head had protruded from the confines of the chair. This head was swiftly followed by a long, sinuous body, which unfolded as the woman stood, knitting still in her hand, staring open-mouthed at the intruder. Ewan stared back as if he had never seen her before. In truth, he never had – not really.

Previously, he had seen her at a distance in the fields or at church but he had never look at her specifically. The overbearing conspicuousness and volume with which the woman's mother conducted herself had completely shielded her from the notice of anyone apart from those who specifically sought out Evelyn's eldest child. Even when Ewan had seen her around the farm, he had paid no attention to her. It was just Mrs Burnley's daughter: someone to avoid for fear she might pass on any little piece of tittle-tattle to her probing mother. She never stood in her own right because she was Evelyn bloody Burnley's daughter. But she stood in her own right now.

How had he missed her? Almost topping six feet, Lilian

Burnley could just about look him in the eye without effort. She was tall and beautifully long-limbed and, as her hands twitched around her knitting, he saw the knitting needles held in long fingers flash in the firelight. A ripple of movement slid through her body as she switched her weight uncertainly from one foot to the other. Her shoulders shifted and a long, thick twist of nut-brown hair slid over her collarbone and came to rest on her chest. And still her eyes shone unblinking at the man standing on the threshold of her kitchen. How had he not noticed her before?

All of this was the thought and realisation of a short moment as Evelyn closed the back door then popped out from behind him full of excitement and bustle.

"Oh Lilian! You're still here."

She barely looked at her daughter who remained unmoved. However, noticing this stillness, Evelyn cast a glace between the two and her expression lost some of its animation, hardening the lines of her face. Evelyn did not like the way Ewan Cameron was looking at her daughter, nor the way her daughter did nothing to break away from his gaze.

"Lilian!" she said sharply, making Ewan jump. "Will you get Mr Cameron some food! By the sound of that belly, the man's half starved!" And then, turning to Ewan, "There's a good man. Now you come and sit down here at the table."

Ewan stood immobile, gawping stupidly at Mrs Burnley before he found enough breath to mumble out the word "Lambs" and gesturing helplessly to his coat.

Evelyn smiled sweetly, grabbing blindly for her daughter and finding an arm. She'd had a thought.

"Lilian will look after them, won't you, Lilian?" She gestured to her daughter who promptly changed tack from the stew-pot and headed straight for the bulge in the chest of Ewan's coat, wiping her hands in the folds of a long apron

18

tied over her skirt.

Ewan found himself involuntarily taking a step backwards. It was a moment before he realised that it was because he was completely unnerved by this woman who had appeared before him. He hugged the lambs to his body and heard himself saying, "No! I have to feed them."

Unfazed, Lilian Burnley simply locked eyes with him and quietly said, "I can feed them." She pulled back the dripping coat and extracted the two lambs with little assistance then turned her face reassuringly back to Ewan. "Don't worry. I feed nearly all of Bertie's orphaned or sick lambs. He doesn't have the patience for it."

Evelyn's body stiffened perceptibly at the slight cast on her son. She huffed. "Rearing ailing babbies is no business for a man."

"I would have said that all animals, big or small, are the business of a farmer," replied Ewan absently as he watched Lilian place the two lambs in a wooden box by the fire. She then turned to a pan covered with a square of muslin which she whipped off before placing the pan on the range to heat. "Not to say," he murmured, tearing his eyes away and focusing on her mother, "that women aren't just as capable of caring for animals as men." He waved his hand in Lilian's general direction to clarify, then glanced to where she was bent over the pan with a hand trailing in slow circles through the milk to stir it and give it an even warming.

"You should take off your coat," she said.

"Sorry?" Ewan stared at her, uncomprehending, thoughts rushing through his tired head at such speed that they all seemed to crush together, jamming up the system so that it ground to a gormless halt.

"Your coat," Lilian replied patiently. "You should take it off. It's dripping on the floor."

Ewan looked down at the flagstone floor. A puddle of

water was forming around his boots, dissolving the mud that caked the soles and streaking the pool with wisps of brown.

He stepped swiftly back out of the mess he had made. "I'm awfully sorry," he mumbled, looking guiltily between the two women.

Evelyn took control of the situation. "Never mind, never mind! You'd be better to take the whole lot off." Catching Ewan's look of horror, she qualified, "The coat and the boots. And maybe the jumper as well. You're drowneded, Mr Cameron."

Ewan's cheeks flushed a little at his own misunderstanding but he covered it up by swiftly stripping off the suggested garments which were then hung beside the fire and began to steam. But Lilian noticed. She had seen the look of panic, the look of relief, the embarrassment and, as she picked up his boots to put them out in the porch by the back door, she again felt him shrink away from her. She was surprised to find that this hurt. She felt his movement acutely and was annoyed, humiliated even, by his obvious dislike of her presence. And yet he watched her. She could feel his gaze touching her skin as she fed the warmed milk to the lambs. It was confusing for her. She prided herself on her ability to read people. Since her mother never allowed her to get a word in edgeways, she took to observing people instead, using her enforced silence to do something else that was just as interesting and informative as the incessant chatter. But for a reason she couldn't quite grasp, Ewan Cameron was different.

She had seen and observed him on many occasions before. Of course she had – he was hard to miss. Mostly, she had seen him doing his utmost to avoid her mother and other women like her. Lilian sympathised. The minutiae of her life had been spread about the parish for years by her own mother and she had no doubts about how other people's lives were dealt with. What Evelyn Burnley's daughter did notice, however, was that Cameron was very good at hiding in plain sight. He was usually present at all the local parish events and a regular at the local shops and markets but, really, she knew almost nothing about him. She knew he was Scottish, but any fool would notice that, given that a Scotch accent coloured the few words he did speak. However, she knew nothing of his background, his likes or his dislikes – apart from the fact that he very clearly disliked her mother. Lilian began to wonder what on earth had possessed him to enter an enclosed space that contained Evelyn Burnley. Perhaps he was unwell, she thought suddenly, casting a worried look over the figure now hunched protectively over a plate of stew the lady of the house had placed in front of him.

He didn't look healthy, that was for sure.

What she could see of his cheeks underneath the profusion of beard had a hollowness about them. Now that he'd removed his coat and pullover, Lilian saw the rumples of his gathered trousers held up around a thin waist by a sturdy belt. There were also dark circles around his eyes which furthered the impression of their depth and the hollowness of his face. However, the enthusiasm and speed with which he ate belied his sickly appearance. Maybe he just wasn't taking care of himself. It was taking its toll, thought Lilian. While he was a strong and determined man built for hard labour, eventually he would burn out. Lilian felt a flutter of panic at the idea.

As she sat studying and musing over their guest, she didn't notice her mother's stream of tattle had ceased and that the room was now silent apart from the sounds of the fire crackling and the large clock on the sideboard. It was a moment before she realised that her mother had, in fact, left the room. Becoming aware of this, Lilian blinked, pulling her

21

head back slightly as if she were pulling her face out of a basin of water. Coming-to once more, she discovered Cameron sitting back in his chair, meal finished, smiling pleasantly at her.

"You're staring, miss. Have I got food in my beard?" He ran his hand ruefully over his hairy chin, still smiling, wariness gone.

He seemed to be finding her absentmindedness amusing. She fought through her fogged mind, desperately searching for something to say to him that wouldn't expose her train of thought. Luckily, her mother re-entered, saving her from coming up with an answer.

"Now, Mr Cameron – oh! Finished already, are we?" She viewed the empty plate with a nod of approval. Very little could please Evelyn more than seeing someone with a healthy appetite. "And what about some cake now? Lilian! Cake for Mr Cameron," she said in a sing-song voice as she plunked an enamel basin down on the table along with a flannel towel. From the basin she took scissors, a pot of shaving soap and a long flat leather case.

Having finished with the two lambs, Lilian quickly washed her hands and did her mother's bidding.

As Ewan ate his cake and was also provided with a mug of strong tea to wash it down, Evelyn busied herself with the basin. She placed it on an upturned egg crate by the fireside chair and proceeded to fill it with a mixture of cold water from a jug on the sideboard and hot from the kettle over the range.

Lilian watched her mother with curiosity then cottoned on to what was happening. "You shouldn't be doing that yet, Mammy." She flicked her fingers at the steaming basin.

"Why not?" replied Evelyn huffily, annoyed by her daughter's interference.

"Well," she cast a questioning eye over Ewan, "if you're planning to shave Mr Cameron here, you'd be better trimming

22

his beard down first."

Ewan stopped chewing to take in the two women as they squared up to one another, ready for an argument. Lilian stood defiant and calm as a variety of emotions swept across her mother's face. The coolness with which Lilian stood there attested to her familiarity with such a clash. She was clearly used to disagreeing with her mother. However, he caught Mrs Burnley's eye when she glanced in his direction and saw the effort it took for her to keep from arguing with her daughter in front of her neighbour. He was right about that. Because fight they did. The animosity between her and her eldest child was her best-kept secret.

"Well, shur, you'd better do it so," snapped Evelyn. But she couldn't help adding, "If you're such an expert."

"I can do it myself, ladies," said Ewan in an attempt to break the tension. He was beginning to regret agreeing to have his beard shaved though he was glad that he had come in for the food at least. Perhaps he could leave now and forget about his beard for another three weeks? But then Evelyn's words earlier came back to him. She had said he looked like a criminal. It had stung and he fought the urge to flinch just remembering the words.

"Now don't be talking nonsense, Mr Cameron," Evelyn said, regaining her composure with effort. "Lilian here will do it for you. She used to shave my husband – God rest him – when he was too tired to do it himself. He said she had a good steady hand. So she shouldn't do you an injury now." Evelyn chortled at her own humour.

Ewan looked to Lilian who smiled weakly and gave a little shrug.

"I – I can do it myself if you want. You don't have to …" he said nervously, tugging at the offending hair. Yet, somehow, he desperately hoped that she would.

Lilian seemed to sense this. Her smile grew crookedly

across her cheek and Ewan noticed that she didn't show her teeth. Maybe they were bad or perhaps she was missing a few. She wouldn't be the first young woman he had come across over the years to have suffered the ill effects of bad diet and poor dental care. But given the general health of the rest of her body he thought that missing teeth were unlikely. God! What did it matter to him?

"No, it's alright. I'll do it."

Ewan felt his body relax in relief. He hadn't realised he'd been holding his breath.

She gestured to the seat by the fire. "Do you want to come and sit here? The light's better and you might dry out a bit more. Your shirt looks damp."

She was correct, of course. Whether it was from the chill or from fatigue, Ewan's body was making known its protest at his abuses. Despite the warmth of the room, a bone-deep cold was setting into him and he was beginning to shiver. Without saying anything further, he stood on heavy legs and shuffled over to the armchair but, before taking his allotted place, he peered into the crate containing the two lambs, both of whom were curled up close together, their little milk-swollen bellies rising and falling in peaceful contentment. With a hum of approval Ewan sat, sighing as he sank into the depths of the seat.

Lillian produced a large sheet of cloth and, with Ewan's assistance, tucked it into his collar to prevent any stray hair from getting into his clothing. Evelyn watched all this with the beady eye of a woman who lived to observe the lives of others and relished the remembrance of every detail. As she looked on, however, she thought that this would perhaps be an encounter that she would not recount to others. In fact, the way the two people in front of her were behaving made her feel quite uncomfortable which was unusual given that she had seen the intimacies of others' lives quite often. There was something different about the way Ewan and her daughter interacted. As far as Evelyn was aware, Lilian had had no previous contact with their Scottish neighbour but there was a familiarity in the way they moved about one another as if they had known each other for a long time. Maybe it was just a case that both were in their thirties and, therefore, more adult in their behaviour. But, then, that wasn't it either. Evelyn had seen individuals much older than either of the two before her who would be unable to conduct themselves so comfortably in such a situation. And, at first, when she brought Mr Cameron into the house, she had felt the tension and their awkwardness around one another. But it wasn't there anymore. It confused Evelyn and made her uneasy.

Lilian, meanwhile, was steadily reclaiming the shape of Ewan's face from the bushy mass that covered it. As she worked, she moved around him the better to trim the shape of his face, sometimes standing to the side, sometimes behind and others directly in front of him. When she was in front of him, Ewan could not help but study her face. It was a long time since he had a woman (or a man) in such proximity to him and he thought that he would have felt deeply uncomfortable had it been anyone but Lilian Burnley with her face inches from his. Without fully realising how much mental and physical strain he had been putting himself under over the last number of weeks, he suddenly felt calmer when he realised its crushing weight was no longer sitting in his chest.

As she moved back and forth, he studied her – the smooth planes of her face that belied her age and the hard labour of rural life. And yet, her face was not flawless. There was a deep horizontal line across her forehead which puckered in concentration as she snipped away at his beard. There was also another mark on her forehead – an inverted teardrop-shaped scar that shone white when caught by the light. Her eyes were in shadow for the most part, their colour unknowable. Her long nut-brown hair was tied in a loose plait that held most of it off her face but the shorter strands around her temples were free, curling around the edge of her face and into her eyes so she had to keep brushing it back.

As she worked, Lilian gently touched his face, tilting his head up and down, side to side. She was nervous but tried to hide it. She had performed a similar duty for her father, but he had been dead more than three years now and she had not laid hands on a man since. Despite her inward trepidation, outwardly she was calm. Her breath was even and her hands steady. But then her hands were always steady. She had never yet found a situation that caused her hands to shake like she had seen her younger sister tremble on her wedding day. Lilian always found it peculiar that her sisters seemed so fearful of their marriages.

In her heart of hearts, Lilian knew that such a day would never come to her but that did not prevent her thinking about how she might act on her wedding day. She was the eldest of the family and she, without any say in the matter, had been selected as the child who would remain at home unmarried to tend her aging mother and the needs of her unwed brother. It wasn't her choice, it was simply the done thing and, though she hated the idea that the rest of her life would be taken up with the mundanities that presently filled it, she accepted her lot in life with as much grace as she could muster. But in truth she was isolated and lonely, constantly fighting against the two people she was to spend the rest of her life with.

For the first time in years, as she shifted around the man who sat in front of her, she thought she might have connected with someone. But then she was so unused to connecting with people maybe she was mistaken. It wasn't as if she didn't have friends, and of course there were her sisters, but they were all people she had known since childhood. It was only natural that she should feel there was a bond between them. She took these relationships for granted because they had existed for so long.

Yet here was a virtual stranger who had appeared on a rainy night in March, awakening in her a feeling that there was perhaps more to life than the familiar and known. And even though Ewan Cameron had done nothing in particular to endear himself to her or give her any indication that their lives, having now converged, would continue to do so, she truly hoped they would. In fact, imagining that she would have to watch Ewan leave in a short time made her feel quite unhappy. Once again, she would be left in the company of her mother who spent the evenings wondering aloud when Bertie would be back from wherever he might have disappeared to.

Finishing trimming his beard, Lilian dipped her fingers in the basin of water her mother had prepared. She flicked them quickly and then dried them on the side of her skirt, much to Evelyn's annoyance since there was a towel beside her. But then, Lilian did things like that – boyish things that no amount of chastisement had ever corrected. Evelyn concluded her daughter did these things now just to irritate her. To Lilian, they were automatic actions as natural as breathing.

Fingers dried, she took the basin to the door and emptied it without looking at her mother. If she had, she would have seen the fury on her face. For Evelyn, it was one thing to be proved wrong about preparing the water, it was another that she made such a show of proving her wrong by throwing the entire basin of water out the door. Not only that, she did it all in front of someone else – someone who was Evelyn's very own guest. She bristled at the indignity of being one-upped by her daughter.

Lilian was oblivious to all of this. She was far too busy beginning to question whether she would be able to shave this new friend she had acquired (for she now saw him as a friend) without accidentally cutting his ear off or something to that effect. She took the kettle of water from the range, filled the basin, added cold water and lathered the shaving soap. As she applied it to Ewan's cheeks, his eyes followed her face until she looked directly into them and smiled her crooked smile. He smiled back. She finished with the soap then paused, cut-throat razor in hand.

"Go on." Ewan cocked his head to one side and lifted an eyebrow in challenge. "I trust you … I think."

Lilian gave a deep humming laugh. "More fool, you," she muttered but she seemed to make her decision as she walked around the chair to stand behind him. "Head up," she said, lightly pulling his forehead back. After that it was just a case of relying on muscle memory. If she had been asked how to shave a man, she wouldn't have been able to explain it. But with blade in hand and a man in front of her, her hands just seemed to know where to go instinctively. She swept the blade in smooth clean strokes, following the contours of his bony face as if she had done it for years. When it came to the trickier parts, she moved to his front once again and Ewan exhaled a long, contented sigh of complete relaxation. He was comfortable in her presence and comforted by her touch. He sank even further into the depths of the armchair, relishing the feeling of being warm, full and dry. Warm, full and dry *and* tired. He felt his eyelids droop as he listened to the scrape of the blade on his flesh, the popping of wet wood in the stove.

He let them fall as a true, deep sleep finally claimed him for the first time in years.

Chapter 3

Enniscorthy was not a town designed to accommodate ordinary folk. Ordinary folk had small children, dodgy knees, a sore back or were simply blighted by the ravages of age and time. Daily lives in the town were blighted by the literal uphill or downhill struggle of traipsing the town's streets on which individuals conducted their business. Residents constantly battled the gradient of the town, looking like cartoon figures as they chuffed up the hill, their bodies sloped forward, or leaned back as they descended, their strides comically extended as the ground fell away beneath them. Now and again poor unfortunates would be seen hurtling down the hill, desperately attempting to force their feet to keep up with their top-heavy bodies until they reached the relatively level surface of the square at the centre of the town which was, in fact, more triangular in shape.

Situated on the River Slaney, the town had been established centuries before making use of the nearby waterway. Given the vast incline of the banks of the river, it was also easily defensible as the town's residents always occupied the higher ground. Seeing this advantage of elevation, Norman settlers capitalised by constructing four storeys worth of castle at the apex of the hill from which one could survey the countryside for miles around and, more importantly, spy vessels coming up the river. The river was also useful as a trade route for small boats travelling the dozen or so miles to Wexford town where the Slaney opened out at the coast into a wide but shallow bay. However, by the fifties, trade along the river had ceased altogether. It was much easier to travel by road. Now the only thing the river was used for was fishing. Men and boys would stand on the humpbacked bridge straddling the river, which sat below the castle, with rods extended hopefully over the edge and baskets and bags at the ready to ferry home whatever they were fortunate enough to catch. More sinister, however, was the dumping of large amounts of waste from the pig factory further upriver which sporadically turned the waters of the Slaney blood-red and acted as a reminder of the town's more violent past.

The castle had also ceased to be of military or defensive use many years before and now lay like an old guard dog, greying and dull-eyed, sitting impassively as it had always done, unwilling to desert its former position of power yet no longer required by anyone. The town itself was also greying, despite its several attempts at ostentation. The Roman Catholic cathedral, St Aidan's, was designed by Augustus Pugin, the man who later became the architect of the Palace of Westminster in London. Another building with similar ideas of its own grandeur was St Senan's Hospital which lay on the outskirts of the town on the road to Wexford.

St Senan's sat in austere isolation on the opposite side of the river – a modern presence that was just as threatening to the town's current inhabitants as the castle had been to visitors centuries before. The vivid orange brickwork of the sprawling three-storey construction stood out like a poisonous blot on the landscape. Its five towers protruded from the surrounding trees, giving the eerie impression that the building was watching, waiting to pounce. Had it been used for something else, the building would have, perhaps, been considered beautiful – architecturally impressive. But St Senan's was a mental institution and therefore tainted by association.

Luckily, however, for the Enniscorthy Church Institute, which was also clad in the lurid orange brickwork of St Senan's, the taint of the mental hospital didn't seem to stretch to the parish building on the opposite side of the river. It was on the corner of Church Street, opposite St Mary's Church of Ireland, at the top of Castle Hill and was the site of many a tea dance. Upstairs there was a large wooden-floored dance hall where many young men and women of the parish met and courted, including several of the Burnley girls. It was also where many of the parish council meetings were held or, rather, governed by one woman.

Astrid Charlton was a woman of indomitable dignity. She was not a local but, in the years since her arrival in the town, had established a formidable reputation as a woman of great ideas, action and, most importantly, execution. If ever there was something needing done, Mrs Charlton was the woman to make it happen. She was rightly viewed as one of the best and most important people in the parish with many admiring her verve and can-do attitude. However, this admiration was rarely followed by an aping of her good example. More often than not, it resulted in a 'Let Mrs Charlton do it' attitude. Not that Astrid minded in the slightest. She loved action and being useful within the community but, more than that, she loved to get things done and done properly.

Astrid had grown up in a household of privilege. The youngest daughter of a wealthy German family, her father a count and her mother from a moneyed industrial family. She had left her home in Eupen on the Belgian-German border at the age of seven to be educated in England in a language and culture completely alien to her. She had cried for days, pined for her nurse and stared blankly when anyone tried to speak to her. But in the unique way children often adapt to challenging situations, within a month or two Astrid had found her feet and began to flourish in her new environment. She came to dread the prospect of going home to Germany for the summer holidays where she was either left on her own or surrounded by family who acted as if she wasn't there. She longed to return to the dormitories, the friends, the sweeping lawns and grand architecture of her true home in England. Indeed, she became so wrapped up in her life there that she would struggle to remember her native language when she went home. It was, therefore, unsurprising that once Astrid finished her schooling, she stayed in England. Moving to London, she became a staple of the young literary and artistic crowd, met a rich, handsome young socialite and was married by the age of twenty-four. But then the Great War broke out in Europe and everything changed.

Being an astute observer of human behaviour, Astrid's father had made plans to take his family out of harm's way. He settled on Ireland as a country that was not too distant from home. It was agreed between her English husband (now a soldier in the British army) and her father that Astrid would join the rest of her family in Ireland as it would be the safest place for her. Anti-German feeling was beginning to take hold and, with her husband fighting on the Front, Astrid would be virtually alone – a foreigner in a country she adopted and thought of as her own. It was something of a shock for her to realise that fellow-feeling did not extend to individuals of a different nationality when one's country was at war with another's. Though she was loath to admit it, she was glad to leave the turmoil of London and the loneliness of her husband's empty house.

It was just as well she left. By the third month of the War, her husband was dead and Astrid was inconsolable. Had she not been surrounded by her family, she was sure she would have gone mad. But they helped her through her grief even though they were struggling to adapt to their new lives. However, what they did not initially realise was that their new lives were to become their permanent lives. By the time the Great War ended, and political wrangling had taken its course, Astrid's family found their home and properties in Eupen had been ceded to Belgium. They lost a vast amount of their wealth and were left to build a perpetual existence in Ireland.

Astrid, now reconciled to her own widowhood, began to pine once again for the cosmopolitan life of literature and art – neither of which she got in the midlands of Ireland. She moved to Dublin, hardly the lively urbane centre that London was, but it was the best she could do in her situation. Yet she still managed to find her "set" within a few short weeks of taking up residence in the most fashionable part of the city.

It was there that Astrid met Laurie Charlton.

Laurence was a tradesman. He was tall, shy, athletic and thirteen years Astrid's senior. Women gravitated towards him and she watched from a distance as he squirmed on receipt of their advances. She wondered why he bothered putting himself through the torture of these evening parties, given that they made him so uncomfortable. It wasn't until later that she understood. Like herself, Laurie was lonely. Widowed two years before, he had moved from the countryside to the city to be closer to his only son who was in school in Dublin. But the urban life was foreign to him and he was lost among a profusion of people. The only company he kept was that of his sparse household, his business acquaintances and the grand folk at such evening parties as Astrid frequented. She never approached him the way others did but soon found that Laurie sought her out and wanted to spend time with her. He was forty-six and

Astrid was thirty-three. Neither expected to find another lover at their age unless that lover was more interested in their money. But both being independently wealthy, Astrid and Laurie met on a level playing field. They encountered one another as mutual admirers of the other's intelligence, self-possession and looks. Both were still attractive, despite their age, and within a few short months were married.

For the next thirty years, Astrid spent every day with Laurie – a diligent wife and loving stepmother to his son Geoffrey. They were happy, moneyed and comfortable in their own little bubble, no longer needing the company of others to feel contentment.

Chapter 4

"Well, I don't see why you let him sleep in my house."

"It's *our* house, Bertie, and I wasn't going to wake him up," she hissed. "Not sure I could have even if I tried. And what harm in letting him sleep here?"

"I don't like it. I don't like coming into my house and finding a stranger stretched out in front of my fire. If you had asked *me*, he wouldn't have been let in in the first place."

"Oh? And where were you then? Because maybe if you'd told us then we would have asked your permission."

There was an angry male sound which was swiftly cut off by the high-pitched tones of Evelyn Burnley who came clattering into the room.

"Lilian, leave your brother alone," she admonished. "Bertram's got enough to do without listening to you bell-ragging."

Bertram Burnley took on a whiney tone that didn't suit a man of his years. "I don't like it, Ma. A stranger in the house. Shur, Jaysus, I thought he'd murdered the pair of yis in yer beds and was waiting for me when I came home."

"Oh, you'd be delighted with that, wouldn't you, Bertie?" Lilian's voice was full of sarcasm. "If the pair of us were dead and gone you wouldn't have anyone *bell-ragging* at you."

"Don't be saying things like that! Shur, that's plain awful, that is, to be going round saying things like that to your brother!" There was a thump. "Oh, now look what you've made me do! I've cracked two eggs."

There was some huffing as Lilian made the reply that it was her mother who had thumped the egg crates onto the table.

Bertie, fed up with the arguing, muttered that he was off outside.

While he hadn't fully grasped what the dispute was about, Ewan was becoming aware of where he was and what was going on around him. Firstly, he was in the Burnleys' house. Secondly, he had somehow managed to fall asleep.

He had regained consciousness but not complete wakefulness while Bertie and Lilian had been arguing but it took him a while to realise who was talking and what was happening. He had teetered on the verge of waking completely, struggling to kick-start his sleep-fuddled mind as he let the hissed conversation of the others wash over him without completely realising the thrust of what they were saying. It was the entry of Mrs Burnley that had brought him around fully but also made him shrink internally in a half-hearted attempt to disappear into the safety of oblivion where Evelyn could not touch him. He held his position in the chair and kept his eyes tight shut as he listened carefully, wondering how he could make his escape. He also wanted to hear what they might say of him next but worried that they might say something he did not want to hear.

However, the next part of the conversation made him a little keener than he had been to wake fully. Lilian spoke first.

"Would you go on, Mammy, and get going! You know the way the Connellys get if you're late." She sounded exasperated.

"But, shur, I can't be leaving you here to deal with *him* on your own, can I?" She spoke in a very loud whisper, designed to carry and, Ewan thought, it might even have been directed at him rather than her daughter. He presumed she was hoping to wake him but he wouldn't give her the satisfaction.

"Are you saying it'll take the two of us to see him off?"

Ewan could hear the smile in Lilian's voice and nearly smiled himself.

"But –" It was almost possible to hear the cogs whirring in Evelyn Burnley's brain as she searched desperately for a reason to stay.

"Well, unless he needs to be carried out, I think I'll be able to manage him," Lilian said confidently. "And besides," she added, "if it comes to heavy lifting, I don't think you'd be a whole load of use what with your bad back." There was a pause. "Would you go on, Mammy! Eta Connelly won't wait forever, you know."

"I know that!" said Evelyn crossly, not bothering to keep her voice down at all. "Fine. I'll go. But you listen here, missy." At this point she dropped her voice, but not so much that Ewan couldn't catch what she was saying. "That's a man of the world there. Now don't you let him try anything funny. Or don't you be getting ideas either now."

"Goodbye, Mammy." There was a cold finality about Lilian's voice.

Her mother gave a little "*humph*" noise but there was a shuffling of feet and the door slammed loudly.

There was silence for a moment then Ewan heard a heavy exhale accompanied by a deep, throaty, rather unfeminine growl. He found her temper quite endearing and afforded himself a quiet little chuckle which ended in a strangled yelp of shock when something cold and wet thrust itself against his hand. It was then he realised that, had he wanted to move before, he would have struggled just as much as he did now. Though someone, presumably Lilian, had tucked a warm blanket around him, he had slept sitting slumped in the armchair in drying clothes and when he had jerked his hand away, felt the jolt of the movement through his entire body. He was stiff and sore. Feeling his age, he thought ruefully as he groaned while gingerly trying to stretch out his aching limbs.

"It was six of one and half a dozen of the other, I'm afraid."

Ewan looked up to find Lilian standing over him, her lips pursed as she tried to hide her amusement. "Eh?" was all his brain could conjure in response.

Lilian laughed out loud. Ewan was rather pleased with himself for provoking such a reaction.

"Well, it was a case of wake you up knowing that you'd likely go off and not sleep at all or letting you stay asleep and wake up stiff as a board." She studied him critically. "Got a few aches, have you?"

Ewan was a little embarrassed by her scrutiny. "I'll do," he said gruffly. It was then he saw what had woken him in the first place. Two large, liquid-brown judgmental eyes stared haughtily at him. He stared blankly back before managing to croak out, "And what are you doing here, lovey?"

The eyes brightened immediately and he heard the slow rhythmic 'thump, thump, thump' of a heavy tail wagging against the mat in front of the range.

"I met her at the back door when I was going out to check your sheep," Lilian said, smiling down at the dog who sat to attention at its master's side. "She was curled up just under the overhang. Couldn't have got any closer if she tried." Lilian ruffled the dog's ears. "I think she was worried about you."

"I left her in the yard when I was going down to the lambing ewes. They can get upset sometimes when they see her." He rubbed the dog's ears but suddenly stopped and stared incredulously at Lilian. "You've been to check on my ewes?"

Lilian shrugged. "Well, you were fast asleep and I thought I'd rather leave you to rest and check them myself. Three lots, isn't it? One in the shed, one in the field by the house and the other in the bottom field. Am I right?"

"Aye … aye, y'are." Ewan raised his hands to scrub his beard but found a bare chin instead. It took him a moment to remember what had happened. "I fell asleep?" He looked to Lilian for confirmation, not quite believing how the last number of hours had progressed. He wondered what time it was and looked for a clock. He knew he'd seen one.

"It's not long after eight," she said, pre-empting him. She turned away and began to bustle about at the kitchen table, clearing crockery and wiping away crumbs, her back to Ewan. "I went around checking the ewes first thing. You have six freshly yeaned from what I could see." She stopped cleaning and looked directly at him. "Four singles and two twins. I hope you don't mind me checking."

"No, no, not at all," he mumbled, looking down at the dog again as he firmly stroked the top of her head.

"She's beautiful." Lilian had come back over to the hearth to check the two lambs in the box and gestured to the dog as she passed. Both lambs, by the looks of things, were newly fed and enjoying the contented slumber that was so easy when bellies were full of milk. "What's her name?"

Ewan smiled down at the dog. For a man who kept himself so emotionally shut off from the world, he found great companionship in his dog. Not only was she an excellent herding sheepdog, she was the creature he told all his plans to first – his friend and confidante through all the loneliness. She did not question him, she did not disobey him and she made him smile and laugh when there was little else in life that did. He loved to watch the joy with which she approached her simple life, uncomplicated by cares of time or money. He loved how she would chase a butterfly across an open field, leaping in the air with wild abandon as she tried to catch it and then return in an instant when he called her to round up his sheep. She was everything he wanted in a companion in life. Or so he had thought.

"Georgie. Her name's Georgie," he said, looking up into Lilian's eyes.

In doing so, he registered the similarities between the gazes of his dog and the very fine woman who stood in front of him. Their eyes had warmth, trust and liveliness, the woman's blue, the dog's brown. Yet, dancing in their depths was also a wariness, an intelligence which led them to study their surroundings, assessing everything. Ewan didn't for a moment think that a woman might find such a comparison unflattering since, in his mind, Georgie was his best friend and he held her in the highest esteem. However, he voiced nothing of his thoughts and did not allow them to show on his face.

"You should have woken me up," he muttered, slightly embarrassed that somebody else had checked his animals, "rather than do it yourself, I mean."

"You think I can't check a few sheep? That I'm not able? Don't you trust me?"

"No!" he said, horrified at the way she had taken his words. "I mean, yes, of course I trust you, it's just ..." He searched vainly for word to show her that his pride was somewhat wounded by his own torpidity.

Lilian saved him. She threw her head back and laughed, exposing all her teeth which he noted, though not absolutely straight, were very healthy-looking.

"I'm sorry, making you squirm on purpose. Bertie would have straight off said I wasn't able, so thank you for thinking I can handle myself. Besides," she went on, "it would have taken a shotgun going off to wake you and since I don't want to set it off in the house, I let you be."

She studied him and Ewan found that, instead of blanching, he simply stayed still and allowed her to carry out her silent inventory of him.

"You looked like you could do with a decent rest for once," she said with a cock of her shoulder. "Now," she added, brightening slightly, "would you be interested in a bit of breakfast?"

He looked at his dog. "I should probably be getting on. I've no doubt you've better things to do than entertain me." And yet, he found he couldn't seem to move. There was true intent behind his answer. He was sure she had enough work to do without him in the way, but he just couldn't bring himself to leave. He realised that he wanted to stay with Lilian. Not for any particular reason, but just to remain in her company a little while longer.

"I'll put on some rashers for you. And some bread to toast."

Before Ewan could launch into a half-hearted protest, Lilian had brushed past him and was placing a heavy-bottomed griddle pan on the range at the same time as she fished for the toasting fork with the other hand. He watched as she scoured the pan with a knob of butter before tossing in three thick rashers of bacon, filling the air with hissing sizzling sounds and the glorious smell of fried meat. Ewan's mouth filled with saliva and his stomach gave an audible rumble.

Lilian turned with an incredulous look and, shaking her head, said, "Lordy! That stomach of yours talks more than you do."

Ewan suddenly heard an impossible sound escape his body: a high-pitched nervous, embarrassed giggle. Lilian's mouth fell open, making him giggle even more. It wasn't long before man and woman dissolved into an uncontrollable fit of laughter for no other reason than it was good to laugh with one another. It was something that was unfamiliar to Ewan.

Lilian finally managed to compose herself just long enough to say, "Oh Jaysus! I'm burning the rashers!" before their eyes met and they were both off once again.

Breakfast was eventually served with only the slightest amount of charring around the edges. Several well-buttered slices of toasted brown bread accompanied the rashers while a steaming pot of tea, fresh milk and a sugar basin formed a nice little semi-circle around his plate – in Ewan's opinion, framing it beautifully. Such a set-up *was* beautiful to Ewan who was highly unused to the luxuries of a normal breakfast and all its trimmings. Sustaining himself was not high on his list of priorities and he therefore rarely had anything more complicated than bread, potatoes, meat and the odd vegetable, all prepared in the rudest fashion. He hadn't the patience for it, so to be cooked for was a rather special thing for him and he was, in fact, quite touched by the thoughtfulness of his hostess.

He hoped, however, that said hostess had not noticed his socks when he stood up to come to the table. His big toe stuck out of the left sock while he could feel the cold of the stone floor on the bare skin of his right heel. Usually he kept on top of darning his holey socks but with the amount of work he was doing, he was hard-pressed to keep them clean never mind whole. At least they were reasonably clean. There were occasions when his socks ended up as muddy as his boots but this, fortunately, was not one of them.

"Eggs!" Lilian said suddenly, making Ewan jump and a large piece of bacon fall off his fork. "I wonder has Mammy left an egg in the place now." She disappeared out of the kitchen before Ewan was sure what was happening, returning with two large brown eggs in her hand, and proceeded to fry them before depositing them onto Ewan's almost empty plate.

"Thank you, Miss Burnley," he said formally, unsure how else he might address her.

She chuckled. "Call me Lili," she said with a smile, refilling his mug of tea and filling one for herself.

"Lili?" he said, cocking his head to one side.

"I don't like *Lilian*," she replied, infusing the name with as much distaste as she could. "Makes me sound like an old maid. But Bertie and Mammy won't call me anything else." She tapped the side of her mug with short fingernails. "I think they just do it to annoy me. They're the only ones who won't call me Lili. And," she looked up, eyes shining with mischievous glee, "secretly Bertie hates being called Bertie, so I just call him that to annoy him too."

"But everyone calls him Bertie," Ewan said, surprised. "I don't think I've heard him called anything else, except by your mother."

Lili nodded. "Oh, I know that. I know what people call him." She paused. "But that doesn't mean he likes it."

Ewan could think of nothing to say to this other than, "Oh," and decided to leave it at that. They lapsed into silence and Georgie took this as her cue to sidle up to her master and give him in a punt in the leg – a gentle reminder there was a willing recipient of the scraps of bacon fat neatly piled at the edge of the plate. He had automatically saved them for Georgie out of habit but, as it was Lili's table, Ewan looked to her for permission. She waved her hand in acquiescence before he picked up a rind of fat and handed it to his dog. Lili reached across taking another rind and called Georgie to her. Never one to reject proffered food, the dog trotted around the table and gently took the food from Lili's fingers, delicately licking off excess grease.

"I think she likes you," said Ewan as Lili fed her another piece of the fat.

Lili smiled. "*I* think she likes food."

"Ah, nothing like a bit of bribery to *make* someone like you," said Ewan sagely.

"And what about her owner?" asked Lili, colouring visibly.

Ewan stayed silent for a moment then said carefully, "Do I require bribery? Or – or are you asking if I, like Georgie here, like you?'

"Both," said Lili. "Neither. Oh Lord, I don't know!" She stood abruptly and began clearing Ewan's dirty plates. He gently reached out with his fingertips and touched them to the back of her hand. She stilled. He couldn't look her in the eye and he was afraid to move even the smallest amount for fear of violating their tiny connection.

"I do like you. *Lili*." He said it so quietly that she could have ignored him altogether but he heard her breath catch and knew she was glad he was brave enough to say it. She had felt it the night before but was so unused to the feeling that she needed to be sure. She flipped her hand over and caught Ewan's fingers briefly in hers then lightly slid her hand out from underneath his, allowing his touch to trail up her fingers before it was gone as she turned away. She bent over the sink, placing her hands flat on the smooth white floor of it.

"I can wash up. The least I can do."

The voice came from right behind her. She laughed shakily. "What type of hostess would I be if I made a guest wash up after themselves?"

"You've already done enough for me." He stood beside her, longing to reach out and touch one of her protruding shoulder blades but, instead, grasped the countertop alongside the sink. "Would you ..." he started and then paused. "Do you ever – that is, would you ever think you might –" He ground to a halt once more. She hadn't changed her position and he found it easier to address the back of her head, finishing the rest of his question in the rush of, "If-you-might-like-to-come-into-town-of-an-evening?" He huffed it all out in one short breath. "With me," he added as an afterthought. His knuckles on the countertop were pearly white, the bones protruding spikily.

There was a long, deafening silence. Ewan wanted to shake her, to prompt some form of response whether positive or ... not. However, though it took most of his willpower, he held fast to the countertop.

Throughout, Lili remained perfectly still – like an animal that knew itself watched by a predator. But it was not Ewan she was afraid of. In fact, sharing this room with the tall Scotsman at her side, she had never felt safer. Eventually, she turned to him, her eyes filled with pain and longing.

"I wish – I want to – it's just –"

Ewan cut her off. "Just not with me." He pushed himself off the counter, propelling himself across the room and was almost at the door when he remembered the lambs. Turning back, he almost collided with Lili who appeared in front of him, hands up in supplication. He couldn't even look at her. He had exposed himself to her and she had rejected him. Couldn't she just let him leave with whatever small amount of dignity he had left?

Lili could see the anger and hurt in his eyes. She didn't dare touch him for fear he might explode right in front of her. She saw, for the first time, that Ewan Cameron also had the potential to be a dangerous man if pushed in the wrong direction. She saw the rawness of his emotions – how, despite being a large and physically tough man, he could easily be hurt. But she had to explain.

"No! You're not going anywhere, yeh hear! Not yet. Not until you've heard me out."

He looked around desperately for some other escape route and she could see the shiny glisten of his eyes as he fought for control. She couldn't let him suffer like this.

"It's not you," she said, her voice barely more than a whisper. "It's Mammy and Bertie."

The look of scorn he threw her cut more deeply than words could have. "What've they got to do with it?" he asked coldly.

"Not saying it would, but if anything … nothing can happen between us. I have to stay here. I have to stay at home and mind Mammy. I – I made a promise." She spoke as she would to soothe an agitated animal. But her heart hammered in her chest.

"A promise to who?" Ewan asked roughly.

"My father." Lili looked down. "He died." It still hurt to think of him but she pushed past the lump in her throat to continue. "Since all my sisters are married off, they can't do it. And it's also a kind of unwritten rule that I mind Bertie until he finds a wife."

Ewan barked a sharp laugh. "Who'd marry *him*?"

Lili was silent for a moment. "Exactly."

Ewan froze. She watched as realisation drained his face of colour. Anger and hurt was replaced by horror.

"I'm tied to him. To both of them. It's not the done thing for … someone like me to be going off with some lad. For someone like me to go … courting. If that's what you were asking. And I made a promise to Daddy." She looked down and noticed that her hands were twisted in the fabric of her skirt and slowly released them to show red and white welts where the material had bitten into her skin. "That doesn't mean I don't want to."

Lili couldn't meet his eye. Unsure how he would take what she said, she thought it best to allow him to deal with it without watching him. She wasn't even sure how *she* took what she was saying. Was she rejecting him? Was she telling him it wasn't possible? Because she wanted it to be possible. She wanted to be herself around someone. She wanted to be herself around him.

Two large, rough hands wrapped themselves around

hers and squeezed firmly. She felt a thrill of security and longing flash through their connected hands like electricity. It was as if this decisive touch fused them together – the north and south of two magnets irrevocably drawn to one another, fixing fast. Her eyes stared dumbly at their linked hands, struggling to come up with an answer to the unspoken question. But her body took over and in one smooth motion, Lili raised her head, stood on tiptoe and kissed the man in front of her.

Ewan hadn't expected it. All he had wanted to do was hold her – let her know that she wasn't alone. Let her know he cared. When she kissed him, he had pulled back momentarily before meeting her lips with his, glad that their brittle surface had been softened by the tea drunk at breakfast. Her lips were soft but that was all he had time to notice before she pulled away from him. He reluctantly permitted her to go, holding onto her hands for a little longer than was strictly necessary.

But Lili had to stop. Kissing him was a stupid thing to do. She had to find space to breathe, to think. She couldn't string him along only to reject him. Where would that lead them? She had to *think*.

Georgie was lying on the mat by the box containing the two lambs, eyeing her master and his companion with deepest suspicion. Lili knelt by her and gently patted her head. The dog's tail thumped slowly on the ground as Lili peered into the crate at the two little creatures sleeping within. Really, she didn't see them at all. Her mind worked furiously as she came up with then discarded various plans between herself and her mother, herself and Bertie and, most importantly, herself and Ewan. But she could not think of him and forget Evelyn and Bertie just as she could not now think of her family without thinking of the man hovering uncertainly behind her. She heard his stockinged feet shuffle quietly against the floor and then stop as he stood still. She

Chapter 5

In the summer of 1948, Astrid and Laurence Charlton returned to Laurie's hometown of Enniscorthy where Geoff, Laurie's son, lived with his wife and two children, managing the family business. Laurie enjoyed the closeness of his son and grandchildren while Astrid began to, once again, build a new set of acquaintances and find her place in this new community. She also clung to Laurie's family with a fierceness that suggested they were of her own flesh and blood. But they weren't. Though they had tried, she and Laurie had never been able to conceive children. It was something Astrid suspected from her first marriage that was later confirmed by her second. She was barren and, apart from one niece and her children, Astrid was the last surviving member of her family.

It was three years after their move to the south-east that Laurie died from cancer at the age of seventy-five. He had been an active, healthy man until he wasn't. His demise had taken only a few short months and Astrid, for the second time in her life, was a widow. As before, widowhood did not suit Astrid. Her grand house at the top of the town echoed as she moved around it and, no matter how many fires were lit or how well stoked they were, the house always felt cold. She sought solace in her activities in the parish. She managed the Church Institute, was involved in the library and also in various knitting, sewing and quilting circles. Yet she still felt lonely and unfulfilled, surrounded by people but disconnected from them. Geoff and his family did visit once a week and were very good to her – including her in family gatherings and so forth – but that still wasn't enough. She wanted company, her own person to share her home, thoughts and secrets with.

The solution to her problem came in the most unfortunate of ways.

Firstly, Astrid broke both her wrist and her hip in one fall. It was the winter after Laurie had died and Astrid was in the middle of helping to deliver Christmas baskets from the Irish Countrywomen's Association to some townsfolk who lived alone – one of her many schemes to occupy her time. The weather that year was cold though not as bad as she had experienced as a child in Germany or '47 in Ireland. Given that there was nothing exceptional about the weather, Astrid did not perhaps take as much care as she should have done. If Enniscorthy had been a town with a normal gradient to its streets perhaps things would not have turned out as they did. But it wasn't and, while trotting down the hill to some of the houses, Astrid slipped on the icy street and found herself tumbling to the ground with such force that she immediately (and quite embarrassingly) burst into tears.

Everybody came to visit Mrs Charlton in her hospital bed. There was a never-ending stream of well-wishers keeping her up to date with local news and an abundance of Christmas cake and mince pies. Though she was grateful for the effort many of them clearly went to, she couldn't help but wonder why people didn't visit her this much when she was well and able to deal with their conversation. As it was, company tired her out and she was glad when the ward closed at night.

For Christmas Day, Geoffrey came to collect her so that she might spend time with family instead of on a hospital ward. Yet, rather than visiting for one day, Geoff's wife Nelly insisted that Astrid remain in the house with them while she recovered. Having never been in a house with children, she dreaded the idea of spending every day in the company of Geoff and Nelly's. Johnny and Winnie were well behaved but were also both under ten. Astrid assumed they would be exhausting to live with. However, being a thoughtful soul, Nelly insisted that the children leave their grandmother alone until she felt well enough to see them. When it was finally decided the two little people could enter the sick room, they were quiet as mice and so gentle when they touched their granny that Astrid laughed aloud and felt quite foolish for her misgivings regarding them.

Both children were a little abashed at first. They had never really had that much contact with their grandmother as it was often the case that they were sent away to play somewhere else when she came. Soon, however, Astrid found herself an object of their fascination. Every few hours, the door to her room would open and two heads would appear one above the other, asking for admittance. Once granted entry, the door would fly open and both children would bound in, then climb onto the covers to listen to Astrid read or tell them stories of her own childhood. But she could not stay with Geoffrey's family forever and too soon the day came when she had to return to the cold, quiet house at the top of the hill.

Not long afterwards, however, Astrid was gifted the opportunity of continued youthful company in the form of a letter from her deceased sister's son-in-law Eric who lived in the west of the country, in County Galway.

Astrid knew very little of her niece or her family. She found it quite peculiar that a man she had never met, connected to her only by marriage, should think to contact her unless something was amiss.

Eric explained their situation with economy. Astrid could see the struggle of a man trying to put into words what the family had gone through in the last number of months. His wife, he explained, was of a "fragile disposition" and had fallen pregnant the previous year with their fourth child. The baby had, unfortunately, died at birth – a great loss to the family, as one could imagine. But the greater loss lay later on when his wife Felicity, drowning in her own sea of grief, became hysterical and completely uncontrollable. She frightened the children, attacked her husband and had taken flight on more than one occasion. However, the most distressing part of the entire saga was the fact that Felicity had now completely rejected her remaining children, wishing only for the company of her dead child. Eric found himself the sole parent of three children, all of whom had been cast aside by their own mother. He did not want to distress the children further by having his wife taken away to the asylum but he did not know what else to do. Lacking alternative familial guidance Eric had, therefore, turned to Astrid for advice.

Had she not spent the last two months in the company of two small children, Astrid would not have made the offer she did. She knew Eric and his family were poor. Her sister had married a man who had squandered everything on drink and horses. Felicity was the only good that had come from the marriage but, because of their circumstances, they could do no good for her. As a child, Felicity had always been delicate of health and mind. It would be best, Astrid said, that the children be removed from her harmful influence and given a chance at a better life – a life Astrid could easily offer them. She therefore proposed that the three surviving children should come to live with her indefinitely so that they might benefit from her influence and the opportunities she could provide. It would also, she added, provide her with some support following her wintertime injury. While her bones were mended, they still ached sometimes and she was also, much to her dismay, nervous of stepping out once again. Perhaps if she had the company of children, they might give her the confidence to get out and about. Or, if she was not inclined to go out herself on messages, she could send a child to fetch them. It would be good for them to have a purpose while they were with her even if that purpose included helping her. She felt a little guilty knowing that her offer to take the children had selfish undertones, but she did not feel guilty enough not to write.

In any event, the reply she got back dampened her excitement somewhat. Eric was "flattered" and "touched" by Astrid's offer to care for his children while he attempted to rehabilitate his wife but felt such an upheaval would do the two youngest children more harm than good. Yet, while he regretted that he could not relinquish all his children, he asked if Astrid would be willing to do him the great service of caring for his eldest daughter. Though she found it strange that Eric would part with the child likely to be of greatest use to him in his current crisis, Astrid discovered why as she read on.

Felicity, though still suffering both physically and mentally, was better than she had been when Eric wrote his original letter. She was now calmer though still weak from the trauma of losing her baby. She now, he wrote, clung to the younger children, finding great comfort in their presence. Eric believed to remove them now would set Felicity back even more. He went on, however, to say that his eldest, though invaluable to him, appeared to cause his wife a considerable amount of distress. The girl, who was now seventeen, had filled the breach during her mother's illness, caring for her younger siblings and her father. But when her mother was strong enough to return to family, Felicity found her daughter's judicious care galling. The young girl's ability was a threat to her mother's position as the head of the household. Or so her mother believed. Felicity had thus been exceedingly hard on her daughter. Being a sensitive soul, this rejection had stung the girl deeply and her father believed it would be prudent to remove her from the situation, both for her own and her mother's sake. It was a chance to get away, see more of the world, to leave her lowly background as a poor clerk's daughter and live in a fine house with a wealthy relation. Though it pained him to admit it, his daughter would go further in the world with the assistance of Astrid Charlton than she would with his.

Over the next two weeks, the arrangements were made. The girl would be sent from her home in the west of the country, all the way to Dublin on the train where she would then transfer to another train and travel down to Enniscorthy. All of this, she would do on her own as the family lacked the funds to send her father as a companion. There was also the issue that Eric could not leave home for too long with no one there to watch his wife. He was sending away the person who usually did that. But it had to be done – for everyone's sake.

Chapter 6

Being the good, understanding child that she was, Eric's daughter accepted her father's diktats without complaint, listening carefully to all his instructions. Though it hurt her to be – as she saw it – cast out, she would not argue with her father. In a way there was some relief in her going away. The last few months with her mother had been the most trying in her life and her life up to then had by no means been easy. This most recent episode was not her mother's first foray into mental sickness, and it had always been up to her to care for the family while her mother dealt with her own issues. What she would really miss, however, was her younger brother and sister. Over the years, she had cared for them more than anyone else. She dreaded to think how the separation would affect them.

When the news finally was broken to the children, it gave rise to floods of tears from all three. It also severely irritated their mother as the two youngsters clung to their elder sister. In a way, Eric was somewhat glad that his daughter was going away. There was no one in the world, he loved more than his wife – not even his own children, though he did care for them as well. And while it hurt to see his daughter go, he knew, in the long run, separation would be better for all of them.

On the day their sister left, the smaller children wept bitterly as their fingers were pried from their sister's clothing. The girl cried silently as she disentangled herself from her siblings and passed them over to her parents. Felicity looked on coldly as she took hold of her younger children. Her eldest took a tentative step towards the group as they waited on the train platform but her mother turned away, the hands of both children firmly clasped in hers. In Felicity's mind, the separation was already complete.

Instead, the girl turned to her father.

He embraced her. "You look after yourself now, love."

"I will," she sniffed.

"You remember where you're going now, yes?"

"I remember, Daddy. Don't worry."

"That's like telling water not to be wet, pet. I'm not going to tell you to be a good girl. I know you are anyway but," he paused, searching for what to say, "I don't know what Mrs Charlton's like. And you don't want to offend her straight off. Just mind yourself with her, Birdy."

She sniffed. "I'll miss that," she said sadly.

"What?"

"Birdy. You always call me Birdy."

"I know," he answered. "But you've got to grow up and own your name at some point. Make it yours and —" he broke off and hugged her tight to him, "be proud of it, Wren."

Wren Stevens was small for her age. It wasn't the sort of thing normally said about seventeen-year-old girls. Usually such descriptions were reserved for children but given that Wren had such a childlike appearance it seemed an appropriate way to describe her. She was barely five foot tall, flat-chested and bony. Her eyes – being the size that eyes generally are – seemed much larger than those of other girls as they shone large in her sharp-featured, delicate little face.

It was these large eyes and the name her mother had given her at birth that led to her father giving her the pet-name Birdy. It suited Wren perfectly: the dainty features, the angular bones, her small size. 'Wren' suited her too but, because of its strangeness, it was rarely used. She was always Birdy Stevens.

Before her birth, husband and wife had agreed that, should they have a girl, the child would be christened Jane. But while in labour, Felicity insisted she had seen a miniscule wren fly around the room and thus decided that her child would be named after the bird. It did not seem to matter to her that no one else had seen the bird. Felicity was so convinced of its existence that she asserted the child be christened under no other name. It caused no end of consternation from both sets of in-laws who attempted – in vain – to talk Felicity out of her strange and, frankly, silly name.

Their protestations were met only by a dreamy, glazed stare and a calm, disconnected voice vowing that the little girl would be called Wren and nothing else. Even the local vicar was brought in to try and persuade the new mother of her folly. However, he was disinclined to tell a new mother her business and, being a keen ornithologist, secretly quite liked the name. And so the baby girl was christened Wren Heidi (after her grandmother) Stevens much to the delight of her mother and the irritation of everyone else.

Her childhood was unremarkable yet punctuated by numerous bouts of her mother's unhappiness and rejection of human contact. It was her father who was her anchor throughout her seventeen years and, between them, they raised the other two children – now eleven and eight years old – since her mother was often unfit to care for herself, never mind the rest of the family. It had, therefore, surprised Wren to find herself sent away. She had taken great pains and pride in her efforts with her little brother and sister. To no longer have care of them felt like a disapproval of what she had done previously. She had constantly been there for them and the reward for her efforts was to be cast out onto the charity of a relative she had never met.

On the train from Dublin to Enniscorthy, Wren's stomach filled with butterflies. She felt so sick at the thought of meeting an old, austere German widow with whom she would have to live for who knew how long. Her own grandmother (this lady's sister), whom everyone referred to as Oma – German for 'Granny' – had terrified Wren as a little girl with her sharp accent, booming voice and large ungentle, pincer-like hands. It had been something of a relief to her child-self to discover that Oma was gone and would not be visiting the house again to pinch her tiny legs and shout over her head, "This child is too thin!" If Mrs Charlton was anything like Oma, Wren wasn't sure she would be able to bear it. But then she would have to because her father had told her to.

It was dark when the train finally pulled into the station in Enniscorthy. Wren wasn't sure what would meet her when she stepped off the carriage – whether it would be the lady herself or someone else. An employee of some kind? A servant? Did this lady have servants? With eyes struggling to adjust to the dim light of the platform, Wren squinted, trying to make out anyone that looked as if they might be waiting for her. She didn't know if it would be a man or a woman, someone old or young. Shyness had always crippled her in public situations and standing on the train platform in an unfamiliar town was at the outer reaches of her capabilities. Indeed, she found once she had descended the steps of the train to the platform, she could not seem to move any further. Rooted to the spot and fighting the rising panic in her chest as other folk bustled about quite oblivious to her struggles, she noticed a woman coming towards her.

The lady looked to be in her late middle years – elegant, well-dressed, with a fresh face and neat hair. On closer inspection, the lady's face betrayed a thin spiderweb of lines around her prominent features hinting at her actual age. She was tall, but then everyone was tall from Wren's perspective. She also had, clasped in one hand, a stylish, slim cane but, as she walked smartly along the platform, she didn't use it much. Coming closer, Wren noticed her hair was a steely grey under her hat and that she had a fine gold chain around her neck attached to a pair of spectacles.

"Miss Stevens? Miss Wren Stevens?" the lady enquired.

"Birdy," Wren blurted out. She could not help it. She wanted something familiar, something less formal. "Everyone calls me Birdy."

The lady seemed a little taken aback but she quickly regained a small smile of welcome. "Birdy?" she asked distinctly to which Wren merely nodded. "Ah yes, I quite understand. I see it now. Well, Birdy, how was your journey?" The lady began to walk away before whirling around to face Wren once again. "But I forgot! I'm Astrid. Astrid Charlton. I'm afraid I don't have another name to go by. Where is your luggage? I'll get a porter to have it dropped up to the house."

She was off. Wren trailed in her wake as Mrs Charlton quickly and efficiently organised everything, her walking stick used more liberally as she picked up speed. Once Wren's luggage was dispatched, her great aunt stopped briefly to slow her breath then turned to her. "I thought we might walk up to the house if you're not too tired. I'm supposed to exercise my damaged hip as much as I'm able so I must walk."

Affirming that she was not so tired as to be unable to walk, Wren fell into step with Astrid, pottering with no great speed down the hill to the bridge that crossed the river. It was quite dark though not cold and the streets were mercifully well-lit. Otherwise, Wren would have felt quite afraid to wander about an unfamiliar town at night-time. But her great-aunt seemed to have no such qualms and set a steady pace, greeting many of the few people they met by name and with a quick nod. Wren noted that those who received Mrs Charlton's acknowledgement redoubled and returned it. The lady was, Wren guessed, well thought of in the locality.

As the incline of the hill picked up, their pace slowed and Astrid relied more heavily on her stick. Wren's shyness prevented her from saying much but Astrid kept up a constant stream of small nothings regarding the town, its history, its people and so on.

Her voice was not at all what Wren had expected. Knowing this lady to be her Oma's sister, she had expected the harsh accent of her grandmother. But this woman had the soft, round vowels of an Englishwoman. There was only the slightest edge to some of her words which Wren only heard because she was taking pains to notice them. This woman was also a good deal more refined than her sister. Where Oma had been rotund and ruddy-cheeked, Astrid was pale and so thin that her clothes seemed a little large for her body. She did not stump along puffing all the while as Oma had. If Wren had not been informed by her father that this woman was Oma's sister, she would not have believed it. She found herself suddenly wondering if some cruel trick had been played on her and the lady wasn't her relation at all. But then no one would go to such trouble to hoodwink her so thoroughly. She had to remind herself of her own insignificance. She was not the heroine in some exotic novel. She was just little old unimportant Birdy. And nothing, she thought to herself, had or was going to happen that would change that.

Chapter 7

Before they got to the house, Astrid thought it might be nice if they became acquainted on neutral ground. She knew from personal experience what it was to be thrust into unfamiliar situations at the behest of others and how uncomfortable it was to be the outsider. The pair, therefore, made a detour on their path to Astrid's home, entering a building just off the main square of the town. Wren didn't notice the name of the place but she did register the fact that there was a large semi-circular overhang above the main door with letters forming the word 'HOTEL' perched on top of it. She also noticed the sickly sugar-candy pink and white of the façade before they were swallowed by the dark wood and thick maroon carpets of the foyer. While Wren trailed half a step behind, Mrs Charlton appeared to know exactly where she was going on her way to the dining room. Once there, both were given a table and menus.

It was more than Wren could take in. She could not remember a time in her life when she had ever been in a hotel, never mind a hotel dining room.

The tables matched the dark wood panelling of the walls as did the upholstery of chairs which were a deep, rich red. If she had looked closely, she would have noticed the cobwebs that swung lazily from the brass light fittings. Or the sagging centres of the chairs, many of which also had frayed braiding which drooped unhappily from the edge of the seat. The floors also had an air of neglect. The once thick muffling carpets were worn almost to the hessian backing so that shoes scuffed along as other diners and waiters walked about. But to the untrained and fascinated eye the place was a vision of luxury.

"Do you like it?" Astrid was watching the girl as she gazed around the room, drinking in all the fantastical details, colouring her eyes with a hue that made them shine brighter and more vivid.

Caught off-guard displaying her innocence, Wren blushed crimson. "I – I just … I've never been in a place like this," she said in hushed, awed tones.

Astrid hid her amusement. It was odd to her, brought up with such privilege, to see wonder expressed at so tawdry and worn a place as the town's only hotel. If she had a choice, she would have taken the girl somewhere else. But there wasn't a choice and besides, the food was passable so the rest mattered little. "It's a quaint little place, isn't it?" was all the praise she could muster for the hotel. "I don't come here very often but I thought it might be nice to have a little celebration of your arrival. Start as we mean to go on. Not," she added, "that we'll be dining out every night of the week. Order what you like," she said with a smile, glancing down at her menu. "My treat."

The onus now on Wren to choose something made her panic. Her eyes skated up and down the page, taking in only disparate words like "lamb," "potatoes" and "ox-tail". She hummed and stuttered again.

Astrid, recognising her discomfort, offered to order for her.

Wren's shoulders slumped in relief. "Yes, please. Only …" she glanced down at the menu again, "only, not lamb. I don't like lamb. Sorry." She felt she should apologise for her contrariness.

Astrid waved it off easily. "No matter," she said. "I'm not that enamoured of it myself. A roast beef supper and tea?"

Wren only nodded and whispered out a, "Yes, thank you."

The food was ordered with a pot of tea and the two women, one young, one old, began to talk. At first, Astrid did the majority of the questioning and speaking, trying to fathom whether the girl was slow or simply shy. As their talk continued, answers became longer, more animated – as physical warmth and human kindness softened Wren's tautness and worry. Astrid realised very quickly that her companion was, in fact, afraid of her and wondered why. But as the girl grew in confidence and tiredness checked her caution, she admitted more to her great-aunt than she would have.

Dinner finished, the pair had tea with some overly sweet biscuits which Astrid nibbled without enjoyment, mostly for fear that Wren would not eat them if she didn't. Being young and not altogether accustomed to sweet things, Wren relished the fare as much as her companion disliked it, and Astrid took pleasure in seeing the girl's happiness. After all, it can't have been easy for the youngster. And from what she gleaned from the girl's talk there were two things that played on Wren's mind.

"I thought you'd be like Oma," Wren had said very quietly (she said everything quietly). "I was looking for someone like her when I got off the train. You're so different."

She had never liked her grandmother. There was no warmth to the woman, no kind granny cuddles, no indulgent smiles. There were only flurries of activity when her visits were announced, weeping from Wren's mother, the boom of her voice announcing her arrival then chaos and bitterness left in the aftermath of her visit. Wren couldn't imagine the woman sitting before her ever being the source of such violent extremes of terror and annoyance. She could not imagine any child would fear to crawl into the lap of this true lady with whom she was now to live. Indeed, Wren could almost imagine curling up to this woman without being rebuffed. She dared to hope that she had found the older, wiser female confidante and adviser she had never had before.

Astrid nodded knowingly. She and Heidi had never got on, even when they were adults. One of the greatest insults Astrid could ever imagine was being positively compared to her older sister who was as dissimilar to her as any stranger plucked off the street. It was a wonder to her that this tiny creature who sat so still and demure in front of her had the same blood in her veins as her elder sister. It seemed Astrid's father's side of the family, who were all thin and fine-boned like her and like Wren, had skipped a generation – or maybe two. Astrid did not know what Felicity, her niece, was like since she had never met her. Curiosity made her ask the girl about her family and it was then that Astrid saw the second of the two things that were foremost in Wren's mind: her siblings.

There was a great warmth and a great sadness in the way she spoke about her family. At first, she made no mention of her parents. Instead, she spoke solely of her little brother Arthur and her sister Olivia or Artie and Oli. She had lived for their amusement, their education, their love. For her, the keenest ache was parting from them not her father and, as Astrid soon discovered, definitely not her mother.

Over the next number of days, as the girl settled into the fine house at the top of the hill, her new guardian began to tease out what Birdy's home life had been like. Poverty, it seemed, was not a far-off prospect in their household hence she had not been sent away to school. Instead, she attended the local technical college which she had left three years previously. There, she had received a rudimentary education in the keeping of a household and the female arts of cooking and sewing. She also gained a basic knowledge of more agricultural pursuits such as butter-churning, the management of chickens and the care of small and young animals. To Wren, all of this had been interesting though not altogether useful as it was aimed at the students from the surrounding countryside rather than those who dwelt in the town such as herself. The most useful part of her education, however, was to do with the care of children.

Once she had ceased attending the local technical college at fourteen, she had taken over the care of Artie and Olivia from her mother, or rather from their neighbour who, it seemed, looked after the children more than their own mother did. Felicity had told her husband that she could not spend another minute cooped up with the two wailing children. Therefore, given that Wren had conveniently just finished her schooling, the woman insisted on finding herself some employment away from home. Eric had acquiesced easily to his wife's wishes, finding her work as an under-secretary but she had disliked her new employment as much as she had been irritated by her children. She had taken to her bed, refusing to get up and go to work, pleading sickness even though the doctor could find nothing wrong.

Every occupation Felicity had she grew tired of, even motherhood. Yet, she was still an expert at telling others how their jobs should be done. When she was out of work, instead of helping Wren – still a child herself – she would sit at the kitchen table or in her bed, nagging and criticising until her eldest daughter sobbed. Felicity was her mother's daughter in that way: she had a criticism for everything but no solutions to problems or praise when they were righted. Worse, however, than all of this were the occasions when she would be overcome with fits of rage which made her scream at the children, frightening them half to death. At such times, the only thing Wren could do was take the children away (usually to their kindly neighbour) while she went to fetch her father. Eric would then drop everything and come home to care for his wife, sometimes for days on end. And while all this was going on, the children lived with their neighbour. Wren told Astrid that her mother suffered "with her nerves" at first and said no more. But as she began to trust the old lady, she gave the details of their frequent exiles to Mrs Rogers' house next door – how difficult it was to please her mother, how hard she worked for Artie and Olivia and so on. Only to be separated from them.

It truly caused Wren physical pain to know that she was not there for her brother and sister. But her mother had cast her aside, bullied and condemned her efforts until she had no belief left in her own abilities. She was glad to leave her mother, but her happiness at leaving would have been so much greater if she could have brought Artie and Olivia with her. But when Eric suggested to his wife that all her children leave, when the option was put before her to be rid of what had burdened her for so many years, Felicity suddenly felt the need to possess them. Except for Wren. From Wren, who was almost grown, there was a threat to Felicity. By removing that threat, Felicity Stevens once more became mistress of her own household. Not that Wren would have attempted to usurp her mother. She was happy to mind the children unimpeded. But she wasn't unimpeded and that was the trouble. So, while it was a struggle to leave, Wren soon began to see that her removal to a new place had the potential to make her very happy. She had a clean slate and in her great-aunt found someone who was willing to engage with her, help improve her knowledge, her prospects and her life.

Astrid was easy to talk to – always open to questions and willing to give advice. She gave Wren plenty to occupy her time but also allowed her freedom to roam the house and – once she got to know it – the town too. Wren became a member of the local Irish Countrywomen's Association and found people her own age with whom she could spend her time when not needed by Astrid. Best of all, however, was the arrangement that Astrid made with Geoffrey that Wren should be allowed to care for his two children (who were of a similar age to her own siblings) a few days every week after school.

Wren had missed the silliness of little people. Though the children did not in any way replace Artie and Olivia, they provided her with something familiar. She loved to spend time with them. Passing several hours in the company of little people was one of the greatest joys she had ever experienced in her life. She loved babies and children and while some girls longed for occupations in offices and shops, all Wren wanted in her life was motherhood. She secretly imagined that the children she cared for were hers – that their lives were constantly in her hands.

However, her imaginings only stretched as far as a family which consisted of herself and several children. The space occupied in reality by a husband was, in her imagination, left completely blank.

Chapter 8

The Burnleys were a fixture of the local community. The family had been prominent in the area for much longer than living memory could account for. With the exception of a few bad eggs which were a feature of every dynasty, the Burnleys were generally respected and liked. However, as is often the case with such families, the name had begun to die out with each successive generation less able to provide male heirs to ensure the name's survival. A combination of reclusive men and large numbers of female offspring meant that, locally at least, the name was preserved only by three of the current stock, two of whom were women with one marrying into the name rather than claiming it as a birth right. Despite three Burnley brothers in the previous generation, with two marrying healthy young women, only one of the brothers had fathered a baby boy to continue the name. Yet, after his birth and well into his early childhood, even his parents thought it unlikely that he would survive long enough to pass the name to his own children.

Being weak and sickly, the boy's father, Leonard Burnley, had the baby baptised shortly after his birth so as not to deny the child a chance of heaven should it succumb as it looked likely to. It was for God, not man, to decide whether to allow the little fiend a place in His holy sanctum should the Lord see fit to claim him, while his mother lay dying in the doctor's house on Weafer Street in Enniscorthy.

The child was christened Bertram Francis Burnley, two forenames that had never before featured in the Burnley family tree. However, it was not a love of innovation that led Len to choose these particular names. In fact, a quick glance over the history of the Burnleys showed the opposite, with Leonard's own name featuring at least four times in the last few generations. It was Len's conscious decision to give his son these names so that should any ill come from his birth, the family could disassociate themselves from the child to some extent even if he did still bear the family surname. True, Len had experienced a great thrill on discovering he had a son. But the aftermath tainted the joy of the arrival because Leonard Burnley loved his wife and his other children too. To him, his family, though distinctly female, was perfect and the thought of this close little group losing its matriarch filled him with horror. He was father to five girls and, despite loving each child deeply, he was at a loss as to how to care for them as their mother did. The thought that this new arrival, the result of Len's own burning need to father a male heir, could steal his wife filled him with guilt at causing such pain, at not being satisfied with what God had already given him. His suffering at the prospect of losing his wife was perhaps, he thought, a divine punishment. It stung him keenly.

However, as the weeks wore on his boy, though sickly, clung to life.

By the time Evelyn recovered enough to return home, she had created an idyllic picture of the family life that awaited her. She expected a doting father, a happy baby boy and five little girls hushed in awe at the tiny being she had brought into the world. But most of all, she expected Leonard's favouritism regarding their eldest child to have abated and been redirected onto the head of their baby son.

For years, Lili had been the apple of her father's eye. It

was he who first realised her hatred of her name and began calling her Lili while encouraging everyone else to do the same. She had always been an earnest, hard-working little girl who spoke and behaved like an adult from a very young age. She was his little woman whereas the rest of the children where his little girls. Len loved her – not that he didn't love the rest of his family – but his first-born held a special place in his heart.

Even before the birth of her son, it irked Evelyn to see this ardent, misplaced affection. Spoiling the child had no function and Evelyn could never condone such special treatment. For her, however, her son was a different kettle of fish. But not for Len.

Len's fervent love of his daughter continued instead of being transferred onto – what Evelyn thought was – a more deserving candidate. Evelyn begrudged her eldest child and began shunning her, criticising where none was warranted and, at the same time, clinging even more closely to her youngest offspring. What Evelyn did not foresee was how her favouring one child would lead to her husband doing the complete opposite. Leonard, though he did not consciously mean to, found fault with his only son more often than he found reason to praise him. He was desperately hard on the boy, wanting him to be a man before his time – wanting a miniature version of himself. He had waited, longed, *hoped* for years that he would have a son to pass his life's work to. Yet he didn't want a boy. He wanted a *man*. However, given the child's ill-health and the fact he spent a large amount of time under the influence of his sisters and ever-present mother, it was impossible that Bertram would be formed in the image of his father. As a small child he was delicate and effeminate. He was prone to crying at the slightest provocation. A grazing of a limb, a harsh word from anyone or a denial of his wishes would send him running to his mother to tell tales on his sisters who, in Evelyn's eyes were always in the wrong if Bertram said so. He would run to her, tears streaming down his face (he discovered at a young age that he could make his eyes leak salty water on command) and bury his head in his mother's skirt. It would then follow that Evelyn would either cuddle the boy if it was a self-inflicted injury or investigate if someone else was involved. She would march to the scene of the crime, Bertram in tow, one hand twined in her skirt, sucking the thumb of the other. He grew to enjoy these little dramas of his own creation and could often be seen smiling around a wet red thumb while peering out from behind his mother's ample posterior.

All this, of course, affected how his sisters saw him. It took time to discover that no matter what they did, whether good or bad, their brother was always against them. It was a case of us and them for Bertram, with 'us' being himself and his mother and the 'them' being everyone else. It followed, therefore, that 'them' decided the best defence was avoidance. All five girls had tried to be kind to their little brother. But when Bertram turned on them, it hurt so much that they forgot the sweet little boy and only saw a vindictive little cretin bent on their ruin. It was these occasions that stayed in their memories, throbbing in their hearts' cores.

Had Bertram allowed it, the five sisters would have loved him unconditionally. But he wouldn't, so they didn't. However, Lili, being more patient than her sisters, dealt with her brother's fits of temper better than the others did. She also had the benefit of her father's unwavering support which made the burden of the boy's behaviour and being her mother's chief skivvy easier to bear. It was perhaps this that led to Lili's staying unmarried in the family home while the rest of the girls all married before reaching their twenty-first birthdays.

Alice – Evelyn and Len's second child – married at

seventeen to a boy she met when attending a technical college while Heather married at twenty to a local farmer ten years her senior. The twins Vera and Sarah, who did everything together, married at nineteen to two brothers whom they met at a parish event in the Church Institute. Both had 'done well' in the eyes of the watching multitudes as the two brothers were the only sons of the local bank manager and, therefore, well-educated, with good prospects. Much to their parents' relief, the twins had married on the same day, saving the expense of two weddings by turning it into one event. Not that the Burnleys didn't struggle as it was. Weddings were an expensive business, especially when Heather and the twins were all married in the space of twelve months.

Throughout her sisters' conversions to matrimonial bliss, Lili remained at home. She tended the house and farm work that women were wont to and also tried to help her parents as they aged and discovered they were perhaps not as capable as they had once been. But her main duty was trying to pacify the arguments that exploded between the three others that remained in the household.

Being the eldest (and only) son in the family, it was understood that once Bertram was old enough, he would take over the running of the farm. He was educated at the best fee-paying school his parents could afford and was then in the first crop of students taken into the newly founded Gurteen Agricultural College.

Though her son's absence took its toll on Evelyn, his education was a constant source of pride for her. Everybody knew he was at boarding school and if they did not, Evelyn was sure to tell them. Len, on the other hand, was not so keen on this high-class education and was sometimes heard to say, "Why does he need to go there? I never did and look at me."

"Would you deny the boy a decent education?" was always Evelyn's reply.

"He can have an education without it costing that bloody much!"

At this juncture, it was up to Lili to head them off, otherwise things would descend into accusations of favouritism or lack thereof.

Part of the reason Evelyn found Bertram's absence so hard to bear was that he was a terrible correspondent. Every evening, she would sit down and tell her son the goings-on of the day and, at the end of every week, she would send the letter to him so that he might not miss anything at home. However, she was lucky if she got more than a half page's response from Bertram.

The truth was that Bertram didn't really care for home. It was only when he went away to school that he saw what he was missing in the dull little farm he would one day inherit. For the first time in his life, people did not know everything there was to know about him. They did not know he was the youngest of six with the rest of his siblings being girls. They did not know he had almost died on several occasions as a sickly and snot-nosed child. Also, for the first time in his life, he wasn't the smallest child in his class. And, most importantly of all, his classmates did not know his mother. Not that Bertram didn't love his mother. He loved her more than he loved anyone. The problem was she was nosey, loud, and seemed incapable of holding her tongue. Bertram privately loved her, but was publicly embarrassed by her.

However, Evelyn's behaviour was not the only thing that was a source of disappointment to her son. The truth was, Bertram hated the way she looked. She was fat where the rest of the family were tall and skinny – all except Bertram himself who, fully grown, didn't quite reach five foot three. But Evelyn could be described as nothing other than dumpy. It pained Bertram to watch her. He loathed seeing the rolls of spare flesh shift lazily under the straining fabric of her clothing. He hated seeing her heaving herself from chairs, puffing out her cheeks which would flush red with the effort of such a simple action. Wherever she went, she was accompanied by her own soundtrack of laboured breathing and a heavy footfall. He wanted his mother to be like one of those mothers who was tall, thin and immaculately dressed instead of the tented figure who waddled unbecomingly around his homestead.

But at school he could forget about his family. At school he belonged. In the dorms there was a wonderful sense of camaraderie between him and his classmates. They bore each other's troubles, shared their provisions sent from home and, every now and then, got into squabbles which were not only entertaining to be part of but also watch from the side-lines as the drama unfolded.

And while he was too small to play in the school's rugby team, the most important team in the entire institution, Bertram found a place elsewhere. In the school rowing team, he was cox for the eights – a job which suited him given that he had inherited his mother's loudness. He was part of something bigger than himself yet all he really had to do was yell at his schoolmates as they did all the heavy lifting. In guiding the team to success, he became something of a celebrity among his peers and found it quite a novelty to be known in his own right rather than because of his family.

Through years of competition, regattas hosted by other schools and various other events, Bertram also discovered something else: alcohol.

While his parents both drank, Bertram had not been exposed to drink himself. But once he started travelling the country with a group of teenage boys, he began to experience the influence of alcohol himself. At first, because of his size, Bertram found it took very little beer to make him feel queasy and lightheaded. In the mornings, he would wake with a violent headache, his brain feeling like it was expanding, pressing on the inside of his skull. Unchecked, Bertram gradually conditioned himself to keep up with the other boys until he could stay with them drink for drink despite being a head shorter and several stone lighter than others in his company. This freedom to drink was part of the reason he decided to continue his studies in a farming college. And then there was the hope that he could become more knowledgeable than his father.

Bertram wasn't ready to go home and face his parents. They made him feel like he was still a boy. He wasn't yet old enough to go out of an evening without their approval. He didn't know how to farm. It was infuriating to him to find himself constantly being told what to do. No one asked his opinions. College was, therefore, his attempt to gain the knowledge necessary to give credence to his opinions. And it was also a chance for him to continue to indulge his other thirst.

What Bertram had not bargained on was the interference of the woman he boarded with in Tipperary. Mrs Dagg was a cousin of the Burnley family's vicar, Reverend Harrington. Evelyn was part of the parish council and, at one of their many meetings happened to mention to Rev Harrington that her son was in need of a place to stay while pursuing his studies. Though well aware of the existence of Mrs Dagg, she allowed the Reverend to helpfully proffer the connection himself. In the eyes of Bertram's mother, a widowed late-middle-aged lady was the perfect babysitter for her darling boy and bound to keep him well fed. He was, she told Mrs Dagg in her letters arranging her son's stay, the best, most well-mannered and quietest of boys that ever lived. And, of course, being a widowed lady, Mrs Dagg would greatly appreciate the stimulating presence of such a fine young man.

Arranged without Bertram consent, he found himself packed off to live in a damp-smelling house with a fussy old woman who provided bland meals and even blander company. He hated the house and he hated Mrs Dagg. By the end of the first fortnight, he had been locked out of the house twice. His hostess refused him a key and would insist that he had to knock on the door to be allowed in whenever he arrived. Therefore, when he arrived home late after a night in the pub with his new friends, the old lady refused to get up to admit him. Another issue Bertram had was that Mrs Dagg was of a deeply religious bent, lecturing him on the benefits of virtue and the cost of sin with particular emphasis on the harms of alcohol and tardiness. But when her sermonising seemed to have no effect on him, she took more decisive action. She wrote to his mother.

It was with a real sense of fear that Evelyn opened the letter addressed to her in Mrs Dagg's handwriting. She hadn't received a letter from Bertram since he had gone to Tipperary so there was quite a commotion when news from there arrived. Worry, however, quickly turned to disgust as Evelyn read the enumeration of her son's sins in black ink. However, her fury was directed towards Mrs Dagg more than anyone else for the simple fact that the woman had criticised her son.

There followed a rather heated though slow correspondence between Mrs Burnley and Mrs Dagg, none of which touched the ears of their subject. Bertram continued on in blissful ignorance of the rift he was causing. He continued to drink and carry on with his friends while drawing Mrs Dagg nearer and nearer to the end of her tether.

The snap finally came when, in a fit of rage at yet again being locked out in the wee small hours, the young Mr Burnley threw a plant pot through the front window of the house and proceeded to join the flowerpot, its contents and a considerable amount of glass into the front room. Understandably terrified, Mrs Dagg had fled the house and woken several neighbours in a state of panic at the thought of a burglar rifling through her worldly possessions. Her acquaintances helpfully formed a party armed with a hockey stick, poker and cricket bat but, upon entering the house, discovered no one other than the good lady's tenant fast asleep on the settee in the front room with a few tiny shards of glass caught in his coat.

Mrs Dagg was incensed. Her lodger had frightened her half to death. He had shattered her window and woken her neighbours. Her greatest source of anger, however, was the fact that he had used her favourite plant pot and its contents of bulbs to do the damage. Seeing the little tubers scattered bare-rooted across the floor was more than enough to make her wish a slow and painful death on the culprit.

It took a great deal of persuasion and grovelling on Bertram's part for him to convince her not to expel him from her house immediately. However, he could not prevent her from cycling to the post office at the other end of the village to telephone Bertram's home. Having made so little headway with his mother, Mrs Dagg changed tack and insisted on speaking to *Mr* Burnley. It took the best part of half an hour to wait for Mr Burnley to be brought to the other end of the telephone line but when he did reluctantly and gruffly speak to his son's landlady, his reaction was worth the wait. Leonard Burnley, a man who had barely travelled past his own county lines travelled all the way to Tipperary to personally deal with the aftermath of his son's escapades. It took Bertram a good half day of arguing with his father to convince him not to turn around and take his son straight home.

The window, by this time repaired, was paid for by Bertram at Len's insistence out of the generous allowance he received from his mother. Another purchase made from his allowance was a new plant pot to rehome the salvaged bulbs. This self-same allowance was then stopped and Bertram was found a job in a grocer's shop to fill his spare time. In Len's view, if his boy was going to make a fool of himself and the family name, he was most certainly not going to do it with his family's money.

The incident was the tipping point for what little relationship existed between Leonard and his son. When Len returned home, he did not speak to his wife about what had taken place but she knew instinctively that an irrevocable change had occurred. It hurt Evelyn deeply to see that her darling boy would never be seen through her eyes by her husband. Evelyn had pinned her hope on a good education improving Leonard's estimation of his son, believing that Bertram was the right person to run the farm once Len could not. Instead, the boy's escapades destroyed his credibility and forever altered his father's opinion of him.

When Bertram finally returned home well-educated in the minutiae of modern farming, there was no warm welcome from his father. But neither was there open animosity. Rather, there was silence. Len withdrew, he listened but hardly ever talked to his son. His ideas were met with nothing but platitudes and noncommittal shrugs. Frustrated and hurt, Bertram was increasingly absent in the evenings when the atmosphere in the house was oppressive. Instead, he spent his time in Fat Lar's public house, keeping company with other locals of an alcoholic and semi-alcoholic disposition. Even his mother was no longer a comfort to him. Her constant interference and cajoling annoyed him. Though he loved her, he wished that she loved him a little less as her expectation became a burden, making him feel inadequate as he constantly fell short. He resented her belief in him so much that he sometimes thought life and his relationship with his father might be improved if his mother wasn't constantly trying to improve it for them.

Leonard, meanwhile, turned to his constant source of comfort and companionship. Lili was the bystander throughout the marriages of his other daughters, throughout the trouble his son brought. He clung to her, confided in her and found solace in her steadiness. Though he could not talk to his wife and spoke very little to his son, Len could converse freely with Lili, voice his opinions honestly without fear of contradiction or a descent into argument. And Lili was by no means an empty vessel into which Leonard poured his thoughts and woes. She was intelligent, knowledgeable and had an excellent sense of humour. She was, quite simply, a wonderful person to talk to. It was just a pity that no one else did other than her father. She was still lowest in her mother's pecking order when it came to what Evelyn thought of her children. They were two very different people but the main issue was that Evelyn took herself very seriously. Everything she did had a certain stateliness to it: the way she collected eggs from the hens, the way she walked into church on Sundays and sat as straight-backed as her bulk would allow, the way she poured tea into a cup. Every movement she made was choreographed from youth and carried through to middle age – ingrained in everything she did. Her speech was also affected and sounded like that of a woman with a much greater level of education and breeding than she actually had. This was nothing out of the ordinary considering many people, men and women, spoke better than they had ever been taught to. The difference with Evelyn was that she overdid it and drew attention to the way she talked by talking down to other people.

On the other hand, Lili took very little seriously, least of all her mother. She never tried to be anything. There were no airs or graces with Lili. Her movements were not studied and there was a natural intelligence rather than any pretention in the way she spoke. Yet there was still a natural elegance to her. She knew how to use her long limbs without thinking. In this way she was like her tall, stringy father who walked like a gentleman, upright and long-striding, despite having lived all his life as a farmer. And though few people ever got to talk to Lili without the constant intervention of her mother, when they did manage to get her on her own, they always came away a little shocked by her unforced erudition.

Despite these differences, the family muddled along together in some form of working order. But then, in the winter of 1950, everything on Bachelor Lane changed.

Leonard had always been friendly with Billy Doyle who worked the middle farm on the lane. They were forever calling on one another for assistance, opinions and, the odd time, they would even head off to the pub. Though Len was usually sensible when it came to drink, there was the odd occasion that he took on board more than was strictly good for him. He could never have been thought of as an alcoholic but that did not mean the people he drank with were not. Billy Doyle was especially notorious for hitting the bottle hard and was gradually selling off fields on the outer reaches of his farm to pay for the habit.

The irony of Billy, however, was that while he was the most unfit man to get behind the wheel of an automobile, he was the only person on the lane to possess a car or, rather, a van. There was a running joke locally that whenever Billy left the pub full as an egg on whiskey, a warning signal should be sent out to anyone between the pub and his home. A year never went by without half a dozen instances of Billy crashing into a ditch, driving into a drain or simply steering straight into the front pier of someone else's house. Countless times irate neighbours had called for him to be put off the road or have his licence revoked only to be reminded that he didn't, in fact, possess a licence and besides he had been put off the road before but to no avail. Billy was the local liability but he was even-tempered, thoughtful and would never see a neighbour without help. Therefore, his problems, while they brought about animosity every now and again, were often forgotten before the week was out. It also did no harm that, having demolished a wall or gateway, he would arrive the next day bringing all the tools to repair it, cap in hand, and a "Terrible sorry, M'm" delivered with a whistle through his front teeth. Nobody could hold a grudge against Billy Doyle for long.

Perhaps it was a pity nobody had.

It was a cold evening in mid-January when Billy, instead of driving past the Burnleys' pulled up, knocked on the door and asked if Mr Burnley would care to join him. It was Evelyn whom he met at the door. With Bertram already absent, she told Billy that Mr Burnley couldn't come that evening. However, Len decided that he would go for a drink (just the one) and to hell with Evelyn's protestations. Usually he would have listened to his wife but on this occasion, he didn't. And if Lili had asked him, he would have stayed put. But she didn't. So he left.

The next morning Billy's van was found upended in a field twenty feet below the road having driven over a ditch and plunged down the other side. Both men were still inside, their bodies chilled by the morning frost. Vaguely spattered with a little blood, the smell of whiskey and stout from the pair was what made the greatest impression on young Paddy Masterson who found them – so much so that he didn't touch a drop for months. To spare the family, he thoughtfully left the doors of the van open to allow the incriminating smell to escape. But everyone knew. Everyone knew what had happened to the two men from the Lane.

Evelyn was inconsolable. Though they spent years at odds about Bertram, Leonard had been her partner for three decades. There was genuine sadness at his loss. Yet her grief was not as acute as she led others to believe. It was, instead, proportionate to what she thought others would expect of Evelyn Burnley at such a tragic time. The locals were impressed by her show and Evelyn was consequently happy. However, as a result of her theatrics, the person who experienced true grief was overlooked. While all the girls in the family felt the loss of their patriarch, it was Lili who suffered the most. Everybody around her had someone. Her mother and brother had each other and her sisters had their husbands and children. But for Lili, the loss of her father was like the loss of a crutch that supported her, gave her confidence and a connection to the world.

Evelyn and Bertram, on the other hand, having abided by what they viewed as an acceptable period of mourning, bounced back higher and much more full of life than ever. Evelyn joined every local committee, chaired as many as other members would allow her to and was out more days in the week than she stayed at home. Bertram began to put into effect all the changes his good education had suggested but his father had resisted, spending money on improvement and generally making the local traders very happy. He also spent more time with his mother on the few evenings she was home – much to her delight – but still found he could have enough trips to the pub every week if he went when she was at her committee meetings.

It followed that Lili was increasing left at home on her own to hold the fort "in case anyone calls". Never one to make many public appearances, after her father's death she became something of a recluse. She was not naturally a shy person nor was she disposed to prefer her own company but circumstance had forced her to be what she was not. Still lost after Len's passing, she simply went through the motions of living. Not even the arrival of a new Scottish neighbour (a bachelor) who bought Billy Doyle's farm three months after the accident was enough to rekindle her interest in life. Even when her mother insisted that they, as a family, go to welcome the newcomer to Bachelor Lane, Lili refused, saying vaguely that she "had jobs to do". However, her reluctance to see their new neighbour had more to do with the fact that she never wanted to set foot inside Billy Doyle's house ever again. If she did, she felt all the memories of his life and, therefore, his death would come flooding back, reminding her of her absent father. She would see a new beginning brought about by this stranger that would slowly erode the memories of what had gone before. She stayed away because she could not bear to relive her loss. She could not bear to think that her father was truly gone.

Chapter 9

There was something funny going on with Ewan Cameron.

There was a difference in the way he went about his trip to the shops in the village twice a week and his collection of bags of meal for his sheep. A smile played about his lips and he was more talkative than was his wont. Not that he said much, but normally he said nothing at all without being directly spoken to. Yes, something had most definitely changed and the local women, especially Evelyn Burnley, where aching to know what.

Evelyn saw herself as something of a local authority on Cameron since he was her nearest neighbour so people began to ask her if anything had happened to him lately. Had he perhaps come into a bit of money? Or, much more interestingly, had he acquired himself a lady friend and, if so, who? Evelyn positively burned with curiosity but couldn't for the life her figure out what had brought about the change which was rather silly considering it was her own daughter. But when it came to anything to do with Lili, Evelyn was wilfully and completely blind. If she had paid attention to her daughter, she would have noticed a change in her too. Even Bertram, who seldom thought anything of his sister, thought there was some alteration in her behaviour but, since his mother said nothing, he dismissed it. Bertram surmised if Evelyn hadn't seen and consequently mentioned something – because Evelyn couldn't see anything without telling everyone about it – then there was nothing in it. His flicker of interest in his sister died out and he returned to ignoring her.

Meanwhile, another man was doing the opposite of ignoring Lili Burnley. After their first meeting, Ewan and Lili saw much, much more of one another than they ever had. However, at Lili's behest, they kept their meetings secret so as not to draw unwanted attention from the locals or, more pressingly, the other Burnleys. This was relatively easy to achieve given that her mother and brother paid little heed to her comings and goings. But just to make sure they suspected nothing, Lili only went out to meet Ewan when the rest of the family were absent.

She always got a little thrill when she saw him standing on the lane waiting for her. He never watched for her. He always gazing out across the fields, hands in his pockets, propped up against the trunk of one of the old ash trees that stood sentinel over the length of the lane. Even at a distance, she could tell he was taking everything in, thinking, planning and improving all the time. His eyes would crease in the corners and he had a far-off look of someone meditating on something important. But then farming was important to him. It was everything to him. Almost. When Lili got close enough, he would catch her movement in his peripheral vision and swiftly push himself upright off the tree using only his shoulder-blades, hands still in his pockets. His movements were powerful and sinuous and as he stood ready to greet her, the preoccupied look would vanish to be replaced by a slow, dazzling smile. He was no longer a man approaching the lower cusp of middle age but a boy flushed with pleasure at the thought of spending time with his girl since he now had time *to* spend.

However, it was early May before they could meet with any regularity. While Ewan's wish to see Lili again was genuine, his situation was less than conducive to spending time gadding about without a thought for his responsibilities – namely dozens of heavily pregnant and newly lambed ewes. Yeaning the ewes took up the majority of his waking hours and quite often disrupted his sleep too. It was a case of the heart being willing but the flesh being too dog-tired to be considered good, or even awake, company. Much to his dismay, Ewan found that he had reached the age where he could drop into a doze if he sat still for long enough. And he just didn't want to be that person in front of Lili.

Ewan found it funny and slightly startling that Lili realised this would be a problem even before he did. On the morning he had asked if he could continue seeing her and she eventually agreed, she had asked only that they give each other time: time for her to figure out how to keep their friendship from prying eyes and time for him to get through the business of lambing his ewes. After all, she reasoned, they had time. Neither were going anywhere and it was unlikely she was going to run off with the milkman in the interim. For starters, she didn't particularly like the milkman.

While Ewan resisted her at first, claiming that he could manage his workload and have time for her, she firmly told him not to be stupid. He couldn't live both of these lives at once. He might have disagreed with someone else but he knew, deep down, that Lili was right. She simply understood him and the way he farmed. It was why he willingly agree with her. She just seemed to have that effect on him: making him see the truth of something instead of being bull-headed and charging on. Ewan, in fact, found it quite unnerving how well she seemed to know him. Perhaps she was more like her mother than he had originally thought – a gossip who knew everyone's business better than they knew it themselves. But no, Lili wasn't like that. And it wasn't the type of knowledge that one picked up nattering to a neighbour in Martin's Grocer's. It was an understanding of humanity, of how people thought and worked, of how they were likely to deal with a situation and, subsequently, how to deal with them. She had totally disarmed him and, had Ewan not realised he had the same effect on her, he would have felt the need to steer clear of Lili Burnley. After all, a person with that sort of power over another could be dangerous. But Ewan thought he was safe with her because she, without doubt, cared for him as he did for her.

Ewan, like Lili, was observant. He doubted if Evelyn Burnley ever saw as much as he did when she beheld a person. He read people in a way that was far too subtle for the likes of Evelyn to understand. For example, where Evelyn saw almost nothing when she viewed Lili – no potential, no intrigue, no interest – Ewan saw everything. There was an intelligence, a strangeness in her eyes that piqued his interest. Her gaze intrigued him in a way that the looks of few women could with their desires and life stories printed on their faces as surely as if it had been done in ink. And yet sometimes when Lili let her guard down, he thought he could see into her soul. He wanted to know her, to know her soul, to talk to her about anything, about everything. And he wanted to touch her. God, he wanted to touch her.

But he hardly ever did. It took restraint not to wrap his long arms around her when she walked up to him like an ethereal being with the sun glowing down the left-hand side of her body, catching the stray wisps of her hair and making them shine gold in the evening light. Georgie almost touched her more than he did. The dog would sit patiently at his feet until she saw Lili coming, ears pricking up as she watched the approaching figure with curiosity. It wasn't until Lili was about twenty feet away that she would get up and trot over to her, wait for a rub and then accompany her new friend to her master's side, looking up at Lili's face all the way. Ewan guessed that, even if he did pluck up the courage to embrace Lili, Georgie would likely be on hand to thrust herself between them so as to make sure they did nothing untoward.

Though Georgie was the animal that would, no doubt, keep them apart if necessary, it was his sheep that had given them an excuse to finally meet once again. When Ewan left that morning with a lamb under each arm, he and Lili had no idea what they were going to do. Lili promised that she would "think of something" but for three weeks Ewan only saw glimpses of her and always accompanied by Evelyn. He did consider calling at the house but that would have led to unwanted prying from Evelyn. And, while he knew Evelyn and Bertie often went out in the evenings, he never knew exactly when. And though he often said to himself, "Today I'll call on Lili," something always happened which meant he had to put off their meeting for yet another day.

It was Lili who finally took the initiative. Ewan was in the middle of some sheep when, looking up at Georgie's warning "*Woof!*", he spotted Lili coming towards him. She waved to him from a distance and he automatically waved back. As she came closer, he saw there was a half-smile on her lips.

"Hello! I've been wondering for a while how those little lambs I fed for you were getting on," she said in a rush. "And so ... here I am," she finished with a self-conscious shrug, her cheeks reddening.

It took a moment for Ewan to realise she was no longer speaking. He was too intent on studying her face. He had been thinking about her so much over the last few weeks that he was unsure whether she would live up to his expectations. But she did more than that. He was struck anew by the way she looked and moved, realizing that his memory had not done her justice.

She looked up from Georgie – who had immediately moved to sit at her side – and he smiled.

"They're doing well. Thriving, in fact," he said warmly.

The tension in Lili's shoulders dropped. She nodded happily and smiled back but then, unsure of him, looked away towards the setting sun. It lit her profile beautifully.

"The sunset's wonderful, isn't it?" Her voice was soft and husky, awed at the pink, yellow and orange-streaked sky. But mostly she was just picking something at random to comment on, feeling shy in his presence.

"Yes," said Ewan but he didn't look at it. Instead, he took advantage of her preoccupation to study her.

Lili knew she was being watched. She turned suddenly and caught him staring. They both blushed and looked away.

Ewan chuckled. "Look at us. We don't seem to know what to do with ourselves. We're a grown man and woman. You'd think we'd have a wee bit of sense by now."

"Just because we're both older doesn't mean we've grown up. Or that we know how to …" Lili waved her hand vaguely between them.

"True," Ewan nodded. "But we can try, don't you think?" He paused fractionally then asked, "Are you busy right now?"

"No. But my mother might look for me after a while. You know the way she is." There was a touch of bitterness in her voice that most people wouldn't have picked up on.

Ewan heard it. "I know. We needn't do anything for very long. If we just go for a quick walk, maybe?"

She liked how he left it as a question. It was up to her. He wasn't going to force it. She nodded. "Yes, alright."

Ewan exhaled with a relieved smile. He waded through a few of the sheep to the edge of the pen and easily swung one lanky leg after the other over the edge. He nearly stood on Lili's toes he landed so close to her. She put her hand on his chest to steady herself and he caught her wrist. Their movements were instinctive but, once both became aware of what they did, they stepped back, nervous once again.

"We don't know what we're doing," Ewan muttered with a rueful shake of his head. He smiled.

Lili smiled back. "No. But we'll learn." She turned and began to walk. "Come on, Georgie!" she called.

Ewan watched Lili walk away for a moment then, in a few long strides, caught up. Falling into step with her, they continued with only the dog and each other for company.

That was how their evening meetings began and proceeded as the spring turned to summer. They would agree to meet two or three times a week and would walk the headlands of Ewan's fields and some of the Burnley farm away from the house. They listened to the birds' songs. They watched together as the leaves of trees and buds of wildflowers in the ditches unfurled, turning the bare brown dull hedges brilliant shades of verdant green spattered with pale blossoms. As they watched nature grow, their relationship grew along with it. Their rambles were safe and comfortable, becoming even more so as their familiarity with one another developed. At first, strolling side by side, they spoke of little other than farming, nature and generic local news. Lili was quite proficient in the latter given that she lived with a veritable font of local scandal. However, when Lili spoke of others, it was not with the glee that always filled Evelyn's voice. Her daughter was more matter-of-fact, more sympathetic and less inclined to judge.

Ewan was glad that his own history hadn't become public currency in the three years he had lived in the community. Before he got to know Lili better, he feared that, should he wish to unburden himself to her, everything he said would find its way to every wagging ear in the county by the end of the week. But now that he was better acquainted with her, he felt able to tell her about himself. As they grew closer, they spoke more openly, touched more freely. It was the easy company of two people who were comfortable in each other's presence. Lili trusted Ewan physically. Ewan, in turn, trusted her emotionally. So often he struggled to confide in anyone but found relief in being open and honest with Lili.

Lili found Ewan equally easy to talk to and did talk quite candidly about how her father's death had affected her. When Len died, she lost her confidant, her closest friend and her ally. As she spoke of her father, Lili began to see the similarities between the living, breathing man who trudged happily beside her and the one she had lost three years before. It was heartening to think that men like her father still existed and one of them happened to live next door. She knew her father would have liked Ewan, and that the Scotsman would have liked Len. It comforted her to think her father might have approved even if her mother never would.

That was one of the reasons things went no further than evening walks for the couple: Evelyn. In truth, Ewan would have quite happily married Lili tomorrow and he was almost certain that Lili, if persuaded, would do the same. But Ewan wouldn't ask. Lili was committed to her family. Her place had always been with them and she wasn't selfish enough to change that, even for Ewan. He didn't resent her loyalty. In fact, he found it quite endearing. He hoped that, one day, he would experience that loyalty for himself. But then he wasn't sure whether she would still care for him if she knew the truth about him.

He had spoken at length on their walks about his home

country and she could tell that he missed Scotland. But he never told her his reason for leaving. Lili dearly wanted to ask him why but felt that, when he was ready, he would tell her himself. She trusted him and, for now, that was enough.

It was getting on for Midsummer's Day and, after one of their evening walks, Lili was taking her leave of Ewan.

Suddenly, he blurted out, "Are you going to the parish dance on the nineteenth?"

Lili was surprised he even asked. "No. Why? Are you?"

He didn't meet her eye, instead scuffing a stone at his feet. "Well," he paused awkwardly, "I was thinking I might want to go. If you came with me."

"But you know we can't be seen together," she said, trying to judge where he was going with this. She had a funny feeling she knew exactly where and tried to head him off. "Think of all the talk there'd be if Ewan Cameron turned up to a dance with Lili Burnley." She gave him a playful nudge and continued, "You'd break the hearts of half the women in the parish – of most the women in the parish," she amended.

"Most of the women in the parish are married," he said with a twisted smile.

"And you think that'd stop half of them," she joshed.

"Anyway," he said, raising his voice slightly to try and get the conversation back on track, "I don't care about the hearts of the parish."

"None of them?" asked Lili.

"Only one," he paused for thought. "Well, two if we're counting mine as well."

"You might want to do that alright, if we're counting."

Ewan took her hand. "Come with me. Please?" He knew he hadn't convinced her when she tried to reply almost immediately. "No, wait. Hear me out. We'll meet somewhere near here and I can take you almost all the way to the parish hall. Then I'll drop you off and we can go in separately. As if we hardly know each other. It'll be as if we meet for the first time at the dance."

He could see that Lili found the prospect appealing. But still there was the fear of being seen in public. She was afraid of the repercussions. Of *talk*. Living with who she lived with, Lili knew what it was like to hear people's personal lives discussed with the flippancy of a conversation concerning the weather. Ewan understood why it was not something she wanted for her own life. But he was also growing restless. While he loved their evening walks and the odd touches and tiny kisses they afforded, he wanted more. He wanted the relationship to grow, to change, to develop into something. Something more.

He had thought about it long and hard and finally concluded a public dance was the way forward. Many local Church of Ireland folk went to them – no matter their age – though most of those who did go were unmarried given that once a marriage occurred, children usually followed – sometimes with suspicious swiftness. Ewan had never been to a dance since leaving home. Indeed, it was an incident that took place at a similar gathering at home in Scotland that had finally caused him to up sticks and move, not only out of the local area but to an entirely different country. But that was different and, though the experience had scarred him more than anyone knew, he did not think such an occurrence was likely a second time round, especially when he had been so careful to withhold any damning information about himself. Discretion had kept him safe for three years. But they had been the loneliest three years of his life. Yet, they had been far from the worst. He had his farm and his animals and they gave him some level of contentedness. But it was no longer enough. He wanted *more*. He wanted Lili.

"So?" he asked delicately.

"'So' what?" she replied a little tersely.

Ewan willed himself to stay patient, not to raise his voice. "Will you come to the dance? With me." He batted his hand through the air as if he was swiping away his own words. "Will you come to the dance, whatever way you *get* there, and once you get there, will you dance with me?" He finished with a huff and turned away from her slightly, gazing out across the fields.

He was fighting the urge to shout, '*Just come, will you!*' in desperation, but he knew he had to stay calm. It was her decision and he had to respect her choices even if quite a few of them were motivated by what her mother and brother might say. He had to remember that Lili shared a roof and bloodlines with these people and, no matter what he thought, she ultimately knew what was best for her. He just hoped he was best. The silence continued. He felt the pressure building inside of him. If she didn't speak soon, he was likely to explode with hope, fear, speech – anything.

A cool, long-fingered hand slipped into his and squeezed tightly. He turned to meet her eyes. Her smile. Relief flooded through him. Lili noticed his shoulders sag and his head drop as the anxiety left him. She reached up on her tippy-toes and rested her forehead against his.

"I'll come," she whispered.

And with that she kissed him on the lips and was gone, running down the lane with her hands outstretched, like a girl in the first flushes of love.

Chapter 10

As spring ended and the summer of 1953 began, Wren settled into her new life in the south-east. Previously, in the west of Ireland, she'd been used to bad weather and gloomy days but in Enniscorthy the sun shone brighter and more often. Prior to her move, she considered herself an indoor person, preferring to work in the kitchen or be near a fire than to experience the feeling of the wind on her face and the sun or rain on her cheeks. Yet now she walked daily, no matter what the weather did – not for errands, not because she had to but because she wanted to. She had been pale and weak of body when she arrived – oppression did that to young girls. But now she had colour in her cheeks, laughed and smiled much more and had vigour and strength in her body from her daily trudges up and down the hills of the town.

In short, Wren blossomed. She was free from the constraints of her family, free of the expectations of those who presumed that her character would remain unchanged. It wasn't until she cast off their influence that she realised how like her namesake she had been: a bird trapped in a cage. Now she was free to explore both herself and the world around her. She realised she was a much gayer person than she had been permitted to be. She was happy to indulge frivolity. She was, in fact, more intelligent that anyone previously gave her credit for. And she also discovered that she loved to read.

There had never been many books in her house as neither of her parents were interested in pursuing such a pleasure. But her auntie (as Wren now called her) had thousands of books and loved to recommend and discuss the stories once they had been read. She discovered the lives of heroes and heroines, different worlds filled with strange people previously unimaginable to her. She also gained a new understanding of relationships between men and women, growing to love the neatly woven tales of courtship wrapped up and nicely presented in the novels she now devoured daily.

However, more and more she also cared for Johnny and Winnie Charlton, Astrid's step-grandchildren, whom she would collect from school or from their home and bring about town with her. Both children were only a few short years away from leaving home to go away to boarding school but they were still exceedingly childlike in the way they played and interacted with Wren though, to their credit, they were always unfailingly polite and well behaved. The only trouble she ever had was not with the children themselves but with their pet: a beagle by the name of Rodney.

Rodney was as spoilt as either of the children but, sadly, had not been given manners along with his privileges. Wren – unused to animals – soon found she had a strong aversion to them if all creatures were as badly behaved as Rodney. What made him so disappointing to her was the fact that some days he behaved impeccably, making her reluctantly fond of him, but on others he was totally uncontrollable and embarrassingly naughty. Yet the children insisted that he accompany them on their strolls around the town and it often fell to Wren to take charge of the dog as he was too strong for the children to lead. This in itself produced funny looks from passers-by as they watched a young girl being towed along by a dog with two children trotting in her wake. Indeed, Wren was sure that her arms must have increased in length since her arrival given that they were hauled out of their sockets on a regular basis. Yet without the existence of the wretched little dog, a peculiar event might never have occurred on the streets of Enniscorthy one afternoon.

Wren had been living in the town for almost four months by the time the heat of June arrived in the district. Despite the warmer weather in that part of the country, it was the first occasion she decided to finally put on one of her summer dresses. She only had two and had been saving them for only the best of weather. The one she wore on this particular day was a cream colour with a tiny pattern of orange-and-yellow flowers with green leaves. It was a dress she had made for herself the year before, drawing on the skills she gained in the technical college and the experience she had from making clothes for her little sister. Her first thought was always to make something for Olivia but the material for this dress had been bought specifically so she could make something for herself. Her father, marvelling at her skill in making clothes for others, had thought to treat her by giving her fabric for herself. However, through diligent measuring and cutting, Wren saved enough material from her own dress to make one for Olivia too. Thinking of this as she walked the streets of the town, she wondered if Olivia was wearing her dress today too or if she had outgrown it already. It was always a wonder to Wren how quickly small children grew and that once they reached adulthood, they simply stopped. But, going back to thoughts of Olivia's dress, she reflected that the weather might not be as favourable at home as it was in Enniscorthy. And there was also the possibility that, knowing Wren made the dress, her mother would prevent Olivia from wearing it. Felicity was funny like that.

Such musings accompanied Wren all the way to the 'Little Charltons' House' as she called it. This was despite the fact that Geoffrey Charlton's house was three times larger than her aunt's. It was simply the appellation she afforded the place when thinking about it in her own mind because the little Charltons lived there and, while she liked Mr Charlton and his wife, it was Johnny and Winnie who were the most important residents to Wren.

Johnny met her at the door when she arrived. He flung it wide and smiled happily on seeing her. Wren was something of a favourite of his. She was pretty and delicate and, being almost of a size with her, Johnny thought himself very important when he walked about town with her. He saw himself as her protector and took great pride in his duty to guard her on their outings, from arrival to departure. Once she left, however, it was a case of Wren having to defend herself because Johnny was invariably engaged elsewhere – usually eating his supper.

"Hallo, Birdy!"' he called cheerfully, followed by an invective of, "Back Rodney! No! *Back*!"

"*Johnny! Close the door! Quickly!*" yelled his mother who came rushing into the hallway looking harried. But she was too late.

Rodney slithered out the door past Johnny's bare knobbly knees and charged along the garden path straight through Wren's outstretched fingers as she dived to close the gate with one hand while trying to catch the dog with the other.

Out the gate, across the road, over a low wall and gone.

Wren, Johnny and his mother all stood helplessly immobile as they watched the dog disappear from view, the sharp point of his white-tipped tail the last part visible as he soared neatly out of sight.

Nelly Charlton was the first to regain her voice. "Oh Johnny! Now look what you've done! No, don't!" she added, catching her son by the back of his starched white collar as he made to follow the dog, nearly throttling him in the process. "Don't you dare go off and get your good clothes all mucky."

"But, Mother –" he began.

She swiftly cut him off. "Don't you 'but Mother' me, young man. It's your own fault. You *know* what Rodney's like. *No! Leave the dog!*" she hissed as he struggled against her vice-like grip, his face going red with agitation.

"*Muuuuummmmyyyyy!*"

"Oh God, *not now*," Nelly muttered as she manhandled Johnny back into the confines of their garden.

"*Mummy! Mummy, where's Rodney gone?*"

Winifred stood in the doorway looking like a cake decorator's confection, all shiny pink bouffant dress and pigtails. She also looked like she was about to burst into tears. Taking in Winnie and Johnny's immaculate clothing, Wren momentarily wondered what the occasion was. Then she remembered that Nelly's mother and father were coming to visit. However, she was almost sure they were supposed to be coming the next day. She asked to be sure.

"My mother and father are coming a day early." It was no wonder she looked harried and was absolutely determined to keep the children out of mischief.

"I'll go and look for Rodney," Wren offered.

Nelly sagged with relief. "Are you sure?"

Wren (reluctantly) nodded.

"Oh, you're such a pet!" Nelly exclaimed, briefly patting Wren's shoulder. She turned and ran flat-footed up the path to the door, shooing the children in front of her calling, "Thank you!" over her shoulder before closing the door.

Wren stood at the end of the garden path with no idea of what to do next.

Her first port of call was the far side of the wall he'd

hopped over and promptly disappeared. She peered tentatively over it, hoping that he was perhaps sniffing around at the base just out of sight and she might get to climb over and catch him. But all she saw was copious amounts of nettles and she wasn't about to go crawling through them to locate the dog. He really wasn't worth it. If he had been stung by every single nettle on the far side of the wall then so be it, he wasn't going to get any sympathy from her. She sighed, pushed off the wall and began to make her way down the pavement towards the centre of the town. It was going to be a long afternoon.

Two hours later, Wren had seen neither hide nor hair of the dog. She was almost at the centre of the town having criss-crossed her way down the hill trying to work out where Rodney was most likely to go when not firmly attached to a person on the other end of a lead. The afternoon drew on, the sun slid around to the west and the wind picked up making the temperature drop. Still in her summer dress, she began to feel the cold as it pebbled her exposed skin with goosebumps. She'd forgotten to bring a cardigan. Muttering what simple curses she knew under her breath as she rubbed her chilly arms, Wren was trotting down Cathedral Street onto the Main Street when she heard a kerfuffle in one of the shops.

She was only a few yards from the bakery when a woman's voice bellowed, *"Oh no ye don't, ye little fecker! Out! Out!"*

Wren felt her stomach drop as she picked up the pace only to have Rodney shoot out of the shop in front of her with his tail between his legs, a bridge roll in his mouth and a large lady brandishing a broom in pursuit.

"Stop him!" she screeched. *"Thief! Stop him."*

"Oh God!" whimpered Wren, mortified. "I'll be back in a moment!"

She called as she flew past the bewildered shopkeeper

and ran after the dog. She wasn't about to let him escape now. She careened down the hill, plimsoll shoes pat-pat-patting on the pavement. He hung a left down Slaney Street and she flew after him, skidding on the corner as she made the turn. But Rodney was already well down the steep street and gaining momentum. He was going to get away from her again, she just knew it.

A young man stepped out of Sheehan's shop halfway down with a paper bag under his arm. Wren acted on impulse. *"Stop him! Please!"* she yelled.

It would never have crossed her mind to address a stranger in normal circumstances. She was just too shy. But on the spur of the moment and in desperation the words left her lips before she had time to realise she was saying them.

A little startled, the young man looked up in time to see a small dog coming towards him pursued by a young girl. Without thinking, he dropped his parcel, bent down, stuck out his arm and neatly caught the dog around the chest, flung his other hand round its middle and lifted it partially off the ground as its momentum carried it through his arm. But he held fast. The dog squirmed a little before going limp. He then wolfed down the roll he had been carrying in four massive gulps, making his cheeks bulge and his neck stretch up so as not to drop a morsel.

By this point, Wren had come puffing to a stop beside them, cheeks flushed and holding her sides. Still crouched over the dog, the young man looked up only to quickly look down again. Wren watched a red flush wash up his neck, up his face all the way to his hairline. Immediately self-conscious, Wren's toes curled, her plimsolled feet pointed in and her hands began clasping and reclasping one another. She didn't know what to do in a situation like this and he wasn't helping her.

The colour began to fade from his cheeks. "Is the dog yours?" he asked.

"Yes – I mean no!" Flustered, she tried to explain. "I – he's – he belongs to ..." She wasn't sure what designation she should give to the Charltons. "Friends of mine," she finished.

He nodded, still not looking up. There was another pause. "Have you a lead for him?" he asked.

That stumped her for a moment. "Oh. No ..."

"Never mind. Here, grab a good hold of his collar." His manner changed perceptibly when he had something to do, but he still didn't raise his eyes to her. Wren wondered suddenly what colour they were. His hair was curly – dirty blond with sun-bleached lighter streaks peeping out from under his cap. He was broad-shouldered – stocky, she thought, but couldn't be quite sure as he hunched over Rodney. Taking hold of the dog's collar, she crouched opposite the young man as he opened his paper bag and produced a large ball of binder twine, took out a penknife, measured off a length and fastened it to Rodney's collar. Once the dog was secured, he stood. Wren took this as her cue to stand as well. When she did, the young man looked directly at her and then away again, his hands playing with the end of the piece of twine attached to the dog.

He was taller than she thought he was when crouched down. While the top half of his body was broad and well-muscled, he had a narrow waist and hips connected to legs that looked too long for the rest of his body. His face was large and slightly boyish but maybe that was because a red glow stained his cheeks. He huffed a little as if he was attempting to say something but thought better of it. He was saved from going any further by the arrival of another young man who stepped out of Sheehan's behind them.

"You right, Robbie?" the second young man asked, not looking at Robbie but instead directing his gaze unblinkingly at Wren. It was a penetrating stare which seemed to take in every inch of her. He then nodded his head

101

a little as if he was letting her know he approved of her before turning his full attention to Robbie. "Well, man, are we off?"

Wren, who had been caught off-guard by this new apparition, looked again at Robbie and found him watching her.

"Yes," Robbie said gruffly. Then, thrusting the string towards Wren, he said, "Here. Watch you don't hurt your hand on the twine," and with that instruction, spun on his heel and set off down Slaney Street. towards the river.

The newcomer, however, paused.

"Will you be alright now?" he asked kindly.

Wren nodded. "Yes, thank you. And … and can you tell your friend thank-you. For his help. And the string."

"I will, of course, no problem at all. Well then," he doffed his cap to her, revealing dark-brown hair slicked back, "'til we meet again, miss."

They took one more lingering look at one another then turned away, she travelling back up the hill while he walked down it to join his friend who stood waiting below them.

However, before Wren reached the top of the street, she heard a voice call.

"*Miss! Miss!*"

Turning, she watched the second man come puffing up the hill towards her, his cap once again in his hand. He looked lean and fit but he had short legs and found the gradient trying. By the time he got to her, he was completely out of breath and she had to wait for him to regain his voice as he bent over with hands on knees.

"My friend – *hoo!* – my friend – Robbie – asked if he might know your name," was what he finally managed to choke out.

"Oh, it's Wren, Wren Stevens," she answered, wondering why he would possibly want to know her name.

"Stevens?" he said quizzically.

"Yes." She looked down at her feet as he smiled good-humouredly back at her.

"Do you ever go to the tea dances in the Church Institute, miss?"

The question caught her off guard. "No. But I've been thinking I'd like go to the next one. I know some other people who go to them so ..."

"Well, maybe myself and Robbie'll see you at the next one then, eh?"

"Maybe, yes," she muttered into her chest.

"Excellent!" he beamed. "See you then, Miss Stevens." He turned once again and began to trip jauntily down the hill.

Wren wondered if what she said had given gave such liveliness to his gait.

"*Sir!*" she called, stopping him in his tracks. He faced her once again. "Might I know your name too?"

He smiled a dazzling smile and began walking nonchalantly backwards, hands in his pockets. "If you dance with me at the next tea dance, I'll tell you!" And with that he swung round and loped down the hill to Robbie, clapping his friend on the shoulder before walking on. But not before looking back once more, a large smile on his face as he drank in every inch of the girl in the orange-and-cream summer dress standing above him.

Chapter 11

It was with a true sense of excitement that Wren anticipated the next dance in the Church Institute. It fizzed in the pit of her stomach and bubbled up through her chest and head at unexpected moments. It made her feel dizzy. Her skin seemed to tingle. She would be occupied at her work and then would suddenly find herself smiling for no apparent reason. It was, in fact, a little disconcerting to her as she had seen her mother do something similar when she was in the middle of one of her bouts of nerve trouble. Felicity's expressions could change with the click of a finger and return to their original state with similar speed. But the real problem was that her moods were just as changeable as her expression, swinging back and forth with frightening rapidity. Wren just hoped the fleeting thoughts that flitted through her mind were not the stuff of Felicity's. She didn't want to be like her mother.

Astrid noticed the change but couldn't put her finger on the cause. She knew it all stemmed from the day Rodney went on his merry jaunt. She heard all about the episode when Wren got home. But she also knew the girl wasn't telling her the whole story. Wren had recounted the escapade in great detail until the very end, finishing with, "And then a man caught him." She had built the story to a crescendo only for it to end in a whimper instead of a bang. She had painted every facet of her story so vividly up to that point that it made Astrid wonder who had caught the dog and why he made such an impact on the girl. She worried for her little Birdy (that was how she now liked to think of her) and what effect a man might have on a child as innocent as she was. Because she was innocent. The most minor of conversations with the girl would tell you that. And Astrid did not know how best to go about educating that innocence. She wasn't even sure she wanted to.

Her suspicions were confirmed within the week when Wren approached her with mumbling apologies and stuttered questions followed by a promise that she wouldn't mind if Astrid didn't want to.

"Don't want to what?" asked Astrid, fighting her impatience as she watched Wren worry the hem of her skirt.

But even that question made the girl balk, shake her head and get up to leave. Curbing her frustration, Astrid said as calmly as she could, "No, darling, what is it?"

Wren coloured noticeably but Astrid kept her face as neutral as possible so as not to scare her great-niece off. Eventually (though it took some not inconsiderable amount of persuasion) Wren asked Astrid if she might have a new dress to go to the Church Institute social on the coming weekend.

Astrid knew Wren had been asked to go to the socials on several occasions by her new friends in Enniscorthy. There were a number of nice young girls around her age who had made a conscious effort to make her feel welcome but, being shy, Wren struggled to socialise with any of them. She was yet to accept the girls' invitations to the socials, merely telling them she "might go" but then deciding against it when the day came. It worried Astrid somewhat to see the child's reserve and fear of society. That mentality was totally alien to someone who attended many London parties in her youth. But, in a way, she was also glad that Wren maintained her childishness and wanted to stay at home with her old aunt rather than go out with her friends. She knew it was wrong, but there was a small part of Astrid that wanted to deny Wren a new dress and keep her at home. But indulgence won out.

"Of course you can, darling. We'll head down the town to get one tomorrow and make an afternoon of it."

It turned out that Wren was unfamiliar with the activity of clothes-shopping since her mother bought all her clothes on days she was well enough to venture outside. They also had very little money which limited their purchases. With Astrid, however, money was no object. It almost embarrassed Wren to see such freedom with coins and bills – all of which was being spent on her. But, by the end of the day, her mortification was tinged with pleasure as she was the proud owner of two new dresses instead of one and a new pair of shoes to boot.

She had been deeply worried about buying dresses as so much of the clothing she wore made her look like a little girl rather than the young woman she wanted to be. Her biggest disappointment was the flatness of her chest which was only exacerbated by the pucker of empty fabric that sat over her sternum with all the dresses her busty mother bought her. But, as always, shopping with Astrid was different. Being a woman who knew the importance of dressing properly, both in terms of how one looked in the eyes of other people and how one felt in the clothes one wore, Wren's aunt took great care to find the right size and shape of garment to fit perfectly.

Wren finally returned home glowing with happiness, her purchases wrapped in tissue paper so that they might not be creased in transit. Before anything else was done, she ran upstairs with her packages and hung both dresses on the door of the wardrobe so that she might sit on the bed and look at them. There was something about happiness that brought out the child in her – the little girl who always wanted a pretty dress to twirl about and dance in. Looking, however, wasn't enough. Soon she was running the fabric through her hands, tracing the patterns with her fingertips, taking it off the hanger and pressing it to her body, taking off her plain cotton dress and getting into the new one. She sat on the edge of the bed in a cream dress with purple flowers tinged with pink the size of tea plates. Lying back on the covers, she felt the cool of the sheet against the bare V of skin between her shoulders as she listened to the rustle of the two fabrics rubbing with her slightest movement. She sat up again and fanned out the skirt of the dress around her.

While she was still perched on the edge of the bed, her skirt circling her hips, Astrid knocked and came in. Seeing the look of pure joy on the girl's face was enough to make the grand old lady's throat close over. It was a gift, she thought, to conjure up so much happiness with something that, in her life of privilege, seemed so little. Again, she feared the girl's innocence yet knew no matter what Birdy asked of her, she would willingly provide it. The child's guilelessness and absolute delight in the small things in life made Astrid want to keep her happy because seeing Birdy in raptures made her happy too.

"Don't crease your dress," was the only warning she gave before closing the door softly behind her.

Chapter 12

On the day of the dance at the Church Institute, Wren was beside herself with a combination of nerves and excitement. Some of the other girls arranged to collect her from home and head down to the hall but when they didn't arrive on time, Astrid almost had to physically restrain Wren to stop her from going on her own. Being young, she worried that the others had forgotten about her, that they were perhaps playing a trick or abandoning her and going on their own merry way.

As it was, the two girls, Mary and Joan, were simply late. They came running up the garden path, giggling and gushing profuse apologies to which Wren replied, "Oh but I didn't notice you were late at all!"

Hearing Wren's airy dismissal of her friends' explanations, Astrid fought to hide her smile. However, it took some effort to maintain a cheerful demeanour as she watched her young charge collect her handbag and cardigan before following her friends out the door. The old lady assumed what she was experiencing were the pangs a mother experienced on seeing off a child on their first day of school: it was another phase in their growing up, another expanse of distance between someone being your child and their own adult. She fought the urge to call her grandniece back – to warn her away from the outside world. But Astrid couldn't do that. Like any mother, she had to let her child go. She had to let Wren grow up.

Wren was, of course, completely oblivious to the inner turmoil of her guardian as she linked arms with her friends and jogged down the hill towards the centre of town. They didn't see many people as it was too early for the general flow of traffic towards the pubs and too late for the usual daytime townspeople to still be out and about. However, once they turned the corner onto Church Street, they became a little more hopeful. A group was beginning to congregate outside the Institute, milling around waiting to go in with friends, smoking, taking in the last rays of sunlight and making their predictions on what the weather of tomorrow would bring.

You could tell that many of the gathered crowd were farmers – in from the local countryside for an evening's entertainment – by their talk of grass growth and milk prices from the creamery. Many were there to court existing sweethearts or pick up new ones. Indeed, while they were still halfway up the street, one of the gathered men in a shirt with sleeves rolled up hollered to them and waved vigorously in greeting. Joan detached herself from Wren's arm and trotted down the street to meet him.

Mary and Wren, however, maintained a more leisurely pace. They passed Joan who was, by that stage, in deep conversation with her young man and continued through the door, proceeding up the stair to take their place on one side of the room while the men assembled on the other. Mary immediately began to converse with another acquaintance giving Wren the opportunity to study the gathered mass of men for the people she was looking for.

Both of the boys she met that day on Slaney Street had stayed in her mind throughout all her preparations for the night. She wasn't sure which of them she wanted to see more. The pair had piqued her curiosity and she had whiled away hours weighing up the pros and cons of each should she come across them again. The first one, Robbie, was much more handsome than the other. Taller and physically more imposing. But Robbie barely managed to string a sentence together. He had been quiet and abrupt in contrast to his loquacious and playful anonymous friend. This unnamed friend lacked Robbie's stature but was not without favourable looks. He was thinner, stringy-looking even, and had dark floppy hair with deep-brown liquid eyes which made Wren feel like her insides where aflutter when she thought of his direct gaze. She hoped both were there so that she might continue to compare them but, if it came to it, she would settle for the presence of one.

Scanning the crowd quickly at first, she felt her stomach drop in disappointment. Neither of them where there. Not to be put off so easily and also to prevent herself from bursting into tears, she examined the crowd once more but slowly this time, studying each face before discarding it.

And there he was. Robbie. She hadn't spotted him the first time as, in her memory, he wore a cap. But now he sat staring into space, capless and not looking particularly comfortable. As she watched, he ruefully ran his palm over his head several times as if he hoped to erase people's gaze by brushing it away. There was a slight pang of regret that he was alone. If she could have chosen only one of them, it would have been the other one. She watched him for a while, trying to decide what she thought of him but soon gave up. In all the time she stared at him, he never looked up. He was a boring subject so Wren eventually found herself being drawn into the conversation between Mary and another young girl. However, once the music started, Wren's night began to improve dramatically. Unbeknownst to her, while her attention was focused on Robbie, she had caught the eye of several young men in the assemblage who wasted no time asking her to dance. Unsure how to rebuff this interest politely, she simply accepted the advances of several men and danced the first three dances with three different partners.

When it came to the fourth dance, however, she got a little surprise as she found herself face to face with Robbie. She had spotted him while she was being whirled around the floor by other boys, knowing exactly where he was since he never moved from his original position. Now he stood in front of her, taller than she remembered (but maybe that was because she had stood uphill from him), and with a pleasant though shy smile on his face.

"Can I have the next dance, miss? If you're not going with anyone else," he added, looking around as if to check that no one else was coming to take her from him.

"Yes – I mean, I'm not dancing with anyone else," she replied.

The smile that broke across his earnest features was something to behold. It transformed his boyish roundness into something far more masculine and grown-up with creases forming around his eyes. It made Wren see the potential in this boyish man. However, just as he was about to lead her into a space on the floor, Wren found her elbow in the grasp of an unfamiliar hand with a corresponding hand also taking hold of Robbie's elbow.

"Ah now, Robbie, I've had my eye on this one since I walked into the room. You're not going to take her off me, are you? You who have all the women after you."

It was the other young man!

He was not exactly as she remembered. His cheeks were a little flushed and his eyes looked a little more vivid than they had on their first meeting. Shorter than Robbie by several inches, he still seemed to have power over his friend as Robbie reluctantly relinquished Wren to his grasp. However, she thought she had detected a small, reddening embarrassment at the mention of "all the women" that were interested in him.

"Another time," he muttered, then turned and abruptly walked away.

The other man smiled at Wren, bowed then led her to the centre of the floor just as the music started up once again. He moved not without some skill but there was a certain studied quality to his footwork as if he lacked natural grace and was simply doing the steps he had been taught.

As they pottered slowly around the floor, Wren asked, "Are you going to tell me your name now? Or is it a secret?"

He laughed then, taking a better hold of her, answered, "It's not a secret. It's Bertram. Bertram Burnley. And you're Wren Stevens, Astrid Charlton's great-niece, aren't you?"

Wren was a little taken aback. She knew she'd given him her name when they first met but wondered how he knew about Auntie Astrid. She realised he must have asked someone about her. She found it quite disconcerting to think someone she didn't know was finding things out about her. She worried about how much he might know of her situation, of her family. One of the reasons she felt so comfortable in her new home was because she was unknown and of little concern to anyone. Maybe people knew more about her than she thought.

"How do you know that?" she finally asked, having allowed her brain to freefall through her worries for a moment.

Bertram smiled reassuringly. He could tell by her face that he had shocked her and he didn't want to scare her off straight away. This was a flighty little bird if he was any judge.

"I think you might know my mother, Evelyn Burnley?

She's in the ICA. She knows Mrs Charlton well and I heard her talking about Mrs Charlton's niece. Mammy said she was a young pretty thing named after a bird but she couldn't remember what one. You're young and pretty so ..." He let the sentence hang delicately as Wren blushed and looked down. He wanted to bring her chin up to make her look into his eyes – to see that he was serious and not simply being flippant or making fun of her – but thought that might be too bold. He would have to be gentle with her. "Two and two, you know." He shrugged. "I may be a farmer but I can just about add two and two!"

That made her look up. She giggled – a high purring sound that seemed to come from deep within her chest. The sound was a bit of a shock to Bertram who momentarily seemed to lose his wits, his face slackening. He wasn't expecting such an unguarded happy sound from the girl who appeared to be so reserved.

As they continued to dance, Wren ventured to speak. "You live on a farm then?"

"Aye," said Bertram enthusiastically. "Inherited it from my father. I'm the only boy, see. Five older sisters. All but the eldest married off. She lives at home with Mammy and me."

"I grew up in the town," Wren said sadly. "I think I'd love to have grown up on a farm. All those animals just ... *there*. I like animals. Well, not Rodney. Rodney's a –" she broke off and huffed crossly.

It was Bertram's turn to laugh. She had such a severe frown on her face from the instant she mentioned the name.

"Rodney's the dog I met you with. He's horrible."

"Ah but if you hadn't had him that day you wouldn't have met me, would you?"

That stumped her for a moment as she considered his point. It was a good one. "But that doesn't stop him from being awful. He's just so naughty."

"In my experience, most animals behave the way humans have taught them to. Or not taught them. I think that might be the problem with your little Rodney. Is he spoilt?"

"Rotten. He belongs to Auntie Astrid's grandchildren and they're terrible with him. Always encouraging him to misbehave. They think it's *funny*." She sounded almost scandalised.

"Well, I can assure you that the animals on my farm are very well behaved," Bertram continued. "And if you should ever want to see them, you're more than welcome to come along and have a look. I could give you the grand tour." He tried to keep the hope in his voice to a minimum. He didn't know her well enough to guess how she might respond. But he needn't have worried.

Her face glowed with feverish anticipation at the prospect. "Oh, I'd love to!" Her knees bounced just like a little girl's as she said it.

It was such a childish gesture, fitting perfectly with her physique, he thought.

"Well, I'm sure we'll manage to get you over some day. It'd have to be a day I'm not too busy though. Give you my full attention and all that, eh?" He smiled but it was a fixed smile.

Not knowing Bertram (or men in general) that well, Wren never noticed. But Bertram's thoughts left him somewhat perturbed. How would he explain inviting a stranger to the farm, especially a young girl, without his mother asking an unmerciful amount of questions? Though he loved his mother dearly, he was not about to introduce this young, easily alarmed girl into the sphere of his mother's indomitable influence. Little Wren Stevens would find herself overwhelmed by the old lady. And Evelyn wouldn't like her – Bertram knew his mother well enough to know that. She was too small and timid for Evelyn who liked people to be large and loud like her. In Evelyn's opinion if someone was reserved or quiet, there was something wrong with them. It was probably why she and Lilian didn't get on that well. Lilian was far too reserved for her mother to think well of her. Funnily enough, Bertram was sure Lilian would love Wren. But Bertram had no interest in gaining Lilian's approval. What his eldest sister thought didn't matter a hoot. Still, he wouldn't be introducing the girl to them any time soon. Not yet.

Chapter 13

It had been several years since Lili had ventured out to one of the parish dances. There were numerous reasons for her avoidance of such occasions but mostly it was to do with the fact that the people she went with previously were, for the most part, married with children.

There was always a jitteriness to the crowds at such events. Some men prowled up and down searching the opposite crowd like feral animals stalking their prey. Women, young and old, stood at one side of the hall forcing casual chat while they waited for one of the lads at the other side of the room to cross the abyss and ask them to dance. When the music struck up, nobody moved until one young chap would stumble forward or, more usually, was pushed as a one-man vanguard to the wave of men who followed across the empty floor as the ladies feigned patience opposite. It was then the turn of some of the wilder young girls to laugh and shove one another as red-faced men approached and asked them to dance. It was just at the same moment they asked a girl to dance that most of them became fascinated by the floor in front of their scuffed, heavily polished, boots. They would start their approach with faces forward only for their heads to steadily droop as they got closer and closer to the women. If the girls didn't care so much about the outcome of the male advance, they surely would have found the sight comical. There were often playful scuffles as their edginess burst forth in shoves and mock punches followed by whoops of laughter and ribald remarks. Nervous titters pealed from the men as much as the high-pitched giggling erupted from the female side of the room until the music drowned out their noise and gave the cue for the dance to begin in earnest.

Sometimes one of the parish council would simply operate a record player but usually there was a proper band at the head of the room churning out various renditions of popular old tunes and sometimes sneaking in a more modern number later in the proceedings when the stuffy traditionalists had gone home to their beds. Everybody could dance a waltz or two, with some of the more ambitious couples attempting basic foxtrots and a few slightly more risqué moves that would have, no doubt, scandalised their mothers.

For Lili, her first few experiences of the dances had been far from comical. To a young girl they were, in truth, quite traumatic. She went through the thrill of seeing men come towards her, clearly with the intention of asking her to dance only for them to veer off in a different direction when they were close to her. It hurt to watch men come forward having searched the faces of the women and singled her out from the masses only for them to change their mind once they were close enough to see her properly. It affected her confidence to watch the hope fade from potential partners' faces when she couldn't figure out what she had done wrong. Did she smell funny? Was she only attractive at a distance? Was she, in fact, really very ugly? It took one of her closest friends, Kitty Porter, to point out what she thought was the main problem.

When the lads stood far away from Lili at the other side of a room, Lili looked like a woman of normal height, especially when sitting down. But once she stood up or a man came closer to her, he would realise that she was actually rather tall – quite often taller than he was himself. If they stood up and danced with Lili, many of the local men would effectively be the lady in the partnership and not many of the boys were willing to endure such emasculation for the sake of a dance with a pretty girl. While the explanation Kitty offered was comforting, it did nothing to alleviate the hurtfulness of the situation and the jealousy she felt towards other more evenly proportioned women. The other issue Lili had with this explanation was that the few tall men who had the elevation to match hers always went for the tiniest women at the gathering. When a man of stature danced in the crowd, it often looked as if he was swaying to the music on his own only for the crowds to part revealing a woman whose nose was no higher than his navel. As the night progressed, Lili would find something similar happen to her as smaller and smaller men tried their luck with her, thinking that she might find such little fellows endearing.

In reality, she found them rather irksome, uncomfortable even, as their short arms would cling to her with a vice-like grip, pulling themselves closer and closer as the dance wore on until their heads were nearly buried in her bosom. It was at that point she would use all her unfeminine strength to push them a safe distance away and claim the need of a trip to the facilities where she would hide out long enough for her erstwhile partner to capture another unsuspecting victim. Lili had quickly grown weary of such bad experiences. While her friends found suitable partners, she became increasingly isolated at these evenings until she was forced – in an attempt to avoid a pursuer – to sit at the old spinsters' table and listen to them reel off the family and relations of every single person on the dance floor. It was the final straw and she hadn't attended a dance since.

But this dance would be different. There was always an air of excitement surrounding the midsummer social in the parish and, this year, Lili allowed herself to be swept up in the swell of chatter and speculation. There was going to be a band coming all the way down from Dublin to play. Every girl in the parish was supposedly buying a new dress from Mrs Sidney's – even the ones who couldn't afford it. In reality, most were browsing the latest fashions before concocting their own versions on a sewing machine at home. Lili absorbed all these conversations but did little to add to them and only gave vague replies when asked if she was attending.

Lili chose to tell her mother she was going only two days before the event when the two of them were alone, Bertie having gone out for the evening. She waited until it was almost their bedtime to tell Evelyn as she knew if she started the evening by telling her, she would have to discuss the social for the rest of the night.

Instead, when her mother stood to leave for her bed, Lili casually said, "Oh, by the way, I'm going to the parish social on Friday night. I'll be out from about half seven."

It had taken her all day to come up with those two sentences and she was relieved when she finally got them out. She did not want to ask Evelyn if she could go. She also did not want to give too much information about why she was going or who with. She was sure her mother's inquisitive mind would pick up on anything she mentioned so she only gave her the barest bones of her plans so as not to arouse suspicion. In any event, she either needn't have worried or had planned well.

Evelyn gave a little *"Humph!"* and said, "Well, if you're going to be out, you'd better take a key. I'll be on my own so I'll be locking the door. Remind me to tell Bertram in the morning."

And with that, she was gone out the door to her bedroom, leaving Lili in a slightly stunned silence.

* * *

Friday arrived and with it came a further burst of anticipation for Lili. She spent the day in a preoccupied haze, imagining the best and worst scenarios. Dancing with Ewan long into the night. Ewan jilting her once they got there, leaving her to sit with the dowdy old spinsters dressed in floral print that was twenty – if not thirty – years out of date. Or, even worse, if he never showed up to collect her from their agreed meeting place. If that happened, she would have to trudge back across the paddocks to sit at home for the rest of the evening and field various enquiries from her mother. She thought if that happened, she would rather spend the night in one of the sheds on the farm than listen to her mother drone on about all the folk who likely made it to the dance. But then, she trusted Ewan and kept telling herself to trust he would keep his word and do as he promised. After all, the whole thing was his idea. He wouldn't let her down … would he?

Supper came and went without event, after which Bertie made his obligatory pilgrimage down to the pub. In his opinion, no girl he met at the local socials would be up to his standards. He had given them up as a bad job after only a few outings. Lili was glad he wouldn't be there because, if he was, he was sure to report everything back to his mammy.

Lili had cleaned her shoes and laid out a dress the night before so all that was left for her to do was put it on then apply a little bit of rouge and lipstick to complete the picture. It was a simple look that belied the amount of time and thought that had gone into it. She took one last look in the mirror before leaving, taking in how the dress hugged her body in the right places. It was a light but vivid blue colour with brown buttons down the front. With it, she wore a brown, plaited, thin leather belt and brown shoes with a two-inch heel. Ordinarily, she never wore heeled shoes to such a gathering as it only exacerbated the problem she had. But tonight, she thought it wouldn't matter. Ewan would still be taller than her but she would now find it even easier to look him in the eye when they danced. Happy as she ever would be with her appearance, she picked up a light little cardigan and her handbag before descending the stairs.

Evelyn was sitting in her usual chair as her daughter walked through. Lili was almost at the door, ready to say goodbye and make a hasty exit when Evelyn called her back.

"Wait a minute there and let me have a look at you."

Lili's mother hauled herself up out of the depths of her chair on the second attempt, rocking her hefty frame back and forth, trying to gain enough momentum to stand. When she did, she viewed her daughter with a critical eye for a moment.

"You always did have a good figure, you know. From your father's side, it was." She gestured to herself. "Well, you never got it from me, did you? Give us a twirl then." Lili did so. "Yes, very nice. But your hair." She tutted. "Now that won't do at all."

Evelyn sat back down as Lili patted her head nervously, unsure what to do. Her mother beckoned. "Come here to me and kneel down. I'll never reach you all the way up there."

Bemused, Lili followed her mother's instruction. No sooner had she knelt on the rug than her mother began stripping her hair of the usual pins that held it in a knot at the back of her head. She never wore it at the base of her skull the way many other women did as she felt it gave off the air of an old maid and, though she was an aging spinster, she wasn't ready to be considered completely unattractive – especially now. She was surprised by the dextrousness of her mother's fingers, considering everything else about her moved so slowly.

Evelyn unwound her daughter's hair and ran her fingers

through it, teasing it out, and split it into separate strands. She began plaiting the hair at the front of Lili's head and wound it around to the back before pinning it in place. She did the same at the other side and finished by rolling the plaits and remaining hair in an elegant twist.

"There. That's a bit more done-up." She placed her hands on her eldest child's shoulders and then removed them. "Off you go then. You don't want to be late."

Taking this as her dismissal, Lili stood, thanked her mother and left.

She was surprised at what her mother had done for her. It was a long time since Evelyn had passed any kind of comment or made any suggestions regarding Lili's appearance. But then there was no occasion to warrant her passing judgement on her daughter. The only places Lili went with any regularity were the local village and to church. All they required was neatness and cleanliness (for some even that was optional) and Lili needed no guidance on that front. She always turned herself out well in terms of clothing and footwear. But, now that her external circumstances were beginning to change, perhaps she should think about reinventing herself a little. A new beginning? But no. She couldn't predict what might happen. Really, very little had happened so far although, having led such an untouched life, every development was significant.

As she walked down the road to their elected meeting-place, her heels clack-clack-clacked on the packed stones and earth of the roadway. She delighted in the rhythmical sound but gave little skips and hops, changing the music of her footfalls. She was jittery, excited.

While kneeling in front of her mother, Lili had heard Ewan rumbling down the lane. She felt her body vibrate in response to the sound of the engine and hoped her mother hadn't noticed.

However, in all her eagerness about the dance, she had not thought of how she might get there with Ewan. The roar as it moved away was somewhat of a dampener on her buoyant spirits. It was the roar of a motorcycle engine.

One of Ewan's prized possessions, aside from his farm and animals, was a large black-and-silver Triumph motorcycle which had been among the belongings he brought from Scotland. He had, in fact, ridden it the entire way from southern Scotland to the south-east of Ireland with a ferry crossing in the middle.

In dressing, Lili hadn't thought of the fact that she would likely be whizzing through the countryside clinging on for dear life on the back of a motorcycle. She had thought about what would flatter her figure, what would not look dowdy or old. She wanted to make an effort and that effort just happened to consist of a dress. Well, she would manage. She had to.

She followed the curve of the road and at the end of it, a short distance away, she spotted him. The motorcycle was parked and Ewan was facing her, leaning casually against the seat, arms folded and ankles crossed. He stood up when he saw her, a smile spreading across his face as his eyes travelled from her toes to the crown of her head. If anyone else had looked at her that way, she would have felt exposed and uncomfortable. But it was Ewan so she was quite pleased with his reaction.

"Hullo," he said, coming to meet her. He held out his hand to her.

She took it and he lifted their entwined fingers up over their heads so that she twirled under his arm, coming to a stop against his chest. Both of them laughed. Ewan wrapped his arms around her, pressing the length of her body against the length of his. Lili's laughter faded. This was completely unknown territory for her and she was unsure what to do.

Pull away? Stay where she was? Ewan saved her from making the decision by reluctantly letting her go and producing something from his pocket. It fluttered in the light evening breeze.

"For you," he said and handed it to her.

His cheeks flushed and he stuffed his hands in his pockets.

It was a scarf covered with large blue, grey and white flowers.

"I thought it might match your eyes."

"And my dress too," said Lili, a little awed by the gift. It was still warm from being in contact with Ewan's body as she ran it through her hands. It slid across her skin as if it consisted of water. She almost expected her hand to be wet after it touched her skin. "It's beautiful," she whispered, leaning in to gently kiss him. "Thank you."

"Maybe you could wear it round your head now. So the wind doesn't ruin your hair."

He watched her neatly fold the scarf and knot it under her chin. She was so pretty, he thought, with her cheeks flushed in excitement and self-consciousness. And her body so lithe and beautifully proportioned.

"Shall we?" He crooked his arm in a gentlemanly fashion and led her to the motorbike. He got on. "Are you happy to sit behind me and hold on around my waist."

"Yes, all right."

Ewan felt a little guilty as he watched her stop for a moment to work out the best way of going about getting on a motorcycle. He had considered asking a neighbour to borrow a car but the idea that he might have Lili Burnley pressed against him with her arms tight around his waist all the way to the parish hall made him reluctant to be utterly gallant. As he felt her arms slide around him, he was glad of his own selfishness.

Chapter 14

Ewan let Lili off the motorbike a little way from the parish hall so that they might arrive separately and not arouse suspicion. This worked quite well for Lili as she hadn't walked far when she spotted a familiar figure coming down a side road towards her. Lili waved and the woman waved back, quickening her pace, and almost trotted straight into Lili when she reached the bottom of the steep path. They steadied one another and hugged, taking a good look at each other. The figure was Kitty Porter, her school friend and one-time neighbour who had married William Porter in her early twenties and moved several miles away to live in wedded bliss. However, all did not go to plan. Within a year, William was ensconced in a sanatorium and within another year he was dead of consumption, leaving Kitty a widow after just two years of marriage – during most of which they had been separated. Other women would have floundered after such a loss so young, but not Kitty. A naturally buoyant and active person, she took William's death on the chin and decided to continue running her husband's farm with the aid of one of her younger brothers and his wife.

Though they hadn't seen each other for several months, she and Lili were still firm friends.

"*Hello!*" she cried, eyes shining with happiness. "Lili

Burnley! Well, I never thought I'd see you at another one of these yokes." She grinned knowingly. "Especially not after the last time with Cecil Howard!" She shrieked out a laugh as they walked along arm in arm and dug her elbow playfully into Lili's side. She had always been loud, confident and full of ribald remarks – but that was one of the reasons Lili was so fond of her.

Kitty could make you happy on the saddest of days, almost always managing to err on the right side of making people laugh rather than upsetting them. She was simply good with people and knew how to act around them, tailoring her humour to suit the occasion but never losing it completely. With a few people, however, she was completely herself and Lili was one of them. They had seen each other's lives unfold and been there when they were needed. They also knew how to press one another's buttons and Kitty had pressed one of Lili's by mentioning Cecil Howard.

At her last parish dance a number of years before, Lili had been persuaded to dance by a short and very rotund man by the name of Cecil Howard. Thinking back, she never could quite remember what made her agree to take the floor with such a person. Kitty had never let her forget it. Cecil was not a local but apparently made a habit of attending the county parish dances in hope of catching an unsuspecting lady friend. He latched on to Lili, quite literally, and refused to let her go despite her resistance, eventually toppling over in the middle of the dancefloor, dragging poor Lili with him. It had been the talk of the parish for weeks and was the reason behind Lili not leaving the house for an entire month, much to her father's and Kitty's amusement.

"Hoping to meet Cecil again, are we?" Kitty cackled. "Well, I suppose beggars can't be choosers, eh?"

"No," Lili answered primly. "I'm meeting someone else there tonight."

That quieted Kitty for a moment. "Really?" she said, surprised.

"Yes."

"*Who?*" she asked, squeezing Lili's arm so tight it was almost painful.

But Lili made no other reply than, "You'll see ..."

By the time they got to the hall, Kitty was bursting with anticipation. Lili was doing her best to remain relaxed but her heart was thundering. They paid at the door and, once inside, made for the gaggle of women – some familiar, others unknown – who sat in groups along the right-hand wall, waiting for the music to begin.

"Where is he?" Kitty hissed, impatiently jamming bony fingers into Lili's side.

"*Ow!*" Lili jerked away. "Just for that, I'm not telling you."

Kitty huffed. "Ah come on, Lil! Don't be such a spoilsport. Where *is* he?" She scrutinised the men who were milling around at the far side of the room. "Oh Lord!" she squawked suddenly. "There's Cecil Howard!"

"No! Where?"

Horrified, Lili scanned the men and, sure enough, there sat Cecil, much larger than she remembered – in lateral rather than vertical terms. Their eyes met and he waved cheerily at her.

"Oh God, no! No, Kit!" She grabbed at her friend's hand. "Kit, promise you'll head him off if he comes anywhere near me. Please!"

"Oh *now* ..." Kitty sat back and folded her arms as if she meant business. "There'd have to be something in it for me if I was to do that for you. For instance, you telling me who's meeting you here. Because I'm still saying it's yon Howard over there." She jerked her head in his direction but Lili didn't want to look that way ever again for fear of giving the man ideas.

She had almost forgotten Ewan was there in the panic that ensued once she spotted Cecil. She knew she needn't worry. Ewan would ask her to dance and then she would spend the night in his company.

"*Hey!*" Kitty snapped her fingers in front of her. "God!" She shook her head. "You're far gone, aren't you?"

"What?"

"The mystery man. You must be far gone over him. You went all glassy-eyed soon as I mentioned him." There was an envious look in Kitty's eyes. She would never begrudge her friend happiness but she still missed William even if, outwardly at least, his death didn't appear to affect her too much. "It's serious, isn't it?"

Lili paused, considering her answer. "Yes," she finally said.

Kitty whistled and got several scandalised looks from a group of old spinsters sitting nearby. "Lili Burnley in love! And here I thought you'd be like that lot over there for the rest of your days." She pointed a thumb in the direction of the disapproving spinsters sitting like a flock of puffed-up little hens.

"I might still be," she said quietly. "Can't leave Mammy and Bertie, can I?"

Kitty flared immediately "That useless eejit! Shur you can't put your life on hold for that wee shi –" The end of her sentence was drowned out by a flurry of huffs and squawks from the spinsters. "Oh whisht!" said Kitty crossly.

Bertie was a bad subject to get Kitty onto. Her loathing of him meant that even the mention of his name was enough to launch her into a lengthy diatribe on every little defect she thought he possessed. On visits to the Burnley house as a child, she experienced the boy's fits of temper and saw what he did to the family. Kitty had watched Lili's life fall by the wayside as the family's energy focused on Bertie. She cared deeply for Lili and she'd be damned before she saw her friend make another sacrifice for a family that would never do her the same courtesy.

The band had made its way up on the stage while Lili and Kitty talked. The energy of the crowd surged as musicians tuned up. As the groups of men moved to and fro, Lili spotted Ewan sitting with a group – all farmers – who seemed to be in serious conversation. He didn't look up but still seemed aware of being watched because the hint of a smile played about his lips. Before, she hadn't really been paying attention to the way he looked. She had other things on her mind – namely how to ride a motorbike in a dress. Now, however, she was free to survey him.

He'd had a haircut for starters, but she'd noticed that before. His hair was short at the back and sides then slightly longer on top. He was also completely clean-shaven making him look much more youthful. He was dressed in a pearl-white shirt, dark-brown tie and a light-brown tweed suit. The fabric was not the heavy tweed of some jackets she saw in the room. She assumed the men that wore them where slowly stewing in their own juices. It was already quite warm in the room what with so many bodies crammed in.

A drumbeat began and was followed by the rest of the band. A small cheer went up from the waiting dancers and their movements became a little more focused. They no longer drifted about looking for ways to kill time but started to home in on who they thought might be a suitable partner. Lili watched the young women pat their hair and straighten their dresses. She saw one girl bend down, hiding behind another, pinching her already heat-flushed cheeks. What a palaver, she thought.

"Lilian Burnley, my dear! And how's your mother?"

The question came from Lili's elbow. She froze for a moment before slowly turning towards the voice. Cecil

Howard stood beside her, rocking genially back and forth on the balls of his feet. Even at the apex of his bounce, he didn't reach her shoulder.

"Come for another round, have you?" said Cecil, extending his hand. "Well, I'm game if you are!'

Kitty gave a high-pitched snort which she turned into a cough, her sparkling eyes fixed on Lili.

Well, she wasn't going to get any help from that quarter, was she, thought Lili. Damn Kitty! She couldn't even think what to say to Cecil who was in full flow telling her about every occasion he had seen a member of her family since their last meeting.

"– and Vera's got a little girl now as well as the two boys. Very pretty child too! Though not as pretty as her auntie, is she?' Cecil chortled heartily, wheezing and dabbing his watering eyes with a multicoloured handkerchief that looked large enough to cover a well-proportioned dinner table. He stuffed it unceremoniously back into the inside pocket of the sports jacket he wore over an open-collared off-white shirt. He continued to chatter as he groped for Lili's hand and began trying to tug her towards the dance floor.

A hand appeared on Cecil's shoulder, stopping him mid-flow. She watched the fingers tighten and, following the hand up the arm, she came face to face with Ewan who smiled wickedly at her before addressing the little man in his clutches.

"Awful sorry, *chum*, but this girl promised to dance with me tonight." His tone was mild and pleasant, but Lili heard the steeliness underneath.

Cecil, it seemed, didn't.

"Ah here, Cameron!" he said indignantly. "Don't they have the same rules off in England as we do here? If a fella asks a girl to dance, then she's his."

"Not," Ewan said icily, "if the girl refuses to dance with

him." Cecil was just forming an answer when Ewan cut in. "And I'm not English, you great lummox. I'm Scottish. Now," he turned pointedly to Lili, "Miss Burnley, would you do me the honour of dancing with me?"

With as much grace as she could manage, faced with an empurpled fat man and a tall, triumphant Scot, she answered, "I'd be delighted, Mr Cameron."

Neatly sidestepping Cecil, who was now doing an excellent impression of a recently landed fish, she took Ewan's hand and they took to the floor.

There were many couples already crowding the floorboards, swaying lazily to the music but, being so tall, she and Ewan cut through the middle and found a space with ease.

As they took their place and Ewan proffered his hand, she asked quite seriously, "Um, you can dance, can't you?"

"Of course I can," he replied and, with that, he took a firm hold of her and spun her in a tight circle.

Lili shrieked, causing no end of funny looks from those close by as she clung to Ewan. She began to giggle girlishly as they performed a half-decent waltz to the music.

"What?" he asked.

"Oh, I don't know," she said. "You, the look on Cecil Howard's face – all of it."

"Howard got what was coming to him, the great oaf. He's such a –"

"Don't start! You're meant to be happy. *I'm* happy. I've never felt so *alive!*" She let go of him and twirled, flaring out the bottom of her dress.

Ewan drank her in. As she spun, he saw her long smooth calves, the jutting boniness of her knee, the pale white softness of her lower thigh – his heart seemed to drop in his chest. It almost hurt. He stepped forward and grabbed Lili gently around the waist. Her back bent to the pressure of his hands, pushing the core of her body close to his as she leaned her head back, extending her long neck so that she could look up into his face. God! he thought. Does she know what she's doing to me?

She did. Lili could see every emotion as it flitted across Ewan's face. The fact that she could see them in the first place told her she was having quite an effect on him. Usually he was so guarded with his expressions. But she knew it took effort for him to remain impassive since he was, really, quite an expressive man. As they danced, their bodies touched and bumped off one another, sometimes accidentally but mostly intentionally. She thought could see into his soul and what she saw both terrified and beguiled her. Lili knew she was losing herself to him and, at that moment in time, she didn't care. This was their night and she was going to enjoy it.

At about ten the music came to a halt and the benches were brought out onto the dance floor. The side door was thrown open and a gust of cool wind flowed into the stifling room. There was a surge of men towards the exit and not a small number of women as they went outside for some cool, fresh air. Lili also knew that a number of the men would be outside urinating on the back wall of the parish hall and in the woods that lay behind it. It was almost part of the tradition that the men went outside to relieve themselves. Several people could also be seen fishing in their jacket and trouser pockets for crumpled packets of cigarettes. The band all sat dangling their legs over the edge of the stage passing fags and matches between them.

At this point, a troop of ladies began to bustle about and organise the refreshments. Women and men now sat together rather than separately, chatting easily, their earlier awkwardness forgotten. As an older woman trooped out with a large red basin of mugs arranged in concentric circles,

Lili, who had linked arms with Ewan, found her other arm clasped in a vice-like grip. She turned to find Kitty staring at her with shining eyes. Lili sighed. She knew she was about to get an earful. She patted Ewan on the arm. He saw her face and then saw Kitty. Smirking, he nodded and left Lili to her fate, making a beeline for one of the many USA biscuit-tins full of sandwiches which were being passed around.

Lili attempted a half-hearted resistance as Kitty dragged her into the kitchen, ignoring protests from various people bringing out tins of buns, cakes and sandwiches. Once Kitty had succeeded in towing her to an alcove at the back of the room, she rounded on Lili.

"Him!" she said, eyes popping for emphasis. "*Him!*"

Lili was a little disconcerted. "Don't you like him?"

"Like him? *Like him?*" Kitty shrieked.

Lili made some shushing motions but Kitty batted her hands away.

"'*Like him*' she says! How could I not *like him*? How could anyone not like *that*?" She gestured to the other room where Ewan's ears were presumably burning. "Most of the women in the parish have been after him since he arrived – even me! How on *earth* did you manage it?" There was awe in Kitty's voice.

Lili shrugged. "I shaved him."

"You what?"

"Mammy brought him to the house one evening, soaked to the skin, with four inches of beard growing out of his chin." She shrugged again, leaning back against the wall and keeping her voice low so that Kitty came forward to hear. "You know how Mammy is. Always interfering in other people's business."

Kitty snorted.

"Anyway, she offered my services as a barber and ... I shaved him," she finished lamely.

133

"That's it?" said Kitty, disappointed.

"Well … no."

"What happened?" Kitty leaned in close. "C'mon! You know you can tell me and it'll go no further."

"Well … he fell asleep by the fire so we just left him there. He didn't wake until morning. It was Saturday so Mammy had to go into town with Eta Connelly to sell her eggs and, well, we were left alone."

"And?"

"We talked."

"*And?*"

"We kissed."

Kitty gave a great whoop and hugged Lili while others looked on in bewilderment. "*You kissed*! When was this?"

Lili tried to shush her again. "A few months ago." She hissed. "Lambing season."

"And what's happened since?" Kitty looked fit to burst with excitement.

"Not much. We go for walks in the evening. Mammy and Bertie don't know, see."

"Ah who cares about that pair of eejits," Kitty scoffed. "What else?"

"Nothing."

"What? You mean you haven't …?" She raised her eyebrows significantly.

"Haven't what?"

"Oh, come on! You know …"

Lili still looked bewildered.

Kitty rolled her eyes in exasperation. "Enjoyed … *carnal knowledge* of one another," she hissed.

Lili was scandalised. "No, we have not! He's a gentleman! He wouldn't –"

"Oh, he *definitely* would! I've seen the way he looks at you. And you at him," she added pointedly. "I would."

"No, you would not, Katherine Porter! You're just saying that to shock me."

"Worked too, didn't it?" Kitty laughed.

She snagged some sandwiches from a tin on the counter and passed a few to Lili who suddenly realised she was ravenous. All that dancing had made her hungry.

"You know what you need to do, Lil?" said Kitty through a mouthful of bread and cheese. "You need to get yourself married off to Ewan Cameron before it's too late. Even if you don't do it for yourself – though I can't see how you wouldn't – do it for all us girls who've been after him since he arrived."

"But he's never asked me. Never even hinted at it. Maybe he doesn't want to.' She was a little hurt when she really thought about it. Maybe he didn't love her. But she was *sure* he did.

"Well, there's one way to find out." And with that, Kitty was gone only to come back moments later hauling Ewan by the cuff of his jacket.

Lili nearly keeled over.

"What? No, Kitty! What are you doing?"

"What do you think I'm doing?" she asked before about-turning to Ewan and setting her jaw. She meant business. "Right, Ewan – You don't mind if I call you Ewan, do you? Why haven't you asked Lili to marry you?"

There was a pause long enough for Lili to appeal to God under her breath before Ewan replied quietly, "Because I know she'd say no."

There was silence. As ever Kitty was the first to regain her voice.

"No, she wouldn't. Would you –"

Ewan cut her off. "You might be right. But I got the impression she'd refuse out of a sense of duty to her mother and brother."

"*What?*"

Lili jumped in. "He's right." He hadn't taken his eyes from her the entire time.

"And you're wrong," he replied simply.

"How?" said both women at once.

That made the edges of Ewan lips quirk upwards.

"You're wrong to put your family before yourself. But then perhaps I'm really the one being selfish. By asking you to put me before them."

Women and a few men were beginning to file back in with empty cups and biscuit tins as they heard the vicar calling out the winner of the spot prize: a box of soap. The three of them stood looking at the goings-on of the kitchen, looking at the floor – looking anywhere but at each other.

"Oh, bugger it," murmured Ewan. He grabbed Lili's hand. "This is never how I imagined it. Lili Burnley, will you marry me?"

Silence. Then Kitty gave a great '*Eeeeeee!*' of excitement and grabbed their hands. "Oh, say yes, Lil. Please say yes! You'd make me so happy if you did." Kitty squeezed her fingers so hard it hurt.

"Aye, she'd make me happy and all," said Ewan dryly, humour twinkling in his eyes as he watched Lili struggle. He wasn't going to help her on this. She'd have to figure it out herself.

Lili couldn't look at either of them. She bowed her head, closing her eyes. She had to think. Their longing was so powerful it threatened to make her rash. And Lili wasn't rash. She thought about things carefully before committing to a fixed plan of action. It was what her father always taught her to do. But she felt her father's philosophies were not designed for the situation she found herself in. If he had been alive, she would have consulted him even though she knew he would have told her it was her decision. Leonard had not been the type of father to interfere with his daughters' choices in men. He had raised good, sensible girls who wouldn't set any store by wastrels. But Leonard was dead and with him went the support system for her mother that would have allowed Lili to leave home and make a life for herself. No matter how independent Evelyn claimed to be, her former illnesses, her still increasing girth and the work she did day in, day out, were all taking their toll. She was less mobile, more out of breath with each step she took. Before, she could stand in the kitchen all day baking and cooking and bustling about. Now she suffered with chronic pain in her back and legs. Evelyn simply wasn't able any more. And while Lili toyed with the possibility of asking her mother to come with her once she married, she knew Evelyn would refuse to leave Bertie. There was also the idea that since she was only living down the lane, Lili could go back and forth between her mother and Ewan. But then she couldn't possibly help to run the two households without stretching herself to breaking point, failing to do a proper job of both and, therefore, incurring the resentment of both homes.

"No," said Lili, emerging from her reverie.

"*No*?" The anger and incredulity were plain in Kitty's voice.

"No," Lili said again, but she didn't look at Kitty. Instead she kept her eyes on Ewan and the bitter smile that twisted his features. "I want to, Ewan. Honestly, I do. But I can't."

"*Why not*?" Kitty whined her question like a child who'd been denied an iced bun.

"Because of her mother," answered Ewan at the same moment as Lili answered: "Because of my mother."

Lili smiled sadly up at him. They were so much in accord with one another and yet they could not be together. For the first time, she felt a lump beginning to form in her throat. She wished something would change and allow her to experience the happiness she imagined as Ewan's wife. She would no longer be under her mother's thumb. She would have a life of living, not of waiting in a constant state of limbo. She would escape the cutting remarks and overarching influence of Bertie. She would no longer stand in his shadow.

But she would. For a while longer at least. And that all depended on whether Ewan would wait for her. She liked to think he would. But she couldn't expect it of him. Just because he'd shown no interest in the local women up until this point didn't mean his interactions with her hadn't opened his mind to the possibility of further relationships. It surely wasn't for the lack of interest that he remained alone. Though she made every attempt not to notice anyone else that evening, Lili was not oblivious to the suggestive postures and batting eyelashes as other women endeavoured to induce Ewan to dance with them instead of constantly with her. They, no doubt, found it the height of insolence that their advances were not only ignored but completely unseen by their quarry. Ewan only had eyes for her.

Calling her back to him, Ewan caught her chin lightly in his work-roughened fingers, making her look into his eyes once again.

"I know you want to. But I won't force you." He paused. "I can wait." Another pause. "I think." He kissed her cheek, turned and walked away.

The two women stood in silence for a time.

Then Kitty rounded on her. "Lili, what do you think you're bloody doing? You can't let him go like that."

"What am I supposed to do?" she asked bitterly. "Grab hold of his sleeve?"

"You know that's not what I mean. You can't reject him, he's …" she searched for an appropriate description, "well," she said with a shrug, "he's Ewan bloody Cameron."

"I'm well aware of that but that doesn't mean I can just up and leave Mammy and Bertie."

"Oh, damn your mother and bloody Bertie! Damn them to hell!" Kitty spat.

"Don't you say that," said Lili coldly. "My mother and Bertie may not be the easiest to live with but they're still family and I'll stand by them, no matter what."

"But why? Can't you see they're ruining your life?"

"They are my life."

"Exactly! Can't you see that's not a good thing?" Kitty was at a loss that Lili didn't understand this.

In truth Lili did understand what her friend was saying but just didn't agree that leaving all of it behind would make her life better. Should she marry, she would carry with her the guilt of leaving her mother. Evelyn would likely be furious with her and, as a consequence, Bertie would follow suit. It would mean that her nearest neighbours – her closest family – would become strangers. And she didn't want that. If she left her home permanently because of marriage, she would like to still be able to walk in and out of the house she grew up in.

The band struck up once more in the other room. Suddenly, Lili felt very tired. "Let's go back in, Kit."

But Kitty wasn't letting her go. "I'm not done yet," she said, folding her arms and swelling indignantly. Like most women, she was smaller than Lili but by no means was she going to give in to her.

"But I am," said Lili shortly. With that, she neatly sidestepped her friend and strode purposefully away. She didn't want to argue anymore.

Once in the hall, she searched the crowd for Ewan. He was sitting on a bench shoved up against the wall with his elbows on his thighs and his hands hanging between his knees. His head was bent and, for one horrifying moment,

Lili thought he was crying. But no. He seemed to sense her presence and looked up. Their eyes made contact for the briefest of moments before he looked away again into the dancers on the floor. He didn't move his hands but slid silently along the bench indicating that she could sit by him. As she walked over, she saw a gaggle of four girls standing nearby with eyes on Ewan. She found it comforting that, as his eyes scoured the room, his gaze did not rest on them. Perhaps he really would wait after all. But then he wasn't looking at her either, so maybe not.

"Do you want to go home?" Lili asked.

"Do you?"

Lili stayed silent.

Ewan sighed heavily then turned to her. "If you don't want to stay then we'll go. But –" he took her hand in his quite unconsciously "– but I'd prefer to use up every little bit of the time we spend together instead of wasting it. So, if you're willing, I'd like to dance with you again. If you're willing."

She smiled, relieved, and stood then led him onto the floor where he took her in his arms.

Chapter 15

Wren spent the rest of the night with Bertram. They danced and sat and had tea together while Bertram kept up a steady stream of conversation, regaling her with tales of daily life on the farm. The only time they were apart was when Wren went to use the bathroom. When she came back, Bertram was craning his neck, searching the crowd. He was so small that, even though he was right on the tips of his toes, the action had virtually no benefit in terms of improving his vantage point. Wren appreciated his predicament as she walked through the crowd, dodging elbows at her shoulders.

She wondered if he was looking for her and felt a little swoop of delight which quickly turned into a blush when she reached him and he asked, "Have you seen Robbie anywhere?"

"No. Why?" she asked, automatically examining the crowd though her own viewpoint was even worse than Bertram's.

"What? Oh, nothing. Just I'm supposed to be giving him a lift home in my car this evening. I haven't seen him for a while is all. Never mind." He led Wren back to a seat.

Once there, however, another man came along and Bertram began to chat to him, leaving Wren to examine the room at her leisure.

Just as her eyes swept across the entrance, Robbie slunk in, his gaze immediately fixing on where Wren sat then turning away. He disappeared to the opposite side of the room, distancing himself from her by using the crowded dance floor. Upset, Wren stood, touched Bertram on the shoulder to let him know she was leaving and set out in the direction Robbie had disappeared. She wasn't sure what she would do if she found him, but knew she had to, even if was only to satisfy her curiosity. There was something about Robbie that drew her, something she didn't yet understand. She liked Bertram, she liked him an awful lot, but he still didn't seem to lure her the way this other young man inexplicably did.

She hadn't made it halfway around the room when she came face to face with him. Robbie stood tall, no longer caring whether he made a good impression. It made him confident and, to Wren, much more attractive. She saw someone totally different to the meek young man she had encountered at the start of the night.

For Robbie, it was a case of knowing the battle was lost. Bertram had taken her from him. He cursed himself for not putting up some sort of fight. Looking back, he couldn't believe he'd just walked away from her. But he had and Bertie bloody Burnley had charmed her. Robbie knew he had no hope. He lacked the natural charisma and self-confidence of Bertie. In a way that took the pressure off him. He didn't have to win her over anymore. But he still wanted to hold her, even if it meant nothing to her.

He proffered his hand, smiled and simply said, "Dance?"

"Yes," replied Wren quietly, sliding her hand into his and feeling him squeeze it firmly. His hand was warm and rough – a safe hand.

The dance was slow. They had moved into the latter end of the night when couples were well-established, more comfortable holding one another close. This, of course, was not the case for Wren and Robbie. There was a moment as the tune started when both of them balked a little. However, regaining his composure, Robbie simply held Wren firmly by the hand and waist but made the compromise of keeping almost the full length of his arm between them.

Dancing with Robbie was very different to dancing with Bertram. Though a heavier build, Robbie was incongruously light on his feet. Bertram, though slimmer, lacked natural coordination. As the music progressed, Wren found herself falling into the space between them, not really noticing her change in position until her nose was almost touching Robbie's sternum. It just seemed so natural to get closer to him, to feel the heat radiating from his body, to smell the masculine odour of his chest. They swayed in perfect synchronicity to the music as if they had done it together a thousand times before. Each seemed to have an innate understanding of the other's body. In that moment, they belonged together.

Though bound up in this first experience of one another, a chance moment when another couple bumped into them caused Wren to look up and catch Bertram staring across the room at her. His gaze was chilling. Gone were the sparkling eyes that danced with latent humour and brightness. Two dark pits seemed to bore into her, slicing through the softer part of her being to her very core. It was like swallowing a scalding hot drink which burnt and blistered her insides as it passed through her. His face was transformed from boyish, rounded joviality to angular, ugly blotchiness. Even at a distance she could see the strain in his jaw as the neck muscles tightened, the veins in his temples protruded as the skin stretched to contain what threatened to burst from beneath. It made Wren automatically step back from Robbie, knowing instinctively that it was her proximity to him that caused such a black look to colour the features of Bertram Burnley. She had never made a man jealous before. Now she knew what it was like. And she didn't like it one little bit.

After that, the evening petered out. Wren said goodbye to both men, making sure she sought out Bertram second. He smiled and nodded at what she said but Wren could see he was still put out by what he witnessed earlier on. Yet, he did have the presence of mind to ask if he might see her again. Relieved that he was not holding her apparent misdemeanour against her, Wren readily agreed to meet him at the next event in the Institute – whenever that might be.

"It can't come soon enough," he murmured, leaning close to her and making her insides flutter, before taking his leave. As he walked away, he looked over his shoulder at her, smiled that dazzling smile, then continued on.

Wren found Mary talking to her cousin. They said their goodbyes, disentangled Joan from the embrace of her young man then descended the stairs out into the cool night. The wind trickling down the street stung Wren's exposed legs and face. She wrapped her cardigan around her as much as she could, crossing her arms to keep in her body heat.

"I wish I knew someone with a car," Mary grumbled. "Might at least stay a bit warm on the road home."

"I know someone with a car," Wren piped up, immediately regretting it as the two women wheeled around to stare at her. "Bertram – Mr Burnley, I mean – has a car. Or, he said he did," she mumbled.

"Where is he then?" squealed Joan, looking around. "Your *Bertram*!" She cackled as she skipped away, delighting in Wren's discomfort.

"He's gone home," she muttered, feeling her face burn. "And he's not *my* Bertram. He's just a boy."

"A boy you spent most of the night with from what *I* saw," teased Mary, warming to Joan's theme. Wren was so spotless a character that they rarely got the opportunity to tease her.

"Aye, I only saw her dance with a couple of lads. And even I danced with more than two people tonight," said Joan. "Did you not want to dance with anyone else? Or was it that he wouldn't let you?"

"I –" Wren thought for a moment. She hadn't noticed not being allowed to dance with others. It was simply a case of Bertram always being by her side. She was flattered by his attention, reckoning he must think very well of her when he stayed so close. Yet now, when she thought about it, maybe his constant presence was just a means of keeping other men away from her. It was a little disconcerting to think she was being cordoned off but also a little exciting to think someone put such effort into keeping her for himself. But then she remembered the look on Bertram's face when he saw her dancing with Robbie. She shuddered. She would have to tread carefully.

The two girls quickly grew tired of trying to provoke some kind of reaction from Wren as, no matter what they said, she managed to stay stoically mute. Her silence meant the others eventually began to discuss the other people at the dance while Wren sank into her own contemplation of the evening as they walked home. She had enjoyed the evening in Bertram's company – loved it even. And yet the few minutes she snatched with Robbie had affected her too. She felt something different when she was with each of them yet both feelings were strong – her thoughts on Bertram perhaps being that bit stronger. Perhaps that superior emotional connection corresponded to the amount of time she spent with both men. And if time directly corresponded to feeling, then what she felt regarding Robbie was much greater. He had touched her indelibly in those few short moments in a way Bertram had not despite being attached to her all evening. Maybe it was just the moment Robbie caught her in. By that stage of the night, she was tired, her defences were down. Or it could have been the music's slow, swaying rhythm that promised romance. Or maybe not. In truth, Wren didn't know enough about her own feelings regarding men to be able to understand what had occurred.

When she got home, her aunt was sitting up by the fire in the parlour, a book drooping from her tired fingers.

"You didn't have to wait up," she admonished, taking the book from the old lady and placing it on the mantelshelf.

"I just wanted to be sure you got back alright," replied Astrid, wincing as she got heavily to her feet. When she stayed too long in one position, her recently mended bones ached, making her movements painful.

Wren immediately went to her aunt's aid, gently supporting her waist as she took as much of the other woman's weight as she could across her shoulders.

"I'm alright, I'm alright," Astrid protested. She hated showing her weakness to anyone. She had been dozing in her chair and had slid down in the seat, twisting her body awkwardly. When she stood, she could feel the blood fizz through her veins as it flowed once again. It felt like too-warm liquid was being forced through her system, pressing hard on her newly healed bones.

Usually when Astrid told Wren she was alright, the girl would cease what she was doing instantly, fading meekly back. But this time she ignored Astrid's protestations. It was surprising to the old lady but she was glad of the help. It also surprised her that Wren hadn't begun to regale her with tales of the evening the moment she walked in the door. Whenever she went anywhere, Wren always came home bursting with news of what she had seen or done. But now she was silent, introspective. There was something grown-up about her discreet aid, as if the child Astrid parted from earlier had not come back. It made the old lady worry about what had happened in the interim. However, she felt it wasn't her place to ask. If Wren wanted to speak to her, she would.

Wren helped her aunt up the stairs to her bedroom. Once there, she helped her undress and get into her nightclothes in virtual silence. When she was done and the lady was safely tucked up in her bed, Astrid, with some difficulty, sat up to stop Wren leaving. Without a word, she took the girl in her arms, embracing her in a way she never had before in the hope that all the love she felt for this girl might flow through her own tightly wound arms and into her great-niece's heart.

"Thank you, sweetheart. For everything." She kissed Wren's cheek then lay back down on her pillow.

Wren stood for a moment watching her begin to breathe evenly in preparation for sleep. She didn't know why, but she knew she wouldn't tell her aunt about the two boys. Not yet, anyway. Time would need to run on a little before she opened that can of worms. She tried vaguely to pull her emotions to the surface but it was no use. Her tired mind protested too strongly and so she found herself slipping lightly out of the bedroom and down the hall to her own room. Once across the threshold, she firmly closed the door on the world. Tomorrow was another day. Tomorrow she would have time to think.

Chapter 16

As summer progressed, Lili continued to go to parish dances with Ewan. Each time she went, she would tell her mother just before Evelyn went to bed and every evening, just before she left, Evelyn would sit with her daughter in front of the fire and plait her hair.

Lili was surprised that her mother didn't ask her any questions about her nights out. About who she saw, who she talked to or who danced with whom. She assumed Evelyn knew she spent these nights in Ewan's company as several of the people who attended the dances were regular correspondents of her mother's. None of them would pass up an opportunity to tell Evelyn Burnley that her daughter was stepping out with the most eligible bachelor in half a dozen parishes. Lili could imagine the glee with which they would inform her mother of her dalliances. They would watch closely for any sign Evelyn was in the dark about the whole affair, hoping they could spread the word that Evelyn Burnley didn't know what went on in her own household. But Evelyn remained impassive throughout, frustrating all the local tattlers with her simple acceptance of her daughter's involvement with such a sought-after gentleman. Of course she knew. Why wouldn't she? Her daughter's affairs were her own was her constant refrain. It was the only sign Evelyn gave of being rattled since everyone's affairs were her concern. Lili was a little disconcerted by her mother's lack of interest. Neither did she know whether her mother approved or disapproved of her liaisons with Ewan but surmised that, since Evelyn hadn't expressed open condemnation, she consented to her daughter stepping out with their neighbour.

Ewan and Lili continued their evening walks when they had time, enjoying the long evenings and good weather of the summer. The sun would heat the ground during the day and as the night drew in, the earth would release its warmth creating a palpable haze that swirled around moving bodies, touching them with tendrils of hot air. When the men took to the fields to make the hay, the blackberries were beginning to lose their white and pink petals, forming hard green lumps that would later turn red then bruised purpley-black. But first, the hay had to be cut, gathered and stacked.

All the local men helped one another out, descending on each other's farms in a rotation that needed no discussion since the order they worked in had remained unchanged for years. The women's involvement was confined to providing the sustenance (which consisted primarily of large amounts of tea, brown bread with butter and fresh tomatoes). The men would return from the fields late in the evening smelling of sweet, dried grass and covered in a fine layer of brown dust which streaked as they washed it off their faces.

On one such evening, Ewan had arranged to meet Lili but, when she arrived at the tree he was not there. He came trudging down the lane about ten minutes later, preceded by Georgie who looked a deal sprightlier than her master.

"She's only showing off," grumbled Ewan when he reached them both. "She's been sleeping under the hay bogie most of the day while the rest of us do all the work out in the heat. Only time she appeared was when the food did."

"Well, I don't suppose she'd be much use wielding a sprong," said Lili.

"Aye, but it's still not fair she gets to laze about all day and I've got to work to earn my keep." He rubbed the dog's ears affectionately. She shuffled towards him while maintaining her sitting position and shoved herself against his leg.

"I think Georgie does quite enough for her keep," Lili said, reaching across to pat the dog's head.

"And don't I as well?" he said, feigning offence.

Lili adopted a serious mien. "Oh, not near enough. What do you do only sit around all day?"

"Oh *really*?" Ewan's whole body seemed to grow and change from languid, overworked farmer to something feline – predatory even – as he advanced slowly on Lili.

She retreated a few steps, tittering nervously. She knew he wouldn't hurt her but that didn't stop him from being imposing. He was quite an impressive sight, sunburnt and tanned, covered in dust with his limbs stretched out ready to capture her. She knew what he was planning to do. And she wasn't at all keen on letting him do it. He had discovered a weakness of hers several weeks before and she had a feeling he was about to exploit it.

In a moment of boyishness while getting over a stile on one of their walks, he had caught her round the waist to swing her down beside him. At this juncture, Lili had almost collapsed nose-first off the stile only for Ewan to save her, half catching, half dropping her onto solid ground and almost overbalancing himself in the process. In his unsteadiness he had staggered several feet away and, on turning around, found Lili doubled over crying. Terrified that he had somehow hurt her in his attempts at romanticism, he rushed over to her.

"Lili! Oh God, Lili! I'm so sorry. It was stupid thing to do. Where does it hurt?"

It was then that his brain managed to catch up with his eyes and his ears. She wasn't crying – she was laughing. Curled up in a ball, her face bright red, in absolute hysterics. Lili, he discovered, was desperately ticklish.

Now he advanced on her, she knew there was no fighting him off but that didn't mean she wasn't going to try. She took a more combative stance, looked him in the eye ... then turned and ran. And she was by no means slow. Her long limbs and athletic physique lent themselves to flight. For a moment she thought she might escape him. She couldn't hear him thudding along behind her at least. But then long arms snaked their way around her stomach, and she found herself captured, held fast up against the lean, dusty, hay-smelling torso of a very large man. Of course she couldn't outrun him. Lili was fast, but he was faster.

"Oh no you don't, hen," he whispered in her ear before drawing his fingers up the sides of her belly.

She reacted immediately, doubling over around his hands, only half registering the little *"Oof!"* he gave when she did so. Again, he could have let her nose-dive into the ground but he held her fast, ready for the reaction this time. He continued to tickle her mercilessly until she was lying on the grass verge giggling like a girl which in turn made him laugh, both overcome. He finished up bent double on the ground beside her shoulder, head bowed, his hand still on her stomach. As they subsided, neither moved. They both took account of where each other's limbs were and suddenly became silent, hardly moving enough to breathe.

Slowly, Ewan lifted his head to look into Lili's face, into her eyes. He saw many things there – uncertainty, openness, a tiny bit of fear and also lust. Instinctively he reached down and kissed her. And she kissed back. He had noticed that, no matter how often they kissed, there was always a reserve to the way Lili kissed him. He knew it wasn't that she didn't want to. But it sometimes felt like she was thinking too much about doing it. There was always the barrier of her thoughts between their lips and, no matter what he did, he could not break through. But now he had. She moved like she had known how to all along, her reserve only a coquettish ruse to make him think her innocent. She was no longer behaving like the innocent. She had finally let go and, in letting go, she grabbed him with such fierceness as to make him half collapse against her, his weight pressing her into the ground. He readjusted his position, placing one knee on the skirt between her legs, sliding his arms around her back between her and the damp evening grass. He pulled her body closer to his, arching her back, pressing the length of her torso against his.

Lili could feel the bones of his ribs, the muscle that covered them, his heart hammering in his chest, the burning heat coming from his body. She should stop. But she wasn't going to. His fingers were firm as they searched up and down the length of her spine creating an answering heat of their own in her body. His sun-baked lips were initially dry when they touched hers but now they were soft and supple as they teased her own. She met each surge of movement from his mouth, opening her lips just as he opened his, tongues touching, dancing just as their bodies had done in so many parish halls. She had thought those subtle touches intimate. Now she realised they were nothing compared to this. She raked her hands down his back and he hissed into her lips, attacking them with renewed vigour.

Neither were sure how long they remained thus but at some point, both became aware of a yapping noise close at hand. Not without considerable effort, Ewan finally broke away from Lili to see where the sound was coming from only to come face to face with Georgie, barking and yipping while hopping about in a state of wild excitement.

"*Och*, Georgie!" he said crossly, rolling off Lili and throwing his spare arm over his eyes. "You've ruined it!"

As she still lay on his other arm, he felt the laugh build in Lili's belly from the vibrations through her back.

"Georgie's the only sensible one among us," she said.

"Hang sense. Oh Lord, I didn't think I'd have the energy for a walk this evening but I thought we'd get a wee bit further than here." He gestured vaguely to the lane and hedges that hemmed it in.

"What had you planned?" Lili rolled onto her front and propping herself up on his chest as if she had done so a hundred times before.

His arm wrapped around her and he ran a hand unconsciously up and down her back. "*Och*, I don't know. Maybe that we'd go up to the house and have tea. A nice sit-down maybe. Christ," he scrubbed his face, "I'm getting old."

"Not old, just tired. You're working hard."

"I thought I didn't work hard at all. Wasn't that how we ended up in this situation?" He waved at their surroundings once more.

"I was only teasing."

"I know, love, I know."

"Maybe we can have tea tomorrow?"

He chuckled. "If I'm honest, I'd prefer we did this again."

She swatted him playfully in the chest.

"*Ow!*" he grumbled.

"Wait," said Lili suddenly. "Hen?"

"Hen?" he answered, confused.

"You called me 'hen'. Why?"

Ewan's chest rumbled. He obviously found it funny. Lili wasn't quite so amused. To her, such an avian appellation suggested she was short, dumpy, prone to incessant chatter and had a tendency to flap about without purpose. In other words, 'hen' was not a flattering epithet. Perhaps Lili had a high opinion of herself, but she didn't believe she exhibited any fowl-like characteristics. Maybe Ewan was just trying to rile her.

After a pause, he answered. "I hadn't realised I even said it. In Scotland, it's a term of endearment. Just something you call someone you love." He kissed her forehead. "Alright ... hen?"

"Alright," she said, copying his Scotch burr.

He chuckled and squeezed her tightly to his chest. They stayed thus for a time until Ewan finally said his shirt was getting damp. He didn't want to catch a chill in the middle of haymaking and he also didn't want his muscles to seize up. The work was hard enough without being stiff. He was an affectionate man but he was also a practical one. Lili sighed, rolled onto her back again and allowed him to sit up then stand. He could already feel the tightness from the moisture in the grass seeping into his shoulders. He would have to change his shirt when he got home. But it had been worth it. He turned around to find Lili still lying on the ground, wisps of hair escaping from the knot at the back of her head, her clothing crumpled and generally in worse order than when they met. He realised he didn't feel the slightest bit guilty. In fact, he was rather pleased.

"Come on, up you get." He proffered his hand.

She grabbed it but resisted as he hauled her up.

"I wish we could stay like this all evening," she groaned, staggering to her feet.

"Well, if you married me, we could spend all night together too," he murmured, rubbing the back of her hand with his thumb.

It was the most suggestive thing he had ever said to her. She didn't know what to say. But he didn't need a reply. He knew how she felt and knew that it would take time. He smiled at her expression and kissed her cheek. "You should get home too. I can feel the damp on your blouse."

She nodded and began walking away in a daze but then turned. "You said you wanted to go up to the house for tea this evening?"

"Aye, I thought we could."

"We'll do that tomorrow. I'll meet you up there at the usual time," she said decisively before continuing on down the lane home.

Chapter 17

The next day was scorching, with nowhere to shade from the burning sun out in the middle of the fields where the men worked. Even Evelyn, who made it her business to visit the men every lunchtime to deliver food and, more pressingly, to hear the talk, was overcome by the heat while out feeding the hens in the yard.

The hen yard was sheltered on all four sides. The square patch of ground where the hens scratched was hemmed in on two sides by the back walls of two barns and high walls at either end which were perfect for preventing the invasion of foxes. However, the whitewashed walls and the enclosed space meant heat couldn't escape from the space as there was no wind to circulate the air. Most of the hens had remained inside in the cool darkness of their shed but Evelyn chose this day (of all days) to clear the ground of droppings and detritus left by her birds.

Not having seen her mother for a while, Lili went out to search for her and found her propped up against one of the walls under an overhanging eave of the roof. Evelyn was sweating profusely and her breathing was laboured. Lili felt a little jolt of fear when she spotted her. She knew her mother struggled more and more these days but she coped quite well considering the state of her health.

Rushing up to her, she found herself saying, "What on earth have you done to yourself?" She sounded angry but it was simply how her fear manifested itself in her voice.

Evelyn flared immediately at the accusatory tone. "Would you go away! There's nothing wrong with me at all! Just a bit hot is all." But her body belied her flippancy as she suddenly clapped a hand to her chest, hissing air out through her teeth.

"What is it?" No response. "Mammy, what is it?"

Evelyn was frightening Lili. Was she having a heart attack? Heart problems were prevalent on her mother's side of the family but Evelyn had always asserted that her heart was as strong as an ox's. Silently Lili had hoped that was true since her mother's heart had to sustain a body akin to that of an ox. Her mother's weight really was a problem.

Evelyn didn't answer Lili's question at once but waited for the pain to subside. "Just a bit of heartburn is all. I've been getting it quite a bit lately. And no," she said, pre-empting the question, "I'm not having a heart attack. Just hot and a bit of heartburn is all. Help me back inside to the cool, will you?"

When she put a helpful arm around her mother's shoulder, Lili could feel the clamminess of Evelyn's skin through the light material of her blouse and was reminded of the dampness of her own blouse following her escapades the night before. She felt heat in her cheeks and knew it was nothing to do with the glare of the sun. It seemed that Ewan was slowly invading every small part of her life. Usually she loved it when these little memories popped into her mind but, at that particular moment, she found the intrusion quite unhelpful.

Once they got into the house, Evelyn decided to lie down in her room to cool off and recoup some of her lost energy. Lili went with her, opening the small windows at opposite ends of the room to try and encourage a cooling through-flow air. The room was one of the coolest in the house. On the eastern side the window was overshadowed by a large deciduous tree which made the space quite dark. The other window opened onto the back yard and was therefore always in the shade. It was the perfect place to put someone suffering from the heat. It was also perfect for Evelyn as it was on the ground floor so she didn't have to climb the stairs. She hadn't been up the stairs for a long time as she simply wasn't able to negotiate its high, steep steps. Lili now did all the housework upstairs. She was never told to, she just saw her mother couldn't.

Evelyn did not emerge for the rest of the day, oscillating between dozing and a wakefulness that allowed her to hear the sounds of the house. She rarely stopped and listened. It was one of the problems with her. Whether it was a case of overworking herself or excessive speaking, Evelyn always did too much, only realizing the truth too late. She knew Lili was worried about her and hated the way her daughter hovered uncertainly. Not only did it annoy Evelyn that it was she who was laid up in bed while Lili was perfectly fine, but her daughter's worry was beginning to infect her mind too. Maybe she *was* seriously ill. But she didn't feel ill. She just felt desperately tired. All she wanted to do was sleep and Lili wasn't helping her on that front.

It was, therefore, a relief when Lili slid into the room and asked, "Would you be alright if I went out for a while?"

Evelyn suppressed a tiny grin. She knew exactly where Lili went, despite the precautions she took. Of course she did: Evelyn knew everything (in her own humble opinion). Though she would have liked to know more about Ewan, regardless of whether he was courting her daughter or not. He had never been forthcoming with her and that irked Evelyn considerably. But she was privately glad that Lili hadn't approached her on the subject of her new attachment.

She therefore had no cause to broach the subject herself. Evelyn was afraid that, if she did, she would push Lili away or give her cause to suggest to her mother that it was time she left and began her own life and her own family. Because the truth was, no matter how many times Evelyn told people she was still capable of managing her workload, she knew her body was giving up on her. She just wasn't able anymore – even with Lili's help – and if Lili went off and married this chap then Evelyn would be on her own. She had to concede that she couldn't carry on without her eldest child's assistance. However, she was confident in the knowledge that Lili would not leave her. Lili would continue to live as per their current arrangement out of a sense of duty. But then Evelyn did not want to discourage her daughter either as it was quite exhilarating for her to think that one of her girls had wrangled the most eligible bachelor in several parishes and also that another woman in her family might lay claim to another property on Bachelor Lane. Evelyn had it all planned.

"Go on. Shur I don't need you to sit by me. Go on and don't be loitering."

Lili left. She felt a little guilty leaving her mother in such a prone state but there really was nothing she could do. And Evelyn had said she could go …

As she walked up the lane towards Ewan's house, her guilt evaporated. She felt excited. She was peeling back another layer of his protective outer shell and getting to know the man beneath. She doubted anyone local knew him as well as she now did but she also knew there was more to unearth. Physically, at least, they were less guarded. The evening before had shown that.

On nearing the house, she found herself a little unsure. Should she go to the front door as a visitor might or around the back? Luckily, the query was answered for her when she got to the gate. Georgie was sitting behind it watching the

159

lane and barked when Lili approached.

Ewan was sitting on the front step soaking up the last of the evening sunshine while absentmindedly rubbing his wet hair with a towel.

"Hello!" He stood as Lili came through the gate. He was barefoot and had the slightly blanched look of someone who had recently been doused in cold water.

"What happened to you?" she asked.

"Nothing. I went for a swim in the river is all. Get all the sweat and dirt off after a day doing hay." He dropped his head and shook it like a dog but it was almost dry so only a fine mist of water droplets hit Lili. He smoothed his hair back with his hand and said, "I do it most evenings."

"I didn't know that," she said, slightly disappointed that she was only discovering this now. She knew he was sometimes dusty and sometimes clean but hadn't really thought how he came to be that way. It just never crossed her mind to ask. "You can swim then?"

"After a fashion," he replied. "One of the corporals taught me when we were stationed beside a lake in Italy."

"In the army?"

He nodded. "During the War," he answered but then looked away.

"I can't swim at all," she offered, noting the sudden tension in his shoulders.

He still did not look at her. "I'll teach you some day. If you want."

It was as if a cloud obscured the sun, casting a shadowy spectre of the past. Lili knew he fought in the War and considered asking him about it but didn't. She wasn't her mother. But then she did want to know more about him – to know him, to *really* know him. She had to ask.

"Why did you join the army?"

It was her turn to avoid his gaze but when she finally

looked up, she found he was not looking at her either. Instead, he was staring at his bare toes as they wiggled on the stone path. He stayed silent. The tiny sounds around them, the twitter of birds and the hiss of the breeze in the trees, seemed like they were amplified to an unbearable degree. Even Georgie stood, unmoving, studying her master for any sign of life.

Unable to bear it any longer, Lili's voice burst through the silence: "Forget I asked. It doesn't matter."

He still didn't speak. Lili began to fear she had done irreparable damage to the trust she had built with him. She was about to tell him she would go home and come back another time when he finally spoke.

She was so relieved to hear his voice she barely registered what he said.

"What was that?"

"I said you'd better come in." He stood aside, allowing her to pass through the door.

The house was not what Lili expected.

When Billy Murphy owned the middle house it had been sparse, tired and grubby. Almost every stick of furniture was older than Billy, sagging and broken – mostly due to his proclivity for knocking things over when drunk. It was also a wonder he had never been burnt alive by the open fire at the end of the room upon which he did all his cooking and which heated the house. The fire was badly designed, sitting in a huge alcove with a tiny flue at the top, resulting in most of the smoke missing the opening completely and purling up and across the ceiling, staining the wooden beams a charred black colour and the white in between a dirty grey. It also resulted in a layer of dust that covered everything. But the worst part had always been the floor, covered as it was in a thick layer of mud and grit that crunched as you walked on it. No one knew if it was a mud floor or just so unclean that the real floor couldn't be seen. Outside had been no better. The exterior walls hadn't been repainted in twenty years and the garden was like a jungle, tangled with a giant, straggling rhododendron and an abundance of briars. It had always been an excellent place for picking blackberries.

But not anymore. One of the first things Ewan had done when he arrived was tear out the rhododendron and with it came much of the briars and overgrown shrubbery. Of an evening, after a day's work on the farm, he would eat his supper then go back out to wage war with the garden.

"Do you want to sit down?"

Lili jumped. Ewan was standing in the doorway just behind her, his head at an awkward angle in order to avoid cracking it off the lintel. She had taken one step into the room then stopped dead to take it all in. Now she got to inspect the interior of his home, Lili was even more impressed. She had noticed the glow of the whitewashed outer walls of the house and now she saw that the fresh paint continued inside. The walls were a warmer colour than the stark white of outside but the ceiling was a shining white alternated with the soot-blackened beams. Part of the reason the ceiling was so white was because the useless open fire had been replaced by a large Victorian range with a flue pipe leading directly to the chimney. Georgie slunk around Lili's legs and made a beeline for a stuffed flattened sack that was in the corner beside the range. She kneaded it with her forepaws, circled twice and lay down.

It was then that Lili noticed what the sack lay on ... a tiled floor. Well, that answers the question of whether or not Billy had a mud floor, she thought. There was, in fact, a checkerboard of red and black tiles covering the entire floor, with no hint of its former state of filthiness. The furniture was new and solidly built. Lili made her way over to one of two low, upholstered chairs with high backs and smooth wooden armrests. The chair facing the door had a slight depression in the middle of the seat and the wood looked a little worn. It was clearly the chair Ewan favoured so she sat in the other one.

The range was just warm enough to keep a kettle hot. Ewan went to the sideboard and brought out cups, plates, bread, butter, jam, sugar and a jug of milk, all of which he put on an upturned crate before placing it between the seats. He went back to the cupboards and produced a teapot, proceeding to spoon in tea then water from the kettle. He went about every task with a domestic familiarity that Lili had never envisaged. Though he was always well-dressed and had good manners, there was something innately outdoor about him. He belonged in the fields with the animals so perfectly. And yet here he was performing all these little jobs so ably without looking out of place at all. He was such an oddity.

He was silent while preparing tea. Lili simply watched him and he let her. He had to let her see him for what he was. Because this might be the first and last time she entered his house willingly.

Finally, he poured the tea, handed her a cup and sat down.

"You've done a lovely job on the house."

"*Hmmm.*" Ewan sat slowly running his index finger repeatedly down his nose. He didn't take his eyes off her.

She felt uncomfortable and looked away. She studied the books on the shelves, the stairs, the table, the chairs – everything but him. They continued in an uncomfortable silence until Ewan finally spoke.

"I never told you how I came to be in the army, did I? No. I haven't told you because I didn't want anyone here to know. To know what happened before I came here. You see, I came here to get away from … things that happened in

Scotland. It's why I joined the army too. That and to serve my country. But I could have done that at home. They needed farmers to feed everyone when cargo ships got caught up in the Atlantic blockade. But I couldn't stay at home because, well, I wasn't wanted there."

He stopped and scrubbed his face with his hands.

"I need to start at the beginning, don't I? I was … married. Once before. When I was a young man – a boy. I –" He stopped. "It wasn't really my choice. It was, well, it was arranged, after a fashion, by my family and the girl's family. Not that I wasn't willing. I was young and cocksure. Thought the sun shone out of my … well, I wanted to be a man and I thought if you were to be a proper man, you needed a wife. So I married the daughter of a neighbouring farmer when I was twenty. She was just gone eighteen. Mabel was her name. You see, the idea was that Mabel and I would marry and unite the adjoining farms and, once her parents died, Mabel and I would keep the farm instead of it going to one of her male cousins. Her father thought marrying her off to me would be the simplest way of keeping his land in the hands of his own bloodline. She was an only child, see. Mabel's father was my father's closest friend and they came up with the plan between them before telling either of us. So that summer Mabel came home from school in Edinburgh and she and her parents came to ours for supper. That's when they told us we were going to be married. We were both very naïve. Neither of us thought to stand up to our parents and say, 'Hold on a minute!' What our parents said to us was law. We – neither of us – were going to go against their wishes. And, well, there was also the fact that she was very pretty … I thought all my Christmases had come at once when I saw her walk down the aisle of the church towards me. I thought she was made for me." He paused. "But she wasn't. We moved into a cottage on one corner of my father's land. They'd been getting it ready for months. I remember I was quite hurt they'd kept it from me – the house, not the wedding plans. No, back then I wasn't clever enough to see the dangers of marrying someone you didn't know. No matter how pretty she might be. The thing with Mabel was that while she may have been beautiful on the outside, there wasn't much else to like about her." He grimaced. "Now, you may think me cruel for saying that but it's difficult for a young man to bide with a woman he can't even have a decent conversation with. She was just … empty? No – that sounds terrible. Distracted?" He tapped his cheek with his finger, thinking. "She was just … not the sort of woman I would have chosen for myself. She had no spark, no verve. She could sit for hours on end doing nothing but looping a piece of ribbon around her finger. I would come in for dinner or for supper and she'd have nothing made. And she wouldn't realise it made me angry. She wouldn't be apologetic, she'd just say 'Oh I didn't realise the time,' or something. Back then –" he dipped his head "back then, I wasn't as … controlled as I am now. I had – have – a temper, a bad one, and sometimes I'd lose it. I never hit her, I'd never do that, but I'd shout and it used to frighten her. When I was angry with her, she'd sometimes go back home to her mother. And then, of course, people began to talk. You know how it is. Something was going on with Ewan Cameron and his *wife*." He said the last word as if it tasted foul. The bitterness and pain were evident. "I had no idea what to do. I was young – I know that's not an excuse – but I had no experience in handling women like her. My mother and sister worked hard, they had a sense of humour, they fitted into my world perfectly. But Mabel didn't. After I'd scared her, once I'd calmed down a bit I'd feel guilty. Because she was a sweet girl. She just didn't understand the world in the same way I did. So I'd try and make it up to her – do things to make her happy. And it worked for a while but then something else would happen, I'd get mad and she'd leave. That's how we carried on for nearly three years. Anyway …" He sat up in his chair.

Lili could tell he was at the business end of the story. She was glad of it. She felt uncomfortable hearing about his past, simply because she was seeing a version of Ewan she didn't know and wasn't sure she would have liked to know.

"Anyway," he said again. "One of times when I lost my temper, I tried to make it up to her by getting electric lights in the house. She'd spent years in school in Edinburgh city and was used to flicking a switch and having light so she hated the poor light from the lamps. The town had electric light so some of the local houses were getting it. I'd originally said no because it was expensive. But then I decided to get it for her to try and make her happy. And it did. She was like a child with a new toy. She just couldn't leave it alone!" He was suddenly angry. "She'd walk into a room and have to switch the light on and off and on and off again. It used to make the bulbs blow and then she'd have to get me to change them which would make me angry again because she was wasting money. So –" He stopped, huffed and continued. "I gave her a real telling-off one time she blew a bulb and told her I wouldn't replace another one. So the next time she blew a bulb, she decided to try and replace it herself and … and …"

He came to a shuddering halt and gasped for breath. He had not spoken of this incident to anyone for years. He didn't want to remember it, so he'd pushed it to the back of his memory and trained himself not to think of it. But now as he forced himself to do the opposite – to examine the whole affair – he felt the agony of it more acutely that he ever had. Now he had years of experience, years of suppressed emotion, years of understanding, which made him see what had happened in a new light. He put his head in his hands and finally carried on.

"She tried to replace the bulb herself," he repeated, voice muffled by his arms. "But she wasn't tall enough to reach. That was part of the reason I used to change the bulbs, see. I was tall enough to reach if I stood on a chair, but Mabel was tiny. Her head barely reached my chest. So when she tried to reach the bulb she couldn't. It was the light in the kitchen so she pulled the table over underneath the socket. But she still wasn't tall enough. So she got a little stool as well and put it on the table."

Lili shifted in her chair. She could see where the story was going and didn't want to hear any more. In her mind's eye, she could see the childish little figure balancing precariously on a stool. She listened to Ewan as he told her about how the table would rock on the uneven flagstones of the kitchen floor if it was moved even a little bit. She found herself standing in a cottage kitchen in the south of Scotland, watching it all. She heard Ewan's voice as if she were underwater. She wanted him to stop but the girl in her imaginings kept moving inevitably forward.

Mabel stood on the stool, a new lightbulb in her hand, legs shaking which, in turn, made the elevation she had cobbled together shake. The girl stretched up, balancing on her toes, reaching for something she would never touch.

Ewan ducking under the door frame, coming into the room in time to see his wife make a final desperate grab for the bulb.

The table tipping violently on the uneven floor. Mabel falling, falling, falling backwards, her back arching, her head leading the rest of her body towards the floor. The lightbulb, popped from her grasp, sailing in a graceful arc towards Ewan whose long arm allowed him to simply scoop it from the air without thinking as he stood rooted to the spot, watching his wife fall.

The resounding *thunk* of a skull hitting a floor.

The table rocking back and forth in the depression of one of the flagstones, slowing down, slowing down, stopping. And then …

Silence.

Lili was the first to break the moment, hissing air between her teeth as tears fell down her cheeks. She saw the girl on the floor and the girl stared back at her with dead, empty eyes.

"I caught the lightbulb," said Ewan finally. "But I should've caught my wife."

Lili couldn't speak, couldn't form words in her brain. All she could think of was the life that had been lost all those years ago for something so pointless. She couldn't help but think of her father's death in among all the other jumbled thoughts. A life wasted just like Mabel's had been. But then there was guilt. Guilt that she, Lili, resented the existence of another woman. Guilt for being relieved that Mabel was gone. Even if her shade still haunted Ewan, the other woman could never come to reclaim him. And then there was pity. Pity for the simple little creature who had been so foolish in life that it led to her premature death. Mabel hadn't belonged in the countryside. She was too soft to cope with a solid country boy like Ewan. She hadn't needed a husband who worked on a farm all day only to come in at night to be waited on. She was not independent enough to cope on her own and, being young, Ewan had been too immature to understand her.

She also pitied Ewan. The boy from twenty years ago and the man that sat across from her now. He was not naturally cruel – she knew that – but he could be abrupt. Sometimes when he was tired or exceedingly busy, he expected people to know what to do just in the same way he did. Lili had watched him even recently instructing younger boys in the finer points of haymaking with patience and a true interest in teaching them. But equally he had struggled to control his temper when some of the men were slap-dash in their approach. He was the sort of person who wanted things done right – something that would have caused no end of problems for his disorganised wife. In a way, both man and wife had been freed from a lifetime of unhappiness by Mabel's death.

"Say something, would you?"

Lili jumped. She had been so wrapped up in her own musings that she had completely forgotten where she was. She came back to consciousness as if she was resurfacing after a time underwater. She expected the world to look different but it was just the same. She expected Ewan to look different but he was still the tall, handsome farmer who lived up Bachelor Lane. He looked the same … but he wasn't. That didn't mean Lili thought less of him, she just knew more of him.

"Say something! *Please!*"

The look of anguish on his face made her speak.

"I still love you."

Her head had screamed so many things at her in that moment but 'I still love you' was the first that reached her lips. Ewan's entire body slumped. He bent over, his chest on his knees and his arms over his head. A dry sob wracked his large frame and, before she knew what she was doing, Lili was on her knees on the floor beside him. She laid her cheek on his shoulder and her arm across his back. It was a weak gesture but it was all she could think to do.

"You believe me then?" His voice was muffled but she heard him nonetheless.

She put her lips to his ear. "Of course I do. Why wouldn't I?"

Ewan was quiet for a moment, then he raised his head.

Lili could see the agony on his face. It broke her heart.

"Because nobody else did," he whispered. "Everyone thought I'd killed her."

Realisation hit Lili like a physical blow. Of course they did. An unhappy marriage, a wife in fear of her husband, a husband with size and strength on his side, no witnesses and Mabel killed changing a lightbulb. She could see how the news would pass from individual to individual with each one putting in their own little details, their own slant on the tragedy. Before the truth of the matter could ever be told, the gospel of the gossips would be hammered home with such conviction that their version of events became the indisputable truth. Lili had seen her mother and friends spin their webs time and time again until rumour had more credence than truth. Lili knew the small communities where truth was in the eyes of beholders, not in the explanations of those directly involved. She doubted whether a small town in Scotland was any different.

"What happened?" she asked quietly.

It took Ewan a moment to speak, his voice hollow. "I was arrested. I … I …" He faltered then carried on. "I was in prison for a time. Until they were forced to let me go. They had no evidence. Only speculation. And, of course, there was gossip. It sounded awfully convincing but, unfortunately for them, it didn't stand up in court. Even though I was released, they still thought I'd done it." He lifted his head and stared straight into her eyes. His own were red-rimmed and shining with unshed tears. "Do you know what it's like to have an entire community turn against you? People you have known all your life, friends since childhood, shopkeepers, relatives. All of them turning against you. Talking behind their hands, going out of their way to avoid you, dragging their children away. It eats away at you, makes you wonder if you'd be better off in jail. And all that time you still haven't been given the chance to grieve about what happened, what you saw – what I saw – that day. So, I did what many young men do when they're ashamed or have their wilfulness checked: I ran away." He sat up in his chair. Lili stayed at his side and he absentmindedly began to stroke her hair. "War had just been declared so I signed up. Got posted to the continent mostly. I was a good soldier. Made my way up through the ranks. Mostly because I didn't get myself killed. But it was also because I didn't think of anything else other than soldiery. I didn't want to think about home. I didn't want to think of the wife I didn't love … *rotting* in a graveyard. So I thought about how to fight, how to channel all my anger and hate at something that deserved it. And war was perfect for that. It saved me. Because I learnt to be a machine. And I learnt control. The army made me a man again."

"What happened? After the War ended."

"I stayed on the continent for a few years. Just drifting around mostly, helping to rebuild. And then I went home. I was older and less hot-headed. And I was gullible enough to believe that people's opinions of me might have changed."

"But they hadn't?"

His free had balled into a fist. "They still believed I murdered my wife."

"But you didn't."

He looked directly at her. "No, I didn't."

Lili rose off the floor and slid onto Ewan's lap. She knew she must have been heavy. Nonetheless, she curled into his chest, placing her palm over his beating heart. Slowly, he folded his arms around her and held her tightly to him.

"And then you came here," she said finally.

"I sold up my part of the farm. I gave the rest of it back to Mabel's father. Funny, aside from my family, he was the only one who believed I didn't do it. He still farms the land, but he has no one to pass it on to," he said sadly. "So, with the money I had, I went searching for a new farm and a fresh start."

They sat for a long time in silence until Lili murmured, "Even though what led you here was terrible, I'm glad you found us."

"So am I." He caught her chin between his thumb and forefinger and kissed her before breathing, "God, I love you, Lili."

Then, for the first time in years, Ewan let go and cried.

Chapter 18

In the weeks that followed her first dance with Robbie and Bertram, Wren's feelings began to untangle themselves, forming into a true emotional connection. This was mainly due to her only ever seeing Bertram. Robbie never came to another dance but Bertram was at all of them. And at each social, he made a point of spending the night with Wren who, for her part, was the epitome of encouragement. Young love made her garrulous and playful. Soon she was joining Joan running down Church Street to meet her beau standing outside the Institute with an elbow leaning up on the grey granite window surround or, for those who weren't quite so tall like Bertram, simply leaning against the vivid orange bricks of the wall. They would kiss happily, enter the arched double doors hand in hand, pay the person at the table and ascend the stairs to the hall where they would dance all night. Bertram in fact, with Wren's assistance, progressed greatly as a dancer. But one thing she quickly realised was that he could not abide being corrected within the earshot of others, especially men. His jaw would snap tight and she would see his entire face strain in an effort to control his irritation.

In moments like that Wren felt the pangs of fear and panic that she always suffered when her mother's mood suddenly shifted with no hint as to what she would do next. Not without some self-will, Bertram would rein in his anger as he watched the change in Wren's face just as she saw the difference in his.

As the blood drained from her face and her pupils dilated, sensations tore through his body, battling one another for superiority. He was ashamed he could scare her like that. He worried he might scare her away. But most of all, and in a way both exciting and disconcerting for him, Bertram felt himself roused by her fear. Luckily, Wren was both too innocent and too preoccupied with trying not to anger him further to notice. He liked that. She may have known more about dancing than he did, but on almost all other fronts, he was the more informed. He liked that he could tell her things and it made him feel important when she marvelled at his intelligence. Because Bertram was intelligent – very much so. But there was also something else to him that wasn't so admirable.

The problem was that Bertram had a chip on his shoulder. Forever the little man, he had to prove himself. He enjoyed spending time with Wren, but it was more for the affection she showed him and the fact she furnished him with a willing listener, than any feelings he had for the girl herself. She was someone who would defer to him, sit and listen as he talked to others without interruption. She was so unlike his strong-willed sister and talkative mother that he began to feel a possessive sort of affection towards this girl. This was the sort of woman he would like to come home to every day – who would leave him to his business without interference. But most of all he wanted someone who wouldn't argue with him. Because he'd had enough of that with his family. He just wanted someone he could get along with – and was pretty – and had a potentially large inheritance from a wealthy aunt. Yes, Wren Stevens appeared to have all the makings of a perfect little wifey.

Bertram knew he had to have her. Over the summer, he spent every free moment in Enniscorthy with her. He went to the dances with her, collecting her from Astrid's house in his car after a day's work. They travelled further afield to the ballroom in Courtown, joining the revels of all the holidaymakers down from Dublin. They also went on walks around town. Sometimes, they simply stayed at Astrid's house, sitting in her lounge, conversing with the old lady but mostly squirrelled away in a corner, talking to one another.

Astrid, for her part, was not sure about Wren's newfound attachment but didn't say anything. If Wren wished to go off for the evening with her young man, Astrid was not going to stop her. Likewise, if the girl wished to bring him home. Affection curbed Astrid's wariness. She was too much invested in her great-niece's happiness to check the activities of the young lovers. Plus, it reminded her of her own relationships. There was also the fact that she had seen the two of them together, observed them keenly and noted that there was nothing untoward between them. Astrid knew the boy's mother and, while she would not willingly converse with the nosey Evelyn Burnley, Bertram came from a respectable family and had a decent living. The boy also gave a good account of himself during their meetings. He asked her permission to take her ward out before suggesting it to Wren. He was polite in Astrid's presence, deferred to her judgement and listened to her opinions. He was also, though small, passably handsome. Astrid could see why Wren found him an attractive prospect, even if she could not see it herself. Mostly, however, Astrid saw Wren and, seeing the change in the girl, conceded that young love was good for her. And Bertram seemed fond of her. Astrid just hoped he wasn't stringing her along. She knew it would be unbearable for Wren if he did anything to hurt her.

It was therefore something of a relief when one Sunday after church, Bertram fell into step with them as they made their way home. He didn't often come to the church in town. Astrid had spotted him entering, cap in hand and looking a little sweaty, but said nothing to Wren. She didn't want the girl fidgeting beside her for the entire service. However, when the last note of the last hymn was sung and they filed out of the church, Astrid couldn't see him anywhere. Perhaps he had gone without speaking to them. Yet, as they walked down Court Street, she heard someone running and turned to find a harried-looking Bertram skidding to a stop behind them.

Wren's face lit up the moment she saw him and her knees jogged in a childish fashion. He smiled charmingly at her and squeezed her outstretched hand but, rather than holding on to it, he let go and proffered his arm to Astrid. She was grateful for his assistance. She still suffered with pains in her newly healed joints, especially after sitting on a cold hard pew in an equally cold church. She noticed a slightly petulant look on Wren's face as they walked. The girl thought her great-aunt had stolen her man. Astrid hid a smile. The child really was changing.

Bertram gabbled constantly as people often do when nervous. Sensing he wanted to say something to her without Wren eavesdropping, Astrid told Wren to run ahead to the house and get the tea things set out. She had to stop herself from laughing aloud when she felt Bertram's arm sag with relief under her own as he watched his girl precede them up the pavement.

When she was out of earshot, Bertram slowed and turned to Astrid.

"I think, Mrs Charlton, you've guessed that I want to talk to you," he began haltingly. Astrid simply nodded. "I'm not sure how to approach this. It's all new to me." He stopped talking, searching for what to say. "You've no doubt noticed that I've a particular fondness for Wren – for your great-niece." He stopped again, looking anywhere but at Astrid.

"She's very fond of you too, Bertram," Astrid proffered, attempting to encourage him. She was fairly sure she knew what was coming but the boy had to get there himself.

"Yes. She is. And given our fondness – love even – I wanted to know who it is I might speak to if I was to ask for her hand in marriage."

Surprised to find a lump rising in her throat, Astrid swallowed. "Well, I suppose the best person to contact would be her father."

Bertram nodded. "Well, then, would it be possible for me to get his address so I can write to him?"

"I'll do you one better," said Astrid. "I'll write to him myself. A kind of introduction and you can put your letter in with mine, save him getting a letter from a total stranger asking to marry his daughter. Is that not a good idea?"

Bertram nodded.

"You can give your letter to me when you're ready. Would that be alright?"

"Yes. Thank you."

"Good," she said approvingly. "Now let's go and have some tea."

Chapter 19

There was something wrong with Evelyn. Ever since her turn in the yard she had been tired and irritable. She would be doing something undemanding and suddenly feel lightheaded. She would begin to sweat, the energy leaving her body, forcing her rest. It was deeply frustrating for a woman whose life was ruled by activity yet now found herself incapable of doing the simplest of jobs.

Lili's presence also irritated her. Her daughter was now everything she wasn't – young, vigorous, capable, sought-after. She couldn't abide Lili flaunting her privileges. Even the way she moved about the kitchen so freely made Evelyn angry. It was as if her child was goading her. She, therefore, lashed out quite regularly, criticising everything Lili did.

But it was not only Lili who experienced her mother's ire. For the first time, Bertram found himself in the firing line. He could hardly ever remember his mother raising her voice to him let alone disapproving of his behaviour. But now she gave out to him for going to the pub, for getting up late (one usually following the other) and for wasting money.

The last of these was a surprise to Lili. She knew her brother spent money with less care than she did but it wasn't until her mother brought up Bertram's spending habits that Lili really paid attention. Her brother seemed to think nothing of spending several pounds on "useful" items only for them to remain unused. He purchased all the latest farming inventions solely for the purpose of appearing to be the grand and innovative farmer when he held court in the pub. What he didn't realise was that every one of the men whose ear he gnawed could see what he could not: Bertram may have been spending money, but he most definitely was not making it.

For Lili, it was her mother's attacks on her brother that scared her most. She was used to Evelyn nit-picking where she was concerned. But this newfound exasperation with Bertram was worrying, not because he didn't deserve it – of course he did – but because it wasn't something Evelyn did. And, of course, being an independent, healthy woman, there was no question of her seeing the doctor. But there *was* something wrong. Lili could feel it in her bones. She just didn't know what.

It was, therefore, with great surprise that Lili was awoken one morning early in September by clattering noises from the kitchen. Sitting up in bed, she listened before sliding out of bed. She shivered before throwing a shawl over her nightgown and putting on a pair of slippers to investigate. Leaving her room, she met Bertie – or rather Bertie's head – poking out the door of his bedroom. His hair stood on end and his eyes were bleary and bloodshot. His youthfulness was the only thing that saved him from looking truly terrible.

"Wha's all the bangin'?" he mumbled.

"Well, it's either Mammy or we're being robbed. Although I'm not sure robbers make that much noise."

He squinted at her, huffed, "Mammy," then retreated, shaking his head.

It was surprising to think her mother was up and working already since she hadn't been awake before Lili for months. Lili was an early riser since being up promptly gave her a better run at the day. It was a habit Evelyn had originally instilled in her but, as her mother aged, she found she couldn't even live by her own rules. What on earth was she doing then, getting up this early to work in the kitchen?

The first thing Lili noticed when she walked in was the temperature. The wave of heat that hit her when she opened the door nearly pushed her backwards. The fire had been built up to a roar in the stove. The table was littered with containers, paper bags, bowls and jars. There was a fog of flour hovering in the air and dusting the tabletop. And in the middle of everything, her front covered in flour was Evelyn, red-faced and sweating with a maniacal gleam in her eye.

"Ah, Lilian! Will you run to the shop and get me a pound of currants? I won't have enough to finish all these fruit cakes."

Lili stood in the doorway, stunned. What was going on? What had changed between the last number of months and today? She found her voice. "What are you doing?"

"I'm making fruit cake and bread for the ICA bake sale," Evelyn answered as if she thought Lili should be well aware of this.

"But, Mammy, the sale's not until the end of next week."

"I know that! Shur didn't I organise it myself?" She began to vigorously beat eggs into sugar and butter. "I want to get ahead of May Lawlor. Otherwise she'll be up telling me all she's done and me not even started."

"But Mammy, the bread'll be mouldy by the time the sale comes."

That made Evelyn pause midway through sifting some flour. "True. But the fruit cakes will keep. They get better with age, a bit like myself."' She giggled wheezily until tears slid down her cheeks. Then, she sat down on a chair with an "*Umph!*" before surveying the mess on the table. Finally, she slowly took in Lili's appearance. "Why're you still in your nightie?"

Lili walked around to sit on the table beside her mother. Evelyn said nothing. She usually would have. She hated Lili sitting on the table.

"Because it's not even six o'clock yet." She felt her mother's forehead. "Mammy, your head's burning."

"Is it only six?" She brushed at the flour covering her front. "Of course my head's hot! It's hot in here." She rose laboriously to her feet and resumed baking but more slowly. Her cheeks no longer looked rosy but instead looked pallid and clammy. "Are you going so?"

"Where?"

"To the shop for currants! Aren't you listening to me at all? Go and get changed!"

"Mammy, the shop won't be open yet. Are you sure you're alright?"

"I'm fine," she snapped. "You can go to the shop when it opens then."

She said no more. Lili had spoiled her merriment and she sulked like a child. But no matter what Lili said, she wouldn't stop. She continued baking until Bertram appeared. Then she immediately abandoned her cakes and began readying her son's breakfast.

Bertram sat at the head of the table, lording it over the mess of baking, restored to his position of importance. Lili went upstairs, dressed quickly and returned to watch her mother, trying to find what had changed between yesterday and now. Maybe it *was* just her mother's insatiable need to better every other woman in the ICA.

But when Bertram got up to leave, Lili followed him outside.

"Bertie!"

"What?" He turned irritably.

"There's something wrong with Mammy."

He looked surprised. "What do you mean? There's

nothing wrong with her. Back to normal, I'd say." He began to walk away. "And about bloody time too."

Lili stood at a loss as to what to do. She wasn't sure what she expected from Bertie but she had hoped he might share her concerns. Evelyn, after all, was Bertram's favourite. But the things Mammy had said to him lately had stung and he therefore felt a coolness towards her. Before, he might have shown due care. Now, he wasn't overly concerned.

"Lilian!"

Lili started and turned to her mother framed in the doorway, hands on hips and elbows pointing backwards since the entrance couldn't accommodate both her heft and arms akimbo.

"What?"

"I asked you to go to the shop and you haven't gone yet. *Go! Now*, please." Evelyn turned about and re-entered the house.

Lili gave in to her mother's chivvying and went to the shop for currants. It was really quite fortunate as she had wanted to go to the grocer's for several days but didn't have the time. Evelyn constantly overburdened her with extra jobs she could never possibly have time to do. She wanted to make chutney with some early windfall apples and needed some vinegar, several pounds of sugar and onions. However, once she completed her shopping, her mind again bent itself towards her mother. She would have to keep a close eye on her. This sudden surge of activity couldn't possibly be sustained. When Evelyn hit the wall, Lili would have to be there to pick up the pieces even though she knew first-hand how little she liked being helped. But the family matriarch would have to accept sooner or later that she was getting old and *needed* help whether it was desired or not.

Evelyn was still hard at it when Lili got back, the smell of freshly baked cakes pervading the air of the kitchen, making

Lili's mouth water. Rather than trying to stop her mother or interfere, she deposited her groceries on the table, separating her own items from those of her mother. She then fetched her overflowing apple basket and heaved it onto a chair at the far end of the kitchen so as not to be in Evelyn's way.

"What are you at?" Evelyn asked, pausing momentarily while weighing out more sugar.

"Making chutney," said Lili. "Want to give me a hand peeling apples?"

Evelyn looked highly affronted. "No, I do not! What would I be doing that for? Shur I haven't half enough cakes made yet."

Lili looked over at the cooling racks on the sideboard. There were already four black-speckled, reddish-brown fruitcakes cooked to perfection in their temperamental oven. There were two more cooking at that very moment and Evelyn was preparing the mixture for two more. Lili fought back the urge to point out there were enough cakes already. Instead, she got a large saucepan and began peeling apples into it, cutting off bad bits and coring them as she went.

"You shouldn't do it like that."

Lili was almost halfway through the basket when her mother spoke. "Oh?"

"You should peel them all then do the chopping and coring at the end. It'd be faster."

It aggravated Evelyn immeasurably to watch her daughter simply shrug off her advice and continue with her own method.

"You're not doing it right!"

"What odds does it make?" asked Lili, shrugging again. "They'll all get peeled and chopped in the end."

Doggedly pursuing her own incontrovertible advice, Evelyn answered with what could be the only logical reply to such an inquiry. "But you're doing it wrong!"

Lili could feel her temper rising. She tried so hard to remain calm around her mother but often found it exceedingly difficult since she could never do anything right. Why was it that she couldn't even peel bloody apples without her mother's criticism? Couldn't the silly old cow just leave her alone? She bit back a retort and continued to stoically dismember the apples with much more vigour than was strictly necessary while Evelyn glowered at her.

It was all to do with Cameron, thought Evelyn. It was that strange neighbour's adverse influence on her daughter that was making Lili less biddable, more opinionated, defiant. She, Evelyn, must remember to pay him a visit and tell him that he was, on no account, to have any further contact with her daughter. She would like to see Lili's face when she told her what she'd done: see how she behaved after she realised the reach of her mother's influence. That would teach Lili to go against her, the ungrateful little besom. There would be tears and bitterness, no doubt, but after the tantrum the old Lili would return, lesson learnt. But first she had to make more cakes.

The morning continued and Lili moved on to chopping onions for the pot, adding sugar, vinegar, sultanas and a piece of root ginger – which she bought especially for the purpose – before heaving it onto the stove. She let it simmer, stirring it every now and then to allow all the fruit to mush to a pulp. She took the apple peels and cores out to the pigs, throwing a few handfuls to the hens who trotted over with squawks of appreciation.

Back inside, she washed jars ready for chutney and heated them by the fire so they would not crack when she poured the preserved fruit into them. An acidic tang filled the air as the apples, onions and vinegar boiled down, permeating nose and mouth so that the taste coated the inside of her cheeks and tongue. It wasn't exactly pleasant but Lili didn't mind. Busying herself decanting the boiled-down fruit into jars, she paid little attention to what Evelyn was doing with her cakes.

She wasn't sure what made her look up at her mother's gasp. It wasn't loud or panicked – it simply wasn't right.

Glancing up at the noise, she locked eyes on Evelyn just in time to see her fall. She hit the floor with such force, the room seemed to shake. Landing half on her back, half on her shoulder, convulsions took her. Lili watched in horror, the final jar still in her hands as her mother's eyes rolled in her head and her neck and arms spasmed. It was as if some invisible force, hiding under the floor, was wrenching a cord wrapped around Evelyn's neck and attempting to drag her through the solid ground. Her bulk rolled, bracing her back against the ground as further spasms made her twitch and thump the floor.

If she had been a smaller, less rotund woman, it likely would have been much more shocking to watch. As it was, the image of her mother writhing on the floor of the kitchen haunted Lili for years afterwards. Evelyn's spine arched, forcing her head into the floor. Her feet and hands flailed, forcefully hitting off the ground, the chair, the sideboard. Yet it was the sound that made it so deeply disturbing. There was the thump of her limbs and the swishing and scuffing of her clothing and the soles of her shoes. But the noise coming from her mouth was worse.

She did not scream. She did not call out.

She gurgled.

There was no form to her sounds. They were just that: sounds. The woman, so vociferous, so chatty – so difficult to stop – was halted now. Incomprehensible glugs emanated from her throat as her tongue flapped back and forth. She fought for air as her windpipe closed and reopened with each spasm, her heavy bosom constricting the airflow into her chest as much as her abnormal bodily movements.

Lili wasn't sure how long the fit lasted. She stood transfixed, terrified and it wasn't until her mother's turn began to subside that she moved.

"Mammy! *Mammy*! No, stop it! Please, Mammy, *please*!"

She had no idea what to do. Nothing in her life had equipped her for this. She knew if someone had a fit you were to roll them onto their side. But as she knelt by her mother, shaking her shoulders, sobbing for her mammy to come back to her, Evelyn continued to twitch. Lili had never seen her mother vulnerable like this – prostrate on the ground, limbs now limp with exhaustion and the after-effects of the fit. Air hissed out of her mouth in shallow, uneven gasps. It was too much to bear.

Lili didn't know how she ended up outside. She just was. Still in her slippers, she wasn't sure if she left the kitchen to get away from the terrifying image of her mother on the floor or to get help for her. She found herself screaming at the top of her lungs, her breath short, as she ran around the house and yard looking for Bertie. No response came so she ran back past the door – her footwear flapping absurdly with every step – and headed for the lane.

In the enclosed yard, her screams echoed back to her, the volume and terror of their sound like a physical pressure on her eardrums. But out on the lane her voice was lost to the ether, swallowed up by the autumn hedges and their rusting leaves. It seemed to take an age for her to see anything living. Her cries had even frightened the birds into silence. Finally, she heard a reply. Turning wildly in search of the sound, she spotted a dog galloping towards her from the opposite direction. It was barking manically and was followed by a man calling her name.

Ewan.

She ran back down the lane towards him and had enough time to register the pale petrified look on his face before colliding with his chest.

"Mammy," she sobbed. "Mammy!"

Ewan could barely hear what she said to him, muffled as it was by his clothing and by the blood pounding in his ears. He had heard her high-pitched wails on the wind, knowing immediately that something was seriously wrong. Downing tools, he took off at a run, her continued shouts spurring him on. He was coming, he was coming! If she would just stop! Each pitiful screech triggering another stabbing fear of what he might find.

He pulled her away from him. Taking a firm hold of her shoulders he surveyed her. She didn't seem ill or injured. "*What*? What is it?"

She squirmed away from him and began running towards her house, all the time crying, "*Mammy, Mammy, Mammy!*"

Ewan followed. He knew it was bad. Composed Lili, precise, cheerful Lili was gone. He knew human nature well enough to simply be led to the cause of such terror without question. Even if you did get someone to speak, their information was often garbled, incomprehensible, hyperbolic. He would find out what it was when he got there. The army had taught him that.

In the army, he discovered in himself a calm that many other men lacked in the face of danger or death. He would be called on in a crisis because the men knew Cameron was a solid bet. Cameron just got on with it. However, this situation was different. He was personally invested in one of the constituent elements of this crisis. He was also no longer at war. This was home.

Lili beat him to the door by several seconds. Ewan rushed in after her, afraid of losing sight of her even for a moment. "*Stay*," he ordered, rushing in the door, pointing an admonitory finger at Georgie who did as she was bid. Sure that Lili had carried on further into the kitchen, he virtually collided with her when he entered.

She was standing with her back to him just inside the door. It took a moment for his eyes to adjust to the change in light between the brightness outside and the dullness of the house. He grabbed both her arms as much to steady himself as to make sure he hadn't thrown her off balance. Holding her as he did, he felt the limpness of a body in shock. Lili was still standing upright but her bones felt almost rubbery. He, no doubt, could have pushed her out of the way and her body would have slid to the side with little resistance. But he didn't. Instead, he held on to her and looked over her shoulder, letting her line of sight guide his own. When he saw what she was looking at, he pushed gently past her without moving her from where she stood and swiftly crossed the room to kneel by Evelyn. She looked bad, that was his first thought, and his diagnosis didn't improve as he made a quick inventory of her immobile form. His brain immediately brought him back to kneeling not on the floor of a kitchen, but on dried earth as he looked over the bodies of young men. When you did that, you looked for where the most amount of blood was coming from and did what you could with inadequate and often dirty materials to stanch wounds while someone beside you screamed, *"Medic! Medic!"*

He mentally shook himself. He was at home in Ireland now and the War was over. This was different. If his fingers had not automatically found the pulse beating weakly in her neck, he would have thought her dead. Evelyn Burnley looked pale, almost bloodless. A clammy sheen gave her face a kind of false glow as the moisture caught the light from the windows. Her clothes where rucked up and crumpled under her. The crown of her head was beginning to swell visibly through the thin, mousy hair where she had braced her bodyweight against the floor. The white skin of the back of her forearms was also turning a livid shade of purple where the weak blood vessels had burst and flooded underneath her stretched skin when banging the ground during her fit.

"How long has she been like this?" he asked and was glad to hear his voice sounded calm.

He was a little surprised when the answer came from directly above him.

"She had a kind of fit," said Lili, her voice expressionless. "I didn't know what to do so I – I ran when she … when she stopped. I didn't know what to do." Her chest began to heave.

He could see she was about to fall apart so he stood and took her by the shoulders. "We're going to have to get her some help," he said. "But first we're going to have to move her off the cold floor. If she's on it too long she'll catch her death."

He regretted his choice of words immediately since he had a feeling little could be done for Evelyn as it was. But at least they could make her comfortable. Lili didn't seem to notice what he'd said. She merely nodded her head numbly.

Stepping back from the two women as he wondered how to proceed, he heard a crunch under his feet. Looking down, he noticed shimmering flecks were scattered across the floor, dancing in the light.

"The jam jar." Lili stared at the ground as if she'd never seen it before. "I was potting up chutney. I must have dropped it when Mammy had her fit. We should move her now." It was all said in the same dream-like tone.

Turning to the prone form beside them, Ewan asked, "Can you take her feet?" Gently, he lifted Evelyn's head onto his chest before sliding his arms under her oxters while Lili took hold of her mother's legs. "Be careful of the glass," he said, glancing at the floor. "Where to?"

"Out the door behind you. To the right opposite the stairs."

"Right. On three. *One, two, three –*"

He had expected Evelyn to be heavy but hadn't anticipated the strain lifting her would put on his limbs. First, his legs screamed in protest as he lifted her from the floor, followed swiftly by his back. By the time he reached the door, he had heard both his shoulders pop. Lili, though she had the lighter end, was also puffing slightly as they manoeuvred her mother through the right-angle turn from kitchen to bedroom door. Once they deposited her on the bed – gratefully – both of them were blowing hard, red-faced and slightly sweaty.

"My God," Ewan heard his own voice speaking before he could stop himself, "she could have lost a bit of weight before getting us to carry her." It was the sort of crass humour he had heard and spoken on a battlefield. He was horrified with himself for voicing his thoughts out loud.

He met Lili's gaze. She saw panic – a plea not to think badly of him for what he said.

"Aye. She's heavy alright." It was all she could think of to say and it was true. Her mother was a great lump of a woman. The physical effort of carrying her, the comfort of actually taking action and Ewan's presence were all calming her. Now, she felt she was able to think, able to help her mother. "We'll have to get her a doctor."

Ewan nodded. "Aye. I'll go on the motorbike." He stuffed his hands in his pockets and looked at the floor, unsure whether he should say something or just go. In dipping his head, he noticed red smudges on the floor. He bent and looked more closely. The smudges led not to Evelyn, but to Lili's left foot.

"Your foot's bleeding."

Lili looked. "It'll be fine. You go."

Just then, there was a clatter in the kitchen. "Lilian! Who owns the dog outside?"

"Bertie!" Lili flew out of the room.

Ewan followed. He didn't want to be left alone with Evelyn. He got to the door in time to hear Lili ask her brother, "And where the bloody *hell* were you?"

Taken aback by such a greeting, Bertie flared immediately. "What's that supposed to mean, ha? And what's *he* doing here?" he hissed, pointing an accusing finger at Ewan who hung back. "What was he doing in Mammy's bedroom? And where's Mammy? And dinner?" he added as an afterthought.

"Mammy's had a turn," replied Lili coldly. "I called and called for you but you never came. Ewan did."

"Ewan? *Ewan*? Since when did he become 'Ewan'?'" sneered Bertie. "Where's Mammy?"

"Through here." Ewan stepped aside to allow Bertie to pass.

Evelyn's son didn't approach the bed. He stood just inside the doorway, looking at his mother. "Oh." He re-entered the kitchen. "Let her sleep it off, I suppose. What's for dinner? And why is there glass everywhere? What did you break this time, Lilian?"

"This time? *This time*?"

Standing behind her, Ewan almost thought he could see her physically swell with indignation.

"Mammy doesn't need sleep. She *needs* a doctor. And if you weren't such a thick-headed cretin as to barely look at her, you'd see it!"

"Oh, for God's sake, if it's so bloody important someone goes, let *him* go!" Bertie waved his hand insolently at Ewan.

"Christ, Bertie! Don't you care about Mammy at all?" she screamed. "If it was the other way round she'd be beside

herself. You didn't see it. You weren't here. Go and fetch the doctor!"

"You go and fetch the doctor!" he yelled back petulantly.

Before anyone but she realised what was happening, Lili was launching herself across the floor at her brother. She recognised a dawning look of shock on his face before her open palm made contact with it. It was a sight to behold. Lili was a head taller than her undersized brother and she also had the advantage of taking him completely by surprise. Then her nails dragged across the side of his face, leaving three parallel vivid red welts on his cheek.

Suddenly, strong arms had her in a vice-like grip. Ewan had wrapped his arms around her chest, pinning her arms to her side. The Scotsman lifted her bodily from the floor, noting to himself that, even though she struggled and wriggled like an eel, at least she was a damn sight lighter than her mother. He dragged her backwards.

"Go and get a bloody doctor!" she screamed.

Bertie hastily went.

Ewan, who still had his arms around Lili's chest, hands tightly gripping her opposite shoulders, released her for fear she would begin to struggle and fight with him as well. When he let go, it seemed the fight left her. He watched as her shoulders sagged.

"My foot hurts," she said quietly.

"Here."

Taking her by the elbows, he led her to a chair. He knelt in front of her then gently took her ankle in his hand. He lifted her foot, keeping the slipper on for fear the glass had gone through the sole. But he could find nothing. While he studied the bottom of the slipper, a drop of blood slid down the side of his finger from inside it. He took the slipper off and found a shard of glass caught in the bottom of her heel. The bottom of her foot was coloured the orangey-red of dried blood and even as he lifted her heel, more dark red liquid welled around the imbedded piece of glass.

"Do you have tweezers? And some Dettol and a bandage?" he asked, glancing at Lili's face. She was viewing her foot critically, her upper lip drawn back in aversion.

"There's some things in the middle drawer of the sideboard."

Ewan swiftly went to the drawer, paying no attention to the glass underfoot with his strong, solid-soled work boots. He came back with a basin of warm water, tweezers, a bandage, cotton wool and Dettol. He took Lili's ankle again, noticing for the first time that she had no socks or tights on; her skin was bare and he got a little thrill from touching it. Silently, he gripped her foot and drew out the piece of glass as gently as he could. Air hissed out through Lili's teeth but she did not pull away and Ewan did not look up. Methodically, he cleaned the wound with warm water and cotton wool, stanching the blood-flow as best he could. He was reminded of a time several months before when they met in this same kitchen, when he sat by the fire and Lili tended to him. Now the roles were reversed. He remembered the warmth and gentleness of her touch – what that touch led to. He hoped that, despite his task, he treated her with the same gentleness she had shown him.

Lili hardly made a sound as he worked. Instead her grip on the edge of her chair became tighter, whitening her knuckles and making the wood of the seat creak. Finally, having swabbed the injury with Dettol and washed the entire foot, Ewan bandaged the gash tightly and efficiently, neatly tucking the end in. Lili viewed the finished job with admiration as he fished the offending shard from the basin of water.

"Where'd you learn to bandage like that?"

"Army," he said shortly. "Is it alright?"

She stood to test her injury.

Ewan immediately put out his hands to support her, catching her by the elbows so they were almost nose to nose. He thought about kissing her but didn't, instead saying, "Don't move too far. The glass."

"I'll sweep it up," she said, making to move.

"*No!*" His voice was a little louder than he intended. "No," he said quietly. "I'll do it. Where's the dustpan and brush?"

Lili watched the tall Scotsman stoop over the brush, dwarfing it as he swept with long smooth strokes, the glass tinkling and scraping across the stone floor. Once he cleared the whole floor he promptly dropped to his knees and looked across it with his head touching the cold stone. A long arm stretched under the table and picked up two stray pieces of glass. Finally collecting up all that remained of the jam jar, Ewan went outside and threw it into the ditch alongside the house. He paused briefly, listening. The world still continued. The birds still sang even though life inside the house was falling apart. Georgie sidled up to him and stretched her head up to his empty palm. He rubbed her absentmindedly as he ruminated on Evelyn's condition.

It was bad. He hadn't said so to Lili for fear that he was wrong but he was almost certain her mother had suffered a stroke. He had seen the effects of one on his great-aunt before at home in Scotland. Lili's description of the fit and what he ascertained himself from his quick examination of Evelyn made him worry that little could be done. If anything made him sure, it was the fact that her face sagged as if some cord had been severed in her cheek. He supposed, in a way, it had. Once they put her in the room, he stood watching as she lay on the bed, spittle slowly leaking out the side of her slack mouth – that mouth that was always moving. Now it was immobile.

He gave the dog a final pat and went back in.

He could just see Lili's back where she stood leaning against the doorframe of Evelyn's room. "Is there anyone who could help you with your mother?" he asked. "One of your sisters maybe?"

"Heather," she said after a moment's thought. "Heather's a good nurse. She'd know what she's doing better than I would."

Ewan knew where she lived. "I'll go and get her, shall I?" he said, turning to leave.

"No!" Lili grabbed his hand. "No, I don't want to be alone in case – in case anything happens with Mammy again."

She squeezed his hand tightly. He gripped hers firmly in return. As they held onto one another, he watched as the paleness in her cheeks was warmed slightly by some colour. She took strength from his presence and his touch. He could have insisted on fetching Lili's sister. But he didn't.

Silently, Lili led him into the room. Evelyn had not moved. There was no tautness in her features. Yet their expressionlessness was further than that of a face relaxed in sleep. The corner of her mouth remained slightly open and a patch of damp was beginning to form on the pillow by her cheek. Lili approached, taking a handkerchief from her pocket, and gently dabbed away the saliva from the side of her mother's face. Looking at her, Lili saw her clothes were still untidy. She set about smartening her up and removed her shoes which she had neglected to do earlier.

"Maybe we should put the cover over her. She might get cold." Ewan was unsure about what to do but nevertheless was wanting to do *something*.

They set about heaving Evelyn's bulk up enough to slide the cover out and put it over her, Lili on one side of the bed and Ewan on the other. She was surprised and touched by the care with which Ewan handled her mother, tucking the cover around her as one might with a sleeping child. And it suddenly struck her that Ewan would make an excellent father. Perhaps, one day, a father to her children. No – she could not possibly think that far ahead while standing over her mother's prostrate form. And she was getting old herself. There was no guarantee she would ever have children. But she still thought Ewan deserved them.

"Would you like some tea?" she asked, trying to turn her mind away from her train of thought.

Ewan fought to hide his smile. Tea: the solution to all ills. Or – he cast a pitying look at Evelyn – the solution to some of them. He put his hand out and led Lili back to the kitchen. "I'll make it." He was already planning to put lots of sugar in Lili's. He was sure she was suffering from shock but was putting on a brave face. Sugar was, in his experience, one of the best and simplest treatments for shock.

As they entered the kitchen, however, both of them were distracted by a smell of burning. "*Mammy's cakes!*" screeched Lili, making Ewan jump. She hobbled quickly across the floor, grabbing a cloth as she went and flung open the oven door. She was engulfed by billowing black smoke which seemed to momentarily swallow her head, making her cough and splutter as she beat it back, trying to find the two ruined cakes underneath.

They were a sorry sight. Rock solid, lumpy black circles from which emanated a sharp smell that irritated the nostrils and left a bitter taste in the mouth. Ewan immediately opened the windows to disperse the smell but it had already got into their clothes and hair. He turned back to the room to see Lili braced on the edge of the table, leaning over the two burnt cakes, staring fixedly at them. Experienced as he was in human grief, he knew what was about to happen before it did and was across the room to take Lili in his arms as she burst into tears. He held her to his chest, rocking her gently from side to side as he murmured into her hair. "I'm here. I'm here."

Once she calmed, he sat her down and made her tea – not without difficulty given that he didn't know where anything was kept. But he didn't want Lili getting up to do it herself so he simply kept quiet and figured it out as he went along. Tea made – and laced with a large quantity of sugar – he and Lili went back into Evelyn where Ewan lifted one of the bedroom chairs to the side of the bed so the daughter could sit by the mother's side. He stayed and stood guard over both women, hand protectively on Lili's shoulder. Looking between the women he wondered, not for the first time, how such a creature as Lili was related to Evelyn Burnley. They were so different in every possible way. Lili quiet, reserved, tall and thin where Evelyn was fat, fond of talk and never thought. Leonard Burnley, he thought, must have been quite a man to father such a daughter. On occasions like this – where he struggled to reconcile Lili's place within the Burnley family – Ewan wished he had met the old man. If father was anything like daughter, Ewan thought he might have loved the man as much as Lili did.

But Leonard was gone and so were the other Burnley sisters. Lili was the only woman left who had been born into the Burnley name and yet she did not really belong to it anymore. With the death of her father, her final tangible tie to her family was severed and she remained in limbo, neither belonging to the house at the bottom of Bachelor Lane nor having anywhere else to go. And that was why it was so important that she should leave them behind and become part of Ewan's family. He would make sure she belonged to him and he to her. They would be together, they would share and they would love. But now? Now what? How would Lili cope with Evelyn? Would she have to forgo their meetings and devote her time to what remained of her mother's life? Should Ewan dare to hope that Evelyn's illness was short, not just for the sake of the lady herself but also her daughter and, shamefully, for his too? Could he really wish her dead? No. He wasn't that cruel or selfish. But, for Lili's sake, he hoped her mother's fate would swing one way or the other rather than remaining undetermined. If the latter happened Lili could spend years caring for an invalid with virtually no chance of recovery, chained to Evelyn's bedpost with no life of her own. He did not want such a burden for Lili and he did not think such an end befitted a vigorous woman like Mrs Burnley.

Eventually, after what seemed like hours of waiting, Bertie arrived back with the doctor. Ewan took the look he got from the youngest Burnley as his cue to leave. Before he did so, however, he asked Lili, "Do you want me to get Heather?"

Bertie answered. "I can get her. You've done enough here for one day."

Lili looked as if she might argue but instead shrugged and turned to talk to the doctor. As Ewan went to leave the room he turned and addressed Lili once more. "You know where I am if you need me. I'll come back later. See how things are." Lili just nodded and, without further ado, he spun on his heel and exited. He did not want to share a room with Bertie.

Once he'd left, however, he did not feel the relief he expected to. Though he continued to work for the rest of the day – and had to work that bit harder to finish because of being side-tracked by the Burnleys' crisis – his mind was preoccupied. He longed to be by Lili's side. He could see the strain she was under – the brave face she put on. She was good at keeping other people happy, even at the expense of her own emotions. He worried that if she found no release, she would eventually fall apart altogether. He was aware that she had suffered similarly when her father died, trying to manage everyone else's grief while neglecting her own. He did it himself when Mabel died: shut off his emotions to deal with the needs and accusations of everyone else. The problem was that once he did that, he couldn't switch them back on again. It was what made him such a good soldier. He was comfortable taking orders because it meant he had no personal connection to anything. Decisions were made for him. He was able to view things dispassionately, carry out his orders and move on without dwelling on what he did. However, the problem was he never seemed to be able to totally supress one emotion: anger.

There were occasions when he found rage ripping through him – an animal lying dormant, fighting to get out. It scalded his veins, made his muscles burn. Sometimes he'd let go – let the rage take him and hang the consequences. More often though, he fought against it, keeping it at bay through sheer willpower. Leaving the army had helped somewhat with his self-control as he was no longer surrounded by large groups of scared, testosterone-fuelled men and boys. Back in the quiet of the countryside, surrounded by animals instead of people, he found a calm and contentment that he had never experienced before and thus decided that was how he would live his life: in his own company, where no one could hurt or anger him. Coming to Ireland was the extremity of his self-enforced isolation and it had worked well up until recently. Not that he never felt lonely. Of course he did. But self-discipline and working every hour God sent prevented him from dwelling on his solitude.

Yet when he finally saw Lili – really saw her – his eyes were opened to his own unhappiness. He surmised that Lili experienced a similar feeling of awakening once they began to spend time together. She had become more animated, more open. He felt a similar change in himself and was almost shocked by the things he found himself telling her.

But he wasn't afraid of this new candidness. On the contrary, he felt more alive now than he had for nearly two decades. It was as if his life before had been lived underwater with all the sounds muffled, the weight of gallons of liquid suppressing the movements of his mind and body. Now, he was free and he did not want to lose that freedom, that light-heartedness. If he did, he thought he might be crushed – drown in the mire of his own mind if forced to live there alone once again. He needed Lili and thought she might need him too, especially now. He did not want to watch her smother her feelings, allow them to fester inside her. He had to be there for her to release her emotions with him if she was not prepared to do it in front of anyone else. And that would mean exposing their relationship to her family.

Ewan doubted the Burnleys were oblivious to Lili's relations with him. They had been seen together publicly on several occasions at dances but she had told him only recently that none of her family mentioned him to her. He was glad of their discretion if not slightly surprised given Evelyn's verbosity. However, there was the issue that if they disclosed their connection at a time when Lili's mother was very seriously ill, the other Burnleys would accuse them of being tactless and selfish. Ewan feared the family might turn on Lili if their relationship came to light at such a sensitive juncture. He did not want to make her life more difficult than it was. He did not want her to become estranged from her sisters after all the work she had done over the years to help the family through its difficult periods. If she became estranged from Bertie, Ewan thought she might be able to cope with his loss. But Lili loved her sisters and he would have to tread lightly if he was to remain on good terms with the women of the family. Whether he remained on any kind of terms with Bertie was, in his opinion, inconsequential. But come what may, he was going to be by Lili's side.

Chapter 20

When the doctor departed after his examination of Evelyn, Lili was left alone in the house with her mother. Bertie had left swiftly after Ewan to fetch Heather so it was up to Lili to bear the doctor's diagnosis in solitude.

It wasn't good. According to Dr Morrissey, Evelyn Burnley was unlikely to make it to the week's end. "You'd best get the vicar over," he said sympathetically. "Get him to say a few prayers for her. It's in His hands now, I'm afraid, not mine."

Evelyn had suffered a massive stroke. Given the state of her health – the strain she put her body under – it was, said Dr Morrissey, a miracle she had gone so long without having an attack. It was then that Lili mentioned the episode some time before during haymaking when Evelyn had her turn in the hen yard.

"Yes," Dr Morrissey nodded. "It's likely that was a minor stroke. A forerunner to this one. Tell me, had she been behaving any differently over the last day or two, leading up to the fit she had this morning?"

Lili told him of her fanatical cake-baking and he nodded again. "*Hmm*, yes, it can happen. They become fixated on a task much as expectant mothers do before a child is born. A kind of flurry of activity before the body changes. Unfortunate, yes, but there's nothing we can do about it now."

He left Lili with instructions to try and make her mother comfortable by keeping her lips wet and keeping her warm. In essence, Lili was to wait for her mother to die. "Sometimes they can last for quite a time," Dr Morrissey told her as he left. "But I think it's almost a mercy if they're fortunate enough to go quickly. We can live in hope, eh?" He smiled and left quietly as Lili took in his words.

Fortunate enough to go quickly. We can live in hope. Both of these were platitudes to give comfort to those left behind and Lili had no doubt that, for some people, these words did make the passing of a loved one easier. But not for her. Instead, she found herself analysing these throwaway clichés. She did not want her mother to "go quickly". She wanted Evelyn to get better. And what was the point of living in hope if the hope was that someone else would die? It seemed like the height of cruelty to live in hope of another's death. Nevertheless, that was how the doctor left and that was what Lili dwelt on for several hours afterwards.

She sat by her mother's bedside, wetting Evelyn's lips with a feather dipped in water, just as the doctor had instructed. Watching her mother's chest rise and fall, she was torn between the hope it would stop, thereby ending Evelyn's ordeal, or keep going in the hope that she might miraculously recover. Every now and then, she got up and wiped the saliva that leaked out of the corner of Evelyn's flaccid mouth but, other than that, it was a case of watching and waiting.

Heather arrived with Bertie in the middle of the afternoon. With them was Reverend Harrington who offered his sympathies with a comforting if business-like air. But then life and death formed a major component of his occupation. He said some simple prayers over Evelyn's motionless form, commending her soul to God, his palm resting gently on her forehead. Afterwards, he shook hands with the three watching Burnleys, promising to keep their mother in his prayers.

"One hopes, at least, that it will be a painless exit, eh? There is that."

Lili offered him tea and some of Evelyn's many fruitcakes before he left but the Reverend declined, saying that he was sure she had enough to be getting on with. Turning to Bertram he asked, "Would you mind awfully taking me back to the vicarage in your car? I'm on a bit of a tight schedule is all."

Bertie followed him meekly out the door. The two sisters listened to the sound of men's muffled voices through the thick walls and wafer-thin windows of the house. They heard a laugh, the car doors opening, closing, the engine starting up, revving too high and then trundling off. After the sound of the car, there was nothing but silence.

Lili was already looking worn, her face drawn tight across her bones and tinged with grey. She listened to herself tell her sister the doctor's prognosis. She spoke calmly and watched as Heather's eyes filled with tears. As she observed her sister's grief, Lili was surprised by her own lack of reaction. She was simply numb. She couldn't let emotion overtake her. She had to stay strong and keep going.

Before leaving to go and do all the neglected work, Lili hugged Heather and gave her the same instructions the doctor had given her earlier. Heather smiled weakly and took her place by their mother's bedside, silently giving Lili permission to leave.

The first thing she did once she left the sickroom was leave the house. She threw herself into her tasks with a single-minded concentration that prevented her brain from dwelling on anything. Collecting eggs, cleaning out the henhouse, feeding a few lame sheep in one of the outbuildings, feeding the pigs, milking the cows – all was done with the dazed kind of precision of someone afraid to explore certain parts of their consciousness. Doing these simple things was safe, familiar – as if things were perfectly normal and Evelyn would saunter out to the back door and call her in to help in the kitchen. But Evelyn did not come to the door. Lili went about her business undisturbed and returned to the house of her own accord to make something for supper.

She poked her head around the bedroom door once she got in. "How is she?"

Heather looked up from gently stroking Evelyn's hand. "No change," she answered, a small sympathetic smile touching the corners of her mouth. Heather had a habit of smiling when she spoke. Even in bad situations like this one, Heather could smile and make those around her feel that little bit better.

"Do you want your tea here or do you want to go home to the boys?"

Heather had two sons and a husband at home which made Lili acutely aware that she was keeping her sister from them.

"They're big enough to take care of themselves," she answered, then added, "Well, Stephen and Dickie are. Whether their daddy is, is another matter altogether. I left them out some bread and jam anyway so they won't starve."

"Alright. Thank you."

It was only when she began to prepare food that she realised they had not eaten dinner at midday as was the family's wont. Knowing Bertie would be hungry, she prepared the dinner as an evening meal instead, automatically cutting up vegetables for three. She panicked slightly when she noticed she was preparing enough food for herself, Bertie and Evelyn but then calmed down when she told herself that the three portions were – of course – for herself and her two siblings.

When he came in to eat, Bertie made to enter his mother's room but thought better of it. Instead, he sat at the table. "How's Mammy?"

"The same," Heather answered as she walked into the kitchen and made a beeline for the range. "God, it's cold in that room," she said, shivering. "I think we should light the fire in there. Keep her comfortable. Bertie, will you do it?"

Bertram looked as if he had been told to kill a pig right there in the kitchen. No one said anything for a moment as both sisters looked to their younger brother. He rearranged his face and nodded jerkily. "Right." He took off determinedly towards his mother's room though he lacked anything to light a fire with, then returned red-faced and mumbling about his need for matches and some twigs. The women felt like laughing but didn't want to annoy him. So both simply turned away and busied themselves at nothing.

Dinner was a quiet affair. Usually there would be discussion of what they'd done during the day, what they'd heard and who they'd met. But none of them could think of a safe subject to talk about as, in their minds, everything related back to their mother. Finally, Heather spoke.

"We need to tell the others."

Neither of the other two spoke. They didn't need to. They knew it had to be done.

"Maybe you could drop me home this evening, Bertie. And then call on the others after? Will you be alright here on your own, Lili?" She caught Lili's hand in her own and squeezed it tightly.

Lili nodded. Then almost inaudibly said, "Ewan might come down and sit with me for a bit."

There was a pause. Both Bertram and Heather stared at

their sister who resolutely kept her eyes on her plate.

As always, it was Heather who said. "That would be good of him." Then she added, "You're sure you don't want one of us to stay as well?"

"I'm sure. Go and tell the others."

Bertie gave the impression that he might say something but a look from Heather was enough to make him swallow his words, a mutinous expression remaining fixed on his boyish face.

In a way, they were a strange family. They had been told that their mother was unlikely to live much longer and yet none of them even considered the possibility that they would not eat a full meal for their dinner. Perhaps it would have been more disrespectful to their mother to fast than it was for them to eat. It was as Evelyn would have wanted even though she lay inert in the room next door.

Once they'd all finished, Lili told the other two to head on. She wanted something to do and clearing up after a meal was the perfect distraction. Heather and Bertie looked in on Evelyn before leaving then departed, leaving Lili on her own in the house with her mother.

Chapter 21

What with one thing and another, it was well after eight o'clock before Ewan finished everything he needed to do, wolfed down some bread and butter and nearly blistered the inside of his mouth trying to gulp down scalding tea. It had started to rain quite heavily so he put on his gabardine coat and a flat cap before whistling to Georgie and heading off down the lane. As he walked towards the Burnleys', he was reminded of another night, not dissimilar to this one, when he had been wrapped in the same coat, pressing onwards through the stinging rain, two lambs held to his chest as he cursed the weather. Suddenly, a woman had appeared out of the darkness. She had persuaded and bullied him into her home while he fought against her. Would he have fought so hard if he knew about the woman who waited within? Really, if he thought about it, he owed his relationship with Lili to Evelyn. And yet, he was also prevented from marrying the woman he loved by that self-same person. Lili's loyalty – though Ewan thought it misguided – would never allow her to marry him. And what if Evelyn died? Would she finally agree to marry him – to share his bed? Or would she come up with another excuse? Did she, in fact, want to marry him at all?

When he got to the house, Lili opened the door to find

Ewan wedged against it, trying to shelter himself from the rain and the runoff from the roof. She didn't say anything. She simply opened it wide, allowing Georgie to snake past both of them, making for the rug in front of the range. The dog circled twice then seemed to smell something that disconcerted her and stopped. She sniffed the air of the room and then the floor in front of the range where Evelyn had collapsed. She circled the patch with caution, whiffling it carefully. Deciding that there was nothing threatening about the smell, though not quite sure what it was, she sat at the far side of the rug before looking at Ewan and Lili standing in the doorway and giving a tiny "*woof*" as if to tell them something wasn't right.

"I know, love," Ewan said quietly to the dog but his hand gently stroked Lili's back. "Heather came, aye?"

"Yes."

"Is she still here?" he asked, glancing around the kitchen as if she might appear.

"No."

"And Bertie?"

"Gone to fetch the others. My sisters."

He nodded, continuing to caress her spine. "Any change?"

"No. Ewan –" She broke off.

Her eyes met his and he saw the pain he had come to try to alleviate. That did not, however, make its existence easier to witness.

"She's dying," Lili finally choked out.

"Aye." He gently rubbed her arm.

He stripped off his wet coat and brought one of the chairs from the kitchen into Evelyn's room. Lili was already there, sitting once again by her mother's bedside. Silently, he placed his chair by hers, sat down and took her free hand, both wordlessly agreeing to begin their vigil. The only time he spoke was when he offered to make tea at ten o'clock.

Otherwise they moved very little. Every now and then Lili got up to wet her mother's lips or straighten imaginary creases in the bedding. While she did this, Ewan put wood on the fire, keeping the room warm and comfortable. He thought at the very least the crackling fire might do something to assuage the dreary sound of the rain as it continued to fall. But then, considering the situation, he doubted the fire had any effect other than to give warmth and cast a dim orange glow about the room.

Lili fell asleep in the small hours of the morning, her head resting on Ewan's shoulder. Wanting her to rest, he did not disturb her even though his shoulder began to ache with the weight of her skull pressing into the jutting bone. With one hand, he flicked a blanket from the end of the bed and covered Lili as best he could without jostling her. Though it strained his eyes to look at her face, which was so near to his, he still tried. It wasn't often one was presented with the opportunity to view an object of desire uninterrupted and at such close quarters. He could feel the warmth of her cheek and the faint mist of her breath through his shirt. She looked so peaceful, her body relaxed – all the day's troubles forgotten in the midst of sleep. His eyes raked the length of her body from head to foot. He'd held that foot this morning, bathed it, bandaged it. A jolt went through him as he thought of it. The smooth softness of her ankle, the contact between his work-roughened hands and her untouched skin. It was not like touching her hands or her face. They had been exposed to the elements and, while he saw them as beautiful, they were weathered, toughened by their life outdoors.

His eyes rested on her bosom as it pushed her blouse in and out. A tiny flick of his finger and he would have the top button undone. Another flick and the second would fall open as well and reveal – what? Well, he knew what. He had been married before, after all. But every woman was different. Mabel's body was almost boyish. She had remained tiny and child-like throughout their marriage, flat-chested and androgynous. That, however, did not mean she was undesirable to him. On the contrary – as a boy of twenty he had not been able to take his hands off her. But therein lay another of their many problems. There could be no spontaneity in his advances towards her. He could not grab her as she passed him in the kitchen to plant a kiss on her cheek. Small and child-like, Mabel was also breakable. The slightest pressure from his fingers would empurple her delicate skin. Each touch of his large farmer's hands left their mark, staining her pale skin for days, making Ewan hate himself even when she told him he wasn't hurting her. Every time he saw the marks, he despised himself even more until, eventually, he feared touching Mabel at all.

It wouldn't be like that with Lili. Ewan wanted to touch her. It made the pit of his stomach burn with desire, even more as he drank in the curves of her body. Because Lili had curves. Her body wasn't like Mabel's angular, sparsely covered frame. There were lumps and bumps, sweeping rises and flowing dips. Her flesh encased bone covered in muscle making her strong and beautifully shaped. And he wanted her.

But not right now. These weren't the thoughts to have by her dying mother's bedside. He looked at Evelyn, silently breathing her way to impending death. Morrissey had said it wouldn't be long. Ewan could have slept. He was tired enough to do so but thought someone should at least be awake to witness Evelyn's final moments should they come during the dark hours. It wasn't the first night-time vigil he had sat through and he doubted it would be his last. Though he struggled with exhaustion during the spring, he usually had the ability to tell himself to stay awake and trust his body to do so. It was a rarity for him to sleep without consciously relinquishing his wakefulness. That was part of the reason he found that first occasion with Lili in the Burnley kitchen during the spring so strange and therefore of note. Lili had to be something special for him to automatically trust himself to her after such a short acquaintance. He let go in her presence because he felt safe. He hoped he could return the favour.

Dawn was just breaking and Ewan was absent-mindedly wondering why Bertie hadn't come back to his sister when Evelyn stirred. A shiver went through her body, immediately drawing his wandering eyes. It was as if she was cold yet he knew that couldn't be the case as he was warm enough and wasn't cocooned in a layer of quilts. The shiver continued, becoming more vigorous, developing into something else. The woman's entire body began to heave, churning the covers as if silently fighting to break free. In a way, she was.

Lili did not wake. Ewan dithered for a moment, unsure whether he should save her from witnessing the turmoil of her mother's final moments. But then, if it were him, he would prefer to see her finally make her peace rather than wake up later to discover she was already gone.

"Lili." Tenderly, he lifted her head from his cramped shoulder. He had a quick stab of fizzing pain as the blood rushed through his crushed veins and arteries but ignored it in favour of trying to ease Lili back into consciousness as gently as he could. She blinked awake. "It's happening. I think she's going."

Lili was on her knees by Evelyn's bed, clasping her mother's writhing hand, holding on fiercely as it jerked away from her. Ewan wasn't sure if she was trying to will her mother to cling to life or purely attempting to tell Evelyn, through nothing but touch, that she was not dying alone. Either way, Evelyn's virtually silent thrashing began to ease

211

until suddenly her entire body juddered to a halt – heart beating its last, lungs making their final gasp and then … nothing.

It stunned Ewan a little – just as it always did when he was confronted by death – to abruptly realise that a body now lay in the same place a living, breathing human being lay just moments before. A bubble of terror rose up through his chest, making him struggle for breath as his heart skittered off, trying to distance itself from the spectre of death that lurked in the room. He could almost feel its cold clammy tendrils snaking across his skin, threatening, or perhaps offering to take him as well. He desperately wanted to leave the room but could not absent himself while Lili still knelt, unmoving, by her mother's bedside. She still clung to Evelyn's hand and Ewan fought the urge to rip the dead woman's fingers from her grasp for fear that death might somehow seep from a deceased being to a living one.

"She's gone, isn't she?"

The birds had already begun their dawn chorus but it wasn't until Lili's words penetrated his ear that he heard anything.

It was the same for her. As if her ears had been filled with water – a great pressure in her head and a great silence.

Ewan got up and felt for Evelyn's pulse to be sure. There was nothing. "Aye. She's gone."

Kneeling beside Lili he tentatively offered her his arms, unsure whether she would want them. She relinquished her mother's hand and slowly collapsed sideways into his chest.

"I'm so sorry, love."

Lili began to sob. Amongst the gasping breaths, he could hear her whispering, *"Oh God, she's gone! Oh God!"*

Ewan couldn't decide whether she said it with sadness or relief. He felt both. "You'll get cold kneeling here," he eventually whispered into her hair. Her sobs had subsided but her breathing was still uneven. He could feel the chill of the stone floor creeping through his own knees and thought it likely that Lili could too only she was too upset to realise.

"*Hmm*," was all she said, but she wrapped her arms more tightly around his neck. Sighing, he slid his arms behind her back and legs and, mentally counting to three, heaved her off the floor onto his lap. She settled into his chest, eyes staring, wide-awake, silent and still.

They were in the same position when Bertie arrived back a couple of hours later with the four remaining Burnley sisters in tow. Ewan was, at first, rather pleased that Lili did not leap up and distance herself from him to maintain the guise that they were simply two uninvolved neighbours, but his happiness quickly faltered when Lili didn't even move when what remained of her family entered the room. He watched helplessly as the sisters trailed in and stopped dead. He was hampered by the considerable weight of a large grown woman, forced to stay seated even though his head was screaming at him to get up, offer his sympathies and beat a hasty retreat. The sisters stood rooted to the spot with Bertie peering sourly around them, unable to pass.

Heather recovered herself first. "Hello … Ewan," she said, the edges of her lips quirking upwards. "Is she …?" She didn't need to continue. Her eyes had travelled past him to the still, white figure that lay amongst the agitated bedcovers.

"Yes," he heard himself say. "She's gone, I'm afraid."

Two of the women standing by the door grabbed each other's hands. Ewan's eyes were drawn by the movement and he was shocked to find a mirror image looking back at him. The twins must be identical, he thought. Meanwhile, Heather crossed to the opposite side of the bed and opened the curtains. She then turned to her mother and kissed her on the forehead. Lili did not move.

"Let's make some breakfast." Heather had tear-tracks down her cheeks but otherwise seemed to be functioning perfectly well. Sarah, Alice and Vera all approached their mother and touched her softly, murmuring Ewan knew not what. Then, as per Heather's suggestion, they filed out, back to the kitchen past Bertie who stood transfixed and whey-faced by the door.

Heather touched him kindly on the shoulder. "Go on, Bertie. Say goodbye."

"She's gone?" He couldn't take his eyes from the bed.

"Yes, pet."

For someone who was viewed by others as a fine young man, Ewan thought Bertie was extremely ugly when he cried. He screwed his face up, wrinkling it like an old man's. Tears caught in these new crevices of his skin and ran horizontally before streaking down his bright-red cheeks. He curled his hands and arms into himself as a child might and, when Heather went to comfort him, pulled away with a little squeal of disgust.

Giving up on her brother, Heather turned to Lili. "Are you coming, Lil? And – Ewan, of course. You'll stay and have some breakfast." It was not a question. It was a statement, as if he were one of the family. Or perhaps it was just that Heather knew her elder sister was unlikely to move unless he did.

No one showed Ewan any animosity during breakfast, not even Bertie who had subsided into a shell-shocked heap at the end of the table. Lili sat beside Ewan, holding his hand under the table. He didn't say anything but kept a close eye on her while listening to the sparse conversation going on around him. She hadn't uttered a word since her family arrived. Her eyes looked dead and empty. He hoped it was just that she was drained and upset by the loss of Evelyn but he also feared that she was withdrawing from him and everyone else. He wanted to do something, to say something to her but didn't know how or what to do under the gaze of her siblings. Fortunately, Georgie came to his rescue. The dog, who had sat in the kitchen by the range so quietly all through the night, came slinking up and lightly rested her head on Lili's thigh. Her tail wagged slowly, sadly, and the whites showed at the bottom of her eyes as she looked up into Lili's face. Georgie didn't beg for anything. She just let Lili know she was there. Ewan watched as Lili began to gently stroke the dog's silky soft head and ears. The tears leaked from her eyes and slid down her cheeks as she smiled wetly at the dog. "You're a good girl," she whispered.

Despite being asked to stay with the family by Heather, Ewan took his leave. However, he made one concession: he left Georgie with Lili. It didn't take any persuasion on his part. When he stood up to go, the dog looked at him but did not move from her place with her head on Lili's knee. It felt wrong to leave but he had his own work to do, his own life to look after. Besides, he did not want to be stuck in a house full of six Burnleys as they planned a funeral. It was no place for him. Surprisingly though, he had not even reached the garden gate when he heard his name being called. For a split second, he thought it was Lili. It sounded like her. But when he turned Heather stood in the doorway.

"Thank you," she said, walking up to him. "Make sure and come back later. I think –" she looked over her shoulder. "I think Lili would like it if you did." With that she gripped his hand firmly, smiled and left him standing at the gate somewhat bemused but also quite pleased.

Heather obviously accepted him. It was a start.

Chapter 22

After her discussion about a marriage proposal with Bertram, Astrid wrote a letter to Eric Stevens in readiness for the arrival of its companion. She expected Bertram to be back in the next few days with his own missive since she imagined he was impatient to propose and make Wren his wife. But he didn't come. An entire week passed and they saw nothing of him even though Wren had expected him. It wasn't likely he was caught up on the farm. He usually managed to get away. Even during haymaking – the busiest time of the summer – he still made his pilgrimage into town. Astrid worried that he struggled so much composing his letter that he had given up the entire thing as a bad job. Or maybe he was simply spending all this time so that he might create the perfect letter to send to his prospective father-in-law. She hoped so.

It put Wren out considerably to think that her man had abandoned her. She desperately tried to think what she might have done wrong to make him disappear without explanation. Bertram was sometimes so changeable that it was difficult to know what he was thought of her. And, when she did think about him – really *think* – Wren realised she knew very little about the man she had spent her entire summer with. She didn't even know where he lived (not exactly), so that she might call on him. She hadn't even met his family so couldn't ask any of them about him either. It left her feeling a little empty to know that so much of her relationship was hollow space, unpeopled by intimate understanding of the person she loved when he knew so much about her.

It wasn't until the end of the week that Wren discovered Bertram had a perfectly good reason to stay away.

Astrid was no longer in the habit of going out on her own, having become so used to Wren's constant presence. However, being in a state of permanent melancholy since Bertram missed one of their scheduled meetings, Wren had pleaded sickness and asked not to go into town that morning. If she had, she would have discovered more of Bertram than she ever could have wallowing in a haze of self-pity.

It was not until Astrid arrived home, puffing and limping heavily having rushed up the hill to deliver her news, that Wren was dragged from the mire of her own thoughts.

"Birdy! Wren, come down here at once!"

The sharpness of her aunt's tone was enough to send Wren scuttling to the top of the stairs like a scolded puppy. She knew she was being petulant, hiding away in her room, but she thought her aunt was sympathetic. Perhaps the old lady had finally lost patience with her.

"Yes, Auntie?" she said timidly, her fingers wrapped nervously in the end of her frock.

"I know why Bertram hasn't been to see us," Astrid said triumphantly. She wasn't usually one for gossip but the relief she felt on hearing what she was sure was the reason for the boy's absence made her a willing relater. "His mother, poor Evelyn Burnley – you remember her from the ICA meetings, don't you? – she died of a stroke at home earlier in the week. Did you hear anything about it?"

Wren, shaking her head in disbelief, was dumbstruck. Her legs seemed to move without thought, bringing her down the stairs to her aunt. It wasn't something she had done – that was her first thought. Uncharitable as it was, she felt a surge of happiness as the anxiety left her. Guilt, however, quickly followed as she realised she felt cheerful at having discovered Bertram's mother was dead. How cruel it was for her to rejoice when he was no doubt heartbroken by her loss! She wished she could go to him – comfort him – but she still had no idea where he lived. All she knew was the reason he was staying away.

"Has the funeral been?"

"It was two days ago," Astrid answered, shaking her head. "If I'd known I would have gone. I didn't know her well but I should have been there as part of the ICA. It would have been right and proper. But no one said anything to me."

Each of them went about her business dwelling on her own personal, silent contemplation until the evening arrived and they sat down with one another as was their wont.

Wren was quiet for a time before suggesting they perhaps send a card of condolence to the Burnley family.

"That would be a good idea," Astrid agreed. "I'll get the address from Mrs Burnley's ICA membership form." She stood and hobbled over to her desk. Her hip was exceedingly painful after her rush up the hill with her news.

"You know where he lives?" Accusation dripped from Wren's voice. She had pondered aloud on numerous occasions where Bertram might live and received no help from her aunt. "Why didn't you tell me?"

Astrid – a little taken aback by the girl's vehemence – said simply, "I don't know where he lives. And I never thought to check his mother's documentation to find out. It wouldn't be my place to share that information with anyone. Not even you, Wren."

Wren coloured immediately. Her aunt's tone of disapproval was subtle but tangible. "Sorry."

"It's alright," Astrid said calmly. "I understand. But you have to too. Be patient. It will all come to rights in the end." She had to stop herself from adding 'I hope'.

She needn't have worried. Within a week, Bertram returned full of apologies for having not contacted them. He was, he said, all muddled up after his mother's death and simply never thought to contact them. Astrid thought this perfectly acceptable, having gone through her own griefs over the years, but Wren was secretly quite upset to learn he had not thought of her in the week just passed. She had done virtually nothing but think of him while they were apart.

His visit was brief and rather awkward as he was not as chatty as usual and neither of the other two were sure what to say to him. However, as he left, he discreetly passed a letter to Astrid without uttering a word. Meeting his steady gaze with her own, she nodded and he inclined his head in return. The wheels had been set in motion.

Chapter 23

Had Lili been aware of her surroundings on the day of her mother's burial, she might have indulged in a rueful little chuckle. If Evelyn had been alive, she would have been in her element at such an event. She would have craned her neck, stood on tiptoe and asked neighbours who every attendee was while maintaining just enough piety to give the appearance of a dutiful mourner. She then would have spent the entirety of the next day discussing who was there, who they were married to, who they were related to, the relatives of whom they were married to … and so on and so forth.

The other thing that would have piqued Evelyn's interest was who was *not* there. As it was, there was no one other than her old cronies to register who was present or absent. Some of the local ICA women didn't come and, to Evelyn, that would have been the height of affrontery.

But Lili wasn't aware of anything – especially not what her mother would have thought of her own funeral. She drifted through the days after Evelyn's death seeing and hearing nothing. She was numb to the world, neither part of it nor absent from it, simply being steered through it by her sisters who, having their own families to loosen their dependence on their mother, found her loss easier to bear. However, once the funeral ended and everyone had left, Lili began to regain the power of her senses. But what she experienced when she emerged from her natural sedation made her long to return to her sensationless state. Everything reminded her of her mother. Being in the kitchen, making food, working in the yard, walking through the garden. It was as if her mother's spectre lived in all the things Lili saw and touched. All the tasks she did were those which Evelyn gave her. All the things she knew how to make were taught to her by her mother. She was everywhere and in everything.

What haunted her most, however, was the knowledge that despite having lived with the woman for thirty years, almost every good memory had a corresponding negative. So much of her life with Evelyn had been lived in mutual irritation at the other's behaviour. Now she was lost without that reference point, even if it was a negative one.

Ewan never saw her. Since the funeral, he had been busy with his sheep, readying them for the rams, repairing fences on the fields, separating the ewes out into different groups and so on. He also wanted to give Lili space. He did not want to impose himself upon her and make her feel like she had to acknowledge that their relationship was now in a transitional period. She would have to decide whether to stay living the life she had for three decades or begin a new one with him. But he did not want his constant presence to force her decision even if he did want her to choose him more than he had ever wanted anything in his life.

However, Ewan was not the only person to see nothing of Lili in the fortnight after her mother's death. When he went down to the village for his weekly provisions, he asked as casually as he could whether anyone had seen her since the funeral. They had not. The family's usual weekly groceries were collected by Bertie and no one had seen her at church that Sunday. The fact that she was not in church raised a few eyebrows given that her mother had died so recently, but most people understood that there must have been a reason for her absence.

By the end of the first week after Evelyn's death, Ewan hadn't even seen Lili at a distance so he made the decision to attend Sunday service at church for the first time in months. He had never really been religious or a great believer in the power of God – for him, church was more of a place to be. If he went, he would often feel calmer as he walked out into the daylight. Yet the problem was allowing himself that hour per week to leave all his work behind. So often, he just could not bring himself to do it – to walk away, to waste an hour on something as unproductive as singing, sitting and listening. Now, however, he had the excuse of Lili to draw him out of his self-imposed exile. When Sunday came, he rushed through the regular morning jobs, trying to have everything done in time so that he might get a quick wash and shave before he left. Despite his hurry, as the hours of the morning progressed, Ewan still found himself running out of time. He made the decision, therefore, after having a quick sniff of his shirt, to have the wash and dispense with the shave. After all, he would not be the only man with a beard. And while he still hated beards, his tolerance was growing in spite of how much they itched. That was something he forgot to tell Lili, he thought. When he recounted his history and the death of Mabel, he had not mentioned the time he spent in prison. During his incarceration, he sat in a cell fearing the worst and all the time he was there he had never had access to a razor. His beard had grown rapidly, unchecked for the first time in his life. Now, every time he saw the reflection of his face completely framed by a bushy mane, he was reminded of that time when he thought his life was over. Over the years, he simply learnt to avoid his reflection which made forgetting about the past that little bit easier. He still had to condition himself not to loathe the feeling of a beard and the look of it when he caught sight of it. But beard or no beard, he was going to church just so that he might catch a glimpse of her across the nave. She didn't even have to look at him. It was just so he could see her and know that she was alright – or as alright as she could be. But she wasn't there. Neither was Bertie, but his absence was not surprising. Like Ewan, church attendance was not high on the youngest Burnley's list of priorities. The only member of the family he saw was Heather with her husband and two boys in tow.

Ewan spent the entirety of the service thinking of all the things he could be doing and worrying about where Lili was. As he sat and stood, mechanically following the sermon but hearing nothing that was said, he formed a plan. If he didn't see Lili by the end of the day, he would go and find her and to hell with giving her space. He did not like to admit it to himself but he was really frightened by her withdrawal. It wasn't good for her, he thought. He knew that self-imposed exile was good for no one because he had lived through it and was now attempting to crawl out the other side into the light.

Afterwards, he did not loiter. He had been sitting near the back of the church and so was one of the first to walk out past Reverend Harrington. He shook the Reverend's hand but did not stay for chitchat, instead lengthening his stride so that he might not find himself cornered by anyone wanting to talk.

He was at the gates of the church when he heard his name being called. He turned and found four people bearing down on him with a woman in the lead. It was Heather, her husband Trevor and their two sons.

"I'm so glad I caught you," she said without preamble, catching hold of his hand and giving it a squeeze. It was a familiar gesture that surprised him. There was something so endearing about Heather's smile – her openness, her friendliness and her acceptance of him. But then there was also trouble in her eyes which made Ewan tense involuntarily and grasp her hand a little harder than he meant to.

"Have you seen Lili?"

They both spoke at the same time, the strain and concern in their voices plain for each other to hear. The two young boys, who had caught up, giggled at the absurdity of it. Their father hushed them disapprovingly but Ewan still caught the trace of amusement on Trevor's face. Ewan liked Trevor. He was ten years older than his wife, grown up, sensible and a good farmer to boot. He was also a very shy man, unlike his wife who was friends with everyone. He took the two boys by the shoulders and steered them past his wife, walking a short distance away so as not to intrude. He began gesturing towards the hedgerow close to where they stood and, though he could not hear Trevor's voice, Ewan knew he was pointing out the various plants that carpeted the ditch. It surprised Ewan when he found the sight tugged painfully at his heart. He wanted to share simple things like that with his own children.

"I thought you might have seen her. You being closer," continued Heather. "I told her to come over the week after the funeral but she never did. Maybe she didn't want to come to our mad house with the boys and Trevor."

Ewan had to hide a smile. He couldn't imagine Trevor ever being mad.

"And between one thing and another I never got to see her. Do you think she's alright?"

Heather looked as worried as Ewan felt.

"I don't know," he answered. "Do you think I should ... check on her? Although maybe it's not my place ..."

"Of course you can. I'm going up there now, I think," she said, making the decision on her feet. "Do you want to come with me?"

Ewan began to speak but then checked himself. Yes, he did want to. Very much. But then he had sworn to himself that he would meet Lili on her terms. Yet, Heather had offered. He could say he was going because of Heather. But he would be lying to himself and he didn't want to do that.

"No, no. You go. But just . . ." he tried to think what message he might pass on. "Just say I was asking for her, aye?" It was innocuous enough to be taken as the general concern of a friend but it was also a reminder that he was still there and still thinking of her. It was enough … for now.

Heather waited a moment, expecting more, then nodded, rubbed Ewan's arm with affection and walked away.

Chapter 24

Ewan spent the rest of his Sunday afternoon catching up on his work – unblocking a clogged drain, retying tarpaulin over one of the hayricks. He also needed to move a group of ewes to a different field. When he went to relocate them, however, he found he not only needed to change the raddle on the two rams in the group but also that three of the ewes were breathing far too fast. It meant putting all the animals into a pen then separating out those five sheep from the rest of the flock, treating the ewes or bringing them back to the yard, followed by putting new raddle markers on the rams. It was not particularly difficult work but it was time-consuming as it meant he had to return to the house to get raddle markers and a drench for the ewes then traipse back to the field to finish the job.

By six o'clock he was almost finished but still had to change the rams' raddles. They were easy to spot with their leather harnesses which also made them easy to catch. Not that Ewan needed help catching them – he was big, strong and had years of practice. As he up-ended the first ram, catching its woolly sides between his knees and wrapping one arm beneath its chin, Georgie, who was sitting outside the pen, gave a soft "*Woof!*" letting him know they were no longer alone. He turned to look and saw a tall thin figure with shockingly pale skin approach. He felt his mouth drop open as he recognised the familiar yet now much more prominent features of Lili Burnley.

Sensing Ewan's preoccupation, the ram gave a violent squirm, punching upwards and almost colliding with Ewan's chin, the horny poll of its head brushing up the side of his face instead as he jerked out of its way. When he'd hushed the ram, he looked up to find Lili standing at the side of the pen, looking not at him but at the sheep huddled at the opposite end. Ewan took his opportunity to study her while she was preoccupied. He was right: she was much thinner. He could see the bones in her face more clearly. The blue veins in her temples shone through the white skin, making her look ill.

"They're a good bunch." Her voice seemed to be disconnected from her body, higher and less forceful.

Ewan grasped at the safe subject. "Aye. These are the bigger ewes. I separated out the smaller ones and put them with a younger ram up the top fields. The grass is a bit better up there."

She stared at the sheep. "Good idea."

Silence.

Finally, she looked at him. "What are you doing?"

"Changing the raddle." He looked around. "Damn."

"What is it?"

"I dropped the marker over there." He pointed at the bright red rectangle of soft wax that he wanted to attach to the harness. It allowed him to see which ewes the ram had covered and also, because he used a blue raddle on the other ram, which ram had covered which ewe. The red marker had been in his pocket but it had obviously fallen out while he wrestled with the sheep.

Wordlessly, Lili slipped into the pen, went over and picked up the marker before handing it to him. She stood and watched as he attached it before releasing the ram.

"Next one," he said. "Do you want to take the second marker? So I don't drop it."

She took it from him without touching his hand, turned and began to slide through the sheep, her eyes on the other ram. "I'll push him towards the corner and you catch him."

They worked together, quickly and efficiently, as if they had spent their lives rehearsing the same scene. He cornered the sheep, upended it, took off the old raddle, handed it to Lili and found the new one in his palm immediately. Finished, he righted the ram and let it skitter away from them, grateful of its release as it buried itself among the other woolly bodies. Ewan stood up straight and brushed past Lili to open the pen. Georgie slid wraith-like past him into the enclosure, rounded up the sheep and pushed them out the gateway.

He leaned on the outside of the pen as wool-covered bodies sped past, some even being so bold as to give a little cat-leap of happiness to celebrate their new-found freedom after their confinement. Lili followed slowly behind, taking up a position that mirrored Ewan's, standing inside the pen, leaning on the top rail. He didn't look at her. Instead, he stared unseeing at the flock now bending to graze.

"You all right?" he asked. It was the first thing he could think to say that didn't stray into deeper, emotional territory.

"No," she said quietly. "Not really."

"I suppose not."

"I just …"

Ewan looked across to see Lili pulling a splinter of wood from the top of the pen.

"I don't know what to do now she's gone." She caught another strip and began pulling that off too. "I hate being on my own with Bertie. I don't know what to do."

Ewan felt a surge of anger towards her. "Yes, you do."

He pushed off the fence and went to collect his jacket hanging on a corner post. How could she say that to him? That she didn't know what to do? Didn't she know how much saying something like that would hurt him? He was there for her, waiting, and she made it sound like she had no one to go to. He stood by the post, clenching his jacket in his fist, staring out across the fields and hills trying to calm himself.

He was breathing heavily through his nose when Lili slid up quietly to stand beside him, her hand almost touching his but not quite. Finally, she stepped forward and stood facing him. He didn't look at her immediately, instead continuing to stare into the middle distance, but eventually he sighed and met her eye. Her lips quirked sadly. She reached a tentative hand up to his face, asking permission. She knew he was angry. She knew what she *wanted* to say but that did not make facing the man she was going to say it to any easier. She did not want to hurt him. Ewan didn't move away from her outstretched hand. Lili gently took hold of his overgrown beard and tugged affectionately, dropping her eyes from his searching gaze. She did not want him to see into her soul. So instead, she tried to distract him.

"Your beard's gone long."

Ewan caught her hand and kissed her knuckles. She didn't react. He fought the urge to suddenly grab hold of her in an attempt to shock her out of her stupor. Yet he wasn't sure if it would work. He thought she might just continue as an emotionless rag doll. Unbidden, the notion came to him that he could, at that very moment, do what he liked to Lili without her resisting. His own thought scared him, as much for her sake as for his own. How could he think that?

"Heather said your beard had gone long," Lili continued, oblivious to the turmoil in Ewan's mind.

"Heather? She visited, did she?"

229

Lili nodded and turned away, her back to him. If he took a small step forward, he would be flush against her and could wrap his arms around her waist. He wanted to. But he didn't.

"She's cross with me. Said she was worried." She paused. "Said you were worried too."

"Yes."

She spun around to look at him. "Come on, let's get rid of that beard."

Before Ewan could reply, she had grabbed his wrist, as one would with an errant child, and began towing him back towards the house. Quickly, he twisted his wrist out of her firm grasp and took her hand in his. She seemed to stutter a moment at the change, then gripped his hand, returning the pressure. They didn't talk. They couldn't. Both of them were as uncomfortable around one another as they had been on the first morning after they met. Neither wanted to begin a conversation. They couldn't talk about something innocuous because both would know the other was trying to force a conversation. Their falseness would be an insult to both their intelligences. They weren't about to get into such an important conversation in the middle of a field in the gathering darkness of an autumn evening. Both of them knew, by some unspoken agreement, that the conversation would happen tonight. But it would be in the confines of Ewan's home where neither of them could walk away.

Georgie trotted ahead of them in the gloaming, Lili wasn't exactly sure where to go so followed the white patches on the dog's back which glowed pale-blue in the dim light. "Have you anything more to do this evening?" she asked when they reached the yard. She stopped and faced Ewan. There was a determined set to her jaw. They were going to talk and she did not want him to have excuses to make a hasty exit.

Something about her confrontational tone irked him. She was clearly still grieving the loss of her mother and he knew he should have felt sorry for her. And he did. But there was also something else niggling at him.

"No." He sounded harsher than he meant to.

He had been starved of her company for too long and now all he wanted was answers. He wanted to know what their future might entail – whether they would spend it together or apart. If it was the latter, he thought, he might as well sell up and move on now. He could not live so close to someone he wanted so much but could not have. He wouldn't be able to cope with Lili choosing to stay with Bertie over the chance of happiness with him.

Bertie. The thought of him further blackened Ewan's musings. So much so that he found himself saying, "What about you? Doesn't *Bertie* need feeding this evening?" before he was even sure the words actually came out of his mouth. *What was he doing?* He had never spoken to her like this. And then it hit him. He was absolutely terrified about what she might say to him next. Anger was always the emotion that ruled him as a young man but as he grew older he had supressed all of his emotions just so he might check the most dangerous of them all. But Lili had awakened so many feelings in him – love, lust, exasperation – that he had lost a handle on his anger. He had lost control of himself. She made him raw and emotional once more.

Hearing this anger in Ewan's voice, Lili's head jerked back a little as if he had taken a swing at her. "I left him bread and ham. He can fend for himself tonight."

Abashed, Ewan just nodded before turning towards the house. He began leading the way to the back door but his steps faltered and he stopped. "Does he know you're here?"

"No."

"Does anyone?"

"No."

Ewan paused. "Is that wise?"

"I don't know. Is it?" There was a bite in Lili's voice. "Why is it unwise? Am I not safe with you?"

"You're never safe with me." The words left him before he could stop them.

Lili stared. All through the summer she spent hours alone with him walking the fields and he had never spoken to her like that. There was something unfamiliar in his eyes – defiance, a challenge and something else that she couldn't put her finger on. Those eyes glowed bright in the dying light. It scared and intrigued her. She had hurt him. She could see it in his every movement, his every address. Would he do her harm? Would she care if he did?

No.

He could do what he wished with her because right now, the only thing in the world she felt a connection to – even if it was somewhat tenuous – was Ewan. Her sisters all had their own families. Her mother was dead, her father too. Even her connection to the farm and the home place, which had always felt as if it were a physical part of her, died with her parents and now she floated unattached to anything corporeal, unable to walk the fields and yard that had been her home for so long. Because now it was just Bertie's.

"Never safe with you." She repeated Ewan's words back to him. "Well then," she began walking towards the house, "let's get it over with, eh? If you're planning to do me mischief. If you kill me like you did your first wife there are several people who might be quite grateful." She turned about to look at him. "Bertie might even send you a 'Thank You' card."

The colour washed from Ewan's face with frightening rapidity. He put his hands to his chest as if he had received a mortal wound and the blood was leaking through his fingers, draining the rosy hew from his cheeks. "Don't –" he choked. "Don't – I didn't kill her. I told you I didn't kill her."

Lili stared deep into his eyes, her own empty of feeling. She did not quite know what she was saying or doing but neither could she stop. In some unconscious way, the words that came from her mouth were a test – a test of his self-control, of how much he cared for her. He said she was not safe with him. She would know the truth of his words even if he killed her in the process. She had to, because she wasn't sure a continuation of her life would be worthwhile if he was not part of it. She couldn't see herself living out her days as Bertie's fool, cook and dairymaid. That would be no life at all.

"I told you I didn't kill her!" Colour flooded his face, squeezing out the tears that were threatening to overflow. He started towards Lili, his movement sudden as if he had been shoved by an invisible force propelling him forward, a wildness in his eyes.

Lili couldn't help it: she flinched. She was angry with herself for it. She wanted to stand firm, to take whatever he threw at her without balking.

Ewan vaguely noticed Lili twitch, her tall frame leaning away from him as he approached. But he kept coming. He grabbed her upper arms roughly and held her tight, his fingers squeezing hard enough to bruise her skin.

"I told you I *didn't* kill her!" He shook her a little, the only release he allowed himself in the midst of his terror. "You said you believed me." His voice broke. "*Tell* me you believe me!" And with that he sank to his knees, dragging Lili down with him into an ungainly heap on the damp yard, their long legs twisting uncomfortably, banging off one another as they fell. "Tell me you believe me," he sobbed, eyes downcast.

Lili's hand snaked up to his face and touched what it could of his bearded cheek. "I believe you. I'm sorry."

233

Ewan gasped a breath of relief, of shock. He squeezed her arms hard again before crushing his lips against hers. She felt the release of all his pain and anguish and met his mouth eagerly, finding her own sense of relief in the fact that he chose to kiss her rather than harm her. He did not want to hurt her. He wanted her to trust him.

And now she did.

"Why did you say that?" he whispered, breaking their kiss and resting his forehead against hers.

She could not answer straight away. She wasn't even sure she knew. But, finally, she said, "Because I didn't know if I could trust you and I wanted to be sure that you loved me. And – and I'm scared and hurt so I hurt you. I'm sorry." Even if the gaining of that knowledge had cost both of them a moment of great stress and pain, Lili felt she now knew the absolute truth of him, even if it did cost her two bruised arms.

"Just …" he struggled to find the words, "just don't do it again."

"I won't. I promise."

Ewan pulled away. For a moment, Lili thought he was going to walk away from her but he stood and proffered his hand. She took it gratefully, peeling herself off the wetness of cobblestones. The ground left a damp and dirty patch down the side and back of her skirt which she brushed ineffectually, craning her head around her shoulder in her attempts to see how bad it was. When she was finished with her inspection and looked round, she almost started back.

Ewan stood inches away from her, their clothes almost touching. Gently, he ran his knuckles down her arm, past her elbow, past her wrist, past her hand and onto her hip. He did the same with the other hand, unfurling his fingers as he came to rest both palms on her hips, dipping his knees slightly so that he was nose to nose with her. Slowly, his hands slid around her hips, around her buttocks and softly down the back of her skirt. He could feel the coldness of the damp fabric on his hands. It made the material cling slightly to her skin so that he could feel the shape of her body through it. He pressed his front against her and she wrapped her arms around his neck just as he wrapped his around her upper thighs, lifting her off the ground. His eyes burned again but, this time, Lili understood. It was the look of desire.

A little shocked by the sudden change in Ewan – whose face was still tear-streaked – Lili didn't know how to deal with this new tenderness and want. He carried her to the back door as if she weighed nothing. But when they got there, he reached up, kissed her lightly on the lips then eased her down onto the doorstep, sliding her body down his as he released her.

"Don't want to bang your head on the lintel." He opened the door. "Or mine." He ducked under the doorframe to follow her in.

Lili had not been in Ewan's house since he told her about his previous life in Scotland. She wasn't sure what she expected but she had not expected it to look exactly the same. Yet it did. Still cosy and immaculately clean.

"Go and get your shaving things. I'll put the kettle on."

Midway towards heading to the scullery to get something to eat, Ewan changed tack and loped up the stairs. He came back a moment later, a bowl in one hand, a neat leather case in the other, with a towel draped over his shoulder. Lili had barely put the kettle on the range before he deposited everything on the crate beside his chair – the case contained a razor, brush and shaving soap – arranging it all with precision then disappearing into the scullery.

"What would you like for supper?" he called.

"Are you hungry?" she asked, opening the cake of shaving soap in readiness for the heating water.

"Yes."

"All right." Lili abandoned her preparations. "Do you want me to cook?"

"No, I can cook."

She followed him into the scullery and looked around, admiring the scrubbed surfaces and clean pots and dishes. "How are you so neat?"

He chuckled. "It's not always this neat, but I try. It's a case of discipline and good training. My mother, the army. You don't forget just because you live alone. Sit down, won't you?" He gestured to a chair by a tiny table shoved against the wall below the window. "Some fried bacon and bread do?"

"Yes."

Lili sat down and watched as Ewan busied himself. It was a novelty not to help. If she was in a kitchen, she worked in it. She did feel a little guilty sitting doing nothing, but Ewan seemed to have everything under control. She marvelled at the ease with which he moved around the confines of the scullery. In Lili's opinion, unless they were sitting down, men often looked thoroughly awkward in a domestic space. Yet Ewan seemed to belong even though his head was a fraction of an inch from hitting the beams in the ceiling. Every move had purpose as he fetched a plate from the sideboard, turned fluidly to the meat safe and took out a side of bacon, brought the bacon (now on the plate) to the table then stretched across to a drawer, pulled out a knife and cut off two generous chunks of meat. He then put the remainder of the bacon back in the safe and, on his way back to the table, collected a wheel of brown bread which he placed on a board with a bread knife and a pat of butter.

"Coming?" he asked as he picked up the plate of meat and the breadboard. Lili stood and followed him out to the range where he took down a heavy-bottomed pan, placed it on the hob to heat and flicked in a knob of butter. The bacon was soon in the pan and it wasn't long before the smell of frying meat wafted around them.

Georgie sat up, her nose and whiskers twitching hopefully. Ewan stretched his foot out to the dog and scratched her chest with his toes. "In a minute, sweetheart," he muttered.

He didn't say anything to Lili. While he was more secure in his understanding of their relationship than he had been for weeks, what she had done outside in the yard – lashing out like that – scared him. He had never seen that side of Lili before. It shocked him. Now he saw that she was just as fallible, just as likely to break, as anyone. Really, it was his own fault. He had put her on a pedestal, thought of her as perfect when, in fact, Lili Burnley was just as human as he was. And, rather than damaging his good opinion of her, it made him all the more determined to love her, to care for her, to make sure she never had to experience such a lonely time as the last few weeks had been for her. She was not perfect, but, for him, she was all the more perfect now he had discovered this. But that did not mean he knew how to approach a normal conversation with her just yet.

Finished cooking, he fetched plates and cutlery and they sat in the sphere of heat emanating from the well-fuelled range, feasting on buttered bread and piping hot bacon. They drank tea with their meal and afterwards Ewan brought out a tin of USA biscuits which he had been given as a gift but never had an occasion to eat them.

They devoured several more biscuits than they should have done while Lili asked about his sheep. He gladly began discussing the different groups of ewes, where he bought the rams from and how he had re-seeded two fields to hopefully have better grass for the lambs next year.

Lili listened, nodding in the right places, asking all the

relevant questions but, really, she simply relaxed. She relaxed in the knowledge that they could sit like this, comfortable in each other's company – that she was no longer alone. But mostly she listened to his voice. The deep, rich sound with its rolling 'r's, quiet yet animated and perfectly clear.

Ewan continued his monologue for a little longer, absentmindedly fondling Georgie's ears and feeding her the fat he had cut off his piece of bacon. Finally, he looked at Lili, noticing her silence. He suddenly felt self-conscious. "Sorry. I didn't mean to go on."

"It's all right. I like to hear you talk." There was a pause then she said, "Shall we get rid of that beard now?"

Ewan's lips quirked. He silently spread his arms wide, offering himself to her, a hint of challenge but also anticipation in his eyes. Unfazed, Lili picked up a scissors from the things Ewan had laid out earlier.

"Lean forward." She placed some newspaper on his lap to catch the excess hair. He obliged and she began to trim the long bristles from his cheeks, chin and neck, moving around the seat to get a better angle just as she had in her own home all those months ago. This time, however, her touch lingered. She held one side of his face as she cropped the other and Ewan – completely comfortable with this intimacy – allowed her to manoeuvre his head without resisting. He gave in to her touch and enjoyed the sensation.

Yet, he was not relaxed. Before, he had fallen asleep as Lili tended to him – lulled into somnolence by abject tiredness, warmth and the first tender care he had received and truly enjoyed since childhood. Now, he wanted to remember every touch, be aware of every movement she made. He watched her skirt sway as she walked around him, thrown from side to side by the easy, loose movement of her hips. It made him want to slide his hand under the skirt and up her leg every time she walked by. And when she stooped he almost writhed with lust as her breath tickled the freshly exposed, sensitive skin of his face and neck. He wondered if she knew how alluring she was.

Once she trimmed his facial hair to her satisfaction, she stood back on the pretence of admiring her handiwork but really to admire the man underneath it. His face really was handsome: the piercing, dancing eyes, the angular bones, the closely cropped beard. But when she took in the entire picture, she had to fight to hide a chuckle. However, she obviously didn't fight hard enough. A small titter escaped her lips. Ewan frowned, disconcerted, and ran his hand over his jaw, worried she had done something to him as a joke when he had been so busy concentrating on her.

"What?" he said defensively.

"Nothing!" said Lili but she began to laugh. "It's just – just you've got this lovely square jaw and then this big untidy mop of hair on top of your head. It just looks a bit … funny." Lili began to giggle. Seeing the expression on his face she moved out of reach and made a half-hearted attempt to cover her mouth with her fist but the damage had already been done.

"Are you laughing at me?" Ewan asked, ruefully running his hands over the crown of his head, leaving three-inch-long strands of hair sticking up at ridiculous angles. Without a care for the hair-covered newspaper on his lap, he began to rise, unfold like a predatory animal.

Lili tittered, backing away. Yet she still managed a convincing show of defiance when she answered, "Of course I'm laughing at you! You look ridiculous!"

Ewan pounced. He was up and out of the chair, catching hold of her before she had taken even half a step. As soon as he had her in his grasp, he wrapped his long arms around her waist, pinning her against his body before kissing her hard on the mouth.

"Well, you'd better cut my hair too then, hadn't you?"

Lili allowed herself to melt into his touch, closing her eyes in anticipation. But then she was alone, his hands gone. She opened her eyes to find Ewan sitting on a stool in front of the stove, looking at her expectantly his eyes dancing, a cheeky grin on his lips.

He handed her the scissors. "Well?"

Gathering herself with as much dignity as she could, Lili took the scissors. "What about your shirt and jumper? They'll get covered in hair."

Ewan looked into Lili's eyes for a moment, trying to find a hint of suggestion in what she said but only found sincerity and guilelessness. Deciding to take matters into his own hands, he shrugged, reached up, took hold of a handful of clothing at the nape of his neck and whipped off both shirt and jumper in one go. He was rather glad that today of all days he had neither a vest nor braces on. He had dressed in a hurry after church and forgone both. As he looked at Lili's rounded eyes, he thought the palaver of removing braces and vest would have rather ruined the shock of his speedy disrobement.

Blinking slightly, Lili drank him in. She had seen Ewan's exposed torso before at a distance, covered in sweat and dust, glowing red from exertion and sunburn during haymaking. But decorum dictated that whenever the men saw women coming, they put their shirts back on to save the women's blushes. But, here, now, there was something so intimate about seeing Ewan bare-chested in front of her, in a small room, beside a range with no one else but her to see it. In the dim light, her eyes travelled from his hands up the length of his arms to his biceps where the freckled, tanned skin abruptly changed to milky white. This paleness continued across his chest and stomach where only the shadows of ribs and curve of muscles coloured his bleached skin. Looking more closely, Lili was surprised by the light smattering of hair on his chest. Given the prodigious growth of his beard, she had expected more. Bertie, she knew, had a very hairy chest yet his facial hair was patchy and slow-growing. It seemed Ewan was the other way around.

She approached slowly. She was staring, but she didn't care. She wanted to memorise every plane, every bump, every curve. And she wanted to touch. She wanted to touch his exposed flesh and feel the heat of his body under her fingertips. Stretching out her hand, Lili brushed her fingers down the groove at the centre of his chest, slowly running them further down to his stomach, his belly button – he caught her fingers. Lili faltered, wondering if she had done something wrong. She went to pull her hand from his but Ewan held on, brought it to his lips and kissed her palm.

"Don't tempt me too much. I'm only human." He kissed her hand again. "Besides, you've got a job to do." He pulled at his hair, making it stand on end again. Lili laughed. "Come on, hen. I'm relying on you to make me look presentable."

"For who?"

"Oh. Now ..." He leaned back, crossing his arms over his chest. "There's this wee lassie. *Very* pretty. A local girl and, between you me, I'm trying to impress her."

Lili slapped his shoulder. "Who are you calling 'wee'?'" She made a show of being affronted, drawing herself up to her not inconsiderable height.

"*Ow!*" Ewan rubbed his shoulder. "What makes you think the lass is you? No, *don't* thump me!" he squawked, cringing away as she drew her hand back threateningly.

"I'd like to know who else it might be. I don't see her here shearing you like one of your sheep. You could stuff a cushion with what's come off your great overgrown noggin!"

There was silence for a moment. Then, suddenly, Ewan exploded with a roar of laughter, rocking back and forth on his stool, making it creak in protest. Lili, standing with her fists on her hips, tried to remain straight-faced but it was not long before she was laughing too. It was impossible to feel anything but happiness when she saw the joy on his face.

When their laughter had finally subsided, Ewan's face sobered completely before he said, "Well, I was wanting to look my best for her because –" he became engrossed in an awn of straw that was stuck to his sock "– because I was going to ask her to marry me."

Lili stopped breathing. He didn't look up but, instead, wiggled his toe in a half-hearted attempt to dislodge the piece of straw.

"Were you?"

"Aye," he replied, still not looking at her.

"And what were you hoping she'd say?"

"Yes, of course. What else?" he huffed.

"Yes."

His head snapped up. "What?"

"You heard me: yes." She was pale but her jaw was set determinedly.

"You mean it?" His voice was much higher than it should have been. He coughed. "Truly?"

"Of course I mean it! I –"

But she got no further. Ewan dragged her down onto her knees and crushed her to his chest, making her go *"Oof!"* as the air went out of her. He was kissing every inch of her face until he found her mouth, paused, then kissed her slowly and tenderly, catching her lips gently between his own.

"Thank you," he finally whispered, resting his forehead on hers.

"Same to you," she replied with a chuckle. "But –"

Ewan groaned.

"*But*," she soldiered on, "we'll have to wait. Just a little while. Until the New Year anyway. Ewan, I don't want to delay either but it'd look bad if I upped and married the neighbour a month or two after my mother dying. We've got to think of what the locals will say."

"Bugger the locals," he grumbled.

"No, no buggering anyone. They're our neighbours, our friends, the people we buy from, sell to. We can't have them turn on us. We have to keep everyone happy."

"What about us being happy?"

"We will be. We just have to wait a little bit longer, that's all."

"That's *all*? Lili, I don't know if I can wait that long." He ran his hand down her side to her hips as he slid off the stool and knelt, just as she did. His fingers skated back past her hips to her buttocks and he slowly pulled her against him. "I can't wait that long. I want you to share my bed. Not next year, not next week, *now*."

She knew asking him to wait wasn't fair. She could *feel* how unfair it was to him as he pressed her body to his. It frightened her a little to know she could have that effect on a man but it also sent a thrill through her and for a moment she thought about giving in to both of their desires.

"I can't." She knew what would happen to the both of them if she fell pregnant. If anything were to tarnish the reputation of the Burnleys and those connected to them, it would take years to overcome. She wanted to, but she couldn't.

"I know," he sighed.

"Soon." She kissed him softly. "Now," she said loudly, firmly extricating herself from his grasp, "About that hair."

He chuckled. "Short back and sides, hen. And you might want to take a bit off the top too."

"I do. Sit up on the stool again."

Lili picked up a comb from the set Ewan had brought down and set to work. After a while, Ewan instructed her to light an oil lamp so that she might not accidentally take off his ear. On impulse, Lili swiftly bent down and lightly nipped his ear with her teeth. Ewan nearly fell off his perch. There ensued several minutes of tickles, doled out as retribution for Lili's boldness, culminating in her lying flat on the floor, gasping for breath with a half-naked Scot hovering over her. But rather than feeling intimidated, she began to giggle.

"What?" he asked.

"You look silly! Your hair's only half cut." She reached up and gently smoothed the hair that flopped forward away from his eyes, only to have it fall back again the moment she let it go. Sitting up, she kissed him then firmly pushed him back onto the stool before lighting the lamps and continuing her barbering.

Lili was glad of the warmth of the range and the golden glow of the lamps. With the darkness of autumn and the drop in temperature, she was always pleased to be inside in the evenings. She thought of the walk home later that night and shivered.

"Cold?" Ewan inquired, reaching up to feel her hand.

"No. Warm. Just thinking I still have to walk home after all this."

"You could stay."

Lili laughed. "Don't tempt me."

"But I want to tempt you," he growled softly, grabbing her hand to kiss her palm.

"Ewan," she warned.

He let go of her hand. "I know. Worth a try."

She leant down to his ear but this time simply whispered, "Soon."

Hair finished, Lili moved on to his beard. Kneeling on a cushion between his knees with his arms loosely wrapping her buttocks, she shaved his face. It took her longer than it would have done had she stood behind him but she enjoyed their closeness and an opportunity to study his face – every scar, every line, every bone.

"How'd you get the scars on your cheekbones?"

His hand automatically went to the pitted skin that marked the points of both. "In the army. Boxing."

"Were you supposed to be boxing?"

"Sometimes." His mouth twisted cheekily. "Sometimes not. I got these in matches though." He gestured to the scars. "And these." He took her hand in his and guided her fingers over holes etched under the tips of his eyebrows. "No one was really silly enough to have a go at me outside a ring. I'm a bit big to be picking a fight with. And I was … different then. Younger. Angrier. And I was a damn good boxer."

"Obviously not good enough to avoid being hit," she said, viewing him critically.

"You *have* to get hit some of the time," he said. "Sometimes you don't get out of the way quick enough. I've fought some good boxers in my time. But I was fearless. I didn't care who hit me back then. I even liked it. No," he corrected, "I liked the *thought* of being hit. Not actually *being* hit. That hurt. But I took it because I wanted to feel *something*. And," he shrugged, "I fought back because I'm competitive and like to win. I like being good at what I do. I was a good soldier and I was a good boxer."

"And a good farmer," said Lili.

"Well, that's it, isn't it? The urge to do everything to the best of your ability." He paused. "It's what I didn't do with Mabel. But I'll do everything I can to be the best husband I can be for you."

"And I'll do the same for you."

He chuckled and gave her buttocks a tender squeeze. "You don't have to, hen. I just want you the way you are."

Chapter 25

Despite Ewan's best attempts to persuade her otherwise, Lili walked home after completing her barbering. Not alone, of course. Ewan insisted on walking back with her. Yet, with every step, her heart grew heavier. She didn't want to go home. Where she lived no longer *was* her home and it was the realisation of this that finally made her see her path now lay along the same road as Ewan's. She was meant to be with him. It made her wish away the coming months so that she might finally experience happiness again. This hope would sustain her through a final winter with her brother. Then, in spring she and Ewan would finally be man and wife.

She thought Bertie would be away drinking as usual and she would be able to slip in without anyone knowing she'd been away. But the light-coloured curtains were glowing golden yellow. Bertie was home.

"Right," she said sadly. She had enjoyed several hours away from her own reality and experienced a taster of what her life might be like when she shared it with Ewan. Every evening wouldn't be like that – she wasn't naïve enough to think that – but life would certainly be better. "I'd better go in."

"I'll see you soon, aye?" he asked, a pained look in his eyes as he tenderly rubbed her arm.

"Aye." She leaned up, gave him one chaste kiss and walked away.

Bertie was sitting by the fire, hunched like a gargoyle, the light of the flames throwing ugly shadows over his face. Given that he was staring morosely into the depths of the blazing wood, Lili thought it best to get past him as quickly as possible. She would not sneak. She wasn't going to feel guilty for her time with Ewan. But neither did she want to engage in any kind of conversation with her brother. She had spotted the half-empty bottle of amber liquid glowing in the half-light by his seat and was under no illusion as to what effect alcohol had on Bertie. He was a mean drunk and Lili knew it.

She was halfway across the room when she heard a sneer. "Think I didn't notice you coming in?"

Lili stopped but didn't reply.

"Well?"

She still remained silent.

"*Well*? Where were you?" he asked, voice thick with alcohol. "*Well*?"

"Out," she said simply, without inflection.

"Out where? With your fancy man, was it? Jaysus, you're quare stupid, do you know that?"

"Oh?" she managed. The scorn on his face irritated her. Deep down she knew she should walk away but somehow her body didn't seem to move.

"Listening to all that comes out of that – that –" he fought to find a word suitably damning, "that *cuckoo!*" he finally slurred triumphantly, a grin spreading across his face at his own apparent insight into the motives of Ewan Cameron.

"Cuckoo?" said Lili evenly but not without considerable effort.

"Well, shur, why else would he want you?" said Bertie as if it was the most obvious thing in the world even though he himself had only just thought of the reason a moment before. "Shur aren't you auld and everything?" he continued with the logic of a man of twenty-four who thought everyone else geriatric. "He's not going to get much use out of you." He was relishing the stony silence and colourless face of his sister. "That must be it, mustn't it? Cod you into thinkin' you mean something to him because he thinks you'll be gettin' this place." He waved hands above his head, vaguely encompassing the house, yard and land owned by the Burnleys or, more specifically, him. "Shur wouldn't you be the one to inherit if anything happened to me? And what's to say something *wouldn't* happen to me with that lad about? And then, shur, when I'm out of the way, what's to stop him murdering you in your bed and all, ha? Didn't you see him nosing about the place and Mammy dying in the room beyond? He was looking over what'd be his one day. And, shur, wouldn't it be perfect for him being beside his farm. All he'd need do would be to get rid of the two of us. He has that look about him, he does. The look of a murderer, doesn't he? What's to stop him? Answer me that!'" He finished with a jab of his finger at Lili and sat back in his chair, arms folded, awaiting a reply.

Fury boiled inside her. Bertie had tainted almost every relationship she had with her home, her friends, her mother and her father. She would be damned if she let him take this one as well. Ewan was hers and she was his. Bertie thought he could delude her into believing the most important person in her life was a con artist. But Lili knew Ewan – all of him – and was prepared to defend him to the last.

Her voice was hard as ice. "You've it all worked out, don't you?"

"I do," answered Bertie happily. "And I'll tell you something I bet you didn't know: he was in the army." Then he added childishly, "Bet you didn't know that, ha?"

"I did," she said shortly. "So?"

"*So* … doesn't it mean he's …" here Bertie paused trying to remember why Ewan's time in the army might be important, "that he's killed people!"

"That's often the case when someone's in the army, yes," Lili replied coolly. "Your point?"

"Well, he'd know what he was doing if he wanted to kill you, wouldn't he?"

Lili laughed harshly. It was either that or scream at her brother. "You don't need to have been in the army to know how to kill someone. I could have killed you a hundred times over if I'd wanted to – no, wait – I *have* wanted to kill you on any number of occasions. But I haven't. Because for some stupid reason I decided not to."

Bertie's feet left the ground as his knees began to draw up to his chest: the defence of a frightened child.

"And do you know something, Bertie, the only thing that's stopped me lacing your tea with rat bait some mornings is knowing that I'm leaving you for good the first chance I get. *And I'm leaving you for him.*"

Bertie's bottom lip began to tremble. He cowered away from her malevolent gaze, sinking as far as he possibly could into the depths of the chair. Drunkenness was beginning to befuddle his brain. He went from aggressor to victim in space of a moment. Before, he had his mother to defend him in his weaker moments when he lost his train of thought or was trumped in an argument. But now he was on his own and for the first time he realised it.

Lili was leaning over him. She wasn't quite aware at what point she moved from the opposite side of the room to standing above her brother. Nor was she aware at which point she realised that this was an argument with her brother that she could finally win. The truth was Lili, just like Bertie, expected to be shushed, expected Evelyn to come to his defence. Lili never stood a chance when it was two against one, especially when one of the opposing party was her mother and, therefore, had the last word on everything.

"What about me?" Bertie finally whispered.

"What *about* you?"

"What – I don't know – but you can't – who'll feed me?" he wailed.

Lili laughed again. It was loud and barking, unfamiliar even to her own ears. "Do you think I care about what you're going to eat when I'm gone?"

"I could come up and eat with you," he broke in hopefully, clearly pleased with his own ingenuity.

Another laugh from Lili. "Not a chance! And don't think I don't know you've been off in town every weekend looking for your next slave. The local girls not good enough for you, eh? You see, in some ways, I'm my mother's daughter. I hear and I listen and I remember. You should hear some of the things said about you, *Bertie*."

"*Don't call me Bertie!*" he roared, standing up, his fists balled at his sides.

However, his change in position didn't really make much difference as all Lili had to do to tower over him was stand up to her full height.

"See! You can't deny it, can you? Off searching for some poor unfortunate who doesn't know the truth of Bertie Burnley: the man tied to his mother's apron strings! The man who drinks himself into a stupor every other night! *The man,*" she screamed, "*who has ruined everything his father built, spent every penny he ever had and now likely doesn't even own the clothes he stands up in! Off to find some poor, unsuspecting little rich girl that's fool enough to have him and his ruined life!*"

Bertie swung at her. If he had been sober, he would have hit her full in the face. If he had been sober, he wouldn't have tried to hit her in the first place. As it was, he missed her by a few inches, his fist sailing across in front of her nose while the rest of his body followed, making him stagger and cling to the armrest of the chair for support. Lili's head automatically snapped back out of the way.

Both of them stood shocked at what he had just done. He always had a temper but had never released it in such a fashion. Neither of them said a word though Bertie knew, deep down, that he should apologise. But his pride wouldn't let him do that.

Lili had enjoyed riling him. With Evelyn gone, the dam burst and twenty years of aggravation and dislike released a torrent of water that lay waste to everything in its path. In the heat of the moment, she had not factored in that there would be a response because there had never been a time when she pushed him enough to discover it. She didn't know what would come next. Now she did. At a loss as to what to do, she did what her brain had been screaming at her to do from the start and made to leave.

"You'll not marry that cuckoo." Bertie's voice was hoarse but crystal clear.

Lili breathed deeply and, without turning, said, "Yes, I will," then left the room before her brother had a chance to reply.

Chapter 26

Something in Bertram had changed. He was no longer a careless, chatty, friendly man. He was now prone to silence. He had a tendency to stare at Wren in a way she found slightly disconcerting. It was as if he thought she would disappear if he blinked. When she sat by him, he would take her hand, squeeze tightly then continue to hold it. It was as if he believed holding on to her would protect her – that the same fate that claimed his mother could be prevented from taking the girl he loved.

Because Bertie was sure he loved her. Wren was the person he wanted to go to now his mother was gone. This young, innocent girl was the one he dreamt of, the one he wanted to tell things to. As he went about his daily business, all the incidents he encountered would be stored away in the, 'I must tell Wren' part of his mind. He had found the human anchor of his world and he did not want to let her go. Yet, when they were face to face, he didn't really want to tell her anything. It just seemed wrong of him to tell this girl the things he would have ordinarily told his mother – like a betrayal of her. His love for Wren was just too entangled with the death of Evelyn for him to act normally around her.

It was October before the pair returned to anything like their previous level of intimacy and it was then that Bertram

Burnley asked Wren Stevens to marry him.

Once he departed, Wren's instant assent was followed by a sick, slightly faint feeling. Yes, she wanted to marry this man but, despite another whole month of acquaintance, she still knew very little about him. She was going to attach herself to a stranger and her imagination suddenly went into overdrive, coming up with the most awful scenarios about how their life together might be. But then there were also good thoughts – daydreams where she would walk hand in hand through grassy fields and sit by the fire on long winter evenings. Sometimes in these visions, they cradled a child between them.

She wasn't sure how it would happen but she knew she wanted her own children. After all, had she not cared for two children already? She was used to it and knew she was good at it – her mother's jealousy was enough to confirm that. But Artie and Olivia were never *her* children.

Wren also longed to see the animals Bertram spoke of so often. So, in a moment of bravery, when Bertram was discussing his plans for the future, she asked if she might come and see his farm.

There was a pause of about ten seconds before Bertram spoke. "All right then. Do you want to come the day after next? For the whole day or just a few hours?"

"Yes! For the day."

She didn't trust herself to say any more. She thought she might burst with excitement. The prospect of visiting a farm was almost more tempting than the thoughts of her impending marriage. Incidentally, they had not discussed a date for their wedding and Wren thought the subject might be broached if they were to spend an entire day in one another's company.

Bertram nodded. "Right. It's settled then."

Once Bertram arrived home, he had some explaining to

do. His first encounter with Wren occurred in the spring and he had spent the summer regularly travelling to and from Enniscorthy to see her … without telling his family. He did sometimes wonder why he didn't just come clean and explain what he was doing. He knew Evelyn wouldn't like Wren and his mother was so involved in every aspect of his business he wanted to keep something – just *one* thing – for himself. But then Evelyn died and the problem of her interference was gone.

When he told Lili quite calmly that he would be bringing his fiancée to visit the next day and could she make dinner for three, Bertram was filled with childish glee observing the look of absolute shock on his sister's face. She could not have looked more stunned if his entire herd of cattle had thundered through the kitchen right under her very nose.

Lili was staring too intently at her brother's face to see anything but his dark eyes gazing evenly back at her.

"You're not serious?" she finally choked out incredulously.

Bertram smiled sardonically. "Of *course* I'm serious. I'm collecting her early tomorrow morning. You'll show her round, won't you?"

"Where will you be?" Lili asked accusingly. She was to have a person placed in her care of whom she knew nothing – didn't know existed! – until minutes earlier. Was she young, old, sensible, foolish, a town girl or a farmer's daughter? Was it someone Lili had met previously but not known they would soon be sisters? Sisters! She was meeting her new sister tomorrow. What if she didn't get on with her? Would that mean she would be effectively banished from her childhood home? She looked around the kitchen, imagining a faceless stranger cooking with the utensils, pans and bowls she always used and felt a sudden sense of possession over the room and its contents. This was *her* kitchen.

"I'll be out working, won't I?" Bertram answered. "She'll be in here mostly, not on the farm so I thought you could show her what you do. Give her an idea of what it'll be like here."

"How very romantic," Lili replied acerbically.

"I'll take her out around the farm after dinner. The afternoon should be enough to see it all. And by then I'll have most of the jobs done. You can look after her for the morning, can't you? See how you get on. You'll be here together after all."

"That's unlikely," said Lili coolly.

"Oh?" Bertram cocked his head. "Be living up the lane with your fancy man, is it?"

"Yes," Lili answered succinctly, then left the room. If he got to marry a perfect stranger, nothing was going to stop her marrying their neighbour.

Chapter 27

Wren's morning got off to a bad start. She was coming down the stairs to meet Bertram in the hall when she heard her aunt ask him what the two of them might be doing for the day.

"Nothing too dangerous, I hope?" Astrid said sternly.

"No, ma'am, nothing like that. She'll be spending most of the day with my sister, Lilian. Lilian can show her about the place while I get on with a few jobs."

Disappointment washed over Wren as she trudged the rest of the way down the stairs. She had expected a day outdoors solely in the company of Bertram and instead she was being pawned off on a total stranger. She sulked silently in the front seat of Bertram's car for almost the entire journey. What did nothing to improve her mood was discovering that they had, on several occasions, passed by the end of the road to the Burnleys' farm on their way to various functions. Bertram never once made the effort to call in home to introduce her to his mother when they passed so close by. Was he embarrassed by her? Did he not want his mother to meet the girl he was intending to marry? And now Evelyn Burnley never would.

As they drove through the high, whitewashed, pillared entrance to the Burnley farm, Wren felt slightly sick as she realised this was the place that was to be her future home.

This sudden nauseating feeling was by no means to do with what the place looked like. For the end of October, the day was quite sunny and made the white walls of the enclosed yard shine with cleanliness. There was no rubbish lying around, no animal droppings and very few animals apart from some ducks burrowing in the dust near a gate in the corner and a cat sunning itself on the window ledge of one of the sheds. The window ledges of the house were adorned with long boxes filled with plants, now past their best but which would, no doubt, look impressive when in full bloom. Either side of the door there were also stone troughs filled with dark soil but lacking any kind of foliage. As Wren viewed the two troughs a very tall, very attractive woman walked out into the yard to greet them.

Immediately, Wren was intimidated by her. Not just because of her size – she towered over them as they stepped out of the car – but because this woman had an air of no-nonsense about her. It made Wren nervous. She feared making a bad impression on her, perhaps turning Bertram's family, or even Bertram himself, against her.

Bertram stood between the two women for a moment then self-consciously introduced them.

"Wren, this is my eldest sister Lilian. Lilian, this is Wren Stevens, Astrid Charlton's great-niece."

Lili extended a large hand which completely engulfed Wren's delicate little fingers. "I prefer Lili, if you don't mind, Wren. Lovely to meet you."

The young girl couldn't even maintain eye-contact, Lili noticed. She looked down a lot, scuffing the ground with her shoes. But the first thing Lili noticed was how young the girl seemed. She had no expectations about what kind of woman her brother would want to marry. Despite living with Bertram, she couldn't claim any knowledge of his likes and dislikes other than his loathing of cooked tomatoes. But to see this child standing in front of her was quite a shock. She looked no older than thirteen or fourteen. Surely her brother wasn't planning on taking a child-bride?

"Right. Well." Bertram looked just as awkward as his future wife but then seemed to compose himself. He stood as tall as he could and said authoritatively, "Right, I'm off. I'll be down in the bottom fields if you need me." And with that, he left the two women to their own devices.

There was an excruciating silence once Bertram disappeared out of sight before Lili finally turned to the girl. "Do you want to come in for some tea? I've just put the kettle on."

Conversation between them was stilted. Knowing nothing about one another, neither knew which subject to broach first for fear of causing an undesired reaction in the other.

Wren spent a good three minutes deliberating whether or not to offer her condolences following the death of Evelyn. Afraid of upsetting Lili, she decided not to. Compared with the luxury she had become used to living with Astrid, the stone floor and tiny dark windows of Lili's kitchen were positively oppressive. As the conversation flagged then eventually sputtered out, the room seemed to darken even further, making Wren want to cry or go home or something other than sit at this stranger's kitchen table.

Lili, who was bustling about the kitchen while trying to keep up her side of the exchange, noticed the girl's growing dejection. She had two options: let the girl sulk for the rest of the day or tell her the truth, which might hurt her but also might bring them closer together. Lili took a punt.

Sitting down opposite the girl, she began. "Look, I'm going to be honest with you. Up until yesterday, I didn't know you existed. The first I heard of you was Bertie telling me he was bringing you here today. If I'd known –" Here she stopped. She couldn't speculate on the past. She had to look to the future. "But I *would* like to get to know you. You're going to be my sister and you're going to get five sisters and a husband in return when you marry Bertie so it would help if we could get along, wouldn't it?"

Wren didn't answer straight away. "He never told you about me?" she finally whispered.

Lili thought she could hear the girl's heart breaking. She was clearly fragile and Lili instinctively grabbed her hand, squeezing it tightly, trying to keep her together. "Bertie and I don't get on at all so he'd have no reason for telling me about you. And our mother – our mother wasn't an easy person. She could be vicious about people. Especially when it comes to people around Bertie. No one was ever good enough for him, not since he was little. Friends, teachers, even us – his sisters – weren't good enough for Mammy. Likely he thought he was protecting you from her. I know I shouldn't be saying that given that she's dead but … it's true."

Wren looked unsure but Lili clasped her hand again, smiling reassuringly.

"So: why don't we spend today getting to know each other? Wouldn't that be a plan?"

Wren nodded and returned Lili's smile though hers was somewhat waterier.

"Right. I'll show you round the place, shall I? Did you bring wellies? No? Never mind, I'll find you something."

What Lili didn't tell Wren was that the pair of boots she gave her had previously belonged to Evelyn as they were the only footwear remotely small enough for the little girl who stood beside her. Yet, where Evelyn had to split the tops of the boots to accommodate her grossly expanded calves, they yawned wide around Wren's spindly shanks, *whup-whup-whupping* comically as she walked.

Lili decided to give her the 'grand tour' – as she laughingly put it – of the place, starting with the yard and garden. This turned out to be an excellent plan as it gave the two women something to talk about. Wren questioned and Lili explained, allowing both of them to gauge one another. Wren marvelled at Lili's knowledge while Lili worried about the girl's ignorance. How was she to take over the running of the yard and house when all she seemed to know was how to cook, clean and look after children? Not that these things didn't have their place in the life of a country wife but their role was so much more than sitting pretty inside a kitchen. Lili grew all the fruit and vegetables in the fields by the garden while also caring for all the animals around the yard. There were the hens, the ducks, sick animals kept close by for observation. The pigs, though relatively self-sufficient, still needed looking after, especially when they had piglets. Lili wouldn't have liked to see the look on Wren's face earlier in the year when a sow had lain on four and crushed them to death. Of course, Lili took no pleasure in finding half a litter dead when she went to feed them in the morning. Nor had she enjoyed dealing with the dead piglets. But she did what was required without fuss because that was what you did living on a farm.

It was in the spring, however, that things got much more challenging and required a toughness Lili thought this girl lacked. She would constantly be traipsing back and forth between the flock and the house checking for any yeaning ewes, helping those that needed assistance when lambing, bottle feeding any ailing lambs … the workload was endless. And while Wren's tiny delicate hands would no doubt be useful when lambing ewes, Lili wasn't convinced the girl would be willing to stick her hand into the middle of all that slime and gunge to pull out an equally slimy lamb. In truth, Lili thought it likely she would simply keel over on the spot if faced with a sheep's behind. But then maybe Lili was wrong since the girl seemed keen to know as much as she could about everything that went on on a farm, even consenting to have a little go at milking one of the cows. Lili made sure it was one of the quieter ladies, unlikely to kick or swing her tail while Wren sat with her cheek to the cow's flank. The animal's udder was quite flaccid since she had been milked already that morning, but it didn't matter when Lili was just teaching her the basics. It was strange, but the girl seemed to have a natural instinct. She murmured softly to the cow, running her hand gently but firmly down the animal's side. She seemed to show no fear but then maybe that was because she didn't understand the danger. However, given that it was only midday and the cows weren't due to be milked properly for another number of hours, they left off and went in to make the dinner.

Here again Lili found Wren surprisingly proficient. Maybe the girl would cope after all. Yet when Bertie arrived back for dinner, there was a palpable tension between the pair, probably not helped by Lili's presence. She wondered if they were often like this or was it something to do with what she had told Wren earlier. But the girl deserved to know what she was getting herself into. Bertie didn't help in the slightest when, finishing his food, he informed her that he had some other jobs to do and that Wren would have to stay with Lili for the rest of the day. This irritated Lili as not only did she feel sorry for the girl, but the first thing she had planned to do once she relinquished her charge was to run up to Ewan to tell him all about her. He had been away the previous day so knew nothing about Bertie's revelations and Lili was bursting to tell him.

After lunch, and since Wren seemed more cheerful outside, they decided to go for a walk up the lane to see the extent of the farm. The girl's mood, so much improved after their morning escapade, had taken a dive, making her sullen and silent, leaving Lili to provide all the conversation.

They had spent over an hour traipsing through fields and around headlands, and were on their way back to the house when Lili stopped mid-monologue, her eyes focused on something in the distance. Wren looked up when she noticed her companion was no longer talking. She looked first at Lili's face and then followed the direction of her gaze. Had she done this the opposite way around, she would have been quite scared. As it was, the expression of pure happiness on Lili's face made her think that the man in the distance – for it was a man – was a friend. That said, Wren had to fight the panic that rose from her belly as they drew nearer together. The man had stopped a little way off and she could tell, even at a distance, that he was staring at her. He was huge, well over a foot taller than her with hollow-looking eyes and dark hair. If she had met him on the street, she would have skirted around him. But here he couldn't be avoided.

Lili left her side before he reached them, jogging forward to meet the stranger before he came upon Wren. Watching closely, Wren saw the man's entire face soften. In that brief moment, he had eyes only for Lili, clasping her hand in his then releasing it as she whispered to him. Whatever she said obviously had to do with Wren as his eyes widened, left Lili's face and locked on hers. It was hard for her not to step back – away from such a piercing gaze.

But then he smiled at her – though not quite the smile he gave Lili – and, walking forward, proffered his hand.

"Ewan Cameron, ma'am. At your service." He rolled his 'r's, making his voice warm like a purr.

His palm and fingers were rough and calloused around Wren's delicate hand but they exuded as much warmth as his expression did. He seemed to know she found him intimidating and was being extra-careful around her. His entire bearing seemed to soften and sink lower – less upright yet still as tall. And, of course, up close he was very handsome. Even though Wren could tell he was much older than her there was something attractive about him.

Alas, Ewan was busy and couldn't stay to chat but as he left, he clasped Wren's hand again, gave it a quick press and put his other hand on her shoulder in a kind of fatherly way.

"I was going to call up this evening," Lili said as he was about to leave. "Will you be done in time?"

Ewan smiled. "I'll make sure I am." With a quick glance at Wren, he kissed Lili swiftly on the lips then made a shushing gesture and winked. Lili slapped him affectionately on the arm and sent him on his way.

As they walked on, Wren looked over her shoulder at the retreating figure.

Lili chuckled. "Yes, he does that to people," she said, also looking back. She then lapsed into silence and seemed to be considering what she was going to say. "You don't need to worry about sharing a house with your husband and his sister, you know. Soon it'll be just you and Bertie in the Gate House. Like it was when my mother and father first moved in all those years ago. Before they filled it with the six of us, that is. It'll be like the start of a new cycle." She paused. "And maybe Ewan and I will be doing the same thing here." They had just stopped at Ewan's house. Both women looked up at its façade before carrying on.

"Do you like children?" Wren asked.

"I'm the eldest of six," Lili smiled crookedly. "I didn't have a choice. I suppose I'm not that fond of babies but I do like them when they get a bit older. That's what I found with my sisters' babbies anyway. Maybe it'd be different with my own. You?"

"I love babies," Wren sighed. "The way they feel, the way they smell but –" Here, she looked around as if someone might overhear her and leaned into Lili. "It's the having them that scares me. All that screaming and – and blood. It must be so painful."

Lili briefly thought about her previous supposition that Wren would not be the sort to lamb ewes. But the girl wasn't finished yet. She had stopped walking and was looking down at her feet, her face aflame. She made a few false starts then it all suddenly came out in a rush.

"Howdoyougetababy?"

Lili didn't think it was possible for Wren to look any redder but her face was so flooded with colour she was beginning to look deeply unhealthy. Lili didn't help her in the slightest by being completely dumbstruck. What a question to ask! And to ask it of a virtual stranger.

"Didn't your mother explain it?" Lili finally said.

Wren shook her head. "Mammy's ... not well."

Lili could almost feel the weight of what was left unsaid behind Wren's answer. There was something wrong there, but all she said was "Oh."

She cast around for some kind of explanation, wondering what her own mother might have said to her when she was younger but couldn't remember anything. Had Evelyn *said* anything? Growing up on a farm and watching animals breed year in, year out gave a person an innate knowledge of reproduction. A ram jumped up on a ewe, got down and a few months later she'd have a lamb. Lili knew there was slightly more to it when humans were involved – or perhaps quite a bit more. She had four married sisters after all and, while it wasn't a common topic of conversation, there were times when it had been discussed. In fact, Lili had shared a conversation with Heather not that long ago about going to bed with a man since she was planning to do just that with Ewan in the not-too-distant future. But how to explain it?

"Have you ever seen animals ... mating?" Lili asked.

"Maybe …" Wren answered uncertainly.

Lili grabbed her hand. "Come on," she said, turning and striding back up the lane. "Ewan has some ewes out with the ram still. Maybe we'll see something and it'll help me explain."

Back they went, traipsing across new fields to some sheep in the distance. When they got there, Lili happened to be in luck. So did the ram. They hadn't been standing there long when he went striding purposefully towards a ewe, sniffed around her, mounted her, did the deed and then wandered off.

Lili thought that was perhaps a good place to start. Her eyes followed the ram as she said, "It's not that quick with people." She looked down at Wren and saw absolute horror on the girl's face. Lili fought the urge not to burst into hysterical giggles. Was it really that horrifying? "People usually do it face to face though. And they lie down. In a bed."

There was still no improvement in Wren's expression. Lili began to fear she was making things worse. The girl looked like she might be sick.

"It's meant to feel … nice. Not painful. Well, actually, the first time it's supposed to be a bit sore but then it's meant to be fine and –" She stopped, helplessly searching for something, anything more to say, but finally settled on, "I'm not making this any better, am I?"

"No … I mean it's … alright … just I … *hmm*," was all Wren managed in reply. It was something of a shock to think of what was required in the creation of offspring.

"But you don't end up pregnant every time. Sometimes …" Now Lili felt herself straying into dangerous territory and scrabbled for a way to save what she was saying. "Sometimes … sometimes people make love for … for … pleasure."

"*Hmm,*" Wren said again. She thought it didn't sound that pleasurable at all. In truth, she didn't want to think about it so she turned away and said, "We should be getting back. Bertram's got to take me back to Auntie Astrid soon."

Lili decided it was probably best to keep quiet and let the girl lead on. She worried she might have said the wrong thing. But with a sick mother and an old great-aunt, Wren's options for discovering the truth about sex were few and far between. Lili couldn't have fobbed her off with some meaningless answer. It wouldn't have been fair. Nor did she want the girl to arrive on her wedding night without any understanding of what was expected. She recoiled inwardly at that thought. She did not want to think of her brother and Wren on their wedding night. It threw up worrying images of this childlike figure sitting on a bed pale as a sheet and frightened of what was to come.

When they got back, Bertie was waiting by the car, impatient to leave. Wren's face flooded with colour when she saw him. She couldn't even look at him. Bertie threw a half accusatory, half quizzical look at Lili who shrugged helplessly at him. They were on their own with it as far as Lili was concerned. It most definitely was not something she was going to discuss with her brother. As he performed a U-turn and drove out the gate, Lili waved the pair off. She hoped Wren would be alright.

Chapter 28

The car was barely out of sight when Lili headed back into the house, her thoughts turning inward. She had been so concerned with managing the onset of Wren's panic, she never really considered what she herself thought about finally going to bed with her future husband. It wasn't something she had really thought about that much because, if she was being honest with herself, she was scared too. She and Ewan had moments which were close to going too far but he always held himself back even though she knew it took real effort. It was thrilling to have all those feelings coursing through her body but it was also only *just* not terrifying. What if she got to that point on her wedding night and couldn't go any further? Would it make Ewan angry if she couldn't go through with it? Would it make him hate her? No – he would never do that. But she didn't want to disappoint him. Because he knew what he was doing. He had been married before, had slept with other women and Lili felt she would have to live up to his previous experiences. She didn't want the shade of his past lovers to overshadow her. She wanted to make him forget them. But would she be able to?

She pottered around the house, flitting from one job to the next but really doing very little. Her lack of definite employment gave her too much time to rake over these thoughts so it was something of a relief when half seven came and she could head up to Ewan. The warmth that coursed through her when she knew she would see him in the next few minutes seemed to wash away her worried thoughts. When the time came, she would not balk.

Grabbing half a loaf of bread for their supper, she wrapped herself in a coat and trotted up the lane. The wind on the path stung at her face, clearing her mind and reminding her of the news she had to share with Ewan. Bertie's impending nuptials were quite a turn-up and Ewan knew virtually nothing about it. He had acquitted himself quite admirably in front of Wren, showing no surprise in discovering that she was Bertie's fiancée. Plus, there was another matter she wanted to talk to him about – a much more personal matter.

When she got to the gate, there was Ewan at the end of the path, leaning casually against the door surround, arms folded, one foot gently rubbing Georgie's belly as she lay prostrate on the ground in front of him. On seeing Lili, the dog scrabbled upright and bounded down the path to meet her. Lili bent down and rubbed her affectionately with one hand, making sure to keep the bread well out of the reach of her inquisitive nose.

She laughed, "I get a better hello from the dog than from you!"

Ewan leisurely pushed off the wall and advanced slowly, sinuously. "How can you say that when I haven't said hello yet?" he asked as he unhurriedly wrapped his long forelimbs around her, pinning her arms to her sides. He smiled crookedly then kissed her, making Georgie dance around them, barking excitedly.

Lili was out of breath when he finally pulled away and asked, "Now who's better?"

"The dog," she gasped. "Definitely the dog."

He laughed and swept her into his arms, lifting her off the ground then over his shoulder before carrying her into the house. Lili was too happy to protest although she did have a little squeal when he slapped her on the bottom before putting her down.

"Well then, woman, what's all this about Bertie getting himself a wife?"

"I knew you'd be bursting to know. But I'm barely in the door! You'll have to let me catch my breath first." She threw herself down in a chair and fanned her face with her hand.

"How can you be out of breath? You didn't even walk in!"

Lili grinned. "You're thinking I knew all about this and never told you, aren't you?"

"It crossed my mind,' he said, sitting down. "Did you not know either then? He hardly just turned up with her, did he?"

"Almost. He announced last night he was bringing his fiancée to see the house and farm since, I suppose, she'll be running it once she marries him."

"Really?" said Ewan sceptically. "She didn't look old enough to be out of school, never mind married."

"She's eighteen."

"Doesn't look it. And how is it you only found out now? Did Evelyn know? Or has it been going on that long?"

"Apparently they met last spring. They've been courting ever since. Mammy and I just assumed he was at the pub but he must have been with her."

Ewan rubbed his face. "I had a bit of turn when I saw the both of you coming down the lane earlier." He paused then said carefully, "From a distance I thought you had Mabel beside you. I nearly turned and ran."

Lili didn't know what to say.

"But up close she's nothing like Mabel. It was only that she was small and dark-haired. Still, gave me the willies," he said, shivering. "When are they getting married?"

"She doesn't know. It could be a while yet."

"Well, we'll beat them to it then," he said, smiling knowingly at Lili.

"You did it then?" she squeaked. "You really did it?"

"Spoke to the good pastor yesterday afternoon. He was a bit reluctant given it's so close to Evelyn's death but we had a good chat and he finally agreed. He'll have to see the both of us first, mind. But really it's three weeks of the banns being called and then we can marry."

Lili whooped happily, jumped up and deposited herself straight into Ewan's lap. He wrapped his arms around her to keep her in place.

After her argument with Bertie when he had called Ewan a cuckoo, she had marched back to Ewan's house the next morning and told him that they were going to get married as soon as possible. She couldn't wait anymore. She was sharing a house with someone that made her life miserable when she could be quarter of a mile away in a house with someone who cared deeply for her. She'd had enough and, despite it being such a short time after her mother's death, she made her decision to marry. Hang the consequences and other people's opinions! They would have a quiet, private ceremony without any fanfare or fuss. Neither of them wanted anything fancy anyway. They wanted a marriage, not a wedding.

"Happy?' Ewan asked, cuddling her to his chest.

"I'll only be happier on the day we're married," Lili replied, reaching up to kiss him.

His chest rumbled with humour. It stopped momentarily then started up again until he gave voice to the sound and chuckled.

"What?" asked Lili.

"You're still holding your loaf of bread."

She was cradled it so tightly that it was beginning to shed crumbs over her cardigan as it frayed around the edges.

"Wrap it in a blanket and you could fool people into thinking it was a child," he said smiling.

Lili's stomach dropped. Children. Her earlier conversation with Wren came flooding back to her. She slid off Ewan's knee and made to head to the kitchen to make them something to eat but Ewan caught her hand. She turned back to him.

"What did I say?' No –" He held up his hand to stop Lili who had begun shaking her head. "I've said something. What is it? Tell me," he urged.

She was grateful he didn't stand. If he had she would have been too intimidated to say anything. Not that she was scared of him. It was just he was such a presence at full height. She faced away to make her confession easier.

"You said about … a child and …" She couldn't settle on the right words to explain herself.

"Go on," he said, gently squeezing her hand.

"I just … having children is a – a scary thing and I assume that we might one day … have children. But I don't know if I can … do it," she finished, face burning.

"Well, childbirth is a frightening thing –" Ewan began but Lili cut him off.

"Not that!" she said impatiently. "It – *it*! The – the going to bed bit," she whispered.

There was silence for a moment before Ewan said, "Oh. That," and nothing more.

Impatient to get a more substantial reply from him she stood to look at him. "Well?" she asked. She could almost see the cogs of his brain working but they seemed to be coming up with nothing.

"I don't know what to say to you, hen. It's – you haven't before, have you?" he said, studying her.

"No, I have not!" she said crossly, making Ewan flap his hands in a panicked attempt to calm her indignant outburst.

"All right! I just had to ask."

"Would it stop you marrying me if I had?" she asked, curious.

"What? No! Of course not. It would be a bit hypocritical if I did, wouldn't it? Since *I've* done *it* before." He saw Lili twitch, her hand curl into a fist. He reached for it and unfurled her fingers, sliding his own into her palm. "That's it, isn't it? I've slept with other women."

"Yes – no! Oh, I don't know, Ewan!" she said, shifting agitatedly. "I'm … just … I'm afraid!" she finished, turning her face away in shame.

Ewan finally stood. But rather than stretch to his full height, he took both Lili's hands in his, bent his knees and brought his face to hers so that they were at eye-level. "Lili, I know it can be frightening but … but I'll do my best to make it easier for you." He smiled gently. "We'll take it slowly. I won't force myself on you. And if you tell me to stop, I will. As long as it takes, Lili, remember that. I'd wait for you forever," then amended, "Well, maybe not forever. But until you feel you're ready."

He waited for a response. Lili eventually sighed and nodded.

"And now," he said, "I'm ready for some supper. Come on and we'll eat your bread before it all ends up in crumbs."

Chapter 29

Just over four weeks later, Lilian Burnley was married to Ewan Cameron in the presence of Lili's family and a few close friends.

There was a small kerfuffle in church on the first Sunday their names were announced. Bertie, who sat beside Lili, nearly choked on his own tongue as he both gasped and tried to speak at the same time. Everyone stared but without the look of abject horror that coloured Bertie's face. Lili kept her eyes stoically to the front throughout. She wasn't sure she could control the laughter that was bubbled up inside her or whether it was the laughter of humour or hysteria. At the very least, she knew she couldn't look at Ewan sitting several rows behind or she would begin giggling uncontrollably right there in the middle of the Sunday congregation.

Bertie was the only member of the family she had not told. Heather was the first to know as she was closest to Lili. Her kindly nature, closeness to Lili and prior approval of Ewan all made Heather the perfect person to test out this piece of news on as, even if she disapproved, she would not do so in a way that would hurt Lili. Luckily, however, Heather did approve and was very willing to help Lili through the task of informing all of her other sisters who might think things were progressing a little too quickly following their mother's death.

No such help was needed when Lili went to tell Kitty Porter, however. Kitty was fit to burst with joy when Lili visited to tell her the news and invite her to the small service. Lili thought she might have bruised ribs after Kitty hugged her and was quite glad when her friend let go to ask, "Will there be any men coming from his side? I might get to nab a handsome Scotsman for myself!"

But there weren't. Ewan wrote to his sister as she was the closest family he had. Though delighted to discover he was finally getting married to the woman he had previously written about, she regretted that she couldn't come to the wedding, given that she had four small children to consider. Ewan only sent her an invitation out of courtesy, knowing that she would be unable to attend so neither he nor Lili were disappointed when her reply came. In fact, both were rather pleased when Ewan opened it and found a letter addressed, *To Lili Burnley (Not You, Ewan!)*. In the letter Ursula welcomed her to the family. She was polite but playful and rather funny, making Lili wish they could meet. Ursula told Lili she was, *"glad someone's finally going to be keeping an eye on him,"* and that, *"between us, we might make an honest man of him yet"*. She finished with the hope that they might visit one another in due course and a warning. *"Don't even try to feed him rhubarb,"* she wrote. *"I did once. There are still stains on my kitchen wall to prove it,"* then signed off, *"All my love and good wishes to you both, Ursula X."*

Ewan had anxiously watched Lili read. "Well?" he asked impatiently.

Lili grinned. "Not a fan of rhubarb, are we?"

The look of horror on Ewan's face was enough to make Lili cackle with glee. So much so that she almost didn't hear him say, "She didn't!!"

"She did. Explain!"

Ewan looked highly embarrassed. "It was an accident," he mumbled. "You know the way brothers and sisters behave. I don't know what she expected when she put a bowl of stewed rhubarb in front of me," he said crossly. "I went to throw it out to the hens and she made a grab for it and, well —" his skin flushed "— I swung it out of her reach and … all over the wall!"

Lili hooted and clapped while Ewan grinned ruefully.

"I really don't like rhubarb."

Lili suddenly looked aggrieved. "And here I was planning to make a big rhubarb tart for our wedding afters."

As it was, Lili didn't make anything for their wedding meal. Instead, all her sisters came together to create a beautiful spread which they all shared at the Gate House. Even though there were more than thirty people there, they had more than enough to go around. But while Lili ate what was put in front of her, it was a struggle. Everything that passed her lips seemed to stick in her throat then sit in her stomach, getting heavier and heavier as the evening progressed to night. Everyone else was in such high spirits that they didn't notice the bride's silence – everyone, that is, except Ewan. He watched her as she became more reserved, less likely to laugh, less likely to look in his direction.

Ewan himself was rather quiet and felt a little out of place among her family. Though he was acquainted with them, they all knew one another well and as the gaiety continued settled into familiar groupings. He would have liked to have had both Coxes from the top of the Lane to talk to but had engaged the boy to see to all his animals while they continued their celebration. Mother and son were not wealthy and, rather than expect a wedding gift from them, Ewan asked that the family's gift be to feed the sheep and cattle as it was the best thing anyone could do for him. However, it meant that, while Mrs Cox was there, her son missed the party at the house and left Ewan without his closest acquaintance.

The party didn't begin to wind down until several children were discovered fast asleep and their parents decided to call it a night. There were a few stragglers – including Kitty Porter – but otherwise the house was virtually cleared when all the youngsters were borne off by their respective guardians. Ewan and Lili had seen everyone off and now stood awkwardly a few feet apart, trying to look anywhere but at each other. Kitty, who had been the life and soul of the party, finally came bounding forward to say goodbye.

Hugging Ewan, much to his surprise, she whispered seriously, "Look after her," then she turned to Lili and hugged her too. "It will be *fine*," she breathed into her friend's ear. "Trust me."

Maybe Ewan wasn't the only one to notice Lili's expression after all.

Finally, Lili looked up and straight into Ewan's eyes. She nodded her head infinitesimally and went to fetch their coats. Ewan helped her with hers before proffering his arm and leading her out into the cold December air. There was no moon but there still seemed to be a glow to the world around them. As their eyes adjusted, they watched their breaths purl before them then disappear on the night wind. Neither spoke. This wasn't the sort of situation where musings on the general state of the weather would tide them over. Instead, they walked in silence.

When they got to the door, Ewan opened it but stopped Lili going in. "It's tradition." He gestured to Lili, arms out, palms up.

Lili smiled. "All right then."

Ewan lifted her up and carried her over the threshold to be greeted by a sleepy Georgie who padded over, head low, tail wagging slowly. Setting Lili down, Ewan lit a lamp by the stove so both could see to kneel either side of the dog and give her a rub. But soon Ewan was up and handing Lili up too. "Would you like me to take your coat?" he said quietly. The house was actually quite cosy. Someone had lit the stove.

Bless Mrs Cox, Ewan thought.

"Yes. Thank you." She shrugged out of her coat.

When he came back, Lili was still standing awkwardly where he left her.

"You can sleep in the spare room tonight if you don't feel … able," he managed to say. He hoped she did not hear the pleading tone in his voice wishing her not to take him up on the offer.

"No," she said dreamily, then more forcefully, "No. I want to."

"Are you sure?"

"Yes."

Ewan nodded. Taking her hand in both of his, he squeezed it tightly before kissing her knuckles and leading her up the stairs. "Wait here," he said at the head of the stairs before disappearing into the darkness to light another lamp by the bed. It cast a soft glow on the centre of the room but didn't reach the far corners. Lili stepped in and noticed that the room was very neat before her attention was drawn back to Ewan. He had removed his jacket and was beginning to unbutton his waistcoat. Lili's stomach dropped. It was really happening.

"Are you going to come here?" he asked softly.

She moved forward even though she was not aware she had told her feet to go anywhere.

"I need help," she mumbled, taking off her shoes. "Buttons in the back of the dress." Heather had done them up for her; twenty-three tiny buttons all with their own neat little loops. It was not a dress designed for getting into alone

– or out of alone.

Despite the size of his hands, his fingers were rather dexterous and while Lili took the pins from her hair, he undid the fastenings. In no time at all, Lili was sliding the garment off her shoulders so that she stood only in her slip and stockings. Picking it up, she draped it carefully over the chair where Ewan had thrown his coat. She felt movement close to her and watched his hand stretch forward to deposit trousers, socks and underwear on the chair as well.

His breath tickled her bare shoulder and she felt the hairs on her arms stand to attention. Gently, he trailed a hand down her side, feeling the warmth and curve of her body through the thin slip. She turned to see him standing only in his shirt and vest. Looking down, she took in long bony feet, and long, slightly hairy legs. He had grooves running up the outside of both thighs were the muscle bugled out from the otherwise skinny shanks.

Involuntarily, her fingers reached out and traced the groove from mid-thigh to bare buttock. Ewan slowly sucked air in through his teeth. Undoing the top few buttons of his shirt, he reached for the collar at the back and quickly whipped off both vest and shirt in one so that he stood completely naked in front of his wife.

Greedily, Lili's eyes raked again and again over his body but were constantly being drawn back to his arousal. Overall, though, he was quite something to behold. His skin was white with a smattering of hair. "You're very muscly," she said, impressed, though her voice was high-pitched.

She placed her palm on the centre of his chest but, taking it in his hand, Ewan moved it slightly to his left. She could feel his heart beating. "Yours," he whispered. "All of it," he gestured to his body, "is yours."

"And I suppose all of this is yours too," Lili said, gesturing to herself.

Ewan grinned a kind of impish, infectious grin before bending slightly to take the hem of Lili's slip in his hands. He asked with his eyes and she nodded before he slowly drew it up and away from her body until she stood in her underwear and stockings. Kneeling in front of her, he held her hips and rested his head on her belly. His hair tickled her sensitive skin. Lili placed a hand on his head like a mother giving a child her blessing. He kissed her belly, sending a shiver through her core. She wasn't sure how long they stayed like that before Ewan's hands tenderly crept downwards, pulling her remaining items of clothing with him. He got to his feet again, hands once more on her hips, tugging her towards him. She went gladly, her hands just as eager to discover his body. Their lips locked and their hands wandered, feeling so many unexplored places on each other's body. Ewan discovered that Lili's ribs and spine were quite prominent while Lili found a star-shaped scar on his abdomen. As she stroked it questioningly, Ewan answered, "The War," before adding, "I was shot." Lili almost drew back but he caught her and held her fast. "I'm still here," he shrugged.

Unsure whether the goose pimples that covered Lili's skin were from the cold or something else (and, if he was honest with himself, because he couldn't wait much longer), he guided her over to the bed before throwing back the cover. Lili cast a wary look at the exposed mattress then another at Ewan. He tried to keep his expression as neutral as possible. She had to make this decision herself.

She had to do it and not just for him. Desire burned bright and hot within her and, if nothing else, her own curiosity was driving her forward. She had to know what it felt like.

Climbing in beside her, Ewan enfolded her in his arms once more. She responded, pressing her front flush against his. She almost recoiled when her cold skin touched his. The heat! He burned like a furnace, instantly heating their small pocket in the icy sheets.

"You're so warm!" she smiled.

"You're so cold!" He shivered for effect, making their bodies rub against one another. That sobered them both rather quickly.

"Make sure not to tickle me," she warned. "I might end up kicking you. By accident of course."

"Of course," he nodded in mock seriousness before his chest began to vibrate.

"What's funny?" she asked, a little put out.

"I once heard a little boy call this 'lying down and tickling'." He grinned. "So I can't promise not to tickle you."

They both sniggered about it for a while afterwards, between kisses and the explorations of wandering limbs. Their legs seemed to become entwined until neither knew which where their own. Finally, Ewan's hand found its way between Lili's legs. She stopped breathing, her entire body going rigid. "It's alright," he whispered. She nodded, believing him as his fingers touched her. She gasped involuntarily at his touch. It was so alien, so intimate, so arousing. She watched his face as he watched hers, gauging her reaction. But soon she lost sight of his face, her eyes half closed, revelling in the sensation, only aware of what his fingers were doing. It was, hypnotic, overwhelming, too cold and too hot all at the same time. She had no idea intimacy would feel as glorious as this.

Ewan smiled crookedly, greedily, at the shining look in her eyes, the heave of her chest. She didn't speak. She didn't need to. Her body told him she wanted him. And he was driven half wild with the need for her, though he did everything within his power to control himself. He had anticipated this moment for so long and now, finally, it was here. He could not have waited much longer and neither could she. They both knew it was time.

Without another word, Ewan rose up, rolling her onto her back as he did so. He placed his hands beside her shoulders, supporting his own weight entirely. Lili opened her legs, her feet finding patches of ice-cold space under the bedclothes. They weren't cold for long.

She felt him at the apex of her thighs before he slowly pushed inside her. She didn't make any noise but screwed up her face as she felt the pinch of pain. It wasn't excruciating but neither was it pleasant. He moved again, rocking forward, making her move her legs wider apart. Unsure, but allowing instinct to take hold, she wrapped her limbs around his, pulling him into her. The feeling was beginning to get better – less pain, more pleasure. She thought vaguely that she might, at another time, really enjoy the sensation.

It took everything Ewan had to go slowly. But he would do it for her. His forearms gave way so that he rested on his elbows, the length of his body stretching the length of hers. He could feel her breasts heave as they pressed into his chest. His eyes were locked on hers – nothing would have made him look away. She was his. She was completely and utterly his. And he was hers. There wasn't anything on earth that would stop him from watching this woman move underneath him just as he moved. At the first sound she made – a sharp "*Ah!*" which made her break eye contact and throw her head back exposing her long neck to him – he gave way. His motions became quicker, more vigorous. Lili's nails dug into his back. As she writhed underneath him, he finished, collapsing onto her in exhaustion and ecstasy.

So stunned by the experience, Lili barely noticed the large man crushing her chest as both of them gasped for air, limbs moving uselessly as the sensations washed through their bodies. Eventually, she became aware of the pressure on her chest and, when gentle pushing didn't work, gave him a good shove in the ribs to displace him.

The action seemed to bring him around somewhat as he rolled off, apologising profusely though his words did seem a little fuzzy round the edges. "Sorry, sorry," he repeated as he attempted to locate all of his limbs. "Sorry. It was – I shouldn't – it –" He stopped himself and closed his eyes, trying to rearrange his garbled thoughts. "It should be better than that," he managed.

"Well, then it will be," said Lili, lovingly. She reached forward for a long and tender kiss. "Next time," she smiled.

Chapter 30

Ewan wasn't normally a heavy sleeper but when he woke the next morning it was like trying to drag his mind and body through mud. He was disorientated, confused. He couldn't quite work out were his legs and arms were. In fact, he couldn't even feel one of his arms which worried him vaguely – but not enough to make him try and figure out why. He was also much warmer than usual which was odd considering it was December. There was also something tickling his cheek and shoulder. But he couldn't muster the energy to do anything about that either.

Then suddenly, with his eyes still closed, he came to. The dead arm, the heat, the hair (because it *was* hair) tickling his cheek. He knew. Cracking an eyelid, he found himself staring at the curve of a brunette head. His right arm was sandwiched between the mattress and a sleeping torso. Her body was flush against his and he could feel the damp, sticky heat of where their flesh pressed together.

Lili. His wife.

She was still asleep. Breathing softly and steadily, his other arm rose and fell with the movements of her chest. He could feel her heartbeat – slow, steady, content. He stretched his neck a little and breathed in the scent of her hair then kissed it gently without waking her. Thinking about how he might free his trapped arm, also without waking her, he heard a banging downstairs. Someone was knocking at the door.

Ewan realised this had awoken him. He hadn't been aware of the sound at the time but hearing it again convinced him that it was the only reason he was awake in the first place. Someone had knocked and wasn't going away. Maybe there was something wrong on the farm. The Cox boy had offered to do the work that morning (he was somewhat embarrassed by offering but it had not stopped him) so perhaps it was him at the door. However, that didn't mean Ewan wasn't put out by the intrusion. It was the morning after his bloody wedding night, for Christ's sake!

He dragged himself out of the bed as gently as possible so as not to disturb his wife. He felt a little thrill even just thinking the word. Lili grumbled sleepily, her hand searching abstractedly for his arms before settling back down. Cheekily, Ewan had a quick peek at her naked form then tucked the blanket around her one-handed to keep her warm. Shaking his dead arm to try and get some feeling back into it, he grabbed a pair of trousers as another impatient rap echoed from below. Angrily shoving his feet into his trouser legs and unable to locate a shirt, he descended the stairs with nothing but the lower half of his body clothed.

The sound was coming from the back door right at the bottom of the stairs. It was the door to the yard so the probability that something was wrong on the farm was beginning to look more likely. Sometimes animals could be so inconvenient.

Another knock came just as Ewan hit the last step of the stairs. Now really annoyed, he wrenched open the door making the hinges screech. He had just enough time to think that he really must oil the hinges when a blast of freezing air hit him in the chest making his skin pimple with gooseflesh. It almost burned it was so cold. And who should be standing on the back step muffled in a coat that looked far too big for him?

"*Bertie?*"

Bertie looked miffed. "I'd think now you're my brother-in-law you'd do me the courtesy of using my proper name," he said irritably.

Equally irritated, Ewan was not in the mood for his gripes. If it had been something to do with the animals, he might have accepted the need for his presence. But watching Bertie lolling outside the door without any kind of urgency made Ewan's blood boil, despite the cold.

"Why?" asked Ewan, fighting the urge to grab Bertie by the lapels of his coat and go nose to nose with him. "Lili calls you Bertie, I'll call you Bertie. So, *Bertie*, what do you want?"

Ewan got some pleasure out of watching Bertie chew the inside of his cheek. He could almost see the cogs turning in the young man's brain, considering whether it was a good idea to challenge an aggravated, semi-clad Scotsman twice his size. He seemed to think better of it. That didn't mean he wasn't going to stick his oar in a little bit.

"I was just out round the yard. Got some nice-looking sheep there."

Ewan was getting cold but he was damned if he was going to start shivering in front of this little pup. He grunted in reply.

Seeing that he wasn't going to get anything out of Ewan, Bertie conceded. "I want to speak to my sister. Lilian.'" He said it importantly as if he wasn't to be denied.

Ewan stared. "Well, I don't have any of your other sisters in here."

Bertie bristled but managed to push past it. "Nevertheless, I want to see her."

"Why?"

"Just get her, would you?" Bertie snapped.

"No." Ewan tried to keep the smugness out of his voice.

"*No?*"

"She's not up yet."

"Not up yet?" He looked genuinely shocked. "But Lilian's always up early." Bertie couldn't seem to fathom her post-wedding torpor. "Just go and get her there. She'll come down." He looked like he might make a dive past Ewan up the stairs to get her himself, but Ewan blocked the door by casually leaning against the door frame.

"Not unless you tell me why." Ewan folded his arms to ward off the cold. Despite the temperature, he was rather enjoying this.

Bertie looked like he might continue arguing but then gave in. "I don't know where she keeps the breakfast things," he said, sticking out his chin defiantly.

Ewan gawped. "Did you look for them?"

"No," he said defensively. "I came here to ask her. Maybe get her to come down and do the breakfast."

Adam's apple bobbing with supressed laughter (it was that or thump Bertie), Ewan closed his eyes to compose himself before giving an answer. "Bertie, tell you what, you go back down there to the house, have a shufty round the kitchen and I'll bet anything you'll find what you're looking for. And once you know where it is, you'll never have to look again."

Incensed, Bertie's eyes bulged. He looked like he might have an aneurism if he stood there much longer. But Ewan had lost interest. He had made his point and now all he wanted to do was get warm again. He knew a good way of doing that, he thought happily.

Buoyed by the prospect, he smiled crookedly at the man on his doorstep said, "Bye, bye, Bertie," and closed the door in his brother-in-law's face.

He was back up the stairs like a shot. Stripping off his trousers and dumping them on the floor, he slid into bed as quickly as he could, his body drawn to the warmth of another's. Happily pressing his chilled flesh to the delicious heat, he wasn't quite prepared for the reaction he got.

There was a strangled gasp from in front of him and suddenly the only body part connected with his was an elbow planted squarely in the softness of his diaphragm. Promptly, Ewan gasped himself. It was a proper clout to the abdomen that left him curled up and struggling for breath, trying not to retch though there was nothing in his stomach to come up. Distantly, he heard what sounded like the agitated gobble of a turkey. As the pain receded, however, he realised it was a female voice saying "*Sorry-sorry-sorry-sorry*" as a hand agitatedly stroked his head. He moaned softly as his breath came more easily. It still hurt but the initial shock was over and he was beginning to enjoy the sensation of frantic hands skimming his hair and face as Lili continued to apologise for her assault on him. Moaning again for effect, he thought he might have a little amusement with her sympathies.

He was right.

"Oh God, Ewan – I'm so sorry! – where does it hurt?" she asked.

Groaning, he gestured to his stomach. He almost gave up the ruse when she threw off the covers. He *was* still cold after all. Quickly, however, he came to the conclusion that it was worth getting cold to see Lili Burnley in the daylight and completely naked in his bed. She hovered over him, long brown hair trailing over her shoulders, pale skin almost luminescent in the chilly blue light of the morning. She was already getting goose pimples on her skin and he longed to rub his hands over her flesh under the pretext of warming her up but really so he could feel her body. And he longed to touch her breasts. He hadn't done that yet and he wanted to so badly.

Still trying to drag herself from the haze of sleep while simultaneously experiencing the shock and thrill of waking up next to Ewan, Lili did the only thing that came into her head: she bent and kissed his stomach. It was, after all, what you did to appease injured children and at that moment it seemed appropriate. Yet it didn't seem to have the desired effect. Ewan continued to groan. However, he did point slightly further up his torso. Obliging, Lili bowed once more and lightly kissed his chest only to hear another moan. She looked up just in time to see Ewan's fingers skate up his breastbone and come to rest on his neck. So that's where this was going. Lili hummed a little chuckle under her breath and kissed his neck. But before his hands could move again, on impulse, she straddled him, making his eyes fly open as she lay the length of her body along his. As her lips pressed against his, he opened them. Their tongues met, knowing instinctively how and where to move. His hands found her soft cool buttocks and squeezed, pulling her up so she had to arch her back to continue their kiss. Her breasts brushed against his chest as he moved her making him groan into her mouth. But this time it was nothing to do with pain. Perfectly positioned, he gently guided her down onto him. He shuddered and broke off the kiss. Lili stilled so he held her, guiding her movement. She began to move without him and sat up a little.

Ewan couldn't resist. Though he kept one hand on Lili's hip, the other found its way to one of her breasts. Soft, warm, it felt divine under his palm, just as he imagined her breasts would. And they were his to touch and kiss and fondle from here on out. You're a lucky bugger, Cameron, he thought before the sights and sensations took over, this time bringing both of them to the point of pure ecstasy and beyond.

Chapter 31

Married life suited Lili. Free from the constraints of her detractors, she found a joy in life she had never conceived of. In the house, she was her own mistress. She did not hear her mother's or Bertie's disapproval. It wasn't that they were especially cruel. It was simply a case of when Lili did something right, they said nothing but when she did wrong, they were quick to criticise. Of course it wasn't right when Lilian did it. What else were they to expect? The benefit of this, however, was it created an individual who strove for perfection. It could have gone either way: their nit-picking could have destroyed her confidence but instead it motivated her. The better she became at things, the less they could criticise. It was her defence mechanism and it had served her relatively well. Now, as Ewan's wife, she experienced the wonder that was an acknowledgement of her efforts. Each morning they woke together and each morning she made breakfast. When she placed the plate on the table, he said "Thank you." Sometimes he wrapped his arm around her waist, patted her bottom affectionately or gave her a kiss. But what really mattered were those two little words. They made Lili's heart glow with happiness. He would never know how much it meant to her. All he ever saw was a small smile, but it was enough for both of them to be happy for much of the morning.

Though neither admitted it, both had worried that the first flush of love would leave them once married life began. It did, but it was replaced by something more profound, more constant. Neither were disappointed by their new intimacy with one another. On the contrary. And it wasn't just when in the house. Lili, because of her upbringing and her nature, spent a lot of her time outdoors. Seeing this, Ewan was only too happy to involve his wife in the running of the farm. He asked her opinions, discussed decisions and listened to what she had to say. She was tall and strong for a woman and was almost as proficient as he was at handling the animals. Of course, Lili also had other things to do so she couldn't spend all her time on the farm. There was far too much to do in the house and garden, as well as almost daily visits down to the Gate House to make sure Bertie didn't starve. He was still her brother after all.

Following the incident the morning after their wedding, Bertie hadn't been to Ewan's (now Ewan and Lili's). Lili had laughed, more out of embarrassment than anything else, though she was angry when Ewan told her what had happened. She knew Bertie would not make things easy for them but, now that she was in a happier situation, she felt it was important to maintain a civil relationship with her brother, even if it was only because he was their neighbour. They came to an unspoken agreement that Lili would stock his cupboards the same way she did her own and at the end of every month, Bertie would pay off any bills Lili had put on his accounts in the local shops. Once he had a wife, however, there would be no need for Lili to provide for him but until then she bought him things she knew were easy to cook and left instructions for him when she thought he might struggle. And whenever she did some baking for herself and Ewan, she always made a little extra and brought it down to the Gate House.

She found it rather strange when delivering goods to the

house. She expected to feel a certain amount of sadness every time she entered the familiar kitchen. Instead, the space now felt alien to her. She didn't belong anymore. Not to the Gate House at least. Ewan's house felt more of a home to her now. Although that was possibly because Bertie did nothing to give the illusion of a lived-in space whereas, between them, Ewan and Lili did what they could to make their house welcoming. And they had a lot of people to welcome. Once they were married and everyone recovered from the shock there was a stream of visitors, well-wishers and snoops to keep the newly wedded couple on their toes for the first month of their marriage. It was quite the novelty for the locals to finally see inside Ewan Cameron's house. Billy Murphy had not been famed for his housekeeping skills so it was always a curiosity whether Mr Cameron improved the place or lived in similar squalor to the house's previous tenant. Needless to say, the locals where quite impressed and, possibly, gained even more respect for the Scot.

It was a good thing too since Lili Burnley was something of a local favourite. It wasn't everyone who could marry the neighbour just a few months after burying their mother and get away with it. Such speedy marriages were not the done thing but, for Lili, people were willing to make an exception. They liked Evelyn Burnley's daughter simply because she was the antithesis of her mother. Evelyn had often been irksome and hard to stomach but her daughter was always kind, polite and willing to stay out of other people's affairs. Locals admired her for it and were therefore much more inclined to overlook some of the more controversial things she did. However, knowing that the newlyweds were the sort to keep themselves to themselves, most people left the Camerons to get on with their lives. The only regular visitors were Lili's family and Kitty Porter but even they did not call often.

Of course, Ewan and Lili had to return these visits so, in the lead up to Christmas, they spent several evenings with other people even though they would have preferred to spend them alone together. Christmas itself was to be spent in Heather's house as she insisted that Lili, Ewan and Bertie came to their get-together. She thought Lili might struggle having her first Christmas without their mother even if she was with a husband she loved. Heather was also of the view that Christmas was a time for families, especially children, and knowing from conversations with Lili that Ewan had spent many Christmases on his own, his new sister-in-law thought he might appreciate and enjoy benefits of marrying into a big family.

Lili was, at first, a little worried about how Ewan might deal with such a family situation. When Lili met him, he had avoided social occasions. But now she realised that fear rather than natural shyness made him keep to himself so she was hopeful he would enjoy a family Christmas. It was arranged, therefore, that on the twenty-fifth Bertie would drive them to Heather and Trevor's house. Though she looked forward to it, Lili prayed that neither her husband or Bertie would say anything to antagonise the other. Her brother was easily offended and Ewan (when it came to Bertie) had a quick temper. Any clashes between them could ruin the day entirely for everyone. Indeed, the only way Lili had found of antagonising her husband – unwittingly, of course – was to talk about her brother. Ewan, it seemed, was willing to accept other peoples' shortcomings but when it came to Bertie Burnley there was nothing that would induce him to think civilly of his brother-in-law. The aversion was strong and she had no urge to fight her brother's corner. Attempting a cordial relationship between Ewan and Bertie was not worth the damage it might do to Lili's marriage. So she kept quiet and hoped.

As luck would have it, her hopes were answered. They were in the car on the way to church before going to Heather's when Bertie informed them that after dinner he was invited to Wren and Mrs Charlton's. The relief Lili felt was immense but she was also a little hurt – for Heather's sake mostly – that their brother chose not to spend Christmas with his family. However, deep down she suspected their day would be the better for his absence even if her thoughts did make her feel a little guilty.

Knowing of the friction between Ewan and Bertie, Heather shrewdly placed them at opposite ends of the table so that distance would provide some small barrier against their animosity. Between the cheerful mood of the day and the attempts of everyone to get along rather than ruin it for one another, their dinner and the hours that followed were almost as joyous as Lili's wedding day. There was such warmth in the house that everyone was infected by it, cocooned in a bubble of pure happiness for the remainder of the day. It also turned out that Ewan had something of a way with children and, rather than spend the afternoon talking farming with Trevor as Lili expected him to, he played with the boys and generally had very little time for anyone else.

Lili watched, fascinated by this previously unseen side to her husband. He liked children. She could see the glow in his eyes as he sat on the floor, his gangly limbs crossed just as Lili's nephews sat cross-legged in front of the fire putting together a jigsaw they received for Christmas. But as much as Lili watched him, he watched the boys. They seemed to enthral him – to the extent that they began to tease him for not making any headway with the jigsaw. It wasn't long before the gentle teasing turned into wrestling and the wrestling into a chase around the house then a chase outside around the farm. By the time it was dark their good clothes were spattered in mud and covered in awns of hay and straw. If it hadn't been Christmas, Heather might have given the boys a good telling-off when they arrived back to the house.

As they travelled home with Bertie later on, Lili thought Ewan was far quieter than usual. She put it down to sharing a car with her brother, but Ewan's silence continued after they left Bertie behind at his house and started up the lane for home.

Searching his face, Lili saw he was preoccupied. Still holding his hand, she swung herself in front of him, blocking his way. He stopped, looking down but not really seeing her.

She cupped his cheek in her hand. "What is it?"

He shook his head infinitesimally and forced a small smile. "Nothing."

"Ewan!" Lili warned.

"Just … I enjoyed spending time with the boys and …"

"And you were wondering if you'd ever have any of your own," she finished for him. He didn't reply. "The thought of it scares me half to death," she admitted quietly.

"Thought of what?"

"Of looking after a tiny human being. Of it growing inside you, bringing it into the world, caring for it, feeding it, clothing it, teaching it. Doesn't it scare you?"

"Yes," he admitted. "But not enough to make me not want it. And if you think about it, we'd likely make better parents than most. Although … although if anything were to happen to you because of it …" he shuddered, "I'd never forgive myself."

"I'm sturdier than most women," Lili answered a little huffily.

He smiled at her pique. "I know that, hen," he said soothingly, giving her a crooked smile that quickly slipped off his face as he looked away. "But it has nothing to do with sturdiness. Look at what happened to your own mother."

She had told Ewan of the circumstances of Bertie's birth before and was not one bit pleased by him bringing it up now. "She lived, didn't she?" she answered shortly, turning away and beginning to walk on up the lane. It was difficult to effectively walk away from Ewan. In a few long strides he was matching her gait step for step.

"Don't make something into an argument when it doesn't have to be," he said evenly.

"I'm not making it into an argument, I'm telling it like it is. Childbirth has its risks. But look at the rewards. And," she added, "I don't suppose there would be anything we could do to stop it happening if it's meant to."

"Except abstinence," Ewan said, wiggling his eyebrows, a smile playing about his lips.

Lili looked serious. "I suppose that's an option," she mused before squawking with laughter at the look of horror on Ewan's face. She bumped their shoulders together. "I don't think either of us would be keen on that."

"No." He was still recovering from Lili's teasing. There was a split second where she had really worried him. But that was part of Lili's charm. She could whip the rug out from under his feet just as he had seen a French waiter do with a tablecloth covered in delph when in a café near Grenoble during the War. The thing about his wife was that she could whip the cloth back into place just as easily and make you laugh about it afterwards. She had that wonderful quality of being safe but also unpredictable. You never knew where her mind would take you but he always trusted her no matter the destination. In its own way, it was quite thrilling – that swooping sensation as the stomach dropped. He loved the jittery feeling of the adrenaline rush. It was part of the reason he had enjoyed being a soldier, though he very rarely admitted it to himself, let alone anyone else. But Ewan didn't want to be a soldier again. He finally felt that the weight of his past was receding into the distance. There was now a future to look forward to. A future with Lili. And he was quite happy with that.

Chapter 32

Bertram had lied.

As he sat alone in his house on Christmas Day, a half-empty bottle of Jameson's whiskey by the leg of his chair, he told himself that it was not a genuine lie. Only the omitting of a truth. Yes, he had been invited to spend Christmas afternoon with Wren and Mrs Charlton. But the invitation had been withdrawn – through no fault of his own – which meant he would have to spend the day with his sisters instead. Or would he? It took him no time at all to ponder over the choice of telling his sisters he, in fact, had another (better) invitation. Their company made him uncomfortable to begin with and, while he could talk farming to their husbands, after a while he always felt they were talking down to him. Both men had almost twenty years on him and he was always of the opinion that they liked to put him in his place and make him feel his youth.

The other issue was that if he told his family he was not spending the afternoon with his future spouse, he would be bombarded with questions and one thing he really didn't want was to tell them the reason the invitation had been rescinded. He did not want to disclose the reason because it would have mortified him to say it. It made him angry just to think about it.

The mother of his future bride was to be committed to an asylum for the mentally ill. Somewhere like St Senan's, he thought – the nuthouse above Enniscorthy.

Wren had spoken to him during their acquaintance of her mother's instability, told him a little of her past behaviour. But he dismissed most of what she said, forgetting almost all of it by the next day. It was the fancy of a little girl, the exaggeration of an overactive imagination with a penchant for melodrama. He had not given any credence to it.

On the day of Lilian's wedding to their neighbour, he had worked himself up into a truly foul humour as he stood waiting and waiting at the back of the church to escort Wren and the old lady to their seats. But neither turned up and neither sent any word to explain their absence. He had glowed with embarrassment as he scuttled down the aisle to his seat just before his eldest sister entered. He was sure everybody was looking at him because they somehow knew he had been left in the lurch.

Afterwards, almost everyone from the service headed back to Bertram's house. There they were joined by more distant acquaintances and relatives before the revelries really began. It was then that Wren arrived. For some reason, she had hitched a lift with Bertram's cousins who lived in Enniscorthy instead of travelling with Astrid who was also invited to the after-party.

The moment she paid the required tribute to Ewan and Lilian, Wren sought out Bertram, grabbed his wrist and hauled him off to one of the empty rooms in the house. Shocked by the girl's sudden forcefulness, Bertram followed without complaint, though a moment before he had been planning to give her the cold shoulder for leaving him alone during the wedding ceremony. As soon as they were away from the celebrations Wren pasted herself against the door, closing it with a snap.

"It's my mother," she said without preamble.

Bertram had never seen heard her so verbose. It was what kept him quiet throughout her account of the events that had occurred in her family during the last number of days. But what disconcerted him most was the blankness of her face, her toneless delivery and her unseeing stare which picked a point on the far wall and hardly seemed to move the entire time she spoke. She said what she said without feeling, numb.

Wren had kept in contact with her father and siblings throughout her time with Astrid so was fairly well informed of the family's progress without her. Having taken control of the maternal needs of the family, Felicity appeared to be coping well. The children were taken to school every morning, appropriately dressed. The house, though not as orderly as when Wren managed it, was quite habitable. Meals were edible though, again, not quite up to the standard of their former cook. Eric related all this information to his daughter in a series of letters, painstakingly written every few days in tiny cramped, barely decipherable writing. He seemed to struggle constantly with trying to balance the love he had for his wife with the affection he had for Wren. He did not want to belittle the care she had taken of the family while his wife had been indisposed. Yet he also did not want to deride his wife's efforts though they were often flawed. Felicity was making a monumental effort to regain her hold on the family – to garner their approval, respect and love which would aid her recovery. But she was not always successful and it was these failings, which built up bit by bit, gnawing away at her fragile self-confidence, that finally made her crack again.

This time it was different. Felicity did not rage or threaten her children. Her routine did not change. Eric came home to a clean house, a cooked meal and a supposedly happy wife and children. When night came, he and his wife went to bed. When he woke the next morning, he gave her sleeping form a peck on the cheek and went to work.

Felicity got up, woke the children, prepared them for school, fed them breakfast, then set off, a small hand in each of hers as she walked them to school.

It was at that point the routine began to unravel.

Instead of turning left at a crossroads to bring the children to the schoolhouse, she passed straight through, apparently oblivious to her mistake.

"Mammy? *Mammy!*" Artie had tugged insistently on his mother's hand, believing in the first place that he was far too old to be holding it.

It took a moment before Felicity cast her vague, empty eyes over her son, a trace of a smile constantly playing on her lips. "*Mmm?*" she questioned, pulled from the deepest of reveries, knowing she had been spoken to but at a loss as to what was said.

"Where are we going?" Artie asked.

Olivia was simply enjoying the unfamiliar surroundings and looking for any cats that might be pottering about the vicinity. Olivia liked cats. She wondered why she had not seen any today. Maybe it was too cold. Her own exposed knees, bare above her long socks, were stinging with the biting chill of the early December morning air. But then did cats feel the cold? She thought they must.

Felicity's mind seemed to be drifting as much as her daughter's since it took her a good deal of time to answer Artie. When she did, she simply said, "You'll see … surprise."

They continued toward the centre of the town – Artie with a growing sense of unease, Olivia frustrated that she had only seen one cat and had not been close enough to pet it and Felicity, it appeared, thinking nothing at all but determinedly continuing on nonetheless. The little boy kept up an almost constant stream of protest. His teacher would be cross. Daddy would be cross. He had a maths test. He was cold. Oli was cold. But Felicity just smiled benignly and muttered, "*Mmm,*" and "Not far now."

Rather than follow the curve of the road towards the town's main street, they followed another road parallel to it. The back doors of several shops were to their left and to their right were the empty façades of warehouses with various piles of debris stacked in front of some and nothing at all in front of others. The cold air and a fine mist drifted up the empty street, curling around them, filling their lungs with a chill that caught their breath with a stab like tiny knives. They met no one as their feet echoed on the uneven square cobbles that marked their way. Artie had never been down this street. He was exploring a new part of his own town and though he was still on edge, knowing that something peculiar was going on, the curiosity of all little boys got the better of him as he studied his unfamiliar surroundings. Once they came to the end of the street, there was plenty more for the two children to look at, though Oli was a shade put out there were still no cats about. Instead, they watched as the hulking forms of ocean-going fishing boats appeared out of the fog, rattling and creaking up against the dock. Their olfactory systems were overloaded with smells of the sea, fish and the rotting flesh of dead sea creatures. Clouds of mist billowed around the docks – sometimes painting the world white, sometimes drifting off so everything was visible if a little hazy round the edges.

Felicity didn't see any of this. She proceeded with as much purpose as before, seemingly knowing her way, never breaking step. Though the place appeared to be deserted, there were a number of men gliding around the dock and slithering over their vessels as if they were part of the metal, part of the wood, part of the dirt and grime, part of the sea. Many of them registered the presence of a strange woman and two children but her movements were so focused, so certain, that none of them disturbed her even if they did glance enquiringly in her direction. But the glances became plain stares when they watched the woman approach the edge of the dock. She never paused but slowly began to disappear from view, first her feet, then her calves. She was descending the stone steps built into the quayside along the river's edge, towing the children with her. The little girl seemed to follow unquestioningly but the boy on the top step was fidgeting and pulling against his mother. There were some sharp words from the mother and she let go of his hand and gave a great heave on his winter coat. Perched on the edge, he overbalanced, arms flailing, and disappeared from view.

All anyone heard was a high-pitched shriek as he plunged into the black waters of the river-mouth.

It was as if a switch had been flicked. The little boy's petrified scream shocking them into consciousness. Men who had been watching proceedings in a dazed fashion were suddenly roused.

The little girl began to wail. Both she and her mother had descended below the level of the dock, the only hint of their whereabouts given by the shrill pipe of the child as she screamed, "*Mammy! Help Artie! Mammy! Mammy!*"

A fisherman stripped off his outer garments on the edge of the dock and jumped into the river just in front of where the boy's head was bobbing with frighteningly less frequency. Catching the boy in his heavy coat with a school satchel on his back, he dragged him to the surface. Some other fishermen threw a rope and float into the water and hauled the man and child to safety.

Felicity had taken her youngest child in her arms and simply continued to walk down the steps until her feet found no more. At first her large coat and skirt billowed out on the surface of the water, buoying her up so that she drifted out, away from the edge, floating. But then her garments began to flounder, fighting for air as they became water-logged, surging around her in a steadily darkening mass.

The little girl continued to scream.

Yet before Felicity's contented, impassive face disappeared below the waterline, a hook caught the collar of her coat, dragging her back to the surface, back to the dockside, back to reality. The child was pried from her grasping arms and hustled away to be stripped of her sodden outer garments and swaddled in a heavy blanket. She joined her brother on the dockside and clung to his outer wrappings just as he clung to hers, rubbing his hands absently up and down to make sure his sister was all there. Watching with a dull understanding of what was unfolding before his eyes as he clung to Olivia, the thought that he was definitely going to miss his mathematics test drifted across Artie's consciousness and he felt a surge of disappointment.

But then his mother started to scream.

It took two men to drag the unwilling Felicity Stevens up onto the steps. As soon as she realised her ambitions had been thwarted, her veneer of calm cracked and disintegrated into a thousand tiny pieces. Her frozen lungs inflated and the sound that came out was filled with the anger, fear, sadness and frustration of someone who believed they had reached the end of the line and were on the verge of absolute freedom – a release from her torment. She had failed, or rather, she had been foiled. These men, these strangers who did not understand her weariness with life had denied her the ultimate release. And she let them know it. As they carried her up the steps she began to squirm, to kick, to convulse, screaming all the while, throwing her body about with the abandon of one who cared little for it. The men clung on grimly, trying not to lose their own footing as they were hurled from side to side on the narrow ledge by Felicity's thrashing body. They were all too relieved and none-too gentle when they were high enough to deposit her flailing form on the dock.

The children cowered away from the creature that had been their mother, huddling back into the waiting arms of a middle-aged fisherman with strong, sure hands who held them close. He had children and a wife of his own. He held them until they were taken from him by some medical people and bundled into the back of a waiting ambulance. He never saw the children again, but often wondered in idle moments what had happened to them.

The children were brought to hospital where they were treated for shock and exposure. The December waters of the river had been freezing. Artie assumed they would see their father soon, but it was not until late in the evening that he arrived, looking ten years older than he had the day before. He had been dealing with his wife. Despite what she had done, it was still her he was drawn to first. On arrival, having made sure all three of them were still alive, he sought out Felicity, taking her hand in his when he finally found where she was in the labyrinthine corridors of the hospital. But she had snatched her fingers from his grasp and turned away.

In that moment Eric's world collapsed. He was angry, distraught, but most of all he felt guilty. More than half of his family had almost drowned that morning and he never saw it coming. He had conditioned himself into believing everything in his world had been fixed, that his wife was healed, contented even, and all it took was the banishment of his eldest daughter. But all was not well. All he had done was lie to himself, ignoring the signs of dissatisfaction and it had almost cost the lives of three people he loved. Coming to an awareness of that knowledge, he realised he could not do it anymore. He could not sustain a family only in name. He could not hold together a neat little world through will alone. He had willed his wife sane, willed her to have children and now felt the absolute guilt of forcing someone so unstable to beget his offspring. He wanted the evidence washed away. He wanted a clean slate. He wanted his folly removed from his gaze. However, when he eventually gave up trying to cajole a response from his silent wife and went to see his children, his viewpoint shifted a little.

The children had to leave. It was as much for their benefit as for his. For one thing, his wife was not going to be able to look after them. She wasn't capable of looking after herself. He had to work and since his job was not well paid, he couldn't afford someone to care for them. He could have asked Wren to come home but she was supposed to be getting married and, though he dearly wished to call her home, he was not going to deny her a chance at the happiness she never found in her own family. And, having no relatives on his own side of the family with the means or the inclination to take on two young children, he looked to his wife's side of the family and began to reconsider the offer made many months before.

Eric knew Astrid Charlton was rich. But he would not demean himself further by asking a relative to bankroll childcare for what remained of his family. This rich lady, however, had offered to take on the responsibility of all of his children – to house them, clothe them, educate them and generally give them a life he never could. She had offered him a solution to his family problems months before but his pride and misguided belief that all would be well made him reject her aid. And two of his children almost died because of it. It was time to swallow his own misgivings and to give all his children – not just his eldest – the chance they deserved, away from the damaging influences of their mother. And away from him.

The next morning, he made the telephone call.

Chapter 33

Astrid Charlton always answered her own telephone since she did not trust anyone else to do it. It was a good thing too given what her nephew-in-law related to her of events the previous day. Yet, rather than accuse his wife for her attempts to kill both herself and their children, Eric simply told the lady that Felicity had a turn and unknowingly tried to harm Artie and Olivia. He was still Felicity's husband and, despite everything, he still loved her. He managed, however, to convey the urgent need for the removal of his children without blackening his wife's character too much. Before he ended his telephone call, the basic arrangements were made.

Wren came down to the hall in her dress for Lili's wedding when the telephone rang, knowing it was her father on the other end of the line. She had expected her aunt to defer to her after the required pleasantries but as the conversation continued and Astrid's features became drawn and her pallor turned a sick grey colour, Wren found herself sliding down the wall opposite the telephone table to sit on the floor as Astrid gave monosyllabic ejaculations every now and again.

When the conversation was clearly drawing to a close the girl looked up, catching Astrid's eye.

"Before you go, Eric, do you want to talk to Wren?" she asked, nodding at the questioning look in the girl's eyes.

Wren scrabbled to her feet, ready to take the receiver but then a flash of annoyance crossed her aunt's face. She thought it was directed at her. But it was at her father. "No?" she said sharply, and even in that one little word, Wren heard the Germanic bite of her great aunt's accent that was so often hidden under gentle sibilance. It only emerged when Astrid was tired or angry. She was most definitely angry. The conversation ended quickly with a few clipped phrases and then a cold, "Good bye."

It fell to Astrid to inform her charge of what had happened over the last two days. Though she could provide few details, she told Wren as gently as she could about her mother's breakdown and her subsequent attempts on the two youngest Stevens children. Knowing so little, Astrid coloured the story with the suggestion that Felicity had physically attacked her own children because that was what she believed had happened. And Wren was not going to contradict her. For one, the girl was in shock and, for another, she knew it wasn't beyond the realms of possibility that her mother would attack the children.

They began to discuss their plan of action for the next day and also raking over what little information they had, analysing it and making conjectures as to what really occurred, the state of the two children and whatever else they could dredge up. Wren admitted more than she ever had about her previous life with her mother. Though she did not realise it, she had wilfully blocked out that part of her life when she left it behind. When she thought of home, she thought of Artie, of Olivia, of her father. Her mother hardly ever figured in her musings.

Ruminating on what she now knew, Wren found tears trickling down her face. She did not feel them coming but once she was aware of their presence there seemed to be no way of stopping them. She cried for herself, she cried for her parents but most of all she cried for Artie and Olivia. She felt so hurt by what she saw as her mother's betrayal. Wren had taken such good care of her brother and sister when her mother could not. Yet when she handed over the reins to her mother – the person who was supposedly the only one truly able to care for them – they had almost died. She was angry too. Angry at her mother for her weaknesses, angry at her father for sending her away when she could have cared for her siblings and angry with herself for abandoning these two defenceless children to their fate while she enjoyed her newfound freedom elsewhere.

Astrid did her best to comfort the girl but once Wren got into her vein of self-flagellation, it seemed there was nothing that could be done to extricate the child from her own misery. The problem was compounded when, picking at the lace edge of her pretty new dress, she had a flash of remembrance. She jumped up screeched, *"The wedding!"* then crumpled again, sobbing uncontrollably.

Unaccustomed to dealing with weeping young women or, for that matter, anyone in such a state, Astrid became quite worried as she tried to cuddle and rub her great-niece – to say something calming. Such situations and brittle emotions were beyond her own experiences of silent stoicism. At first, she trod carefully, using the gently-gently approach but, after an extended period of wailing, something in Astrid snapped. It might have been because she believed it was the best way to drag Wren out of her depression. Or it might have been because her hip was aching with sitting on the arm of the girl's chair.

After a particularly loud keen, Astrid stood. Gritting her teeth to stop herself from grunting in pain, she said, *"Right! Enough!"*

The sharpness in her voice made the air catch in Wren's throat. She spluttered then lapsed into shocked silence. Her aunt had never even raised her voice to her before. She was not banking on Astrid's sympathy but nor did she expect anger. She was about to dissolve once again when Astrid caught her on the brink.

"No," her aunt said firmly. "No. That's enough now. Crying serves absolutely no purpose in this situation. Why cry? For yourself? For your mother's lost wits? For Arthur and Olivia? If you're crying for yourself, is that not just selfish? You cannot claim the situation as your own. You cannot blame yourself for something that happening a hundred miles away. And anyway – here, now – this is Lili Burnley's day and you should be drying your eyes and getting on with it for her sake. If you're crying for your mother, don't bother. She cannot hear you and tears won't bring her wits back. From what you've told me, if you cried in front of her, she would be furious rather than gratified. And if it's for your brother and sister, yes, they've been through a terrible ordeal but they're both still alive and as well as can be expected. And they're coming here to live with me! You should be rejoicing, not weeping on my armchair. You have to be strong, child. You have to grow up. Have some backbone, for everyone's sake."

It was the longest and most critical personal speech Astrid had ever given her: rational and supremely Germanic. It may have been cruel – Wren certainly thought it was – but she fell silent, only snivelling when her nose dripped. In truth, Astrid's words were exactly what she needed. Having grown up with such an emotionally unstable role-model, Wren was inclined to take everything to heart. Astrid finally felt it would benefit her charge to think, to really *think*, and lend a bit of perspective to the situation. The girl had to grow up, to be rational and deal with the situations life threw at her. Astrid wasn't going to be there to guide her, especially now she was getting married. She had to stand firm on her own.

By the time Wren composed herself and washed her face, she had missed the start of the wedding ceremony and she and Astrid decided to skip it. It was for that reason that she finally cornered Bertram in his mother's old bedroom to explain what was going on. Astrid did not come to the party because she was making arrangements for their journey back to Wren's home-place. Wren was unsure how long they would be staying – whether they would collect the children and leave immediately or have a protracted visit. "I don't even know if you can come for Christmas like we discussed," she told him. However, there was none of the whiney, simpering little girl about her. She was not apologising for the change to their plans. Nor was she scared about telling him. She was plainly stating the truth of the matter.

Used to taking control of situations involving his fiancée, Bertram was completely thrown. He wasn't sure what he should do or say but Wren turned to the door and said, "Come on, we'd better go back out before we're missed," and she was gone.

Fighting the urge to shake himself, Bertram took a deep breath and followed her out of the room into the melee of the party. For the rest of the evening he was in a kind of suspended state which made him quiet, distracted and passably polite – all the things Lili could have wanted from him on her wedding day.

Bertram was left on his own to brood. In the ensuing weeks, he heard from Wren only once. She would be staying for several weeks at her father's while she and her great-aunt made preparations to remove Artie and Olivia from their home and bring them to Enniscorthy. Unsure of how much care the children needed (he had been told their ages but couldn't recall them), he worried that Wren would feel obliged to stay with her aunt and care for her siblings. If that was the case, what would happen to her plans to marry him? Would she feel her duty was to her family or to him? When he thought that she might not choose him, anger would course through him. He wanted her. He had let his guard down and shown her that. And – though he hardly ever admitted it to himself – he needed the dowry Astrid was providing to tide over his finances for the next year. If she rejected him now – not only would his pride be irreparably damaged, he would likely come close to losing his farm as well.

He also wondered if she would ask to bring the children with her if she still agreed to marry him. That idea filled him with unhappiness. He was not going to share his wife with two little brats no matter how much they meant to her. Plus, he really did not have the money to support two children. If he thought about it, he was barely sure he had enough money to support himself, never mind a wife. He preferred not to think about it.

But all this conjecture led to nothing except wasting of the dark hours of the evening with speculation. The person he really needed to talk to had not spoken to him in weeks and he was not going to be the one who made the first move. His pride would not let him do that. Wren would have to come to him with the solution and in the meantime, all he could do was wait for it.

Chapter 34

As it was, the first week in January was nearly over before Wren was face to face with her fiancé once more. It had been just under a month since she left him at Lili and Ewan's wedding – a lost little boy in a sea of familiar faces. The way he reacted to what she told him, the way he wandered around the house, from room to room without purpose – she had never seen him so unsure of himself. Usually he moved through a crowd with assurance and it was she who trailed in his wake, clueless about how to behave. It seemed he was simply too preoccupied to project his air of self-possession. And though he was somewhat shocked by the realisation that his sister had really married and was leaving him to fend for himself, he was more surprised by Wren's behaviour. It gave him a lot to think about – the whole outlook of his future shifted in the space of a few short hours.

Wren changed that day too. She had broken down completely on hearing her mother had tried to harm her siblings. If her guardian had continued to treat her with sympathy, she would have wallowed in grief and self-pity for weeks. Astrid's no-nonsense approach awoke something in Wren. Or perhaps snuffed something out. Though shy and timid, she was also prone to high emotion. Her aunt's words acted like an electrical shock, sizzling down her nerves and

313

through her brain, burning out that element of her which was so heavily influenced by her highly-strung mother. It was like she was a new woman, a child no longer. In a few moments of speech from Astrid and the consideration that followed, Wren made a decision: to be more. To be more would not be easy but, if she made a concerted effort and her aunt agreed to help her, Wren believed it was possible to reinvent herself. To become more active, more forthright, more self-sufficient, to really *think* before she allowed the tears to flow or let herself be hurt by those around her. She had to develop – as Astrid put it – backbone.

On their drive in Astrid's motor car to collect the children, Wren was relatively quiet for long parts of the journey as she began to re-evaluate her life with new perspective. Astrid let her. She was confident Wren was not wallowing but was taking the advice she had been given to heart and was reassessing the world accordingly. The girl was intelligent and young enough to change for the better. And though she was sweet and gentle, she needed mental strength to deal with what the world threw at her.

When they finally arrived late at night (it had taken them almost fourteen hours with more than half a dozen stops on the way), they were fit for nothing but their beds. Eric kissed his daughter and shook hands with his wife's aunt before carrying their cases to the children's bedroom. There were no children in the house. Artie and Olivia were still in the hospital so each of the women had a bed to themselves.

Though tired but glad to see him, Eric noted that there was a coolness to his daughter. Gone was the flittery little girl in handmade clothes who jumped at loud noises. Instead, a young woman stood before him. A woman. It was this realisation more than anything over the past few terrible days that shook Eric to the core and made him want to break down and cry. Wren did not need him to make her decisions and there was no cause for him to hold her hand. She did not need him.

In that moment, standing in the cramped hall of his house with these two strangers, Eric hated Astrid Charlton. She had stripped his little girl from him and replaced her with a stranger. However, when they went to bed, he chided himself for being selfish. Because that was what it was. Like many parents, he wanted his children to stay as children forever and blamed whomever he could when they made the natural progression from youth to adulthood. In this case, it was Mrs Charlton and he felt the urge to send both Astrid and his daughter back to where they came from. He would find a way to care for his wife and remaining children on his own. But common sense returned as the sleepless night wore on. Though he fought the knowledge that he really could not raise his children alone, he finally resigned himself to the fact that a life with their great-aunt would be better than any life he could give them, no matter how much it stung to admit it.

Eric was exceptionally stiff and formal with the two women when they woke the next morning. One of the reasons was that he was put out by the late hour they slept to. It wasn't their norm to waste the morning but, not knowing that, Eric assumed lazy mornings were their habit and resented such indulgent behaviour. He knew Wren lacked an occupation – other than caring for her great-aunt – and that had appeared perfectly acceptable to him. But now he began to wonder if he was allowing his daughter to live the life of a woman above her station. Perhaps she expected to be waited on. Perhaps she now looked down on him and his economically challenged life. For the umpteenth time he considered bringing her back – keeping her with him to mind the children once again rather than send them all away. He could do it too, he thought. All he had to do was ask and Wren would oblige. He was still her father. But then where would that leave them? She would come back, but even if she did so willingly, she would eventually hate him for his interference. He would be ripping her from the place where she had blossomed – stepped out from under her mother's shadow and become her own person. He would be taking her from the comfort of unearned wealth and replacing it with near-poverty. Because if he had to house, feed and clothe three children, that was exactly where they would be: on the verge of destitution. Though Felicity was still in the regular hospital, she would soon be transferred to a psychiatric facility and, though he could have sent her to the one in town, he had decided to send her to a hospital a distance away in the country even though it was considerably more expensive. He wanted to give her a soothing, rural setting rather than the cramped, dark and frankly spooky conditions of the institution in the town. And given his decision to make this outlay, maintaining the rest of the family would be nigh-on impossible.

By the time the women finished breakfast, Eric was fidgeting with impatience. He had wanted to go the hospital first thing but now it would be nearly half ten by the time they walked there. He had not factored in Astrid's car which meant they got there a little after ten but, rather than coming in to visit her new charges, Astrid begged leave to run an errand or two in town. Eric waved his hand in a kind of do-what-you-want attitude and turned away. No matter what she did, the old lady was going to provoke his ire. He turned about and stalked into the hospital with Wren running to catch up.

They visited the children first and found Artie sitting on Olivia's bed reading to her. When he spotted his elder sister,

Artie shouted, *"Birdy!"* and launched himself off the bed. But as soon as he hit the ground, he staggered. He still made a good fist of hurrying towards her but his movements were not those of a boundlessly energetic young boy. He was stiff and ungainly – effects of the bone-deep cold and his tumble into the water. It did not, however, stop him from throwing his arms around Wren's middle and squeezing her for all he was worth. She was a little startled by the fact that he was now almost of a height with her. Meanwhile Olivia was struggling to disentangle herself from a cocoon of blankets pasting her firmly to the mattress. It looked as if someone had intentionally tucked the blankets in too tightly so as to prevent an untimely escape. Knowing Oli and how restless she was, Wren thought it was a distinct possibility that some frustrated nurse had done exactly that.

Once Oli freed herself and hugged her sister, the three of them settled in to chatter about all that had happened since seeing one another earlier in the year. There were tales of many falls and scraped knees and arguments they had with one another. She admired some drawings they had done while in their beds and was also obliged to read a few cards decorating their bedside lockers. She was also compelled to stare into their gaping mouths as both pointed out their newly acquired adult teeth and squeal appropriately when Oli flicked a loose tooth with her tongue.

Nothing was said about what had happened to them.

After chattering for a while, Wren noticed Olivia was flagging. It had been a tough two days on the children. Eric, who sat silently beside the bed observing his children, stood. "Come on now, back to bed or the matron will be after us." The children whinged a little but their father waved his hand to indicate there would be no discussion. "You'll be out of here soon, I promise," he added quietly, settling the blankets (a little more loosely) around his youngest.

Once Wren said goodbye to her siblings, she followed her father out of the ward, down several corridors and two flights of stairs until they came to another room. Felicity was sitting up in the bed, looking out the window. Wren halted as she was about to enter. She was unsure how her mother would react to her being there. Previous fears of her mother flooding back, threatening to choke her. But then Astrid's voice whispered 'backbone' in her ear making her straighten her spine and continue into the room. Wren knew her mother had been drugged so it wasn't much of a shock to see the vacant expression on Felicity's face. It made her look haggard and older than she was. Wren was not sure, however, if it was the effects of the medication or her attempted drowning that made her look so grey. Perhaps it was a combination of both since the children didn't look particularly well either.

Eric walked up to his wife and took her hand. "Felicity," he said quietly.

It seemed to take her an age to turn her head yet, when she did, her gaze drifted past her husband and focused hazily on Wren. Her mouth opened as if to speak but all that came out was a slow exhalation of air. She gently but firmly extracted her hand from Eric's grasp and managed to form the word, "Who?" after several attempts.

Though her father was about to answer for her Wren spoke up. "It's me, Mammy. Wren. Birdy."

Felicity cocked her head like she was sizing up the girl standing before her. "*Hmmm,*" she said, then looked away and gave a snort. "*You.*"

Wren almost recoiled. She was not sure her mother could have squeezed any more contempt into that single word. But Wren held firm and approached her mother once more. "I came to see you —" She didn't get any further.

Felicity's hand rose as if it was being pulled by a string

and flicked sharply at the wrist, gesturing to the door. "Get out," she said in an absent but clear voice.

Wren wasn't going to fight with her. There was no point trying to be rational with someone like her mother, especially when she was drug-addled as well as unhinged. With dignity, she turned on her heel and left, steps not faltering, her chin neither up nor down. It was a matter-of-fact exit. Finding a seat on the corridor, she sat and waited for her father. She did not cry. She did not brood. She sat. And she waited.

Artie and Olivia came home the day after Wren's visit. Though clearly shaken, they seemed determined to forget their trauma and enjoy their time with their sister. However, Wren was not always with them since Astrid had organised a room for herself and her ward in a guest house. The night spent in a child's bed had not been kind to Astrid who had sunk deep into the soft mattress and woke with stiff shoulders and an aching hip. She did not fancy sharing a single bed with a squirming child, especially when that bed was so uncomfortable in the first place. Aside from her comfort, she also thought it prudent to prevent the household from reverting to its old ways with all three children and their father together. A big change was coming in the lives of the two little ones and Astrid felt it important to begin this period of change from the off.

Every day, the two women visited the house to look after the children when Eric went to work. The week after, the children went back to school to finish out the term before the Christmas holidays and also to say goodbye to their teachers and friends. Wren and her aunt spent the time preparing things for the children's imminent departure but also packing up the rest of the house. Eric had made the decision to leave. Both Wren and Astrid thought it a rather rash and final thing to do – as if he was resigning himself to his family's complete and permanent disintegration. He was moving into a lodging house in town superintended by a matronly old lady which housed many of his work colleagues. It left no room for his children to return and that seemed to be the way he wanted it. Even while they were all still together, he appeared to be making a conscious effort to distance himself from the children. Or maybe he had been making a conscious effort to play the part of the loving father all along and no longer saw the point in trying.

Several times a week, he visited his wife.

Christmas Day was a strange affair. Wren was determined it should be the best Christmas the children could ever have – blotting out what happened in the weeks before. She was at the house early to prepare the food (Astrid bought and paid for everything) and to make sure all the presents were laid out nicely under the tree (again Astrid). The old lady gave her niece free rein to buy what she liked but Wren still insisted on running everything by her for approval. Eric did not contribute to the preparations but neither did he stand in Wren's way. He didn't really contribute to anything anymore.

Once presents were doled out and unwrapped, their dinner was served. Eric wolfed his down, stood up, announced he was going to see Felicity then left. He did not arrive back until eleven that night but, when he did, he looked a lot more content than he had earlier. He whistled under his breath and even kissed Wren on the cheek when he came in. She smelt alcohol on his breath. God knew she had no idea about the needs of a man but knowing that her father had chosen to spend Christmas Day with a bottle rather than his own children discoloured the ardent love of a daughter for her daddy.

They left the next day, car piled high with boxes of

belongings and the children wedged in the backseat alongside their possessions. In the free moments during their stay, Astrid had taught Wren how to drive the car so on their way down they shared the driving, making the trip go a little faster as they did not have to stop and rest Astrid's hip. However, it was full dark by the time they were driving along the top of Enniscorthy town to the house.

It was all Wren could do to stay awake and cheerful for the sake of her siblings as she led them up to their rooms. Ever trying to be the grown-up, Artie solemnly – if a little sleepily – told Wren he could ready himself for bed so she continued on with Olivia's semi-conscious form heavy in her arms. Once Wren stripped her of her travel clothes and put Oli in a nightie, she settled her into bed, brushing the hair from the child's forehead. Looking down at the little girl, breathing so softly, so evenly, Wren experienced a feeling of utter peace. But it was quickly chased away by a worrying thought. *God, I hope they'll be happy here*, she prayed as she left the room, leaving the door open behind her.

Chapter 35

No matter how much Astrid and Wren tried to make the children's transition as smooth as possible, they expected problems and got them.

If they were simply two children who had never travelled outside of their hometown only to leave it and travel a hundred miles to live among strangers, they might have adapted more quickly. But they weren't. They were two children recovering from attempts on their lives now living in an unfamiliar house.

Being of some importance in the local social scene, what seemed like hundreds of visitors came to reacquaint themselves with Astrid on her return. And of course, the children had to be viewed as well. They were called in at a certain point in every visitation to be introduced to Mrs-So-And-So who would view them critically, comment on their appearance (the one they heard most often was how small they were), then dismiss them to some low seat in a corner of the room. They would stay there until Astrid was irked enough by their fidgetiness to send them away again.

Mrs Charlton had never spent long periods of time with young children. Her experiences of them were mostly in passing, when their primary carer was always someone else. Now she had two children of her own but was too old to adapt to their youth quickly. Her own childhood was no use as an example since it had been rigidly controlled by the strict maxim that children were seen and not heard. She did not know what to do with them so it fell to Wren to care for them – both day and night.

While sleeping at home in the same room, Artie and Olivia had managed to comfort one another when dealing with their issues. But now in unfamiliar, separate rooms, their sleep was more disturbed than ever. Their surroundings felt wrong and both experienced vivid nightmares. More than once in the first week the entire household was woken in the small hours by the shrill screams of Olivia as she thrashed about in her bedding. Sleeping next door, it fell to Wren to calm them (since Artie was equally afflicted by these sinister dreams) and try to lull them back to sleep. Usually by the time she entered their rooms, they had woken themselves but their breathing would still be ragged and their hair would be plastered to their glistening foreheads. She would then have to change their nightshirts which were always drenched with sweat and stuck to their skin. More often than not, if it was Olivia who woke, Wren would have to share her bed for the rest of the night, stroking her back and running her fingers soothingly through the child's fine hair.

It was a struggle for Wren to see the damage inflicted on her siblings. But she stayed strong for their sake, trying to make their transition to a new home as smooth as possible. And though Astrid did help with the practicalities of organising a new school for the children, Wren had to prepare their school uniforms and supplies while simultaneously bringing the children around the town with her.

It was for this reason that she virtually forgot about contacting Bertram – she had enough to occupy her mind. Her thoughts touched on him every now and then, but they were quickly swept aside when another crisis presented itself in the form of two young children. New Year had come and gone by the time Wren asked to borrow the car one evening to visit Bertram.

She never thought to check Bertram would be there so, when she reached the house, she found the gates to the yard closed and his car gone. She parked in the gateway and had a quick look around the house and yard but there was no light anywhere. Standing in the middle of the yard, she experienced a moment's indecision. Should she go or should she wait? She turned on the spot and spied a light in the distance. It bobbed and danced as the person carrying it moved away. It blinked as the person passed a tree then turned and disappeared. From her previous visit to the farm, she guessed that the person had gone into Ewan Cameron's house. On a whim, she struck out and walked up the lane. Perhaps Bertram was at his sister's new house, or if not, his sister might know where he was. And besides, Wren liked the idea of seeing Lili again, even if Ewan scared her a little.

Before, she never would have walked in an unfamiliar place in the dark but now it didn't seem so bad. The night air was so quiet and clear that it felt like she was breathing in something sweeter, richer, than normal air. She heard the vague murmur of the bare branches creaking in the gentle breeze and heard some sheep calling to one another a distance away.

She was just turning into the path to Ewan and Lili's house, when the sweep of headlights caught her peripheral vision. A car pulled up at the gate of the Gate House then moved on and turned up the lane to stop at the back door of the house. She knew it was Bertram and since it was him and not his sister she had come to see, she headed back down the lane. She was a little put out, however, by the restlessness of the trees and the dry, dead overgrown vegetation as it scraped along the path in the wind. The air itself seemed to twist and writhe as it moved down the lane, its voice sobbing words of hurt and pain. Wren shivered and hurried her steps. Maybe venturing out in the dark by herself was not such a good plan. She reached the house at a trot and hammered on the door a little harder than she ought to have. It was a moment before it was swung open with no small amount of force. Bertram stood in the dim light of the interior, his face flushed and his eyes shining. As he stared down at her, she thought he might topple straight into her chest. He looked so unsteady, she almost put a hand out to keep him upright.

Wren had not been sure whether she would want to kiss Bertram, hug him, or simply be held by him when she saw him again. As it was, she did not want to do any of those things. The expression on his face made her keep her distance. He appeared to be warring between happiness and anger, giving him a pained-looking leer. They stood in silence contemplating one another. Eventually, Bertram gave a tiny jerk of his head, the rest of his body following whether by design or because his balance was so problematic.

"Suppose you'd better come in," he said gruffly, preceding her into the kitchen.

She followed him – a little reluctantly – into the dingy room. It wasn't half as clean as when he shared it with his sister. In the dim light cast by a lone lamp hanging on one side of the chimney breast, she could see the kitchen table was covered in crumbs. The range looked very sad. The door was open and a few glowing embers were half-heartedly trying to burn three fresh logs but were only managing some sluggishly ascending opaque smoke. Bertram threw himself down in one chair by the range with a grunt and gestured to the other chair.

Wren sat. She kept her coat on. Unable to think of anything to say she asked, "How have you been?"

Bertram stared at her, an incredulous look on his face

before turning to study the smoking wood with a snort. "'How have you been?' she asks. I barely hear from her in weeks and all I get is 'How have you been?'" He hadn't been sure what emotion would come to the fore – relief or anger. It seemed anger was winning out. "Well, for a while I wondered if she was dead since I'd heard nothing but then Robbie tells me he saw her in town before New Year's and yet I still hear nothing. So I'm starting to wonder what I've done wrong or whether she even wants to marry me anymore and if she doesn't, is she too much of a coward to tell me and –" He ran out of breath, huffed and continued. "And well – well, I don't know what's going on. I'm hale and hearty by the way, not that you seemed to care until now."

"You know I had to go home," she replied quietly. Bertram snorted again but Wren persisted. "Artie and Olivia weren't very well – they're still not – but they had to finish the school term before moving."

"How are they?" Bertram asked tightly, knowing he should ask but not really wanting to.

"They're … struggling. They hide it well – Artie especially – but it's been difficult. Imagine your mother –" she searched for the right word, "betraying you the way my mammy did."

"Can't imagine it," Bertram said, shaking his head. Now he was over the initial anger of seeing her, relief rose to the surface. He was just glad she was finally there.

He slid out of his chair, took up the poker and tried to revive the fire, but as he pushed himself back into his seat, a thought occurred to him. She had not answered his query as to whether they were still engaged. The anger flicked again.

"So why didn't you tell me this before now?" he asked.

Wren cast about for an answer. "I don't know. Everything just seemed to get ahead of me. Christmas, New Year. It all came up so quickly. And I was trying to do my best for Artie and Olivia. But I didn't know how to help them. I still don't."

It hurt her to admit that. She felt a surge of grief pushing its way up through her chest to her throat and swallowed hard to force it back down. She looked into the flames, hoping the heat would dry away unshed tears resting on her eyelids. She tried so hard to be strong for her siblings – to set an example to the household that they were moving forward. In all that time no one had asked Wren if she was alright. The two children were everyone's priority. Everyone's grief and hurt was relative to theirs. Given the trauma Artie and Oli suffered, perhaps no one else had the right to feel pain or feel sorry for themselves. Yet, in reality, it wasn't easy for anyone. But Wren did hope she might find comfort or a sympathetic ear with Bertram. Apparently, that was wishful thinking.

Bertram was getting impatient. "And what about us?"

"Well, that's up to you," Wren said evenly.

Bertram was already shaking his head. "I don't think so. There's two of us in this. Or, at least, there was. Now I'm not so sure."

"Do you still want to marry me?" Wren asked baldly.

"Do *you* still want to marry *me*?" he asked in return.

Wren considered.

He didn't like that one little bit. She should have just answered him.

He was about to call off the entire thing when she said, "Yes."

That took the wind out of his sails. He was about to explode. Let her know all the pain her rejection caused him, the embarrassment. But she cut him off with the one little affirmative.

"Oh … Good." However, a bad thought crossed his mind. "But what about your brother and sister?"

"Auntie Astrid is hiring a nanny to care for them. And they're going to school in town too. I won't be needed." That saddened her a little, but she smiled and continued. "Auntie Astrid says I've got to live my life, keep going with the plans I've made. And the first of those was marrying you. So I suppose we'd best get on with it."

She looked at Bertram expectantly. He stared back. Alcohol and tiredness were fogging his brain. He had taken in very little of what his fiancée had just said. "What? *Hmm* ... yes . . . whatever you think."

Wren twitched, annoyed. But he didn't notice. "So if I said we get married at the end of next month you'd be happy?"

He shrugged. "Yes. Whatever you say."

"Then I'll organise the banns and a few other things and we're set?"

"Aye," he nodded in solemn assent, sinking back into the depths of the chair. She could have asked him anything and he would have agreed. Since the main question had been answered, all others didn't matter and, therefore, didn't require his attention. He barely noticed when Wren stood up to leave.

"I'll go then, shall I?" she asked loudly.

"What? *Hmm?* Yes, yes. Fine." Something in his brain told him to stand so he did, moving like a string-operated puppet. He made liberal use of the chair's arm to steady himself. Leaning in to the girl opposite him, he lightly held her elbow and gave her a wet peck on the cheek.

Wren fought the urge to wipe her face. She let herself out the back door and walked around to the car. She had expected him to be angry. She knew from experience that his temper was tricky. But she hoped he would express some kindness and sympathy after the initial breaking of the ice. It seemed, however, that he was too self-absorbed to concern himself with incidents and responsibilities that coloured her life. As she drove home, she hoped he would show more concern for her in the future.

Chapter 36

On the 28th of February 1954, Wren and Bertram married. Unlike the previous wedding in the family a few months before, this was a wedding that seemed to be witnessed by half the county. Proceedings were held in St. Mary's Church of Ireland in Enniscorthy town, much to Wren's delight since the Church Institute – the place where so much of their courtship took place – was directly opposite. Part of the reason they got married in St. Mary's was that it was by far the biggest of the local churches. The other reason was that Astrid Charlton took it upon herself to organise the entire event. And if there was one thing Astrid was excellent at, it was organising a party.

From the day after Wren arrived home from her visit to Bertram, Astrid set aside several hours of each day to planning and preparation for their impending marriage. She wanted it to be a social highlight of the year and talked about for years to come. She felt Wren deserved to have such a memory given the difficulties of the past months. The girl had given herself to her family's needs and now it was time for something that was about her. And her bridegroom. But really the wedding was the bride's day and that was just as Astrid intended.

The wedding brought great cheer into a household that

was struggling to find the goodness in life. Somewhat to her relief, Astrid found Artie and Oli loved to be consulted during her planning sessions. She asked their opinions on colours, flowers and food, watching them relish the distraction. Nothing seemed to please them more than scattering whatever samples Astrid was considering across the floor before plonking themselves in the middle of the mess. Oli usually sat on Artie's crossed legs as they opined the merits of one product, the deficiency of another. It was fascinating to listen to the intelligence of their chatter and the seriousness with which they tackled the task at hand. Finally, decision made, they plucked the article from the floor, holding it between them, before presenting it ceremoniously to Wren and Astrid, deeming it their favourite.

Not only were the children included in the preparations, they were included in the ceremony itself with Oli a flower girl and Artie the page boy. However, Artie's other duty – a much more important one – was given to him on the eve of the wedding.

Eric wasn't coming.

He had accepted Wren's invitation initially and agreed to arrive a few days early to be fitted with a suit and so on but the day before the wedding he rang Astrid's house amid the flurry of activity to inform them that he wouldn't make the wedding after all. Something to do with not getting time off work and his wife having another turn while incarcerated in her institution. It was rather a poor excuse. The truth was Eric now believed it was best for both himself and his children to sever ties completely. They were free from the burden of a mad mother and useless father and he was free to become anything he wanted now that he had been released from the encumbrance of dependants. He could reinvent himself as the single man. Going to the wedding would just remind him of his own failings. Better to stay at home and think of other things than put himself or anyone else through it.

Wren teetered on the verge of being deeply upset by her father's absence but, spotting the signs of a crumbling resolve, Astrid quickly proposed that Artie be the one to walk Wren down the aisle. It was a suggestion that surprised Wren with its oddity. Having a young boy give you away was not the done thing at all. But, as Astrid pointed out, Artie was the closest male relative she had and even if he was younger than her, he was still her brother. Better that Artie, an important man in her life – even if he was only a little man – give her away instead of a perpetually absent father. Astrid, therefore, insisted that it was Wren who informed the boy of his new duty. She thought it might cheer both of them up and, of course, she was right.

When Wren went to tell him, he was in bed reading a book. She sat on the eiderdown and first told him that their father would not be able to come. Artie nodded solemnly as if to say he expected as much. He didn't give any indication that such information upset him. However, when she told him he would be walking her down the aisle the next day, the boy's face altered completely. Rarely had she seen such utter joy animate his narrow young face.

At first all he could say was "Oh ... oh ... oh" but eventually his shiny eyes met Wren's and he said with absolute sincerity, "I won't let you down."

They hugged and said good night to one another after that. A little later as Wren closed the door on her own bedroom, she thought it was worth her father not coming just to see the happiness it brought the little boy sleeping next door.

The wedding went off without a hitch. One of Bertram's cousins was employed as best man, while Mary and Joan, who had accompanied Wren to her first Church Institute dance, were the bridesmaids.

Since Bertram had organised his brother-in-law and another neighbour to look after the farm for the rest of the week, the new Mr and Mrs Burnley were free to spend a couple of days with some of Bertram's relations in Dublin.

After a grand party in Astrid's house, the newlyweds were waved onto the bus by a very merry party. They sat opposite Bertram's second cousins, Gloria and John, who were accompanying them back to Dublin. It was their house the new Burnleys would be staying in and they would apparently have the upstairs of the townhouse to themselves.

On the journey up, there was a lot of giggling and remarks verging on impertinence from Gloria and John who were both rotund, red-faced and far gone with drink. They were two people very like Evelyn Burnley but they were also heavy drinkers which meant their tongues were looser, their manners coarser. It was something of a relief, therefore, when Bertram finally snapped shut the door to their room, muffling the titters and hoots that were still continuing in the steadily darkening corridor outside. There was a scuffle and a thump from the far side of the door as Gloria and John drunkenly felt their way down the dimly lit staircase. And then silence.

"Thank Christ," Bertram said grimly, leaning against the door with his hands in his pockets.

Wren stood awkwardly in the middle of the room, her hands slowly clasping and unclasping the sides of her dress. It was a nervous habit she had never managed to shake. She looked anywhere but at Bertram. And there was plenty to look at. The room was stuffed with all manner of trumperies: mismatched furniture, floral-printed carpet, floral bedspread, floral wallpaper and curtains. There was even a vase of flowers on the washstand. It had the effect of making the room look like it was constantly moving as the patterns appeared to buzz. The furniture itself was abundant, with half a dozen chairs pushed up against the wall in between the larger items such as the washstand, two chests of drawers, a bedside table and the bed itself. The flowers, Wren supposed, were an attempt to mask the scent of dust and mould that permeated the room. Gloria had said they never used the room though it was spacious.

"Take off your clothes."

It took a moment for Wren to realise Bertram was speaking to her. It took an even longer moment for her to grasp what he said. When she did, she just stared at him. He remained impassive, propped against the door with his hands in his pockets. She looked down at her frock. She had changed before leaving Astrid's house because she didn't want to wear her wedding dress on the bus. She did a little double take when she realised the garment also had a floral pattern. She blended into the surroundings perfectly! Yet, after the thought flitted through her mind, she became aware of what her husband (how strange it seemed to call him that, even in her head!) had said to her. All these thoughts moved sluggishly through her head.

Bertram stayed silent throughout, waiting expectantly.

She looked at him quizzically.

He widened his eyes in an expression that said "Well?"

Very unsure of the situation but knowing she had to obey the man who stood in front of her, she clumsily began undoing the buttons of her dress. Quickly, she rued the number of them down her front as well as the fact that they were stiff with newness. They stretched all the way from her collar to her navel but once she got part of the way down, she gave up and grabbed the hem of her dress, dragging it up and over her head. She held onto the dress, keeping it in front of her so as to hide as much of her body as she could.

She still had a slip and underwear on but she felt exposed, uncomfortable. She couldn't help but hunch her shoulders and cover up. The room wasn't particularly warm either making goose bumps crawl up her skin just as Bertram's eyes raked across her exposed flesh.

Still leaning against the door, he said, "Come on. Everything."

Wren stared. Her voice had deserted her. Imploring him with her eyes to see her discomfort, she was met by an impassive stare back. Shaking out the dress in front of her, using those last few moments to hide behind it, she began to fold it carefully for putting away.

"Don't bother with that rubbish," he snapped impatiently. "Just put it away and get on with it, will you?"

Shocked by his tone she jumped and dropped the frock on the floor. With shaking, jittery hands she removed her slip but then came the decision to remove either her brassiere or her briefs first. She paused a moment too long for her nerves to handle and – worried that he would snap at her again – ripped off the brassiere before divesting herself of her final garments, taking her stockings off with her last item of underwear. She stood, desperately trying to cover herself with her arms and hands, shivering in the middle of the claustrophobic print-explosion room.

"Let me see you. All of you."

She dropped her hands, fighting against every instinct to cover up again. Bertram casually pushed off the door, hands still in his pockets, and walked up to Wren, gazing intently at her body while ignoring her face. He walked around her then turned away, taking off his jacket without looking at his wife.

"Get into bed."

Wren darted across the room, grabbed the top of the covers and slid in as quickly as she could. She almost jumped straight back out but embarrassment stopped her.

The sheets were freezing and felt like cold water pressed up against her unaccustomed bare flesh. She almost didn't dare watch Bertram as he undressed methodically, without the slightest hint of shame or concern. Would he be angry if he caught her looking?

Finally folding all his clothing, he turned and caught Wren observing. She immediately looked away. He laughed. "Go on." He stepped up to the side of the bed. "Take a good look." He stretched nonchalantly, while keeping an eye firmly fixed on Wren's perturbed expression. He laughed again. "I'm well made. Don't you worry."

The male body in its entirety wasn't at all as attractive as she thought it might be. Now that he had turned to face her, she saw Bertram was very hairy. Coarse-looking dark-coloured bristles covered his chest and ran down the centre of his belly to where – she jumped past that for now. His legs were also exceedingly hairy and, unlike his forearms where the hair was bleached a lighter colour by constant exposure to sunlight, they were dark with heavy growth. He also had a distinct pot belly which had been completely hidden by his clothing. His distended lower abdomen was also accompanied by pale white fleshy hips that looked almost like discoloured dough. And given the general area her eyes were focused on, she couldn't help but notice *it*.

His … *thing* protruded from a profusion of curly black hair and as she looked, it twitched. Her breath caught in shock. She looked away. She didn't want to see it anymore. And yet, like most things gross or terrifying it drew her gaze once more. It moved. She had no idea that could happen – that it appeared to have a life of its own. She desperately tried to remember what Lili had told her, what she had seen with the sheep, but all she could see was the *thing* in front of her. Everything else fled from her mind, leaving her stranded and alone.

Bored and put out by his wife's less than enthusiastic reception of his nakedness, Bertram turned as abruptly as his growing erection would allow him to and went over to turn out the light. It took him a moment to regain his boundaries before finding his way back to the bed in the darkness. Whipping back the covers, he slid in.

The cold air once again hit Wren as her husband climbed in beside her. Her heart was hammering in her chest and her breathing was ragged. She was terrified. What was more, she couldn't see anything. But she could feel everything. His hands, mercifully, were warm. However, every part of her body he touched tingled as if something unpleasant had grazed her bare skin. She could not move to shake off these traces of his searching fingers. Every movement she made was forced by his hands as he silently pulled her stiff legs apart. Again, his fingers intruded and she stifled a cry as well as the urge to push him away. Sensing her reluctance, Bertram abandoned his explorations and clasped her upper arms in his hands. Without a word, he pushed inside her.

Wren writhed, cringing away from the painful new sensation. And it was painful – agony in fact. She clamped her teeth shut but the sound still reverberated in her chest and throat. Tears coursed down her temples, following her jawline before sliding down her neck to wet her hair. She could feel the dampness of her crying soaking into the pillow as her entire body moved with the vigour of her husband's movement. His hands were still clamped down on her arms, squeezing so hard she could no longer feel the ends of her fingers. She willed herself to concentrate on the tickling sensation of her tears on her neck rather than the pain everywhere else. And she prayed. She prayed it would end.

It did. And quickly too. But the damage had been done. As he reached the end, Bertram let go of her arms and rested his damp forehead on Wren's. The blood flowed back into her hands and she fought not to cry out once again as her fingertips seemed to expand to bursting point with the tide of excess – though much-needed – blood. He kissed her on the lips then rolled off her. Seeking some space that wasn't occupied by him, Wren went to move away but his arms snaked tight around her waist, clasping her to him. He kissed her shoulder once, twice then sighed and began to breathe heavily.

Wren continued to sob silently until, exhausted and hurting all over, she slept.

She woke before he did. The sun was making the room glow with cold, bleaching light. Wren wondered why it was so bright but then realised they had not pulled the curtains when they came in.

Hardly daring to look, she noted he had rolled away from her during the night, releasing her from his grip. Yet she stayed on her side, afraid to move in case a fresh wave of pain hit her. Everything that had happened since the door closed the night before had changed her once again. And not for the better. The ordeal of the night before wiped away the strides she had made to improve herself over the last few months. Without conscious awareness, she reverted to the scared little girl – the girl she thought she had buried for good. As tears yet again began to slide down her cheeks, she fought against the overwhelming urge to sob uncontrollably. This was surely not the way a marriage should start. This, surely, was not love. She continued to cry quietly for a time before getting some sort of fragile grip on herself. She did not want to be near him anymore.

With that resolve, she silently swung her legs from under the covers, placing her feet on the carpet. She was sore. Mercifully, however, the pain was not as bad as the night before. This was pain she could cope with even if it was more than her slight little body had previously handled. As she stood on shaky limbs, she took a deep breath and looked down.

The light from the window gave her skin a blue-white tinge in the cold air. She looked ugly to her own eyes and that was not counting the damage of the night before. Her arms were heavily bruised, with bands of purple colouring her flesh just above the elbow. She could almost trace the marks of individual fingers where his hands had griped her like pincers, grinding the delicate limbs caught between them. She always bruised easily and knew it would take a long time for the marks to fade from purple to black, to purple again, then green and yellow. Her eyes travelled further down and she almost lost control again.

There was bruising. She didn't need to see it to know it was there. She *couldn't* see it in the first place. The insides of her legs were covered in – She looked away, searching for her slip. She didn't want to see anymore. Diving into the garment, fearing someone might somehow observe her from the window (even though they were on the second storey), she covered up the evidence of the night before. Spotting the jug and washbasin on the stand, she went over and poured out some water before wetting a flannel. Without looking, she began to wipe away the traces from the night. Or, at least as much of it as she could. The icy water stung her aches, leaving a dull persistent throb in its wake as if the cold had roused her pain from an uneasy sleep. As she continued, she turned the water an orangey-red as flecks of dried blood dissolved. All the while, Bertram slept on.

Once she finished, she was faced with another dilemma: what to do with the water. She did not want anyone else to see the evidence. Picking up the bowl, she swithered as to whether to throw it out the window and have done with it or find a bathroom. Knowing the latter would be best, she put down the bowl and put on a dressing gown that was draped over one of the chairs. It was far too big for her but, as long as it covered everything, she did not mind. Listening intently for noises below, she eventually opened the door carefully and headed down the stairs.

Luckily, she found a bathroom at the bottom of the first flight. Closing the door, she rid herself of her burden and felt herself relax a little. Rinsing the basin, she put it down and perched carefully on the edge of a cast-iron bath sitting in state at the far side of the room. She vaguely thought how wonderful it would be to have a bath right now – to rinse away all the residue, to drown the demons – but knew there would be no hot water at this time in the morning.

Getting up to leave, she caught her own reflection in the mirror. She almost burst into tears again. There were blue-coloured bags under her eyes from lack of sleep and excess waterworks. Her skin was blotchy from the heat, stress and moisture of the night before and there were still shiny tracks from her tears sticking to her temples like the glistening tracks of a snail. She immediately turned on the tap in order to wash her face and heard the ominous clang and gurgle of the plumbing grinding into life. The tap glugged before sputtering a pressurised jet of water into the sink that splashed back out, soaking the front of her dressing gown. She gave a little shriek and jump back.

"Are you all right, dear?"

The well-meant enquiry was enough to make Wren jump again as, heart pounding, she fought to turn off the tap.

A soft knock sounded against the door.

"*Just a minute!*" Wren called as she scrubbed forcefully at her face with cold water.

"Take all the time you need, dear, I'm in no rush. Just checking you're not in need of anything."

Gloria's voice was a little hoarse but there was a geniality to her tone which calmed Wren enough for her to finish drying her face before leaving the room. However, as she put her hand on the doorknob, she wondered how she would face the woman on the other side. She was tainted now, bruised, bloodied – unclean.

No: she was a married woman, not a girl anymore. She opened the door and came face to face with Gloria's ample bosom.

"Hello, dear!" Gloria croaked. "How are you this morning? Lovely morning, by the way." Her bright smile faltered a little when she looked at Wren properly. "A little bit sore are we, my dear?" Her tone was much softer now. She reached out and rubbed a consoling hand down the girl's arm. Wren flinched. Gloria had caught a bruise.

Concerned, the woman said, "Come down now for a bit of breakfast, lovey." Taking Wren's hand and patting it firmly, she led the girl down to the kitchen saying, "Breakfast, that's what you need."

Gloria set to work frying rashers of bacon and scrambling eggs as well as boiling a kettle for tea. Wren perched at the table and watched, glad the woman seemed to have the tact not to speak. She was not able for chit-chat. Not right now.

Placing a plate stacked with buttered bread, egg and bacon in front of each of them, Gloria sat. Though reluctant at first, Wren found she was ravenous and, following Gloria's enthusiastic example, she made her way through the contents of her plate. Putting her knife and fork together, Gloria studied the girl sitting opposite her. "It gets easier, my dear. Better even. It just … takes some getting used to." She patted Wren on the hand and heaved herself up. "Now," she said, picking up her mug of tea, "I must see if that man of mine is up yet. Maybe you might do the same." She smiled encouragingly. "I'm sure you have some fun planned over the next few days, eh?"

Chapter 37

Their stay in Dublin was short but hectic. On the first morning, they travelled into the city centre and went shopping. Bertram needed a new pair of good shoes and Gloria had suggested a place called Switzer's on Grafton Street so it was there they went. Afterwards, with his new shoes parcelled up in brown paper and string, they strolled hand in hand down to the river, crossing over to O'Connell Street, up to Nelson's Column and then along Henry Street.

It was along there that Bertram spotted a plummy-red coat in the window of Arnott's.

"Would you like that coat?" he asked his wife, suddenly pulling her to a halt in front of the window display.

Wren gaped. Why would he ask her that? Was it a test? What answer would he be satisfied with, she wondered? "It looks expensive," she mumbled, looking away.

It was a lovely coat. If she looked at it too long, she might be inclined to go and press her nose against the glass.

"*You* don't have to buy it," he said, rolling his eyes. "I'd buy it for you. Do you want it?"

She stood on the street mouthing like a fish for so long that he grabbed hold of her hand and towed her into the shop. Walking up to the first server he saw, he announced, "I'm here to buy that reddy-looking coat in the window for my wife. We got married yesterday."

After congratulations from the woman at the counter, she led them to where there was a large display of coats and selected the garment in question. Picking out the smallest one available so Wren didn't end up looking like a child who had raided her mother's wardrobe, she suggested she try the item on for size.

Bertram's smile flickered for a moment as he watched Wren unbutton and remove her own coat. He had seen the bruises that morning. However, he relaxed when he realised she had a cardigan on over her dress.

"Do you want to take off the cardigan too? Make sure it's a good fit?" the server asked.

"No, no," Wren answered smartly. "I'd probably be wearing a cardie or a jumper under it anyway."

Bertram smiled warmly at her but she looked away, focusing on the coat.

It was beautiful. The dark red was set off by a black fur collar and glossy black buttons the size of half-crowns. It nipped in tight at the waist and then flared out at the hips. The lady helped her into it then guided her over to a mirror.

Wren was fascinated by her own reflection. A pale girl – no: she was a woman now – stared dully back at her. Her skin looked very white, still framed as it was by her dark hair and the black fur collar of the coat which tickled her chin. If she were a little taller, she thought, she might look like one of those famous actresses in the pictures. She was certainly dressed to look the part.

"Oh, doesn't she just look a picture!" exclaimed the woman, clapping her hands as she and Bertram looked Wren up and down.

"Doesn't she just," said Bertram wonderingly.

Wren was decidedly happier as she made her way back to

Gloria and John's for lunch with the package under her arm. Bertram had offered to carry it for her but she clung to the purchase with such fervour that he shrugged and left her with it. She spent the entire bus journey across town taking surreptitious glances under the paper. Every now and again, when she touched the soft fabric, her face would transform momentarily, splitting into a child-like grin of pure delight. And, of course, Bertram was pleased he had managed to make her so happy.

After their purchases were duly admired by Bertram's relatives and they had lunch, they set off once again to Phoenix Park and the zoo. They wandered around hand in hand, clutching at one another, pointing and squawking in delight at what they saw. It was an adventure for both and, buoyed by their good mood from earlier in the day, they reverted to childishness, running from enclosure to enclosure to gawp at the exotic creatures.

But as the afternoon wore on Wren's good humour began to wane. As she viewed animal after animal in cage after cage, she began to think of her own little prison: the room she was to share again with Bertram that night. But unlike the animals, once the gate was closed, their keeper left them alone to dwell on their own thoughts. Her keeper stayed with her. She was trapped in their room, for him to do as he pleased with her. It left her cold despite wearing her brand-new red coat.

As she walked around in her husband's wake, she realised she just had to accept her fate and get on with it. But on the bus journey back, she was once again overcome as she thought of the pile of sheets she'd stripped off the bed in the morning, and figuring out how she was going to change them without asking where the spare sheets were. She had been horrified when she pulled back the covers on the bed that morning to discover she had stained the bedding.

Bertram had paused midway through dressing to look too before simply turning away and muttering what sounded suspiciously like "Good" as he did so. But when they arrived back and she hurried upstairs to the room, thinking what she might do, she found the bed already dressed with fresh sheets, and the soiled bundle she had stuffed out of sight behind a chair had been removed as well. She quietly blessed Gloria and hurried back downstairs to dinner.

However, after eating, Wren fought a rising sense of dread as bedtime crept closer. Luckily, Gloria and John were now considerably less merry but still happy and polite which meant conversation flowed more freely and was much less embarrassing than the evening before. They also did not force Wren to join in with their chatter. She was an immovable object, able to sit in silence with her own worries while the others spent the evening contentedly talking of nothing in particular.

But when the time came, the new bride need not have worried. That night, Bertram barely looked at her as they got ready for bed and once they climbed into their respective sides, he simply turned over and went to sleep.

After another hectic day bustling around the city and visiting two museums and some of Bertram's extended family, Wren waited again with some apprehension for her husband to climb into bed. But, again, he simply kissed her goodnight, rolled over and was breathing heavily within minutes.

She then stayed awake worrying and wondering whether she had done something wrong. Was Bertram angry with her? Had she displeased him in some way? Was this what every marriage bed was like? The fretting lasted for what seemed like hours until finally she dropped off into an uneasy sleep.

However, in the wee hours she came to with a panicked feeling that she was suffocating.

Waking slowly and attempting to throw off the weight that constricted her she found, as she tried to free her compressed chest or even her arms so as to push or pull herself upright, that her wrists were also immobile.

"*Would. You. Ever. Stop. Fidgeting.*" The words came out between his teeth which were inches from her ear. "You keep kicking me in your bloody sleep. You're driving me mad." He shoved her into the mattress a little to get his point across.

Wren gasped, petrified. "I'm sorry," she whimpered, as her sleepy mind desperately tried to find something to placate him with.

"*Stop wriggling. You're making me –*"

He didn't need to finish. She knew what she was making him do. She could feel it. She didn't want it to happen. She tried to come up with something, anything to stop him. But she drew a blank.

Gloria was right: it was not as bad as the first time or, at least, it wasn't as painful. In another way, it was worse than the first time. The knowing what was coming, the painful grating of dry skin on dry skin, the fact that it lasted longer than the first time. He held her down again, this time his hands on her wrists. Absently, she wondered how she would hide the bruises since they were so much further down. He would be angry with her if she exposed them. She would have to be careful.

When it was over, he wrapped his arms around her as he had done before. "Now go to sleep," he said. "And don't move."

She didn't do either.

Chapter 38

When they arrived back in Enniscorthy, the first thing the couple did was call to Astrid's before heading out to Bachelor Lane. What Wren really wanted was to see Artie and Oli once they arrived home from school. She had worried about them when she was away. But she needn't have. According to Astrid, they were only a little upset on the first night but then rallied and had improved since her departure. It hurt to discover they were doing better without her but then Wren chastised herself for being so unkind. It was good they were getting better and it was good she got to see it when they got home. To their home. Astrid's house was not her home anymore. She was going to her new home. With her new husband. On her own.

The first thing she noticed when she walked in the door at Bachelor Lane – she was a little disappointed he did not carry her – was that the room was much cleaner than the last time. Somebody had given the place a thorough going-over, returning it to its former state and she was sure it was not Bertram. She would have to thank Lili. It was the perfect excuse for a prompt visit. Not that she needed an excuse. Living close to Lili was one of the things she was most looking forward to in her new home. She and her husband seemed to be a shining example of the model couple, from the little Wren had seen of them. She loved to watch them interact. The small looks and touches, the charged energy which seemed to pass between them. There was a time when she believed that might be possible with Bertram. But not anymore.

Her perception of him had changed and she had not really noticed it until their trip away. The man she fell in love with over the summer was not the man she came to know during winter and spring. He changed after his mother's death – became harder, more disparaging. And, determined to find the approval of another human soul when her own family had rejected her, she had latched onto him blindly, unaware of the faults that had been staring her in the face from the start. Now she saw his true self. The man she met before was the fallacy, not the one she knew now. Yet still she continued with her engagement, her marriage. Why? Did she think or hope that he would magically change back to the person she had fallen for if she gave herself to him completely? Perhaps. In truth, it was more likely she was too immature to know how to extricate herself from the situation she found herself in. She continued to delude herself with a hoped-for reality rather than a genuine one.

Now she saw it. Standing in the kitchen of her new home as Bertram disappeared with their bags, the curtain was finally stripped back. The actuality of her life hit her with the force of a hammer blow. She sat suddenly on a chair. This was now her life and she was going to sink or swim. Either let the child in her crumble under the weight of her situation – descend into useless grief and self-pity – or do as Astrid said and grow up, accept her lot and strive to make the best of it.

With positive thoughts of tackling her lot, she ascended the stairs to the bridal chamber, head held high, ready for what was waiting in the days and months to come.

Life at the Gate House quickly settled into a routine. It was not a routine Wren particularly enjoyed but she was going to make what she could of it for her own sake and for the sake of the people who cared for her. Not Bertram. While he did care, it was not in the way a husband should. He valued her for what she did but not necessarily for herself. She could cook and clean. She caught on to the tasks around the yard pretty quickly and she acted as a willing go-between when Bertram wanted anything from his sister. And, of course, there was what went on in their bedroom.

It still wasn't getting any better and she was still waking up with livid bruises. She had known early on that Bertram had a temper, a violent streak – that he enjoyed being able to scare her. Perhaps it was something to do with her being small enough and naïve enough for him to intimidate. Perhaps it was simply the novelty of being a small man drunk on newfound power. Perhaps it was just plain drunkenness. She had never realised how much he drank. Alcohol consumption was something she never really came across in her isolated little existence prior to knowing Bertram. Now she experienced the full effects of alcohol without ever touching a drop herself. Drink made Bertram irritable and irrational. When he came home from the pub or even on the evenings he drank at home, she had to choreograph a very careful dance around him: not talking too much or too little, not moving too much, not making loud noises, not coughing into silences, not knitting too quickly – the list of things she learnt not to do seemed to be endless. And it continued when they went to bed. Sometimes he wanted to talk, sometimes he wanted absolute silence. Sometimes he wanted to hold her, sometimes he'd lash out if she even touched him by accident. And sometimes he wanted … something else. Worst, however, were the nights when she woke him tossing and turning in her sleep. She often woke him unintentionally by striking him in her sleep only to be woken by him hitting her back. Occasionally it was nothing more than a dig to make her move away. But sometimes it was more, especially when he had been drinking. Those incidents, while rare, left her with bruises that took weeks to fade.

On one occasion, she moved to another bedroom once Bertram fell asleep but on waking to find her gone his anger was frightening. That did not prevent him from sometimes leaving her alone to sleep in their room while he departed to his old bedroom on the nights he came home late from the pub. On those nights, Wren thanked God for the chance of a restful sleep. It wasn't easy for her to surrender herself to the oblivion of true rest with the fear of what might occur during the night in a shared bed. But she had to sleep no matter how hard she sometimes fought it. Those nights alone were all that allowed her to keep going during those first few months. Otherwise, she would have burned out completely.

Yet it was not the fact that he did such things to her that hurt most. He knew what he did was wrong but still did it anyway. Yes, he was often cold and dismissive but there were occasions when he could be loving. But they were so fleeting that the truth of him was, in her experience, the worse side of him. His acts of contrition – sometimes consisting of presents like the red coat from Arnotts – though heartfelt for half a day or so, were not enough to make up for the rest of his behaviour. Sometimes, remorse and apology came with sobriety, sometimes with drunkenness. She never knew which it would be when he walked in the door.

One such incident transpired about three months into their marriage. It was past midnight at the end of May when a drunken Bertram shook Wren awake with a lamp in one hand and strange look on his face. She thought there was a little guilt in his expression but mostly it was anticipation and smug self-satisfaction.

"Got you a present."

She could smell spirits on his breath and tried not to jerk back. She knew he would be cross if she did.

Grinning in the lamplight – which gave his features a hollow, ghoulish shadow – he deposited something black and hairy on the blanket. It squeaked.

This time Wren really did recoil, throwing back the covers and leaping from the bed. "*What –?*" she choked, horrified, as Bertram snatched it out from under the upended bedclothes.

"*Don't hurt it!*" he scolded, shocked by her reaction. His face crumpled with hurt. "Don't you like it?"

"What *is* it?" she asked, poised to run from the room in case whatever it was came towards her.

Bertram carefully placed the small furry ball on the bed once more. When he removed his hand, the ball struck out on ungainly legs and immediately toppled over with a yelp – whether because of its youth or the uneven surface of soft bed coverings.

The little creature had Wren on her knees within a moment.

"*A puppy!*" she said with wonder as it tried and failed to stand again.

It gave another whimper. She stretched out her finger. The pup batted at it with its forepaws then took a gentle nip at the proffered digit.

Meeting her husband's gaze, in hushed tones Wren asked, "Is it for me?"

"She. *She*. Of course, she's for you because you're a she and she's a she too, see? Clever, ain't it?" Bertram looked very pleased with himself but the happiness slid from his face as the dog gave several yaps in a row. Suddenly, a look of disgust crossed his face. "If it's going to start that, it can go outside."

"*No!*" said Wren loudly, eliciting another protest from the puppy. She snatched it off the bed and cuddled it to her chest. It was pleasantly warm and soft to touch. "No. It'll only be worse if you do that. And it might run away. I'll keep it with me."

"And what about me?" Bertram asked.

"Well, you can either stay here or go," Wren answered shortly. She didn't have the patience for him at this time of night and she wanted to properly inspect her puppy. She thought he might argue but instead he huffed and left the room, slamming the door behind him.

Wren looked at the dog. For the first time in months she felt an utter calm descend upon her. As the little animal pottered about the room examining its surroundings, all her attention and energies focused on it, wiping out painful and worrying thoughts. She couldn't have been gifted a better distraction. So wrapped up in her own unhappiness, she had forgotten what it was like to take enjoyment from the little things in life. Yes, overall her lot had not brought her the contentment she'd thought it would but there was still good in her life.

And now, with the addition of this little lady, there was even more good in her life.

Then the pup squatted to piddle on the floor.

The dog was perhaps a little way off completely good yet.

Chapter 39

The next few days were something of a challenge. The pup, who Wren christened Tess, was not trained in any way and, given Wren had never owned an animal, there was a great deal of trial and error involved. She didn't even know what to feed it. Sometime around mid-afternoon on the first day she succumbed to her cluelessness, picked up her puppy and took it to Ewan and Lili's. There, she was given so many instructions as to the proper care and training of a young sheepdog (Ewan informed her of the breed), she asked for a pencil and paper to write it down.

When she got Tess back to the house, however, things began to get a little chaotic once again – so much so, Bertram's supper was late which he was none too pleased about.

Muttering something that sounded like "Damn dog" he added, "I'll send it back if it means I won't be getting my supper when I come in of an evening. And me after working all day."

"Send her away and you'll get no dinner at all," Wren muttered back.

She had already fallen in love with the dog. In that fleeting moment, she thought she might go with the dog if it was sent away.

Bertram heard her but did not reply. He accepted his

dinner when it arrived and they ate in silence.

One thing Bertram was adamant about, however, was that the puppy would sleep downstairs. It was something Ewan had also told her to do. With great reluctance, she shut Tess in the scullery with some old blankets and newspaper. This, of course, the puppy found deeply upsetting. It took all Wren's self-control not to go down and comfort her. Wren had never been so glad to see morning. But when she opened the door, she wasn't glad at all. The puppy had torn the paper to pieces, ripped the blanket and chewed the door surround. It amazed her that one little animal could do so much damage. Forgetting that the little creature in front of her was just a puppy she chastised it roundly then shoved it out the door. She took great pride in the cleanliness of the house and the dog was ruining it. Unfortunately, however, after cleaning up she set about her usual morning routine without a thought for the puppy, its existence temporarily erased from her mind as familiarity took over. It was, therefore, well over an hour before she remembered to let the puppy back in.

But Tess was not there.

The bottom of Wren's stomach seemed to disappear as she ran around the garden and yard calling the puppy's name. Out onto the road, up the lane, climbing gates to look into the fields. Yet no sign of the puppy. Terrible scenarios flitted through her head as she sobbed the puppy's name into empty space. Perhaps Tess had been hit by one of the few cars on the road or trampled by cattle or had fallen into a river and drowned. It all festered in her head so that by the time she reached Lili's, she was in such a state she could barely speak.

After Lili calmed her a little, she managed, "Tess! *Gone!*" then began to sob again.

"Oh dear!" Lili sympathised. "Well, I haven't seen her, I'm afraid. Have you been up to the top farm? Maybe she went home."

"But she's not at home. I checked all around."

"Not your home, hers," Lili answered patiently. "Coxes'."

"What?" Wren momentarily forgot to be upset in her confusion.

"Coxes' at the top of the lane. That's where Bertie got her, isn't it? I know they had puppies for sale anyway."

"I don't know! He just gave her to me."

"That's where she'll have gone. Back home. Go on up there and I'd say you'll find her."

Wren looked sceptical.

"Do you want me to go with you?" Lili asked kindly.

"No, no!" Wren didn't want to be considered completely incapable. After all, it didn't take two of them to retrieve a puppy.

A little calmer now she had a purpose, Wren set off up the lane, going further than she ever had before. Following a curve in her path, she was faced with a house. It was a little distance away but even at that she could see it was very neat. There were window boxes on each sill and pots bursting with early summer colour flanking the front door. Hens pecked in the cobblestones and a terrier scratched at an earthy patch a little further away. Spotting Wren, the little dog came flying towards her barking frantically, a little ball of protective, aggressive energy. Faltering in her forward march, Wren stopped at the entrance to the yard, worried that her bare ankles might fall prey to the eager teeth of this tiny guardian. She was saved, however, by the appearance of a woman with greying hair at the door of the house.

"*Oi-now, come-away-outta-that!*" she shouted across the yard, making the dog skid to a halt. "*Here, dog!*" She clapped her hand against her thigh then added "Hello!", waving to her human visitor.

Wren recognised her from her wedding. "Hello, Mrs Cox! He won't bite, will he?'

"Ah no, pet, he's harmless. Are you just here for an auld visit or can I help you with anything?"

"I think she's looking for this little lady, Mam."

The voice came from the right of the yard. A man in a low-peaked cap stood a little way off and in his arms was . . .

"*Tess!*" Wren began to hurry towards her puppy with the other dog hot on her heels. But then she stopped dead. The young man holding the dog was none other than . . .

"Robbie?"

"We'll have to stop meeting like this," he said freely, meeting her eye with a smile. "Me catching dogs for you," he clarified. "That's how we met the last time, remember? Catching Rodney. Make a habit of losing dogs, do you?"

"I do not! I –" but she stopped when she caught the expression on his face. He was making fun of her.

"Don't think we've ever been properly introduced," he said, shifting the dog and proffering his hand. "Robbie Cox."

Wren shook it, noting the latent strength in his grip and the warmth of his large hand. For such a compact young man, he did have very large hands. She was completely thrown, however, by the difference in his behaviour. He was speaking to her, looking at her. She barely recognised the confident character in front of her even if his appearance was familiar. His hair, however, was a good deal longer and wilder than it was when she had first encountered him. Maybe, she thought, he was a little like Samson in the Bible – his wild and free hair was linked to a freedom and openness in his manner. Where was the boy who walked away from her when they met in town?

He seemed to be following the same train of thought because he suddenly didn't seem to be able to meet her eye.

Handing her the puppy, he muttered, "Of course, you know my mother."

Now Wren was forced to approach the woman out of

politeness. "I'm so sorry, Mrs Cox. I knew you were a neighbour but I'd no idea you lived up here when we met at my wedding."

"Not to worry, pet." The lady patted Wren's arm. "I'm glad to know you now. I was surprised young Bertie didn't bring you up for a visit after."

Wren noticed Robbie turn away sharply at the mention of Bertram.

His mother, however, continued oblivious. "But, shur, now we've been properly introduced you can come visit me yourself. Won't you come on in for a drop of tea? I've just put the water on for Robbie's elevenses."

Without waiting for an answer, Mrs Cox bustled off into the house, leaving her son and their visitor in an awkward silence. Robbie gestured for Wren to precede him and they entered the house which was cool and, like the kitchen in the Gate House, quite dark – although she did note it had a rather pretty tiled floor.

Sitting down at the table with the dog on her lap, Wren turned to Robbie. "I don't remember seeing you at the wedding. Were you there?"

"No," his mother answered. "He wasn't. And he could have been if he'd wanted to at all." She managed to sound cross and affectionate at the same time.

Robbie's face flamed. "I didn't have time what with minding Mr Cameron's and Bertie's places for the day." He said it quickly while looking intently out the window.

His mother made a "*Pfft*" sound but said no more. Instead, she turned the conversation to Wren, asking innocuous questions about her honeymoon, how she was settling in and how she found country life after growing up in a town.

Then came a more difficult question. "And what about your family?"

It was a legitimate question for any kindly neighbour to ask but up until that point Wren had somehow managed to avoid it. That is, she avoided it with everyone apart from Lili and Ewan. But she did not want to think of that conversation. She pushed it to the back of her mind.

"My mother's been very ill for a number of years. We thought she was getting better so my father sent me to live with my great-aunt. I think you'll maybe know Astrid Charlton?"

Mrs Cox nodded.

"But she fell ill again not long before Christmas. My father works so there was no one to look after Artie and Olivia – my younger brother and sister – so Auntie Astrid's taken them in."

"Wasn't that very good of her!" Mrs Cox smiled. "Artie ... that wouldn't be the handsome young man who walked you up the aisle, would it?"

Relief flooded through Wren. At least the woman had not asked what her mother's illness was. She knew Bertram would be furious if she told anyone what was really wrong with her mother. Yet for some reason she suddenly felt the urge to tell these strangers anyway. She no longer wanted to hide the secret. She was fed up doing things because Bertram wanted her to do them.

But no, she couldn't. She shouldn't. She was only a few months (no matter how long they felt) into marriage and here she was, already looking for ways to defy her husband. However, Mrs Cox had asked her about her Artie and good manners as well as her pride in her brother made her latch onto that particular conversational thread.

"Yes, that was Artie ..."

Wren spent over half an hour in the Coxes' kitchen. Robbie contributed very little to the conversation but she found his mother very easy to talk to. On standing to go, she was gladly pressed into another visit and asked that Mrs Cox might come down to visit her some morning too.

Carrying Tess, she found herself leaving the house in a much happier mood that when she entered it. Robbie stood to follow her out. She expected him to disappear back to the yard but instead he fell into step with her. She thought perhaps he wanted to speak to her, but he said nothing. In vain she searched for something to say but found her thoughts moved with glacial slowness.

Finally, once they were well down the lane and out of sight of the house, he spoke.

"You should put the dog down."

Wren came to a halt. The pup, though not particularly large, was beginning to weigh on her arms. She placed her gently on the lane and Tess immediately bounded off after a butterfly flitting lazily above her.

Making to follow her, Wren found her forearm held by Robbie. She looked into his face but found he wasn't looking back. Anger flared deep within Wren's chest. All the frustration that had been building up inside her without a safe outlet seemed to focus itself on the young man who stood in front of her. What did he want with her when he could not even meet her eye? Why did he follow her? Why should he stop her? Why had he walked away from her on that first night? Why did she listen to him when he told her to put Tess down? Now she had nothing to cling to, nothing to shield her. She was laid bare so her only form of defence was attack. She yanked her arm from his light grasp.

"*What?*" she shouted. "*What do you want, Robbie? You can't even look at me! Come on, what is it?*"

Shocked by her apparently unprovoked vitriol, Robbie's head snapped up and his eyes widened in surprise. "I was just thinking," he said mildly.

"Really?" Wren snapped. "About what?"

He hesitated then said simply, "I was wondering why you seemed embarrassed when you told Mammy your mother was ill."

She felt the colour drain from her face. "What ... what do you mean?"

He shrugged. "What I said. I could see it in your face. I was wondering what was wrong." His eyes focused on hers with unwavering concern. "Are *you* alright?" There was a warmth, a kindness, a quiet insistence in the way he said it.

She liked the fact that he stressed '*you*'. He wanted to know how *she* was but all she could do was mouth wordlessly. Could he truly tell something was wrong? And now, with her silence, she was almost certainly confirming his suspicions.

"She's ill," she began with an attempt at conviction but even to her own ears it sounded false. "I ... she ... she's not physically ill, she just ..."

"Has a troubled mind."

"Yes."

"It must be hard for you. For all of you."

"We manage," she answered shortly. "But ... but sometimes –" She looked down. She did not want to admit how hard it was.

"Hey." He caught her under the chin with his forefinger, so this time it was she met his gaze.

There was an instant when they looked into the darkness of one another's eyes. She was caught off guard. His eyes! How had she not noticed his eyes before? Though his brows were the same dirty blond as his hair, his eyelashes were dark, almost black, as they framed irises of the most perfect light blue. Maybe she hadn't noticed because he'd spent so much time looking anywhere but at her.

Then Robbie leaned in and kissed her.

His skin was very smooth. That was the first thing she noticed with her face just inches from his. His visage was that of a man who did not often have to shave – boyish yet not soft of feature. There was definition in his cheeks that had come to fruition since she had first known him. He was more of a man now. Why hadn't noticed that straight away? His lips were soft on hers yet they moved insistently. She had not expected him to know how to kiss. She hadn't even thought about … well, she *had*, but she was not even going to admit that to herself. His hand cupped her jaw as the other slipped around her waist. Involuntarily, her body seemed to lean against him, answering him, kissing him back.

She broke the kiss and shoved him away.

His breath was as ragged as hers as they stood a little distance apart, gauging the reaction of the other.

Wren was the first to get her voice back. "What was *that*?" she said shrilly. "What do you bloody well think you're *doing*?" She never said 'bloody' but circumstances seemed to warrant it.

Robbie rubbed both hands one after the other through his hair then brought them forward, swiping his curly fringe down his forehead only for it to spring back up, as unruly as it had been before. Puffing out his cheeks, he shrugged.

"Don't you shrug at me, Robbie Cox!" she shrieked. She was boiling with anger. How dare he! *How dare he!* Who did he think he was? Who did he think *she* was? Someone who just took what men dealt her lying down? Well, she did with Bertram, but she didn't want to think about that. No one else was going to take advantage of her.

Spinning away, she stormed off down the lane. She had not travelled a dozen paces when he caught hold of her arm. Without thinking, Wren whirled around to him, her palm open, and let her hand connect with his jaw. She had never slapped someone – not even Artie or Oli. She was shocked how much it hurt. Her palm stung viciously but she made herself focus on the pain. She was not afraid of it. It made her strong.

Robbie cupped his own jaw just as he had hers but not before Wren saw the ugly bright red that patchily coloured his skin. "*Ow!*" he whispered, surprise keen in his voice.

Wren suddenly felt horribly ashamed. She had hit someone. Had he really deserved it?

"I'm so sorry," she said, meaning it. "I shouldn't have done that. I –"

Tess appeared at their feet. Rather than reply, Robbie knelt down and began rubbing the dog, leaving Wren to stand awkwardly over them. She wondered whether he was crying yet trying to hide it from her. However, when he did speak, there was no hitch in his voice.

"I've wanted to kiss you since you stood over me – just as you do now – on the first day I met you," he said hoarsely before looking up. His eyes were full of pain. "You don't know how often I've cursed myself for not fighting for you. For letting *him* take you."

Wren couldn't speak. How did one respond to such a declaration?

As it turned out, she did not need to. Robbie finished patting the dog, stood without looking at her and walked away. But she couldn't let him leave without saying anything.

"Robbie . . . you shouldn't have done that," she called, touching her lips, remembering his kiss. "You can't."

He turned, a bitter smile on his face. "Are you telling me you don't want me to?"

She tried to say, 'No, I don't,' but the words caught in her throat. A flash of his touch scorched through her mind and left her speechless. She tried to tell the lie but it refused to pass her lips. Sensing her uncertainty, he took three large strides to stand toe to toe with her then kissed her again.

Wren pushed him away again. "*No!* Don't. *Please* don't!"

"Why not?"

"Because you're too late!" she hissed, shoving him in the chest. "Because I'm *married!*"

"So? Do you love him?"

She searched for an answer. There wasn't one. She thought about her feelings for her husband and all that stretched out in front of her was a yawning chasm that she did not dare approach for fear it would swallow her whole.

"I'm married," she repeated. Even to her it sounded weak.

It wasn't enough to make him stop. He clutched her to him again and crushed her lips with his own. She tried to push him away but his hands were on her spine, strong and insistent, confining her, pressing her close to him. Yet he did not hurt her. Though she struggled against his proximity, his strength was measured – enough to hold her but not to harm her. Try as she might, she only seemed to get closer to him until she stopped struggling and kissed him back. His movements were unrelenting, inescapable, wonderful. She had never experienced such a sensuous explosion of emotions as his tongue flicked at her lips and his firm body seemed to envelop hers. She could get lost in the feel of him.

Tess barked.

Wren pulled away. He did not stop her.

As she walked blindly from him, he called after her.

"I'll see you again!"

It wasn't a question. He knew she felt it too.

Chapter 40

Try as she might over the next few days, Wren could not shake the memories and feelings of her encounter with Robbie. She did her best to focus on other things and, to an observer, she appeared to go about her business as usual. She put a great deal of energy into training Tess, being sure to keep a close eye on her for fear she went walkabout again. She found the puppy willing enough to listen to her but struggled somewhat to control her instincts to run after anything that moved. But it wasn't enough. Though she threw herself into the mundanities of work and the novelty of her new dog, she kept harking back. The only thing that could keep it from the forefront of her mind was meditation on the subject she usually tried to avoid.

Since she had thought about it while in the Coxes' kitchen, her first meeting with Lili and Ewan after becoming Mrs Burnley kept resurfacing for her to pick apart.

Six days after she took up residence on Bachelor Lane, she managed a visit to her sister-in-law. Lili had come down to the house the day after Wren arrived with a basket of items to put in the larder but Bertram came in just as the two women were about to make tea, curtailing her visit. Lili stayed a few more minutes but, knowing when her company was unwanted, left before the kettle had even boiled. It upset

Wren to discover the animosity that existed between the siblings. Though she knew they did not get on particularly well, things had become markedly worse. She hoped she was not the cause of the hostilities.

When she finally did visit Lili, it was only because Bertram wasn't at home. He had gone to the mart that day and wasn't back even though it was well past suppertime. Fed up with waiting and longing for company, Wren walked up to the Camerons' to find them eating their own supper.

Though she had offered to leave, Wren found herself being gently steered into a seat at the table and presented with a mug of tea while she was told, "No, we haven't seen you in long enough. You're not going anywhere."

"I think she's been avoiding us," Ewan said, grinning. "Do you think we scared her away, hen?"

"Oh maybe, maybe. You're an awful scary-looking yoke. Especially when you've got a great shaggy beard hiding the bottom half of your face."

Though the exchange was short, Wren couldn't help but envy the humour and playfulness of the couple who sat in front of her. They were so comfortable with one another. One would think they had been together for years instead of months. She simply could not envisage ever having that kind of relationship with Bertram.

"How long has it been since you've been here?" Ewan asked. "You were at our wedding and then we saw neither hide nor hair of you until just before your own. And Lili had the biscuits baked for when you came and everything."

"Did we really frighten you off or has Bertie been keeping you all to himself?"

"I wasn't here," Wren said, surprised.

Her companions both paused mid-chew. "Oh?" said Lili.

"I had to go home. My mother, she …" Wren stopped. How much should she say?

"Oh. We didn't know. What happened?" Lili asked gently, sensing something was amiss.

"Didn't Bertram tell you?"

A glance passed between Lili and Ewan.

"No," Lili said slowly. "Bertie didn't tell us anything."

Wren felt cold. He hadn't said anything. He had not saved her the difficulty of explaining what happened to her family. How that part of her life imploded over the past few months.

"Nothing?" she finally managed.

"Not a word." Lili shook her head. "Why? What happened, pet?"

"My mother she – she nearly drowned my brother and sister. She walked across town and straight off the harbour wall and into the sea with Artie and Oli."

The silent shock that greeted her was crushing. She wanted one of them to say something but they seemed lost for words.

"When?" Ewan choked out.

"The day before your wedding. I left the day after with Auntie Astrid. We were there for nearly a month."

"Were you back for Christmas?" Lili asked suddenly.

"No. Why?"

Lili and Ewan exchanged a loaded glance.

"Why?" Then, with more urgency, "*Why?*"

"Bertie told us he was spending Christmas afternoon with you and your aunt," Ewan said gently. "We had no idea you were gone."

"Why would he do that?" she asked stupidly.

Ewan threw his hands up in an 'I have no idea' gesture. Lili, however, had another concern.

Catching hold of Wren's hand, she squeezed it. "Your mother – is she alright? I noticed neither of your parents were at the wedding but I didn't want to ask on the day ..."

Lili let the question hang but held Wren's hand as the girl searched an answer. She cursed Bertram for being so cowardly as to not even tell his own sister what had happened. But then was it cowardice? Or was it embarrassment? Was he mortified to attach himself to someone with a mother who lacked mental soundness? Did he believe that people would think less of Wren – less of him – if they knew the truth of Felicity?

"Mammy's in a mental hospital. Auntie Astrid took Artie and Oli. They're living in Enniscorthy with her now. Otherwise I would have had to go back home and live with them."

"Oh Lord!" Lili said sympathetically. "You've not told anyone?"

"I thought people knew. I thought Bertram would tell them."

Lili huffed. "Bertie doesn't do anything he can't see the benefit of for himself."

Ewan frowned at her but turned to Wren. "You said she tried to … drown your brother and sister. That'd be the boy who walked you up the church and the little flower girl?"

"Yes. They were saved by some fishermen apparently. Otherwise …" She couldn't continue. She had thought about the 'what ifs' of her mother's actions. Even though she knew it was unhealthy, she could not completely overrule that part of her prone to see the worst of situations – the part of her that Astrid had tried to discourage. But in a situation as drastic as this one, it was only natural that she should struggle. She shook these notions from her head. "They've settled in well with Astrid. And they seem to like school too. I'm going into town to visit them all tomorrow."

She did not stay very long after that. She had hoped to spend an hour or two in the Camerons' company and forget about her troubles. Instead, the encounter only added to them. It took her days to process what she discovered on her visit and she became noticeably withdrawn. Bertram demanded to know what was wrong on several occasions but she would not tell him she had visited his sister. There was no need to exacerbate the enmity he felt for the Camerons.

Slowly, the initial upset Wren felt at discovering Bertram had not explained her absence turned to latent anger. They had barely been married two weeks when she made her visit to Lili and Ewan so by the time May came around and she met Robbie again, what feelings she retained for Bertram had evaporated. She had discovered his true character which she had been inexplicably blind to during their courtship. How had she never realised his coldness and self-serving attitude? How did she breeze over the anger and the brutal streak of possessiveness? She also wondered what the point of this possessiveness was and what his interest in her really was. Why did he pick her? She had been blind enough to believe that it was because he loved her but that clearly was not the case. If he did have some level of affection for her, he had a strange way of showing it. Gifts where all well and good but they did not make up for his behaviour the rest of the time.

She and Bertram existed separately within the same sphere, only coming together when necessary. She learnt the ways of a farmer's wife quickly but instead of learning them from her husband, she learned with Lili or Ewan. They were kind and patient with her in a way Bertram rarely was. She studied with them on their farm and brought her knowledge home to her own work, just as she had when she wanted to know how to train Tess.

It was a good system. Trips up the lane to the Camerons' got Wren out of the oppressive gloom of the Gate House, gave her company she enjoyed and the knowledge she needed to work. And the better her work, the less cause for complaint and criticism Bertram had. The truth was, despite her husband's dislike of others' methods, Lili and Ewan knew what they were doing. They taught her well but she also had an inbuilt love of animals which helped enormously. It was part of the reason she was so happy when Bertram brought her Tess. The animals up to that point were all outside apart from the few occasions when they brought in ailing lambs. Wren always experienced a thrill when she heard these creatures snuffle and bleat as they lay in an egg box by the fire. When they were put outside again, it was as if the happiness of the household left with them. Once Tess arrived, Wren had constant companionship. And, despite the troubling incident with Robbie, she felt a great deal happier having a canine companion at her knee.

After her meeting with Robbie, Wren worried about seeing him again. She had to remind herself that she had spent several months on the Lane without seeing him at all so avoidance would be relatively easy. Yet she also could not help but believe that Robbie had been making a conscious effort to avoid *her* until she barged unknowingly into his yard looking for the puppy he sold to her husband. She even wondered whether Robbie intentionally sold the dog to Bertram in the hope that it might lead her to him. But that was just a silly thought.

So Wren went about her business with as much gusto as she could muster yet found the physical work of the house and farm did not occupy enough of her thoughts to offer a complete distraction. Instead, she learnt to allow her fantasies free rein internally while maintaining impassivity on the outside. And that was how it would remain: a fantasy. She had vowed in a church in front of God and witnesses to be faithful to Bertram. And she would be faithful because – despite everything – it was the right thing to do.

But that did not mean it would be easy.

Chapter 41

Time in the young Mrs Burnley's new life seemed to have a strange quality. She could look back at something that happened yesterday and believe it could have been months ago just as something that had occurred a fortnight past could feel like yesterday. Some days stretched and yawned in front of her, making her clock-watch until she had to lie it face down to escape the frustration of its slow crawl. On other occasions she would find a morning disappear to the open sky as she worked outdoors. On those occasions she had to rush back to the house to prepare a dinner for twelve or one o'clock with only fifteen minutes to make it. And though their relationship was strained at best, Wren simply could not bring herself to serve dinner late, no matter how much she resented the man who ate it. Even though she sometimes wanted to, she could not be that petty as it was the one thing Bertram always managed to do right: come rain, hail or shine, he always turned up for dinner on time.

It took a while for Wren to master the art of timing when it came to making food. The solution she found, instead of slaving over fresh meals every day, was to cook a large lump of meat at the start of the week which they would cut slices from and eat cold. In the morning, after breakfast, the first thing she did was prepare the vegetables: peel potatoes, dig carrots out of the sandpit in the garden, cut a head of cabbage from the veg patch. It meant that no matter how late she came in, all she needed to do was boil the veg and their meal would be ready. However, Wren discovered having some buttered slices of bread on the table when Bertram came in was a good precaution to take. Instead of getting annoyed about his dinner not being ready, her husband would sit quietly at the table munching his way through thick slices of soda bread until the food was served. Covertly watching the business-like way Bertram demolished the bread and butter, Wren thought he was perhaps quite happy with this arrangement. She came to recognise the look of disappointment on his face when he arrived in to a dinner served on time sans a starter of bread and butter. So to maintain the peace and hopefully curry favour, Wren always had the plate of bread and butter ready, no matter what time dinner was.

The week after her encounter with Robbie, Wren was bustling around the parlour setting the table and getting dinner ready. She was down on her hands and knees searching for a dropped fork under the dresser when she noticed a terrible smell from the direction of the doorway. Sitting up, thinking it was Tess who had likely rolled in something dead – or worse brought it into the house – she found Robbie leaning against the door frame, a satisfied smile on his face. The look he gave her made her leap to her feet in a fluster.

"What are you doing here?" She banged the retrieved fork down on the table with a lot more force than was necessary.

"I brought him in for dinner," Bertram answered as he side-stepped his companion. "Is it a problem?"

Though he asked the question, Wren knew by his tone how to answer. "No," but then added, "Lord almighty, the smell of you!"

"We're cleaning out the cattle sheds," Bertram clarified.

"We fare stink though, Bertie," Robbie said, sniffing his shirt. "I wonder would Mrs Burnley, give us a sup of hot water to have a bit of a wash." He was fighting a large smile and his eyes shone with such avidity that Wren could not look at him.

She handed Bertram the kettle and some soap. "Wash out at the pump. The pair of you would only make a mess of the house."

Wordlessly, Bertram took the kettle and the two men traipsed back out to the yard. Wren set about buttering more bread since she didn't really have enough vegetables for three even though there was a good lump of cooked meat left.

After a while, there was a call from the yard. Bertram. She hadn't heard what he said so went out to see what the matter was.

There in the centre of the cobblestones by the pump stood the two men, both without their shirts as they washed their chests and armpits. One was dark and skinny, the other fair and broad. Both had prominent tan lines around their necks and biceps even though it was only the start of the summer. Both were dripping wet having scrubbed their hair and faces with soap and water.

Wren stood and stared. But not at her husband.

Turning to shout again, Bertram showed his surprise. "Oh. You're there. Run in and get us some towels and clean shirts there. We're done for the day with that job."

Dumbly, Wren ascended the stairs to fetch the items. It took her no time at all to locate them but on her way back down she stopped at the cubby window halfway up the flight. From it, she had an unimpeded view of the water pump. The two of them were continuing to wash themselves half-heartedly simply for something to do while they waited. She could not help comparing them: the man she married and the man she didn't. She had seen all there was to see of Bertram and knew it was not as favourable as his fully clothed form suggested. Robbie, on the other hand, was a man whose physical form could be appreciated.

Clothed, he looked stocky, half-naked, he just looked muscular. His bone structure was built for size. Though not large, he looked remarkably strong, his chest defined, his stomach flat, his shoulders rounded with muscle – the build of someone with the potential to run to fat if he did not work so hard. But he definitely was not fat. She could see the shadow of his lower ribs straining the skin of his torso. Wren smiled to herself as she concluded that he was the sort of man who could – if the horse grew weary – pull the cart himself.

Bertram gestured and the two men crossed the yard to come in. Wren hurried down the last few steps to meet them as they entered.

"There you are!" Bertram huffed. "It's fierce cold out there without a shirt on."

Wren silently handed the two men towels and clean shirts without meeting their eyes. She could feel their gazes on her and it made her uncomfortable. "I don't know if there's enough cabbage for the two of you but there's plenty meat and I've readied up some extra bread and butter for you."

Bertram gave a hum of appreciation before sliding past Wren into the parlour and setting about devouring the food waiting on the table. Wren watched from the doorway until she felt a hand slide gently up her arm. Shaking it off, she followed her husband.

Both men ate hungrily then cleaned their plates with the remaining slices of bread. Throughout the meal, there was talk about people she did not know, places she had never been and the current prices for this and that at the various marts around the county. Wren listened, absorbing all of it, but didn't contribute. She was interested to hear all she could about farming but Bertram had very little interest in talking to her about the live weight of bullocks and the price of freshly calved heifers. It was nice, for once, to hear easy-flowing conversation at the dinner table instead of scattered comments and monosyllabic answers. Afterwards, they all had tea and fruitcake. Fruitcake was something Wren knew she made well but that did not prevent her from glowing with pride when Robbie informed her it was some of the best fruitcake he'd ever tasted. For a moment, she forgot to be angry with him. She forgot she wasn't supposed to look at him.

It was as if she had been hit in the stomach. All the air seemed to leave her system as his eyes bored into hers. There was so much in his eyes: warmth, pleading, love, lust, challenge. She could not look away. How did he do that? How could he have such an effect on her? Was she weak? Her husband sat within feet of them and yet she was making a fool of herself thinking of the other man. How could she be so stupid! She wrenched herself away, shaking her head. And it all started over a compliment about her fruitcake! It was impossible to feel any more ridiculous as the shame burned her insides.

What's wrong with me? she thought.

After the men left, Wren cleared up in a daze, her head filled with guilt, confusion, frustration and longing. She was not married four months and she was already entertaining thoughts about another man. She was still supposed to be in the honeymoon phase of unconditional and irrational love yet when she looked at her husband – or even thought about him – she just felt cold.

She knew she shouldn't think of Robbie, but she did. She wondered whether things would have been better with him. Her experiences of intimacy had so far been distinctly unpleasant. She did not know if other peoples' experiences were any better since she was too embarrassed to ask anyone. She also did not want to try and explain her own experiences to someone else, because she hated to think about them and because they left her feeling dirty and degraded. Surely love wasn't meant to feel like that?

The two people she knew who, like herself, had recently married did not give off any signals of discomfort or fear when they spoke about or even saw their partners. On the contrary: both Lili and Joan, Wren's friend from town, seemed to look forward to the company of their men. They found happiness in helping them, doing things for them. And they were loved in return. Their men made the effort to be appreciative, to show their affection, their *love*. That was what love looked like and Wren knew she did not have it or feel it.

That evening after supper, Bertram announced he was going out.

"Where?" It was something that Wren had asked before. She always got an irritated look in return and the same answer.

"The pub. Why?"

"Just wondering."

Bertram seemed to war with himself for a moment before asking, "Are you wanting to come?"

Wren stared. He had never offered to take her before. She wondered was he shamming. It hadn't sounded like it.

"No," she muttered.

Bertram visibly exhaled. "Right. Bye then." He walked by her to leave, seemed to toy with the idea of giving her a goodbye kiss but thought better of it. Perhaps he felt the waning of her affections as much as she felt his.

Wren was quite happy to be left alone as she sat by the fire, Tess curled at her feet, finding happiness in her knitting, sewing and reading.

Bertram was gone less than an hour when there was a knock at the back door. Tess lifted her head, woofed half-heartedly and scrambled up to investigate.

"No, Tess," Wren admonished. If she opened the back door, she might not see the dog until morning.

Closing Tess in the parlour, she went to do the investigating herself.

It was Robbie.

"What –?"

"*Shhh*," he whispered, coming in and shutting the door behind him.

She was far too close to him. There was a door behind both of them, stairs to her left and another door to her right. Calmly, he removed his jacket and hung it on a peg, took off his boots and left them neatly by the wall.

"I know you feel it too," he breathed. His arms wrapped around her waist and in a moment she heard the door behind her rattle as she collided with it. On the other side, Tess whined and scratched.

His hands seemed to be everywhere. His lips kissing hers, her neck, her cheek, her collar bone, her chest. It was too much. He'd been standing outside the door and then suddenly he was inside and all of this was happening. She couldn't think, she couldn't speak, she could only feel.

She had never felt anything like this. She was in his arms. He lifted her clean off the ground. Instinctively, she wrapped her arms and legs around him. He opened the door to Evelyn Burnley's old room, taking Wren with him.

It was then that she began to protest.

"No. *No*. We can't."

But still she couldn't stop kissing him. Robbie did not stop either.

"Bertram," she finally said, pushing herself away but he still held her.

"Bertram's not here," he said.

She knew he wasn't. And yet the fear that he might return terrified her. If Bertram walked in on a scene like this, what might he do? All she knew was it would not be pretty.

Letting her go, Robbie went over to the bedroom door, closed and locked it.

She should have felt fear being locked in a room with a man she had met less than half a dozen times but, instead, a sense of calm washed over her. Slowly, he approached her but rather than hold her again, he ran his hands down the collar of her dress to rest at the top button. Looking her directly in the eye, questioning without speaking, he began to undo the buttons. Wren didn't protest. Instead, she tentatively reached up to the buttons on his shirt – the shirt she had given him earlier that very day – and began to do the same. Though it was intimate, it was slightly awkward. All of it was done in silence apart from the odd mumbled hum of appreciation. Neither of them was sure what to say or do. It was all very stilted and uncertain: who should undo Robbie's trousers (he did), who should be the first to bare all (she did). But it was still exciting. A new experience, a realisation of the fantasies both had endured for days.

It was so different for Wren. Where Bertram's gaze had been critical, there was a tenderness and a look of pleasure on Robbie's face as he drank her in. Yet there was also the promise of something much more sensuous. He moved fluidly as he slid towards her, catching her bare waist in his hot calloused fingers before guiding himself around her until he stood behind her. His hands slid across her belly, pulling her close to him before creeping up to fondle her small breasts. The heat and pressure of his body against hers made her legs feel weak. He wanted her and she wanted him.

"How do you want it?" he breathed, tickling her ear as he brushed the lobe with his lips.

376

She turned to face him. "Like this."

Backing into the bed, she pulled Robbie with her so that he had to kneel either side of her legs on the quilt. There was an awkward shimmy up the bed followed by an even more awkward climbing over legs as Wren changed position so that she could wrap her legs around Robbie's hips. His hands began to roam freely across her body, charting unfamiliar territory. There was wonder in his eyes as he looked on her – just looked. He ceded control to her. This was her decision now. He had started proceedings but he was not going to have her say it was all his doing or that he forced himself on her. He knew he was placing them in a precarious situation but he was not going to be the only one claiming responsibility. Both were culpable. And both of them were ready. Wren had never felt more ready in her life. So with steady hands she guided him into her and felt the burning heat of skin on skin as they touched each other as intimately as two human beings possibly could. He gasped and she could see his pupils dilate in the dim light.

It had never been so smooth, so easy, for Wren. They fitted together perfectly. He barely moved inside her and yet she knew instinctively that this man was her other half. After a moment, he cautiously shifted and tested the feel of her. Wren gently used her legs to pull him closer. He rocked gently and groaned.

"Keep going," she whispered, stroking his cheek with her hand. She caught the dampness of his sweat on her fingertips and watched with fascination as more beaded on his forehead. She had never seen Bertram sweat at all. But then she realised that Robbie was straining to maintain control. It was taking everything he had not to allow the animal impulses to take over and really move.

She stretched up and kissed him.

"Let go," she told him.

He did. His body took over. The feeling of her crushed against him, inside and out was enough to drive him wild. However, he still retained enough of himself to have concern for the woman who moved with him, stroke for stroke, caressing her body, feeling her, loving her. He knew of no other way to show it, to prove it than to try and make her experience the ecstasy he was experiencing himself.

She writhed and groaned beneath him, pulling him deeper and deeper.

And then it was over.

They lay silent on the bed afterwards, too hot to draw the blanket over themselves. Though they were both naturally shy about their bodies, neither covered up, enjoying the touch of skin on skin, idly stroking one another. They had been far too free and intimate with one another to give way to embarrassment now. In truth, they were fascinated with one another's forms. Robbie lay propped on his elbow beside Wren. He watched his hand trail across her bare skin, investigating every inch, remembering every dip and rise, every reaction to his touch. Wren watched too. There was something so calming about observing his steady fingertips brush her skin leaving the fine down of hair standing to attention in their wake. It was so easy, so comfortable, so familiar, so arousing.

She rolled on to her side, mirroring his position, and pushed his shoulder so that he lay under her wandering hand. She began the same process with him, bolder with her explorations of him than she had ever been of her husband. Though she could tell Robbie was torn between pushing her away and surrendering to her touch, she kept going regardless. She had never had a willing male subject or a male she wanted to study as much as she wanted to examine Robbie. And since he *was* willing, she was taking full advantage of him. Caught in the moment, she straddled him.

His hands automatically went to her hips and gently palpated her buttocks. "Again?"

She smiled, bending down to kiss him thoroughly. "Don't you want to? Or are you not able to keep up?" she asked coyly, sitting up and arching her back.

She did not wait for his answer, instead lowering herself onto him. She had never been on top before. It felt different. Better. But then it all felt so much better with Robbie. It made her want to shed tears of happiness, laugh with delight. She cried out with sheer joy. The sound made him sit up so that they were nose to nose. She didn't know you could do that either. His hand clasped her shoulder blades as her fingernails grazed his back, pressed chest to chest, stomach to stomach. And then they kissed until they couldn't breathe.

When it was over, they stayed sitting, wrapped around one another, skin glued to skin by perspiration. They barely spoke, asking each other questions with their eyes and hands as they continued to caress one another. They would never be done with exploring each other's bodies.

Wren tried to feel guilty but couldn't. She knew Robbie didn't. She also knew what they had done was wrong. They had committed a crime against a holy vow, a legal vow. And yet, how could it be wrong when it felt so right? They were meant to be together. There was no doubt in either of their minds.

"What are we going to do?" Wren finally asked, her voice hollow, muffled against Robbie's shoulder.

"Don't know," he sighed, adding, "m' Birdy." He was tired, his words sluggish.

Wren felt a little quiver of pleasure when he used her pet name. She wondered how he knew it. It was a while since she had heard it. She had forgotten how much she liked being called by it.

"Bertram can never know."

"Bertie can go and stuff it!" Robbie said angrily. "And I suppose these are from him." Even in the dull twilight, he could pick out the fading bruises on her skin and did so, gently rubbing a fingertip over each one.

"He can never know," was all she said in reply.

He sighed again. "Aye."

Eventually Wren managed to push, "You'd better go," past her unwilling lips.

She reluctantly let go, pushing herself away. She sat naked on the edge of the bed and watched him dress. As she did, a pain blossomed in the centre of her chest and burned so acutely she had to fight not to tell him to stay. However, when he finally kissed her before turning to go, she said, "Wait."

Getting up, she dressed hurriedly. Though she did not hear Bertram come back, she had not been listening for him either. She was too engrossed in Robbie. Unlocking the door, she quickly checked for any noise before entering the parlour. Tess was sitting sat in front of the hearth and gave Wren a baleful stare when she walked in.

"Don't look at me like that," Wren said irritably. "Robbie, you can come out."

"Who were you talking to?" Robbie asked.

"Dog," Wren said shortly.

On spotting Robbie, Tess slunk over for a pat and was duly given one. "Good girl," he whispered to her. "Now you look after your mammy." And with that, he turned, gave Wren a lingering kiss and disappeared into the night.

He did not realise what he said to the dog had knocked the wind out of Wren.

Mammy.

What if she was now pregnant with Robbie's child?

Chapter 42

Lili was pregnant. She was sure of it. She had not yet visited the doctor but her body told her enough to know the truth. She was going to have Ewan's baby. She could not have been more elated. Or terrified. She was not young and childbearing was a young woman's game – especially for a first-time mother. Of course, she knew women her own age who were still producing children on a frighteningly regular basis. A woman down the road called Mag Doyle was on her fifteenth now and she was several years older than Lili. But then Mag was not a prime example of successful motherhood since she had lost three babies at birth and nearly died twice herself. She could not have been more than forty yet she looked far too old to be dandling a baby on her hip while trailing several others in her wake. Children had sapped the life out of her – those that lived and those that died – making her worn with worry and cares. Yet, she raised good, honest, hardworking children who were clean, polite and well-fed while living on a pittance. Despite her hardships, Mag was a good and well-loved mother. So perhaps she was a parent that Lili could admire.

She hadn't told anyone else yet, not even Ewan. For now, it was her own little secret. This tiny little flutter of life that sat low in her belly, a buzz of warmth that was with her always, waking her in the morning and sending her to sleep at night. Very early on, she thought she could feel it moving but told herself that it was only her imagination. Then she was sure she could feel it – a kind of internal tickle that made her giggle like a little girl with shock and pleasure.

She found herself daydreaming about the child she would have: a little being with light hair that would darken to the brown of its father over time. It would have brown eyes just as he did. Those eyes would be looking at her soon, she thought. In a few short months she would meet his gaze. Because it would be a boy, of course. And he would eventually grow up to be tall and strong like his parents. But what would his name be?

She had to keep catching herself in these fantasies – there was far too much that could go wrong in the interim – they were too detailed, too perfect and too open to the pitfalls of reality where so much could disappoint her by not living up to her imaginings. But then this was *her* child. Nothing about it could possibly disappoint her. Yet she kept telling herself not to think of it. But that didn't stop her vividly colouring her future with a perfect child at its centre.

As midsummer crept onwards, so did her pregnancy. She finally persuaded herself to go to the doctor while she was in town one day and was told she was between four and five months pregnant. Her child would therefore be born around late October just before the hard winter began to set in. The harshness of the last months of the year were no time to be carrying a child. If she had the baby in October, it also meant she would still be able to help Ewan on the farm once winter set in and there was more work to be done. She could carry the child out onto the farm with her if needed. Although when she thought about it more, she realised that a child would feel the cold more acutely, just as delicate skin was sensitive to the sun in summer. There would also be the issue of drying a baby's clothes and nappies when they couldn't be hung out every day. But she would have to just get on with it. Another worry she sometimes entertained was that they would make terrible, neglectful parents. There was always so much to occupy her workday she wondered how either of them would find the time to care for a child. But these were silly thoughts. She knew they would be loving parents. She kept repeating to herself that other people much less able and far less sensible than herself and Ewan were parents and they seemed to manage.

She was sure Ewan began to notice but still she said nothing. He said nothing to her either but sometimes he would hold her in bed and gently stroke the curve of her stomach. She knew he was bursting to say something to her, but for some reason he didn't. Usually they talked about everything but there was something that stopped them from bringing the subject out into the open. Maybe they both had the subconscious belief that once they talked about it, it would all become real or that they might curse the child by finally acknowledging its existence. Everything muddled along quite nicely when they acted normally so perhaps it was best for them to continue in the same vein.

However, during haymaking in July, Ewan finally cracked. The weather was hot and the work was dusty, leaving a fine layer of dirt on all the men since everything in the air stuck to them as they sweated. Usually, Ewan would have gone straight down to the river after a day's work but, instead, he remembered a promise: to teach Lili to swim. He also remembered their meeting on the lane that followed and it made him smile as he thought of it. He experienced the promise of what was to come that evening and now it had been realised. He shared a bed with Lili and enjoyed it more than he ever thought possible. And now there was the possibility of – no: he could not think about it. What if he were wrong? Or what if something happened to Lili? It would be his fault. He had already lost one wife. He did not want to lose another, not to childbirth, not to *his* child. But then he dearly wanted a child too. But he couldn't think of that.

He came upon Lili in the garden, bending over the veg patch. Quietly leaning on the wall of the house, he got Georgie to sit beside him as he admired the body of his wife and the vigour with which she worked. She had not slowed down at all recently so maybe she wasn't …

"Hello!" she said with some surprise as she straightened up and spotted him.

"Hullo, hen. I've come to take you down to the river to swim. If you still want to learn."

She brushed off her hands and smiled. "Yes! I'll go and get towels and fresh clothes."

As they pottered down the field hand in hand, Ewan was reminded of the days of their courtship and the walks they took in the evenings while getting to know one another. He wondered if she missed those days and asked her.

"Not really. They're nice when they do happen though." She snaked her arm around his waist and leaned her head against his shoulder. "I've got you all the time now. I don't need to walk through the fields with you to know I'm happy or that I love you. It was never a case of where we were. All that mattered to me was that we were out here together. Just you and me …"

For a split second, he thought she was going to say more but she didn't.

The place where Ewan swam was above a narrow section in the river where the water had cut a large slow-moving meander deep into the bank. Because the water pooled there, it was perfect for swimming – deep enough to stand but not so deep that it would be a struggle for a novice.

Breaking away from Lili a short distance before they reached the bank, he began to undress, leaving a trail of garments as he continued walking. Lili faltered behind him, stooping to pick up the clothes he left. By the time he reached the bank, he was completely naked and without breaking step, he dived straight in.

Lili found herself at a standstill, gawking at her husband's semi-clad then unclad form. He's mine! she thought with a swoop of joy.

His head popped up at the edge. "Are you going to just stand there or are you coming in?"

Lili gathered herself, went over and knelt in front of him. He reached up, kissed her then undid the plait at the base of her neck so that her hair flowed over her shoulders. Slowly, he brought his arms around her back and pulled her – fully clothed – into the water. Lili was not sure she had ever experienced a greater physical shock to her entire body. Her lungs seemed to contract, sinking into the depths of her body, seeking warmth.

"*God Al-lllll-mighty it's cold!*" she gasped, spluttering as she made panicky attempts to find her footing.

Ewan held her firmly, giving her time to calm and begin to breathe evenly again. "Relax," he soothed her. "Just lie back and relax."

"Don't let go of me!"

"I'm not going to let go of you. Do you think I want you to drown?"

Lili slapped water in his grinning face but obeyed, allowing him to support her as she lay back to look at the bright blue sky with its wispy white clouds. Without thinking, she began to swish her arms and legs through the water. Her movement pulled her away from Ewan and he let her go watching as she floated in the water, a dreamy look in her eyes. She appeared so serene – her skin given a white cast by the water and her dark hair floating in long tendrils about her head. It was as if she were an otherworldly being he'd just happened upon, floating in the curve of the river.

Suddenly, a bird flew up out of a tree, squawking indignantly. The spell was broken. Lili floundered and splashed for a moment before Ewan reached her, scooping her into his arms. He held her close.

"You promised not to let me go!" she admonished, clinging to him.

"You were managing fine on your own. Don't overthink it," he smiled. "Lie out flat again. You'll be fine. You're able to float. I can't even do that."

"You can't?" Lili ginned triumphantly. She felt rather pleased with herself being able to do something Ewan couldn't. She stretched out in the water once again.

At first, Ewan kept his eyes on her face as he talked to her, explaining the different swimming strokes as Lili continued to float just out of reach of his hands. But then his gaze travelled down the length of her body still clad in her old print work dress. The material clung to her skin, accentuating every rise and fall of her form – especially the curve of her swollen belly.

Without thinking, Ewan placed one hand on his wife's lower back and the other on her stomach. He did no more until Lili put her hand over his. Her eyes met his and she smiled.

"It's true then? You really are …?" He could not bring himself to say it.

Neither could she. "It's true," she said simply.

He stared at her in awe. "It's true," he whispered.

He gathered her to him and they clung to one another until Lili said she was getting cold.

Ewan carried her to the bank then climbed out. It took him a long time to get dressed since he could not help but watch Lili as she divested herself of her sopping dress and underclothes before towelling herself dry. She did not try to hide her body from him now. Instead, she toyed with him, knowing he was staring at her, pulling the towel a little too high, a little too low, revealing a little too much. Once she had finished, she put a dry towel on the grass and lay on it, gloriously naked, allowing the warmth of the evening sun to heat her water-cooled skin and dry her tangled hair. Ewan came over to lie beside her and, taking her hand, he held it to his chest. Neither of them knew how long they stayed that way, whether they dozed off or whether they were simply drifting in a happy haze of daydreams. Finally, they both got up, dressed and began to make their way home.

However, as they sauntered up one of the hayfields, they saw something that woke them from their blissful little reverie.

And the thing was, they each saw different things.

Just as Lili suddenly perked up and said, "Wren," Ewan blinked rapidly and said, "Robbie."

Husband and wife turned to each other, perplexed. "What?"

"Robbie's over there," Ewan said, pointing him out.

"Wren's over there – standing just along from the gate. Or, at least, I think it's her," Lili replied, squinting.

Ewan nodded, spotting the girl himself.

"Should we call out to them, do you think?" she asked, inflating her lungs to shout.

"*No!*" Ewan hissed, clapping a hand over Lili's mouth. "Behind here," he said, dragging her to the far side of a nearby hayrick.

"*What?*" spluttered Lili indignantly as Ewan made violent shushing motions.

"There's something going on," Ewan said quietly, peering around the edge of the rick.

"*What's going on?*" She couldn't understand why they were hiding from their friends.

"Come here." He took her hand and dragged her in front of him. "Look at them, the way they're moving. She can't keep still and he's almost running. And see that? They both keep looking around them as if they're hoping not to be seen."

"How can you tell they're hoping not to be seen?"

"Army," he shrugged.

"How did the army teach you that?"

"The army didn't, the War did," he said impatiently. "You learn to look at people, watch them, study them, see who looks shifty ... They're up to something."

"What?"

"We'll find out, won't we?"

They watched. As the other two got closer and closer to one another, Lili had to fight the urge to turn into Ewan's chest and hide her face. She knew he was right. She watched with a hollow sense of horror as Wren and Robbie met. Even at a distance she could see the passion of their embrace. It felt so wrong to spy on them like this but then what *they* were doing was wrong too. "*No,*" she heard herself whisper. It was then that she realised she was crying. She cared for Robbie and Wren and wanted them both to be happy. But that happiness was not something they could have together. Wren was married to her brother and Robbie could have any girl he wanted, except the one in his arms. "No, no, *no*! How could they be so *stupid*?" She gave in and turned to Ewan.

He held her silently. He did not have any answers but, unlike Lili, he couldn't seem to look away. The dumb show he was witnessing held a kind of sick fascination for him. These two sensible, quiet people seemed the most unlikely of folk to do something immoral or bad. The unpredictability of human nature, he thought, would never cease to amaze him. He was disappointed in the behaviour of his young friend.

Ewan had been surprised when Robbie was not Bertie's best man at the wedding since they appeared to be closer friends than Bertie and his cousin. Giving in to curiosity, he had asked Robbie who had said something about "not wanting to see the Stevens girl marry *him*". Having admitted this, Robbie had asked the older man's advice about what to do when the girl he was "sweet on" moved in only a short distance away. Ewan's counsel was blunt: *stay away*. "Time will cool the affection you had for her and you'll move on to someone else." Even to his own ears, his suggestion sounded like a cop-out. Would his affection for Lili have cooled with distance? The truth was he did not take the boy's emotions seriously. He assumed it was just young love, foolish and short-lived. Now he saw how wrong he had been.

Oblivious to their audience, despite several more furtive glances around them, the pair disappeared through a ditch further along the field. It took some time for the Camerons to unfreeze themselves and continue up the hill. The warm, cheerful bubble they inhabited had burst or perhaps shrivelled up, depressing them both with cares and worries neither should have been party to. It was clear what was going on – any fool could see that. But the problem was no fool was meant to see it. Now Lili and Ewan knew, they were left with the dilemma of keeping the secret or exposing the antics of these two young people. And then there was the difficulty of meeting both parties and knowing their secret. How would they face them? What would they say? Would they bring it up? Their comfortable, knowable little world had suddenly become complicated through no fault of their own. While Ewan was quite philosophical about what they witnessed, concluding that other people could make their own mistakes without involving him, Lili was nothing short of incensed. She had not seen as much of the world or human nature as her husband and was, therefore, scandalised by the behaviour of two people she loved and trusted. She saw it as a betrayal of not only her brother but also herself. That the two of them should be so thoughtless as to carry on with such an affair – an affair on Bachelor Lane! – showed what little regard they had for their friends, their family, their duty. It was selfish and unforgivable.

Lili also could not forgive them for ruining the joy of her evening with Ewan. It had been so perfect – swimming in the river, lying naked in the sun, sharing news of the baby. No matter how hard she tried to get back to that state of bliss it was gone. It made her irritable and snappish.

They got back to the house and Ewan watched silently as she went about slamming the dinner things on the table, waiting for the right moment to calm her down. When she had no more cutlery or tableware to abuse, Ewan sensed his moment and opened his mouth to speak.

"Don't bother." Lili cut him off. "They're making fools of themselves and of me and you and everyone who knows them. And Bertie," she added as an afterthought. "So you're not going to talk me out of being mad."

"I'm not going to try," he said evenly. "You've every right to be angry. But I will say that if it were you and me, would you have even thought about other folk's opinions?"

"I wouldn't have married one man if I loved another!"

"Yes, but you're sensible, you have age and experience on your side. Wren is young. Barely more than a child. Do you really think she knows her own mind? Do you really think she or Robbie could control themselves when they were thrown together? Could we?"

"Do you know this sounds mighty like you trying to calm me down," Lili said haughtily.

"I'm just trying to give you some perspective. They're

young and foolish. They might get their comeuppance. They might not. What I'm saying is, it's their choice. Let them on with it. They can make a mess of their lives but not ours. We go on as before. Despite what we saw, it's got nothing to do with us."

He folded his arms, waiting for a reply. He could see Lili warring with herself, trying to maintain her righteous anger. Then her shoulders sagged, and she slumped into a chair, defeated.

"I'll never be able to look at the pair of them the same way again."

"And you think I will?" Ewan sighed wearily. "We must get on with our own lives, as if it hadn't happened. It's got nothing to do with us," he repeated. "We've other things to think about now." He slid off his chair and knelt at Lili's feet. Gently he placed his hand then his cheek on Lili's abdomen. "Like our baby."

Lili sighed and stroked his hair. "Yes. Let's think of the baby."

Chapter 43

Wren wasn't sure if she was being very brave or very foolish. She preferred not to think about it at all. Instead, she thought about Robbie. She loved him. She loved him even though he had walked away from her more than once. She loved him despite the fact he abandoned her to a marriage with Bertie. She ignored the fact that he had ignored her. Because he said he loved her and she believed him. They loved one another. She could tell by the way he kissed her, touched her. They were meant to be together. And in one way they were – as together as it was physically possible for two people to be. But in other respects, they could not be further apart.

Wren was married to another man and, though she despised it, she could not deny him his marital rights when he approached her. To outsiders, her marriage was seen as Wren Burnley's true life whereas, in her reality, it was the biggest lie of all. Her real life was in the moments she snatched with Robbie. The torrid passion, promises and actions played out for less than an hour every week were what she lived for, what she dreamed of at night and thought of during the day.

And yet, she could not openly acknowledge her adoration for Robbie. Her obsession with him was hers alone – not to be shared in a letter or talked about in a conversation.

All that burned inside her had no outlet. It was consuming her, silent and unseen.

And then she heard about Mary.

Mary Thorpe was Wren's friend from her days living in town with Astrid. She was the only girl out of the threesome of herself, Wren and Joan who was still unmarried. But the talk about town was that her status as a spinster would soon change. At first, Wren was oblivious to the improving prospects of her old friend but on a visit to town, she found herself having a conversation with Astrid that was more acutely painful to Wren than the old lady would ever know.

'Did you hear about young Mary Thorpe?' Astrid asked as she refilled Wren's teacup. After the initial flurry of excitement at their sister's arrival, Artie and Olivia left the two alone.

"No. What about her?"

Wren was not in a gossiping mood. She was not in a conversational mood either. She hadn't been for weeks. Ordinary people simply got in the way of her fantasies and it took a great deal of concentration for her to refrain from mentioning anything of what was secretly going on in her life to them. It seemed confession was always on the tip of her tongue, ready to tumble out in an idle moment only to be snatched back, leaving Wren jittery with nerves and the adrenaline of admitting something so thrilling and so wrong.

Hearing the snappishness in her great-niece's reply, Astrid paused for a moment to take a long hard look at her. Something had changed. The old lady couldn't put her finger on it but the girl who was once so quiet, so shy and mild-mannered had transformed into someone harsher, more aloof, less caring. Astrid found herself grieving for the loss of the girl she had known. Marriage had changed her and not for the better. The improvements she made to herself after the incident in December had been usurped by something else. The curtness, the coldness of her manner was, to Astrid, frighteningly like the behaviour Felicity Stevens displayed when they met. She found herself praying to God Almighty that it would not develop any further. Astrid did not want to see Wren lost to the hysteria that had claimed the girl's mother.

"Well," Astrid, said lightly, pursuing her conversation as flippantly as possible to get it over and done with, "she's – how do you say it? – doing a line? – with your neighbour."

Wren managed to muster the reply, "Oh? Which neighbour?"

"The Cox boy. Martha Cox's son."

Wren's cup shattered when it hit the floor.

A cry of dismay escaped Astrid's lips. "Oh Wren! Look what you've done!"

Wren bent her head to the floor but saw nothing. She had to be told to move her feet when the maid came in to mop up the spill. Her mind was reeling. Robbie and Mary? No, it wasn't possible. But then Astrid had said 'the Cox boy'. Martha's son. Did she have another?

"What's his name? The Cox boy."

"Martha's son? Robbie, isn't it? Or Robert?"

Astrid was not really interested anymore. She was furious that Wren had broken a cup that was part of a full, undamaged set. She would have been angry with her anyway, smashed cup or no. The girl's attitude was all wrong. In her own youth, Astrid saw many over-privileged youngsters rebel in their teenage years – become difficult, rude and careless. It appeared marriage brought out the latent troublesome teen in Wren, replacing the caring, thoughtful girl of half a year ago. She had even been short and dismissive with her own siblings. No wonder they tired of her visit so quickly. Standing in the middle of the room, Astrid turned to Wren with hands on hips and said bluntly,

"What's wrong?"

Wren expression was stony. "Nothing."

Astrid laughed harshly. "Don't take me for a fool, girl. There's something going on and I'll be damned if I'm going to sit here with you in a – a cream puff."

Wren cracked a smile at the phrase.

Even Astrid softened a little but she wasn't going to be distracted. "Well?"

Wren soured immediately. "You wouldn't understand."

"I understand a lot more than you think, girly."

"Stop calling me that!" Wren looked wild. "I'm not a *girl*! I'm a married woman."

"Behaving like a girl!"

"You don't know what it's like!"

"No?"

"*No!*" Breathing fast, Wren looked at her aunt who was as impassive as ever. Astrid's coolness frustrated her but she held her tongue, afraid of what she might admit to or say next. She exhaled carefully then spoke what was partially the truth. "I hate my husband. He is ... not a good man."

"Hate is a very strong word –"

"That doesn't mean it's not true, though. He's a bad man. And he drinks too much."

There was a pause where neither of them spoke.

Astrid sighed. "You're not the first and you won't be the last woman to find your husband is not the man you thought you married." She thought for another moment. "I don't know the ins and outs of the situation but perhaps there's something you can do to improve –"

"There's nothing I can do."

"But surely some wifely kindness would help."

"Don't you think I've tried? Don't you think I've tried to be a good wife to him. It's no use."

"And what else are you to do? You say you've 'tried'.

Your marriage is barely half a year old yet you speak in the past tense. Marriage is a bond for life, you cannot give it up after a few months. It must be worked on constantly. You can't just decide you no longer like it as if you were a child grown tired of their new toy."

"He's not a toy, he's a man!"

"Yes, he's a man. He's a human being with flaws and problems and likes and dislikes. And you're exactly like him in that sense."

"*I'm nothing like him!*" Wren replied vehemently.

"*You are.* You have flaws just as everyone else in the world does and yet, he married you. *Married.* You spoke the vows and so did he. You said 'till death us do part' and so did he. You are bound to him from here on out, whether you like him or no."

"What's to say his out won't be sooner than mine."

In all the time she had known her aunt, Wren didn't think she had ever seen the woman look so shocked. Astrid herself was not even sure she had ever been so shocked. She had heard cruel things – evil things – before, but they came from expected quarters: people in whom she recognised an immoral bent. They did not come from formerly innocent teenage girls who had shared her home. There was something deeply unsettling about the child who sat in front of her. Her eyes glittered maliciously but the rest of her face remained blank. Yet, it was the coldness in her tone, the malevolence and the violence with which it was thrown into the silent room that chilled Astrid to the core. She could feel her own fear creeping up her spine. It was a terrifying sensation that would have made a lesser woman recoil.

Astrid was not a lesser woman.

Her temper flared in a way it had not since her passionate, stubborn youth. Before she knew it, she was on her feet again, fists clenched by her sides, her entire body shaking. "How dare you! *How dare you!*" she spat. "How dare you say such a thing about anyone, never mind your husband. He may not be what you dreamed of as a little girl but he is far better – *far better* – than so many others. He has money, land, a comfortable home. And while he might not always treat you right, he has given you so much. What about that beautiful coat from your honeymoon, *hmm*? He gave you the car to drive yourself into town. What about your dog? Your darling dog who means the world to you. What sort of husband would give you such gifts and deserve to be cursed to an early death by his wife?"

"He was drunk when he gave me Tess! Stotious."

"And yet, even in that state he still thought to bring you the dog, knowing you would like it. Love it, in fact." Astrid laughed harshly as a new thought occurred to her. "You were so young and naïve that you believed the fairy stories about perfect marriages and wedded bliss. God forgive me for not educating you in the realities of life."

By this time, Wren was on her feet too. The comment about her naivety scalded her more than anything else Astrid said since it was true. She burned with embarrassment as she remembered the awkward conversation with Lili so many months before when the depths of her own innocence had been plumbed. She fought against the suggestion her own mind formed: that she was out of her depth. She had worked her way into a situation it would be nigh-on impossible to escape from unscathed and all because she had not thought sensibly about the dilemma she was now squarely in the middle of. What on earth was she to do? Not give in to Astrid for starters. She had her pride, after all.

"You forget how much of *reality* I've seen. You don't live with my mother and escape *reality*."

"*That's exactly the reason you escaped reality!*" Astrid roared. "Your mother was away with the fairies, believing in a life that wasn't there at all. Now you're spending your time searching for a life that isn't there either. You're becoming your mother's daughter. And if you're not careful you'll end up the same place as her talking the way you do about Bertram. You're talking about his *death*, Wren. People have been locked away for so much less."

The two women stood across the room from each other, Astrid's words hanging in the space between them, vibrating in the silence that followed. The old lady had crossed some invisible line. She could have told her great-niece so many things and Wren would have taken them in, mulled them over and come up with some kind of retort. But not that. There wasn't an answer Wren was prepared to give to her aunt for that slight. Instead, she collected her coat and, without another word, left the house forgetting to even say goodbye to her brother and sister.

Chapter 44

In a life spent reaffirming her own reality while the woman who was meant to teach her the ways of life struggled to hold on to hers, Wren thought it would be impossible to feel any more disconnected from the world and the people in it than she did while living with her mother. She was wrong. She had broken with Astrid and, consequently, was unable to visit either Artie or Olivia. She was also making a point of not seeing Robbie since her discovery on that same day regarding her lover and Mary Thorpe. Bertram was as unattractive as ever and now Lili seemed to be avoiding her as well. She had been to the house twice in the last week. Both times she knocked but received no answer even though she was sure the house was occupied.

Though she enjoyed being alone, loneliness was something else entirely. She had no one to share things with – to reiterate the minutiae of Tess's comical behaviour, to talk to about day-to-day life. She thought her voice might die for lack of use. She could not look forward to visiting people or their coming to see her in return. She was truly and utterly alone: a concept she never fully understood until now. Yet part of her solitude was by choice. Robbie wanted to see her. She, however, did not want to see him.

They had a system whereby a white sea stone was left at

the end of Wren's garden wall whenever one or the other was free to meet that evening. They had a prearranged meeting place in one of the fields before they went on to one house or the other to spend their time alone in comfort. The white stone had been sitting on the wall for over a week now but no matter how often Wren's resolve weakened, it never broke. She was not going to see him. He'd lied to her, strung her along, while enjoying liaisons with another girl. And the girl wasn't even a stranger. She had been one of Wren's closest friends when she lived in town. The girls had not spoken in several months but Wren still saw Robbie's actions as the ultimate betrayal while conveniently forgetting her own. She was, instead, sinking into an abyss of self-pity, anger and unhappiness. Even Bertram seemed unsure how to deal with this new unpredictable woman who snarled answers to simple questions and shook off every conciliatory touch. He did not know what to do so he did what any sane man would do in similar circumstances: he avoided her. It suited Wren perfectly. She could wallow and rage alone without having to police her emotions. She took to walking the fields, storming around the headlands with a switch stick in her hand which she used to abuse the foliage in the ditches. Tess wisely kept her distance. Even she was not exempt from Wren's wrath. Mistress was just as likely to snarl at her beloved dog as at her husband. Her mind was so addled with anger and hurt, she no longer knew what she was doing or saying anymore.

This agitation led her to wander without knowing where she was, often bringing her miles away from home without any clue how she got there. She would then have to figure out how to get home while also attempting to push away remembrances that this was the sort of thing her mother was prone to do. She felt guilty, worried and angry with herself. Because if there was one thing she never wanted to be, it was her mother.

One evening, Bertram had gone to the pub as usual, leaving Wren to her own devices. She set off shortly after he left and walked blindly through the fields, Tess gambolling along with her but keeping a safe distance from the arc of her mistress's stick. Mulling over everything that had happened to her in the last number of months, Wren was completely in a world of her own, unaware of where her feet took her. She heard nothing, said nothing and saw nothing apart from the narrow view in front of her.

It was therefore quite a shock to her when she found someone's hand around her arm. Instinctively she yanked away, the switch coming up to strike her assailant before she even saw him. She became aware of who it was just as her stick hit him in the neck. Wren watched as the blood slowly rose to the surface where the tip of the switch sliced through the weathered skin of his throat. The shining red slid slowly down into the collar of his shirt and blossomed like a flower as it seeped through the material.

"What was that for?" Robbie shouted roughly, clamping his hand over the wound.

"What were *you* doing sneaking up on me?" she snapped back. She was perturbed by her own actions but anger overcame her concern for him.

"You're in a field full of bullocks. *My* field of bullocks. Are you trying to get yourself killed or what?"

Suddenly, Wren became aware that they had an audience of shiny-eyed cattle – quite large shiny-eyed cattle. Many of them were snorting with curiosity, their noses sniffing out this strange new entity in their midst. One put its head down, snorting and skipped towards the dog. Tess yapped crossly and they danced and bucked out of her way, with some of them coming directly towards Wren and Robbie.

Wren screamed and grabbed Robbie, using him as a shield.

401

"*Dog!*" Robbie roared, then "*Gid up on outta that!*" to the cattle who shied away from him. But their blood was up now. And Tess was not helping in the slightest as she charged through them barking and snapping at their heels. "*Dog!*" Robbie bawled again.

Cursing under his breath, he picked Wren up without looking at her and unceremoniously dumped her on top of the ditch before wading through the cattle to shoo Tess away. The dog sensed his anger and slunk over to Wren while the bullocks continued to cavort. Robbie stood watching the animals canter across the field.

"What were you *thinking* walking through them?"

Wren didn't answer.

"Well?"

"I wasn't minding where I was going," was the only explanation she could muster.

Robbie looked to be on the verge of speaking his mind but refrained. Instead he put a hand to his neck once again and hissed when he pulled it away and saw the blood on his palm. The wound was beginning to clot but at the slightest movement of his head fresh blood welled up and seeped through the opening.

"What did you do that for?" he asked bitterly.

"You sneaked up on me. You could have been anyone."

"I didn't *sneak up* on you. I was calling you the entire way across the field."

Wren stared in disbelief. "I never heard you."

"Clearly," he snorted. "Come on." He hopped up on the ditch then off the other side before holding out a hand to help Wren down. "*Come on,*" he said impatiently. "You can't stay up there for ever."

She put her hand in his but, instead of guiding her down he gave a yank causing her to trip down the bank straight into his chest. His arms wrapped around her, pinning her to him. "You've been avoiding me," he whispered into her ear.

With all her might, Wren shoved him away. She did not like the way he looked at her.

She would have been glad to still be holding her switch but she had dropped it in the commotion. "I have my reasons," she said coldly then turned on her heel and walked away.

He caught her in a few strides, lifting her off the ground.

"Let me go!" she spat but he simply caught her around the thighs and wedged her stomach uncomfortably over his shoulder. She screamed and kicked and hit him but his arm simply squeezed her tighter. She knew where she was now and knew where he was taking her.

Sure enough, it was not long before they were crossing the yard to his house. He still hadn't said anything to her. She redoubled her efforts to wriggle free of his clutches but he was not letting go. He was hurting her. He had never done that before and she was starting to feel afraid. However, once they got into the house, he put her down, making sure to keep himself between her and the door.

"Well?" He folded his arms and leaned casually against the wall. His stance belied his mood. He radiated anger and tension.

She stood up straight, throwing back her shoulders. She was not going to let someone else push her around. "So what if I've been avoiding you? I have my reasons."

"Which are?"

"*Mary Thorpe!*"

She expected denial or perhaps some soothing words to calm her temper.

Instead he snorted. "What about her?"

"*Don't laugh at me!*" she screamed shrilly, striking out at him as tears welled in her eyes.

He caught one forearm then the other as she flailed

ineffectually at him before shoving her back against the wall, his entire body pinning her upright. He crushed his lips to hers, forcing her head back with a smack against the plaster behind her. She felt it for a moment and then forgot the pain altogether. No wonder she'd been unhappy over the past number of weeks. Denying herself the sensation of Robbie's body pressed against hers had driven her mad. Or perhaps it was the feeling of him next to her that simply made her forget all her anger and frustration. She forgot as she bit his lip, kissing back, rough and needy.

They did not make it to a bedroom. Wren hitched her legs around his hips as she tore feverishly at his shirt. She may have ripped it but she didn't know. His hands followed her thighs, rucking up her skirt as he walked blindly through the door into the sitting room. There on his mother's good hearth rug he tore off her undergarments and had her while both were still almost fully clothed.

By the time they had finished much later in the evening both of them lay naked in a tangle of quilts and embroidered cushions requisitioned from the sofa and armchairs. His mother was away visiting her sister in Laois. Both were drowsy as they clung to one another, cocooned in their makeshift bedding. But something stopped Wren from drifting off into blissful oblivion. Something niggled. Something did not feel right. It wasn't her body. That felt better than it had for a long time and most of her mind seemed to be at peace too. Yet something demanded her attention and it was a name: *Mary Thorpe*.

At that moment, Robbie nuzzled his head into her shoulder. Wren felt a powerful wave of revulsion at his touch – as if ants were crawling across her skin. She pushed him away and sat up, eyeing him with wariness.

"Why did you do that?"

"Do what?" he mumbled. "Whatever it was, you seemed to like it."

She saw him smile with satisfaction, eyes still closed.

She had liked it. God help her, she really had. But she had not wanted it. He dragged her to the house then forced himself on her and her treacherous body had responded to his advances willingly. Instinct and familiarity took over, making a fool of her when she needed to stand her ground. She had allowed herself to be used. Realising her body's weakness, Wren felt more dirty and dishonest than she ever had for deceiving her husband. What had just happened wasn't love, it was carnality exercised to its zenith. Robbie had not made love to her. He had used her and done it gladly.

"Why did you make me do that?" She was fighting the desire to go completely to pieces in front of him.

With a huff of exasperation, he opened his eyes before dragging himself into a sitting position. "You seemed willing enough," he said blandly.

A squeak of indignation squeezed past her lips. But suddenly the horror of realisation came crashing down on her. What Astrid told her, what she figured out herself and what had happened between them just now all added up to one conclusion in her mind. "You've been making a fool out of me all along, haven't you?"

"What?" he snapped.

"All this! The taking me to bed, the telling me you loved me – *all of it*. You were just manipulating me while all along you didn't care for me. You only had thoughts of Mary Thorpe."

"*Stop saying her name!*" he yelled. "Why do you keep coming back to Mary, ha? What's this sudden obsession with her? Yes, I go to the dances with her and yes, I give her the odd kiss now and again, but she doesn't mean anything to me. You're the one I care about, not her."

"Then why are you going off to the socials with her? Why not –"

"You? *Because you're married, for God's sake!*" he hissed.

"I wasn't going to say that!" She was up on her feet, snatching at clothes trying to find her own. But they all seemed to belong to Robbie. "Why not just alone? You could dance with all the girls and not just her."

"Because Mary's nice and I like her." He was on his feet now too but rather than ruin his glorious nakedness by bending down to search for his trousers, he stayed upright.

"So you're going to play her for the fool instead of me, is it?"

"God, every way I turn I'm going to be doing something wrong, aren't I?" He ran his hands through his hair in exasperation rather than grabbing Wren to give her a good shake.

"What *are* you doing, Robbie?" she asked. "Because I've got people telling me you and Mary are going to be married."

"So what if we were? You're married, aren't you? Why can't I?" His mouth was running away with him. He didn't want to say these things. He already knew she could bring out the best in him. Now he discovered she could bring out the worst too.

Wren recoiled as if he had slapped her. The answer she really wanted to give him was no, he couldn't marry. Yet she knew how hypocritical that was. If he was having a relationship with his friend's spouse what was to stop her doing the same thing? But Robbie was hers. She was not prepared to share him with anyone. And yet, he shared her with another man. She wondered how he coped. She was sure she couldn't. Then, she hit upon the difference. When Robbie came to her, she was already married. He knew what he was getting involved in but did it anyway. Whereas, for

Wren, Robbie had surrendered himself to her willingly, pledged love to her alone. She had always been someone else's as well as his, but Robbie had always been just hers. Or so she believed.

"I don't want you to see Mary anymore. I don't want you to hurt her," she said so firmly she almost believed it herself.

Robbie gave a bark of derision. "Is that so? Well, if that's the case I don't want you to see Bertie anymore."

"Oh, for God's *sake*. Don't be so *stupid*! He's my husband! I can't just up and leave. I made *vows*."

"Aye, to love, honour and keep him. And are they going well for you?"

This time, she caught him off-guard. For the second time in her life, she hit him square in the face.

She slapped hard for a small woman, snapping his head back as the tinny sound of open palm on cheek died in the confines of the little room. At the sound, Wren seemed to snap out of the bedlam of her own mind and she became aware of what she had done. If that alone had not been enough, the look on Robbie's face was enough to sober her.

"D'you know what it is, *Wren*?" He never called her by her given name. "You were forever having to do other people's bidding and now that someone's done yours it's gone to your head. Well, you know what, pet? I'm not sure I want to do your bidding anymore."

Wren mouthed ineffectually as he continued.

"This isn't a game. You may think it's great gas to go running around with the neighbour and to hell with the consequences, but have you ever thought of the future, ha? Because sometimes it's all I think about. In the here and now this all seems right but in the cold light of day we don't have a future. There's nowhere for us to go with this."

"There is. There *is*!" she said, clutching desperately at his arm but he shook her off.

"No, there isn't! You're married and you'll stay married. This is your reality and mine. Wake up to it and stop living in a dream."

There it was again. That word. *Reality.* Everybody seemed to be throwing it at her, thinking she didn't understand. "I do *not* live in a dream. I know exactly what we're doing. But we can make it work, I know we can." Why was she begging? She had provoked the argument and now she was the one trying to defuse it.

He laughed humourlessly. "God, you really are a child sometimes, do you know that? The world doesn't right itself just because you want it to."

"*Don't call me a child!*" she screamed.

"Why not? You're behaving like one."

"And you take children to bed, do you?" Her voice was like ice.

The look on his face suggested she had slapped him again.

"Don't you dare say things like that," he said hollowly. He finally bent and began gathering clothes to put on. "I think you should go," he said, leaving the room.

"I'm pregnant," she called after him in desperation.

He stopped dead. His bare shoulders went rigid as marble and he stood unmoving for what seemed like an eternity. Then, he turned to face her, his face ash-grey. "Then I wish you joy." He turned to leave again.

"It could be yours!"

"And it could be his." He walked out.

She followed him, tears now streaming silently down her cheeks. She had not meant to tell him. It just slipped out. But now she needed him to acknowledge what she said – to take an interest, to react, to feel something.

"Don't walk away from this. Don't walk away from me," she begged.

He ignored her.

She made one last attempt. "I'll tell him."

That got his attention. His head snapped around as colour flooded back into his face. "Don't," he said with some control, "be so bloody stupid."

"Why not? He should know, after all. I doubt he'd want to raise another man's baby. But who knows – maybe he would? I should at least give him the choice, don't you think?" She was goading him, trying to break him, force him to stay with her and continue their liaisons.

"If you do," he said quietly, "I'll deny it. Tell them it's all a figment of your imagination. They'd cart you off to the mental before the day was out."

All her malevolence evaporated. "You wouldn't."

"You may want to ruin your life but you're not ruining mine along with it. I've got my mother and the farm to think of."

How could he be so coldhearted? This was not the man that she loved – who professed to love *her*. 'Because this is the *real world*,' said a snide little voice in her head. Whenever she was with Robbie, she *wasn't* in the real world – anything seemed possible, even a future. It was only when she left him that her actuality returned and she saw what a mess she was involved in. She had to leave, to get away from him so she could think clearly. But she could not let him have the last word.

Quelling the lump that rose in her throat, Wren drew herself up to her full height, looked Robbie straight in the eye and used a word she had never used before.

"You *bastard*. You absolute *bastard*."

With that, she left the house, collecting Tess from outside the door as she marched down the lane to her home. As she crossed the yard, she did not look back or break her stride. Nor did she hear anyone calling or chasing after her. He was letting her go. Though she was torn between the hope that he would either beg her forgiveness or never show his face to her again, a pang of pure pain shot through her body as she continued down the lane. It was over – it was all over. He was leaving her to her fate with Bertie – Bertram.

Her breathing became shallow as if her clothes were too tight, constricting her chest as she stumbled on blindly following the path in front of her. How had it come to this? How had she chosen two men so wrong for her? She was foolish, blind, romantic and it had led her to her current position threading her way along a country lane, pregnant and wanting to die. She could not go on. She could not go home after everything that had happened. She was tainted, broken and unfit to see or be seen by anyone. She could not go home to her father. She couldn't even go to Astrid. She was alone. And yet, she still found herself on the path to the front door of the Gate House, opening it and going in. She thought she had nowhere, but her body still recognised a place of safety – a place where she belonged – even if her mind refused to acknowledge it.

She had somewhere to go. She just did not want to be there.

Chapter 45

Wren barely saw Bertram the next day. Before she was up, he had gone to the mart in town to buy some hoggets to put in lamb over the autumn. She wondered vaguely what he might buy them with. Shortly after marrying Bertram she realised that though he had a wealth of land, in terms of monetary wealth he was dirt poor. She concluded that he must be using more of the generous dowry Astrid bequeathed them. Or, at least, Wren had thought it generous. She assumed the money would last them the first few years of their marriage, making things comfortable for them. But at the rate Bertie was spending, they would be lucky if it lasted them twelve months.

He wasn't back for dinner or supper either, which left Wren to tend the stock that needed fed and check the ones in the fields. While she worked, she usually chattered endlessly to the animals and especially to Tess. But she drifted around her tasks in silently, the dog trailing in her wake. With the distance of time and a night's sleep, her emotions seemed to have drained from her body. There was nothing there. Her mind had shut down over night, blocking out the hurt. She was numb. The haze of her thoughts was just enough for her to go about her work without thinking of anything else. Even when she sat down by the range that evening, she could not bring herself to pick up some sewing or even a book. She only sat and stared unseeing as the light faded, as if it was being sucked out of the room through the tiny window below the stairs.

She was completely unaware of her surroundings until a light flared in her peripheral vision.

"*Wren!*"

Bertram stood in the middle of the room with a lamp. He expected her to jump but instead she turned her head slowly – like a mechanised puppet, eyes unseeing. She didn't look at him. She looked straight through him.

It unnerved him somewhat so that his admonishing, "Christ God, Wren, did you not hear me call you?" came out much softer than he had intended it to. He hoped to shake her out of her trance with a harsh reminder of reality but because of the way he spoke it, his words had little effect on her. Several half-formed thoughts began to chase each other through his alcohol-hazed mind, most of them dangerous. Was this what happened to his mother-in-law? A seemingly sane if exceedingly innocent girl whose mind liquefied after a few short months of marriage. Could the same possibly be happening to his wife? Perhaps it was like mother, like daughter. If so, what familial weaknesses had he wed himself to? He did not think he could bear the shame of a wife committed to St Senan's. He couldn't imagine the embarrassment of visiting her, what people would say. And then there was the thought of how he would live without the benefits of a wife. Could he possibly forfeit the advantages of someone to feed him, clothe him, care for him, share his bed? Maybe he could manage her frailty himself and keep her at home. Or maybe she was not mad and it was just a case of his not being used to the company of women who were not his sisters.

Lost in his musings, it was he who missed the next words spoken. "What's that?" he asked, resurfacing.

"I said, I'm going to have a baby."

Silence.

Each stared at the other.

Bertram's thoughts began to pinwheel madly about his brain. He turned and walked away. Wren said something under her breath as he did so.

"What?" he said rather irritably. He'd heard the words but his reeling mind did not seem to be able to find meaning in them.

"Nothing," She seemed a little surprised, in fact, that he'd heard her at all.

Eventually, Bertram managed to latch on to one thought that flitted by. "You're having a baby." He stated it matter-of-factly enough but his face slowly began to alter as he clung to this knowledge for all he was worth. A baby! *A real baby!* He was going to be a father! Yet something jarred that last thought, making it cloudy and somehow unreal. But *what*?

It was impossible. Two minds, addled for different reasons, were trying and failing to communicate with one another. Desperately seeking to understand, Bertram went to move closer to her but only managed a few steps when his knees gave way. Untroubled by his new position, he shuffled forwards so that he knelt in front of his wife.

If he had stayed upright, he would never have seen the mark.

"What's that?" he asked, squinting at the juncture between her neck and shoulder.

"What's what?" she replied, brought to some consciousness by his closeness. She looked down at herself but saw nothing.

"*That*," he said impatiently, touching the point with his finger. She yelped and recoiled. He cocked an eyebrow. "Just there."

"Well, I don't know, do I?"

She didn't like him swaying unsteadily in front of her, looking as if he might suddenly pitch forward into her lap. She also felt uneasy as Bertram's gelid eye bore into her neck. Suddenly, with greater speed and accuracy than she thought it possible for him to have, he grabbed her jaw, forcing it up and to the left. He did pitch forward then but it was not a drunken sway. He was staring intently and closely at the mark. Slowly, he again extended a pointing finger and stabbed it into Wren's flesh. It hurt.

Now she remembered. She remembered another man's mouth biting, sucking, kissing her flesh. Robbie's mouth. She jerked back and attempted to clap her hand onto it, but Bertram held fast and batted her hand away with ease. She could not tear her eyes away from his face as she watched it, inches from her own, turn white with rage.

"What have you done?" The absolute cold fury that radiated from him made his voice shake, hushed with wrath. His hand moved down, caught her by the throat and lifted her from the chair as he rose to his feet. She clawed at his hand as it tightened on her windpipe. He was leaning into her, forcing her to bend backwards as her calves pressed against the front of the seat. She clung to his arm to support herself.

Sensing her mistress's unease, Tess came forward and woofed in warning. Bertram turned to the dog, face twisted like gargoyle, and hissed an inhuman sound through his teeth, making the dog cower behind a chair leg. Wren wished she could do the same.

"*Please*," she choked out, tears streaming from the outside corners of her eyes.

He sneered. "Please what, *hmm*? *Please what*? Go on, tell me! And while you're at it you can tell me who gave you this."

Two fingers slid down and pressed against the bruise. She could almost feel each individual tooth-mark as he dug

414

his fingertips in. A flash of memory accompanied the touch but it was the memory of another man. A passionate caress instead of a violent one.

Lips had caught her skin, not fingertips. He had one incisor longer than the other and she had felt the uneven pressure of the bite when his mouth had latched onto her neck during their love-making the evening before. She could see the soot-blackened ceiling, the dark oak beams, feel the quilts beneath her, hear them as they scrubbed against the carpeted floor.

She gasped for breath but it was for a different reason to the night before. Bertram's hand tightened as he gave her a little shake. He dipped his head forward just like Robbie had but rather than kiss her, he hissed one word in her ear.

"*Who?*"

Wren managed to give a tiny shake of her head before his grip squeezed her to immobility. She clamped her mouth shut as if he might be able to extract the truth from the depths of her throat.

His eyes blazed. "*Who?*" he roared.

Her head was beginning to pound. So were her eyes. The edges of her vision were turning red as she began to scrape with her ineffectual short nails at his flesh. The absurd thought that she shouldn't bite them popped into her head as she did so, quickly stifled by rising panic. And just as the panic rose, threatening to bubble over, he twisted to the side, heaving her from her chair. He was strong enough to lower her down with one hand but he was also drunk. Her weight, small as it was, dragged them both to the floor with Bertram on top while Wren was forced to cling to his forearm for support, trying to save herself from the heavy fall. She began to kick wildly but he shook her again, banging her head on the ground, making her stop.

It was then that she saw the tears streaming down his

face. In that unguarded moment, there was nothing but agony in his eyes. She had hurt him more than he ever hurt her and she knew it. Now she feared he might redress the balance as his face contorted against his own grief, trying and failing to mask his emotion. She looked at his expression and realised he could kill her. But then he took his hand from her throat, leaving her gasping like a landed fish. He leaned over her, placing his palms on either side of her face with just too much pressure to be tender. She could feel the tension in his body where he touched her. His teeth were bared in a frightening leer. His tears pattered on her face as they fell, mingling with her own as they ran into her hair and down the sides and back of her neck.

"*Why?*" he sobbed through his clenched jaw.

"Because you don't love me and he did." She did not know where the petrified whisper came from. It seemed to emanate from her own lips.

His face contorted again as he reared over her. He grabbed a fistful of her hair. "*Who?*"

He slammed her head against the floor.

Wren tasted blood. She had bitten her tongue. Tiny white stars drifted across her vision.

"*Who?*" He threw her head against the flagstones once more.

She couldn't see properly. The white dots had been joined by blue ones. The back of her skull was screaming in protest. But it wasn't over. Again and again he threw her head back, asking the same question, not waiting for an answer. Tess barked and nipped at his jumper but he swung and batted her off. Coming back to Wren, he swung and hit her in the face. Then again and again. She was a rag doll beneath his raging fists. Blood, saliva and tears spattered across the floor either side of her head. Finally, he grabbed her by the shoulders, lifting her bodily.

She screamed incoherently.

Bertram screamed too. One word: "*Who?*"

"*Robbie!*" She screamed back.

Bertram dropped her. Her skull made a sickening clunk as it hit the stone. She lay still. He didn't notice. He did not hear anything other than the tinnitus in his ears, ringing with the name of his friend. A high-pitched whine that repeated '*Robbie, Robbie, Robbie*'. Standing in the centre of the room, the name washed through his body, roaring through his empty chest, buzzing right to his extremities. Quite calmly, he stepped over the prostrate figure of his wife without looking down, collected his coat and left the house to silence punctuated only by the sound of a dog whimpering and scratching her motionless mistress.

Chapter 46

The sky over the lane was pink, yellow and gold even though the sun had dipped below the horizon – beautiful even to those who lived their daily lives in nature. However, there was also an eerie silence at odds with the beautiful sky. It was only when the south-east horizon was seen, that the quiet was explained. Dark-blue and twisting like an agitated sea, a great band of cloud rolled across the fields, darkening everything below then swallowing it in a grey misty deluge.

Ewan hissed through his teeth with distaste as the wind preceding the clouds whipped at the end of his jacket. It was tied with string about his middle since the fastenings had worn through. He wished he had put on the new coat Lili had given him. But it looked so clean and new he just could not bring himself to do farm work in it so persevered with the old one. He muttered mutinously to himself as he trudged onwards towards the rain. He had to move a flock of about thirty sheep to a new field and had spent a good deal of the day at an auction for rams up the country. He'd been hoping to be home sooner, but it took longer than expected to find two suitable young rams for the price he wanted to pay. He should have moved the sheep first thing when he came home instead of telling Lili about his day, but he loved regaling her with tales of the people he met and the things he saw.

When the rain finally engulfed him, he was shooing his ewes through a gateway. It was heavy and ice cold, pelting his exposed skin like grit. He hunched his shoulders with distaste as it ran down the back of his neck, soaking into the collar of his shirt. He was glad when he could finally turn for home.

Looking back on that day years later, he always wondered if the chill he felt walking up the lane was due to the cold wind and driving rain at his back or something else. Did his senses pick up on some subtle shift in the disturbed atmosphere around him or was it down to his awareness of Georgie and the trust he put in her senses? Trotting up the lane ahead of him, the dog stopped at the gate to the Burnley house. She cocked her head with curiosity and sniffed the air before darting into the garden.

"Georgie!" Ewan hissed. He did not want to go anywhere near the Burnleys. If he did, Wren would no doubt ask him about Lili. Bertie would not ask him anything at all. No one could do stony silence better than Bertie Burnley, Ewan thought bitterly. Then he stopped. The front door was open, rain spilling over the threshold. Odd, he thought. Perhaps the wind had blown it in and they had not noticed. Seemed unlikely though. He dithered just inside the gate. Should he continue home or be a good neighbour and close the door? His strongest inclination was to leave and let them clear up the mess of water and debris in the morning. Yet, he felt a pang of guilt for such a thought. Wren was young, foolish, naïve and many other things besides, but she didn't deserve deliberate unkindness.

He could have just closed the door and been on his way. He might never have entered the house at all. But he did.

Once, while serving in the army, he had been in a company which entered a deserted village in Greece after the retreat of the Italian army. They went from building to building searching for traces of life – allied or enemy. When the initial sweep was over, he and a few other soldiers were given the task of moving from house to house, seeking provisions and securing the area before they moved on. One house stood out from the others since it had flowering window boxes bringing colour to the stark whitewash of the walls. But the flowers were parched and wilting in the heat. Inside, they found the body of a young woman, killed for who knew what reason. The men had crowded into the small kitchen one after the other to see what had happened but once they did, they all stood in silence, left too cold by the horror of what they saw to speak. Finally, one young private had uttered the words all the gathered men were thinking.

Standing in the kitchen of a rural house just minutes away from his own home, Ewan found himself echoing the words of that private.

"Fucking hell."

Chapter 47

Robbie had slept in. He had not done it in years. His mother often told him she could set her clock by him since he seemed to have such a knack for timekeeping. But after the fight he was restless, agitated, unable to order his thoughts enough to lay his head on a pillow and sleep. He stayed up late, wandering aimlessly around the house and yard, checking and rechecking gates, trying to empty his mind of the horrible scene a few hours before. When he finally did sleep in the late hours of the morning, it was deep and thankfully dreamless. But, once he awoke, his mind returned to the turmoil of the night before.

Thinking back over all the things he said, he wanted to escape his own skin. He was disgusted with himself. She had brought out the worst in him – worse than even he knew he was capable of. He was not naturally vicious or even mildly confrontational. But he had entangled himself in a situation far beyond his ken. Out of his depth, he lashed out at the one person who understood their predicament, who was there with him. She was lost, confused and scared just as he was. He was scared for her, scared his mother would find out – scared for himself. He had been friends with Bertie for as long as he could remember and while he knew very well that the man had his faults, he did not want to destroy that friendship. At the very least, it would make being neighbours difficult, at the worst … well, he didn't really want to think about the worst. Perhaps the worst had happened already. He had broken the heart of the woman he loved and possibly his own in the process. Yet he could not seem to figure out any way of fixing things since what they had done was wrong in the first place. Maybe he could learn to forget the whole thing – carry on with life and Mary Thorpe.

Mary was his mother's idea. He wondered if his mother had steered him toward the girl because she knew or sensed his attachment to Wren. Or possibly he was just paranoid. He liked Mary but she was not the girl for him. She was a good, kind soul yet there was something lacking. She would quite happily hold his hand sitting in silence all evening at a dance just watching the other couples. All she wanted was a secure marriage that allowed her to be a mother, run to fat and generally stay inside. She was a town girl through and through.

In comparison, despite her urban upbringing, there was something wild in Wren. Not everyone saw it. But Robbie did. She belonged to nature. She never looked more at home than with hay on her clothes, mud on her boots, trudging through a field. In fact, the previous evening, he stood and watched her storm through his field with a glow of pleasure before realising she was in with a group of his cattle. He panicked, shouted at her and it all fell apart. Well, almost. They had the respite of their lovemaking in the middle of all the chaos and it was the best, most passionate, he had ever had.

Unlike many men from his background, Robbie was not completely innocent. When he attended boarding school in Dublin, there had been a brief period of two weeks when he caused complete uproar by running off with a wealthy married woman twenty years his senior. They had lived in a hotel on her husband's money detached from all worldly cares – only interested in sleeping, eating and lovemaking. But soon the decadence and thrill wore off. She realised he was an innocent little country boy looking for a mother-substitute and he realised his lover was just another man's unfulfilled wife. They had parted and never met again. Robbie returned, cowed by the experience and vowing to himself never to get mixed up in such a terrible mess again: the mess of becoming entangled with a married woman. Because he knew from his time in that hotel room that such a relationship would never work. And yet he could not shake the joy, the seductive power of intimacy, the feel of skin on skin. That early sexual experience gave him an education that most grown men would never have. It gave him an urge to seek out such closeness again. But the experience had been strange. Even if his younger self had tried to believe it at the start, there was no love between them. There was just a kind of detached pleasure felt only by his body. With Wren, he felt it to his very soul. And yet, he had pushed her away.

He aimlessly drifted from one job to the next all day, completing nothing. It was dusk and had started to rain by the time he remembered to check the field of bullocks where he had found Wren the day before. In the half-light of the evening, he could barely see the misshapen humps that were his cattle. All he could make out were the patches of white which stood out in stark contrast against the black of the hedge. They were huddled in a curve of the ditch near the bottom of the field, completely indistinguishable from one another.

He had not worn a coat (he wasn't sure why not) so by the time he was heading back to the house, his jumper and trousers were wet through, clinging to his skin and making his movements slow. However, when he got to the front yard he sped up, focusing more than he had all day.

The front door was open and, despite his addled state,

he was sure he had closed it. Standing on the threshold, he was certain there was someone inside. Had his mother returned? Surely not. And, besides, the trail of mess on the floor was something his mother would never leave behind her. Muddy, watery footprints shone from the tiled floor. Robbie peered cautiously into the darkness of his house but could see nothing. Reaching blindly behind him, he picked up his mother's garden spade standing by the door. No bugger was going to sneak about his house without him doing something about it. Lighting the lamp in the porch, he took a firm hold of it in one hand with the spade in the other and pushed the door of the kitchen open to reveal a dark shape standing by the fireplace.

Robbie exhaled with relief.

"Jesus God! Bertie, you frightened the bejesus out of me."

Putting down the lamp, he went over to the fire. Bertie was leaning on the mantelpiece staring into the flameless grate.

"Why didn't you put some more wood on the fire? Or light a lamp?" Robbie asked, flicking his hand impatiently to get Bertie out of the way as he put the spade against the wall.

He knelt down on the hearth and raked the embers before piling on some fresh wood. Bertie was silent throughout.

"What are you doing here anyway, Bertie?"

He looked up at his neighbour properly for the first time and noticed that he was just as wet as he was. The cuffs of his shirt were dripping on the tiles and his hair was plastered against his skull. Robbie doubted he looked any better but at least he was dripping all over the floor of his own house, not someone else's. He would have to mop the tiles. They were his mother's pride and joy – shiny red and black tiles he had laid the summer before only to discover that when they got wet, they were as slippery as ice. The novelty of the tiles had worn off for Robbie somewhat since he had to come in in his socks if there was even the slightest whiff of damp on his boots. However, he was not going to wander about in his stocking soles now. He would just have to watch his step and clean up the mess in the morning.

Bertie was still standing above him. Irked by his friend's elevated position, Robbie stood, stretching to his full height to stand over Bertie. "What're you doing here, Bertie?" he asked again.

Bertie seemed to be weighing up his reply, cocking his head to one side as if trying to decide on an answer. "Come to see you."

Robbie snorted, turning away. "Well, you've seen me now, haven't you?"

He was chilled and wanted to change his shirt. There was an airing cupboard beside the fireplace that contained a change of clothes for him, put by for occasions such as this one. He opened the door for his dry shirt.

He never got it.

Chapter 48

She weighed even less than he thought she would. There really was nothing to the rag-doll body that hung limp in his arms as he pulled her close to his chest. He had covered her with his own coat before bringing her outside – partly because he did not want her to get wet but also because he was afraid of what he might see if he looked again. He wasn't even sure she was breathing anymore. She had been when he knelt on the floor beside her, large hands fluttering over her tiny body checking for signs of life. But now his own half-run as he carried her to his home prevented him from feeling the expansion of her lungs.

Tess kept pace with him as he splashed up the lane. She had been cowering under the table, whining, crying, when he went in but as soon as he lifted the body the dog was by his side, hackles raised in warning. He paid no attention to her, just as he didn't now.

He was calling to Lili before he even turned into the path to their house. He shouldered his way through the door, not caring whether he broke the lock, and met Lili lumbering down the stairs to meet him. Her questioning look turned to one of pale-faced horror as he lay his bundle on the chaise longue he had bought for her beside the fire. His right sleeve was red with blood from the wound in the back of Wren's head. Lili's eyes dwelt for a moment on the stain before Ewan simply said, "Hers."

He hovered, uncertain, as Lili knelt beside the girl performing a quick inventory. Initially, he had acted quickly, glad to move and do something. Now he had stopped he felt sure he should be doing *something* but could not figure out what. Then Lili probed gently at the wound and Wren whimpered. Relief flooded through both as Wren's eyelids flickered and she groaned again. Lili peered closely at the gash in the back of Wren's head, cautiously peeling away strands of blood-matted hair to get a better look.

"Is her skull damaged?" she asked, carefully lighting the area with a table lamp. "Or just lots of blood?"

"Head wounds bleed like a stuck pig," Ewan offered. "I've seen it. You have to put pressure on the wound. Stop the bleeding."

"Get me some bandages then. And maybe a towel."

Provided with employment, Ewan swiftly and gladly did as he was asked. Once Lili was in position pressing a towel firmly to Wren's head, Ewan bustled about heating water and changing his sopping clothes. He thought both he and Wren could do with being cleaned up a bit. And Lili would no doubt need water to wash the wound too. He was hanging the kettle when Lili spoke.

"Where did you find her?"

"In the house. The door was open."

"Bertie?" The question held so much. Was he a victim too? Perhaps he was lying dead on the floor of her old home. Or was he there at all? Lili knew he often stayed out late. But then there was the other possibility. Had he done this?

"Yes." Ewan answered what was unspoken.

"God Almighty," Lili whispered, horrified. She gently stroked the hair off Wren's face. "God *Almighty!*"

Just then, a sharp bark made them both jump. It was

followed up by a whine and scratch. Georgie was snuffling at the base of the door and Ewan realised that Tess was locked out. Ewan obliged the dog and let her in. Ignoring Georgie's greeting she went straight to Wren and licked the girl's hand with a whine.

"'*ess.*" It was the tiniest of sounds. Wren's hand twitched and Tess ducked her head under it so that Wren could stroke the soft fur on the crown of her skull. A single tear leaked from the corner of her eye. "*Ow!*"

"*Shhh* . . . there now, you'll be fine. We're here. You're safe." Lili gently squeezed the girl's hand, but she threw a worried look at Ewan.

"Aye, you're safe here. You both are." He placed a large comforting hand on Lili's shoulder and another on the clasped hands of the two women. He had been sure to lock the door after letting the dog in. It was one thing to further risk the life of his sister-in-law but on no account would he risk Lili or their baby. At least he had spotted Bertie's gun still propped up in the corner of the porch as he left. Wherever he went after almost killing his wife, he did not take the gun with him. Ewan wondered where he had gone. Had he run away? He'd better have. Rage was shimmering beneath the surface of Ewan's exterior calm. If he had not felt the need to stay with the two women, he would likely have gone on the hunt for Bertie.

Wren was beginning to move restlessly, her heels dragging across the seat of the chaise longue. She gasped when she turned her head, but Lili continued to press the towel to the wound as blood turned the off-white material to deep, vivid red.

"'*o-ie. 'o-ie.*" She pushed the sound out through immobile lips then grunted in frustration.

"I know it hurts, lovie, I know. Don't speak, pet. Save your strength." Lili used a cloth to wipe away the tears spilling from Wren's heavy-lidded eyes. She was fighting back tears of her own.

Wren gritted her teeth. "No," she said clearly. "'obbie. Bertie gun fur 'obbie."

Lili and Ewan looked at one another then comprehension dawned on Lili's face. "Bertie's gone for Robbie?"

"*Mmm.*" Wren seemed to be struggling but her eyes, though glassy, were fixed pleadingly on Lili's.

"You told him!" Lili said horrified. "My God, *you told him*! *Why*?"

"*No!*" Wren didn't even bother to wonder how Lili knew. "Fund out. Go. 'lease. 'obbie."

"Robbie'll have to take care of himself, darlin'," Ewan said gently. "I'm staying here with you two."

Wren wailed and jerked her head away, almost dislodging the towel but then she quietened.

Time crept on. Wren's uneven breath began to deepen and become more regular but Ewan insisted she did not sleep so he and Lili talked about nothing while keeping an eye on her. They both tried to appear calm and carry on normally so as not to upset her. Ewan even cooked some supper for them while Lili finally removed the towel and bandaged Wren's head. But both were wound tight as a drum, tensing at every unfamiliar sound, moving like strangers in their own house.

It was past ten o'clock when the two dogs perked up, ears pointing, eyes facing the door. Georgie stood and gave one sharp bark of warning. It didn't stop the person outside trying the handle of the locked door. They all watched it turn and stick, firmly closed.

"*Ewan! Ewan! It's me. It's Robbie! Let me in. Please!*"

Ewan was across the floor in a flash with the poker in his hand. He gripped it firmly then opened the door.

Robbie tumbled in, blundering halfway across the room

before managing to stop himself. He moved awkwardly, his hand cradled against his stomach. The red blotches on the front of his clothing and the wide-eyed sweatiness of his face made him look positively terrifying.

Lili was at the other side of the room, the bloody towels wadded in her hands, staring open-mouthed, rooted to the spot. He staggered towards her and grabbed her wrist with his good hand.

"Wren?"

"'obbie!"

He turned on hearing her voice.

Robbie's look of relief turned to horror as he took in the bandaged head and rag-doll form of his lover. Hobbling over, he found his knees and back unwilling to bend. He was afraid to touch her. She looked so broken. Yet she still had the wherewithal to extend a hand to him. He clasped it in his and held tight. Neither of them cared who was watching.

Lili and Ewan were deeply uncomfortable. It was the type of intimate exchange no one else was meant to see. It was the truth of Robbie and Wren's relationship. It was not something born purely out of boredom or discontentment. It was real love, real passion. For a moment Ewan felt sorry for Bertie.

"Bertie." The name caught in her mind, surging to the surface. Where was he? Had Robbie seen him? Why was Robbie battered and bloodied?

Robbie froze. His shoulders stiffened. He grunted in pain but said nothing.

Ewan stepped between his wife and the others. He had seen men coil like a spring ready for attack before.

"Robbie," he said calmly, quietly, "where's Bertie?"

Robbie did not speak. He kept his back to both of them as he stroked Wren's cheek. Finally, he turned and they saw his face was streaked with tears, red with the effort of holding in his sobs.

"He's –" He couldn't do it. He couldn't tell them. The words caught in his throat. It seemed to close over. Closing his eyes so he didn't have to see their faces, he began to sob uncontrollably. "God forgive me! Lord God forgive me ..."

Chapter 49

The blow had caught Robbie completely unawares in the small of the back. All the air went out of his body just as his knees buckled. He didn't make a sound. There wasn't enough air in his body. Twisting as he fell, Robbie saw Bertie standing over him with his mother's shovel in his hand. He had hit him with the flat blade of his own shovel.

It was this – the fact that he had been attacked with his own implement – which made Robbie force air into his lungs and launch himself at Bertie's knees. He had played rugby in school so knew how to tackle properly but, in this instance, there was no method. There was only rage. He sent Bertie crashing to the ground with a roar, wanting only to bring the other man down to his level. He would not be beaten to a pulp curled up on the floor like a child.

Bertie held fast to the spade and swung it again once, missing Robbie's face by a fraction of an inch. Robbie threw himself backwards out of reach, scrabbling on feet, hands and buttocks across the floor to the wall which he used to push himself upright. The pain in his back was almost unnoticeable. His fight instinct kicked in, dulling the sense of his own body while making him hyper-aware of everything around him. He watched Bertie stagger to his feet, cursing all the while and caught the gist of some of it.

"She told you." The calm steadiness of his own voice surprised him, faced as he was with a man wielding a shovel.

"Aye. She did." Hatred radiated from Bertie. His eyes shone like adamants in the soft light. "And now I'm going to kill you." He smiled, the flames of the fire hollowing out his eye sockets so that it seemed a skull was staring back at Robbie. "Kill you, just like I killed her."

For a split second both men stopped. Stopped moving, stopped breathing.

"*No!*" Robbie exhaled.

"I don't know," Bertie answered. The shock was plain in his voice. His own words had been an ice-cold wake-up to what he was saying, what he was doing. The red anger seemed to ebb from his system, clearing his clouded vision as he took in the white face filled with pain that stood before him. What was he doing? What had he done?

"You don't know? You don't *know*? How can you not know? What have you done?" The questions poured from Robbie's mouth, his voice growing in volume as the anger that leaked from Bertie's body soaked into his. "*What have you done?*" he screeched, advancing on his friend.

Instinct made Bertie raise the spade as Robbie's fists came swing towards him. There was a judder through the length of the handle as the blade parried Robbie's first blow. Robbie screamed in anger and agony as his knuckles shattered, bursting the skin and spitting blood from the wounds onto the floor. He made a grab for the spade as Bertie dithered over whether to attack or retreat. They had both been the instigators of this mess but one of them had to make the decision to stop. And it was not going to be Robbie.

As Bertie backed away, Robbie grabbed for the spade, ignoring the searing pain of his broken hand. They were almost nose to nose, teeth bared over the shaft of the implement as they wrestled for it, both pulling in opposite directions. But suddenly, Robbie changed tactics and gave an almighty shove.

It surprised them both and, abruptly, neither of them had a footing. Their eyes locked for a moment, panicked, before both of them crashed to the ground. Robbie felt the sting as his knees collided with the floor but it was the quiver that went through the shovel handle and his ruined hand that made him cry out.

Bertie did not cry out at all.

They had lost their footing on his mother's damned tiles. Robbie had landed on top of Bertie, knocking the air out of him. Or so Robbie thought. Then he saw the reflection of the fire's flames in unblinking eyes.

For the second time, he pushed himself off and away from his friend, only stopping when he collided with the wall. "Bertie?" he whispered. "Bertram?"

He stayed against the wall for a long time watching for a twitch of a finger, an expansion of the chest. Nothing. Bertie stayed in just the same position he had fallen in, eyes open, staring at a world he would never see again.

Eventually, something seemed to come to the surface of Robbie's mind – something that was not the horror lying in front of him.

Wren.

He tried to stand but his body was empty. The bones of his legs were not there and yet he could feel the pain in both his knees. It took a monumental effort to simply stand, never mind move. However, once he did get his feet under him, the first thing he did was turn away from the body on the floor. He did not want to see it anymore. He wanted to get away from it.

It was still raining outside. With one hand, he awkwardly draped a coat over his shoulders. For some stupid reason it now seemed important not to get wet as he set out down the lane once again. His movements were not hurried – mostly because the adrenaline was wearing off and he was now aware of the fact that he was in considerable pain: his knees, his back, his hand. He did not want to look at his hand. He had caught a glimpse of it before. It made him feel even more queasy and lightheaded than he already did. Terrified of what was behind him, terrified by what was in front of him, all he could do was place one foot in front of the other.

The door of the Gate House was open too, a lamp still burning in the kitchen. There was no one there. There was, however, clear signs of a scuffle. And blood. Lots of blood. But no Wren.

Picking up the lamp, Robbie's dizziness returned with alarming force as he swept the beam across the black pool of semi-dried blood. She had not walked away from this. Someone had carried her away. Someone with big feet by the looks of the prints on the floor.

Ewan.

Chapter 50

Lili was not aware of when she sat down. Yet as silence fell, she found she was no longer standing beside Ewan. She was in a chair and he was behind her, hands on her shoulders. She did not know if he was offering her comfort or restraining her. Probably both. Right now, all she wanted to do was hurt the snivelling boy who crouched in front of her. She followed his actions with distaste as he swept an already soaked sleeve under his nose for the umpteenth time. He looked so pitiful and yet she had no pity for him. She had only hatred.

He had killed her brother.

The man she considered a friend, the man she thought of as her brother's friend had killed him. True, Lili never got on with Bertie. There were times when they loathed one another. And yet, he was still her brother. Was. Gone now. Never to be again. But she did not cry. Instead, she felt as if there was no water in her body; parched, too hot, solid, immobile stone. The world she knew fell away leaving a dry barren landscape in front of and behind her. She could not comprehend it at all.

"Say something," Robbie pleaded. "Anything."

She did not want to oblige but his words animated her frozen limbs. She shook off Ewan's restraining hands, turned about and walked out the door into the dark of the night. Georgie went with her – a spectral presence that shadowed but never touched her. She knew better. She followed her mistress across the soaked yard to the cow shed and sat sentry in the hay where Lili subsided behind the door. It was so peaceful surrounded by the warmth of beasts all breathing evenly as they contentedly munched on the sweet, fragrant hay. Despite having the fire on in the house, the room was ice cold. Out here it was calming. It felt more like home. She was alone for some time before a shaft of light from a lantern split the cracks in the door.

Ewan stepped in. He knew her so well, he did not have to look for her. Carefully closing the door behind him, he came and sat beside her.

"How?" she finally asked.

"Bertie came at him with a shovel. They fought, Bertie fell backwards. He's got no idea what happened. Thinks Bertie must have hit his head."

"Definitely … dead?"

"He seems sure." Ewan huffed out a breath. "I think I'll have to go and check."

Lili thought for a moment then nodded. But there was something else. She sensed Ewan was on the verge of saying something but was unsure he should.

"What?" she asked.

"I don't know what to do."

"What do you mean?" Her voice was sharp. There was more and she knew it.

"I can't do it."

"What?"

"I can't turn him in." He knew she would be angry but he also knew he could not condemn his friend for accidentally killing a man intent on murdering him. The kitchen setting, the loss of footing, the bang on the head: it all reminded him of Mabel. He had not touched his wife but he had watched her slip, fall, bang her head, move no more. The two situations were different but, in his mind, Ewan could not help but connect them. He saw Robbie as himself in this instance. Even though the boy admitted fighting with Bertie, he had not intentionally caused his death – he was, like Ewan, a horrified bystander. Almost. Ewan could not denounce his friend. There was also a part of him that felt Bertie deserved what he got for what he had done to Wren and for attacking Robbie in the first place. It was Bertie's fault. Almost. True, Robbie was enjoying relations with his wife but having seen Wren with both men, he could hardly blame her for throwing over her husband in favour of Robbie. They were all young, foolish people who barely knew their own minds. And they had paid the price.

He tried to explain this to Lili who sat stony-faced in front of him, until his words petered out half in fear, half in hope.

"You want me to allow the man who killed my brother to go unpunished? The man who *killed* him to strut around as if nothing ever happened?"

"I don't think Robbie ever strutted –"

"That's not the point!" she screamed, shooting to her feet to tower over him.

He was shocked by the speed with which such an ungainly figure as his pregnant wife could move. He held up his hands to pacify her but she batted them away. He stood, catching hold of her. Though she tried to shake him off he held fast.

"Do you trust me?"

"I thought I did!" She struggled against him but he gripped her.

"Do you, or don't you?"

"Yes!" she spat reluctantly.

438

"I can't send him to the police. I know what it's like. It would break him –"

"And so it bloody well should –"

"But I can't," he said firmly. "Wren needs him."

"She could have had my brother, but *he* went off and killed him."

"We both knew they weren't suitable for one another. It was never going to end well. You said yourself that Bertie would eat her alive. And, as you see, he almost killed her, Lili."

She didn't respond.

"Wren's pregnant," he said.

Lili stared at him. A baby. *Another* baby. Just like the one that grew inside her. What a world to bring a child into! It was one emotion too many. She sat down suddenly, defeated. All the fight went out of her. It was like she was watching herself from afar. She realised she had not shed a single tear over the death of her brother. Perhaps she should try, she thought absently. "Is it Bertie's?"

Ewan sat too. "She doesn't know – but she thinks it's Robbie's."

"Thinks or wants it to be?"

"I didn't ask." He picked some hay off his trousers. "She'll need help."

"We can help."

"We'll be struggling as it is when you foal. How do you expect us to care for our own farm and hers, as well as helping with a new-born baby?"

"We'd figure something out!" she answered, but it was more to say something against his calm rationality than to show conviction.

"We can't do it," he said firmly. "But Robbie can."

"So you're going to keep him out of prison, keep him from the hangman, to look after a farm?"

"Yes," Ewan answered simply. "That and he doesn't deserve prison or the hangman. It was an accident. His conscience will haunt him enough to make him suffer for what he's done. I know mine did."

"Robbie is not you, Ewan!" Lili exclaimed.

"No. He's not. But all I have to guide me is my own experience and intuition and that tells me this is the right thing to do. Look at the situation from the outside. Allow your brother to die accidentally rather than drunk and cuckolded. Allow Wren to have a baby that won't be whispered about as it grows up. Don't stain her with adultery for the rest of her life. She can't help being young and stupid. Don't stain us, or your family, or her family or Robbie's. Keep the secret, let it be a tragic accident rather than the parish's scandal of the century."

Lili opened her mouth several times to say something. She did not like it but knew he would have an answer to any argument she had. Finally, the tears began to well and overflow, coursing down her cheeks to spatter the front of her cardigan.

"Damn you, Ewan," she sobbed. "I really hate you sometimes."

He wrapped his long, strong arms around her. She let him, burying her face in his chest as the sobs wracked her body. He kissed her hair, breathing in the smell of it and, despite the situation, he smiled.

"Good thing it is then that I always love you, hen."

Epilogue

1972

The Church Institute was closing. Not in the sense that it was closing completely but it was closing in the only way that mattered to most people: the monthly socials were to be no more.

For years the numbers had dwindled since so many people born and reared within a ten-mile radius upped and left for England never to come back. On the occasions when the emigrants returned home, their appearances were marred by incidents of drunkenness and misbehaviour as they threw their newly earned cash about with reckless abandon. The dances had increasingly been populated by drunks and unhappy confrontations. As the reputation of the dances grew worse, more and more people avoided the quaint little gatherings once frequented by their parents in favour of nights in the pub. They sat drinking and talking in the fog of cigarette smoke, slowly forgetting their taste for tea and sandwiches at the interval, neglecting the steps of the dances they once knew so well, overlooking the happy past of the Institute.

Then the Institute announced they were holding the final Friday night dance.

There was uproar in the community. Many spoke of the end of an era, the death of a tradition that went back decades. But the truth was the Church Institute had been slowly dying for years. That, however, did not stop every Church of Ireland soul within twenty miles descending on the building for that final Friday night. Young and old, married and unmarried – it did not matter. Everybody came.

Among their number were two boys – men really – going to the Institute dance for the first and last time.

Both were well – if simply – dressed. Their hands, though well-scrubbed, appeared soiled to anyone who studied them, dirt ingrained deep within their skin. Their faces, necks and exposed arms were toasted a soft brown by constant exposure to the elements. One had a prominent spray of freckles across his nose and cheeks. Though clearly youthful, they both bore the stains of hard, outdoor work. Another reason these two men were noticed – and people noticed, especially the young women – was that one of the pair was exceptionally tall. He entered the room by ducking through the door then extending to his full height. It made folks look.

The truth was, he had no need to duck through the door into the dance hall. But he was so used to doing it – and aware of the effect it had on those in the room – that he did it anyway. And they continued to look since he possessed such an arresting face: angular bones, dark hair and a wide, inviting smile. He drew the eye and drew people in.

His freckled friend – though more modest than his companion – was no less visible. He possessed a different brand of handsomeness. He was shorter – but then everyone in the room was shorter than his friend – yet his body seemed more mature having grown out of the youthful lankiness that clung to his comrade. However, his face was still rounded by boyishness enhanced by the spatter of freckles and the curly dirty blond of his hair. And though his expression was open, the hunch of his shoulders betrayed his discomfort while his friend's expansive gestures and quick laugh showed him to be in his element.

Though not alike, the casual observer might have surmised that the two were brothers given the way they interacted. They had that male closeness of familiarity, unconsciously knowing what the other was thinking and feeling. It was as if they were two halves of the same being when together but could be completely their own person when separated.

The taller of the two was Iain and, somewhat to his disgust, he had been given the job of chaperoning his two younger sisters. However, the two girls were equally disgusted by their brother's hovering. They did not like the way he stuck so closely to them since he was, no doubt, driving away potential friends, admirers and dance partners. Iain was, in fact, quite a scary personage to behold if you did not know him. He also did not mind warding off unwanted attention from his sisters. He rather enjoyed it. This was partly because it annoyed his sisters and partly because he cared a great deal for them but he only let them think it was the former that made him shadow them so diligently.

Both Iain and his companion had been given strict instructions from Iain's mother to keep an eye on the girls, otherwise she would flay them all alive.

"Don't worry, Ma, Bernie and I'll keep them straight." He directed an evil grin at his sisters.

"Give him a slap for me, Bernie," said Iain's mother.

Bernie reached up and walloped his friend as per her instructions.

"That's child cruelty, that is," Iain whined, ruefully rubbing the back of his skull.

"No, it's not," his mother answered. "He hit you and last time I checked you're a man not a babby."

It was the sort of playful conversation that was common in Iain's house. It was also part of the reason Bernie spent so much time there. He enjoyed the time he spent there, not just because his best friend lived there but because he loved feeling like part of the family – being a surrogate brother and son to all of them.

Bernie stood watching the two girls now talking to some young men. He had a vague idea that he might know them which was then confirmed by Iain bounding up to give one of them a hug, calling him by his name. And as neatly as that he had hijacked his sisters' conversation, much to their disgust.

Lucy, the younger of the two sisters, came storming over to Bernie. "Damn the bugger!" she hissed, throwing herself against the wall beside him. He hid his grin in the palm of his hand. She was staring malevolently in Iain's direction. "Can't you do something about him? He's driving us mad."

The girls rarely spoke of themselves alone. They were always a pair. But that was understandable given they were twins. The two of them were also used to catching people's eyes since only those who knew them well could tell them apart. Bernie was one of them. Even at a distance he could tell that Lucy was an inch taller while her sister, Diane, had a slightly hen-toed right foot and always rested the left one when she stood. Lucy was his favourite. She had always been the one to seek him out when they were playing as children, always the one who wanted him to carry her piggy-back unlike Diane who favoured her brother. He smiled at her. She was of a height with him in her heeled shoes.

"What do you want me to do? Dot him on the head and drag him out?"

"Preferably," she said conversationally.

He laughed. "Not sure your mammy would approve."

She pursed her lips. "No, I suppose not. But you've got to do *something*. He's ruining all our fun."

"He's your brother. Isn't that what brothers are supposed to do?"

"You don't."

"I'm not your brother though."

She took his hand and gave it a squeeze. "Yes, you are."

He was touched. So much so that he felt a lump rising in his throat. It was true that they all lived like one big happy family but he always had the nagging suspicion that he was viewed as the poor relation. Apparently not. He gave her hand a grateful squeeze back then cleared his throat and returned to the issue at hand.

"Find him a girl to distract him and then you can do whatever you like."

She pondered for a moment then nodded. "Will I get you one as well?" she asked, grinning impishly.

"Can if you like." He smirked back.

In a flash, she was gone, catching Diane – who was on her way over – by the hand and dragging her through the crowd.

Bernie had to admire the speed with which the girls worked. Within minutes they had returned with two girls, depositing the unsuspecting newcomers in front of Iain and Bernie with hasty introductions before slipping back through the crowd and being swallowed up by the swirling mass of people. There was an awkward little pause as they all sized one another up. Bernie's eyes met those of the smaller of the two girls and they smiled tentatively at one another.

"Let's dance," said Iain, grabbing his girl by the hand and swinging her onto the dance floor. She squawked a laugh as she lost her balance and Iain caught her. Bernie, being a little shy, gestured for his companion to precede him onto the floor where they took up their position in a tight little space which pressed them closer than either of them would have considered comfortable but, given the situation, seemed perfectly acceptable. The song was rather slow and quiet so they began to talk.

"You're Fiona, yes?" The introductions had been so hurried he wasn't even sure which girl was which.

"Yes. And you're Bernie, aren't you?"

"*Mmm*, that's me. Are you local? I don't recognise you."

"I'm from out the Lyre road. Do you know it?"

"Not well. But I know a few lads from out there who play rugby. Brothers."

She grinned. "They're probably mine. I'm Fiona Anderson."

"Nigel and Mervyn Anderson? I know them well." Bernie relaxed immediately. This girl was from familiar stock. Her brothers played rugby with him and farmed with their father so she couldn't be that difficult to talk to.

"I don't recognise your name from the team lists. Do you go by Bernie or Bernard?"

At this his skin flushed a dull red. "Bernie's my nickname," he muttered.

"Oh? What's your real name?"

He struggled for a moment. "I don't like my name."

"Oh, come on! It can't be that bad, surely!"

"Trust me, it is." He shook his head and shivered. He really did hate it.

"Is it something biblical? It's not Judas, is it? Or Jesus?" She looked horrified at the thought but he could tell she was teasing him.

Usually he wouldn't give in to such probing but he reckoned this girl might not tease him the way some people did. He had gone by Bernie since he was five years old. Iain had rechristened him to stop other pupils in their school from making fun of him. It was something he was eternally grateful to his friend for.

He sighed. "My name's Peregrine Burnley."

She stared at him, incredulous. "What?"

"I know."

"No."

"Yes."

"Really?" She looked so sympathetic.

"Anyway." Talk of his name made him uncomfortable. He had never really forgiven his mother for it. Maybe it was his name that made his relationship with his mother so difficult. No – it was much more than that.

Luckily, Fiona was not one to pursue a subject that made the other party uncomfortable so for the rest of the evening, they danced, chatted with the others and generally enjoyed the last social at the Church Institute. When the booing subsided into cheering and clapping after the end of the final song, those who had lasted the course drifted in an untidy trail to the chip shop, buoyed by the happy atmosphere of the Institute while lamenting the fact that it was all over.

Bernie found himself walking with Fiona. Once they had queued and purchased their chips (Bernie gallantly bought her a bag) they wandered down from the square to the river's edge along with many others.

"So," Fiona began as they munched their way through their bags, "how did you get a name like Peregrine? Or am I not allowed to ask?"

He had a chip halfway to his mouth but threw it back in the bag. "My mother's called Wren."

"That's a lovely name for a girl," Fiona said encouragingly.

"Pity there's not a male equivalent then." He worried the top of his bag so that it split and spilled chips over the newspaper it was wrapped in. Tutting, he dumped the entire bag into the paper. "I don't get on with my mother," he said apologetically when he saw the worried look on Fiona's face. "Talking about her … makes me angry."

She could have changed the subject but, sensing Bernie really wanted to tell *someone* about his mother, she asked, "Why?"

"Lots of reasons. My name firstly. And she sort of … abandoned me as a child. I was pretty much raised by my Aunt Lili. Or at least I thought she was my aunt." He looked away, but not before Fiona saw the hurt in his eyes. "My dad died in a farming accident before I was born. Fell getting over a gate and hit his head." He felt like adding, "Or that was the man I thought was my dad." Then he heard the words escape his lips and realised he had, in fact, said them aloud.

Fiona stared.

"Anyway, she married him about ten years ago now. Mam did. My godfather. My real dad. So then I found out my godfather was actually my father, then Mam married him and my actual father became my stepfather." He shook his head. "Following?"

"Just about," she answered. No wonder he was resentful. If she was struggling to follow, imagine living that life.

"When they told me, I–I got very angry."

Fiona could see the pain of the memory written on his face.

"After that, I went to my aunt's house – well, she's not actually my aunt – and I asked if I could live with her when I wasn't away at school." He smiled as the good memory washed away the bad. "She never even thought about saying no. I stayed there that night and lived there until I turned eighteen and moved into my mother's old house. She lives with her husband now, see. But I'm in and out of Lili's house every day and Iain and I help one another out all the time. And his dad, Ewan. He's helped me and taught me a lot."

They were both silent for a time, munching on their chips.

"But that was just the final straw," Bernie muttered. "I said Lili raised me and she did. Mammy ... Mammy was ... ill when I was born. Not physically sick. Suffered with her nerves."

At this, he looked down the river to where the mental institution stood high on the hill, serenely looking down on its future victims across the water. He remembered collecting his mother from Senan's for the last time with his Uncle Ewan. He had been so excited to see her again, to have the freedom to bury his nose in her sweet-smelling soft brown hair every night when they sat by the fire – just him and his mammy, the way it always was. He wanted to run to her when she came through the door to meet them but had stood rooted to the spot by the sight of her. Her hair was lank and unwashed. She had always been thin but at that time she was emaciated. And her eyes ... her eyes had been dead, glassy, shadowed by black circles. She had cried silently the entire way home and he cried too, sitting in the passenger seat beside his uncle. Ewan had held his hand for the whole journey. His mother spoke only to tell Ewan one thing.

"Take me to Robbie," she sobbed as they approached Bachelor Lane.

She had collapsed into Robbie's arms when he came out to meet the car. Neither of them had said anything. He had bundled his former lover to him and carried her into the house without a backward glance. Ewan drove back to his house with his neighbours' child sitting beside him. When he cut the engine, he had lifted the little boy onto his knee and cradled him as they both sobbed. He had then dried them both off with his handkerchief before leading the boy back into the house. Lili had looked askance at the pair of them when they entered. She had cared for him without complaint every time his mother wound up in Senan's but, whenever Wren was home, the boy stayed with his mother.

Heading off his wife's questions, Ewan simply put a hand on Bernie's shoulder and said, "He's going to be staying with us a little while longer."

He stayed for five years. Then, at the age of twelve, he moved back in with his mother before moving out again permanently when he was fourteen. It was a difficult period but most of the time the Cameron family made him forget that. They made him part of their family. In fact, he was more a part of the Cameron family than he ever was of his own mother and father's.

Bernie always thought that was strange. He was the only offspring these two people had and yet, while both of them loved him, there were also times that he seemed to repulse them. He would sometimes catch them unawares when they were looking at him and see the sorrow in their eyes. It was so confusing and hurtful as a child to see the pain when they watched him. And because of it, he tried so hard to be the best little boy he could be, to please everyone. He was helpful to his mother who so often struggled to keep going, who could spend entire days weeping constantly, pushing away her child's little hands extended in desperate, instinctive attempts to comfort her. Bernie could rarely pacify her. Only Robbie seemed to have a knack of calming her. Sometimes, Bernie was sent for him. Sometimes, he simply walked up the lane on tired little legs and got Robbie himself. On these occasions, his godfather would pick him up and bring him back down the lane where he would tuck the boy up in bed. When Robbie did this, he always kissed Bernie's forehead then made sure the old sheepdog, Tess, was lying on the foot of the bed before disappearing back downstairs to deal with the boy's mother. Bernie wondered if he tucked her up in bed too.

These occurrences were always so strange to child-Bernie. Of course, back then, he had no idea who this man really was. He was just the man up the lane and that was it. Still, Bernie always got a little thrill out of the affection the man showed him. But he was also a little frightened by him. There was always an aura of sadness that emanated from Robbie Cox that even a child could pick up on. And then there was his hand. Robbie did almost everything with his left hand – from picking up his tired son to tucking him in – since his right hand was a twisted lumpy mess of stiff, badly mended bone and scarred skin. The hand both fascinated and repulsed Bernie. It looked so deformed and painful that he wondered how his godfather could use it at all. Yet Robbie still farmed and farmed well. But when he worked, he always favoured his left hand.

That right hand.

All Bernie's family trouble seemed to stem from that. Even now as a grown man he tried not to look at it. It reminded him too much of that horrible day.

As a very small boy, Bernie had often been with Robbie on the farm, helping with what little he could do but, mostly, he would watch his godfather work. In a moment of childish curiosity on a day that was proving to be very boring to a little boy, he asked about his godfather's hand. He never got an answer. Instead, Robbie had turned on him, grabbed him by the upper arm and dragged him back to his mother, shouting incoherently about never asking questions and how nothing happened to his hand.

"*I don't want him.*" That was what Robbie said to Wren as he shoved a terrified, wailing child into the parlour.

Wren had pleaded, sobbed and pawed at Robbie until he finally roared in her face, "*He asked about my hand.*" The tears streamed down Robbie's face as he whirled about and left Bernie and his mother crying on the floor.

Wren was committed to St Senan's for the last time two days later. Bernie had been taken in by Lili and Ewan since Robbie could not even look at his godson, never mind take care of him. In subsequent years, their relations were almost completely ruined by the revelation that Robbie was Bernie's father. Yet as maturity came to Bernie, he grew to accept both his parents – to like them. But he would never be as close to his real parents as he was to all the Camerons. And now, despite his bewildering upbringing, here he was, a young man with good friends, a happy working life on his farm and a future ahead of him that was up to him to shape, not anyone else. He wanted to move forward, away from the past and continue what was good in his life. That was what he told Fiona as they sat and watched the sun rise over Enniscorthy town.

Bernie lapsed into silence after a while and was beginning to wonder whether the others had gone home without him. Iain drove them in and was meant to drive them all home again too. But if they could not find him, what was to say the Cameron siblings had not abandoned him? There it was: that constant, nagging feeling of being the 'other' among the four of them. But they would hardly do that to him, would they?

He shrugged to himself. It wasn't the end of the world if they left him behind. He could walk up the hill and ask Uncle Artie to drop him home. Or he could ask to borrow his ancient great-aunt's car. But he would have to wait for her to wake up before doing that. And he knew she slept late in her old age. If he waited for her to wake, he would be home terribly late.

"There you are! We've been looking all over for you. Oh, hello, Fiona!" It was Lucy. "Iain wants to get home to milk.

Do you want to stay here or come home with us?"

Bernie looked from one girl to other. He had his own cows to milk too but knew Iain would do it if he asked. On the other hand, what would he do if he stayed? Go up to his great-aunt's? He had spilled his guts to this stranger and could not think what else to say or do. Yet, he still wanted to stay with her. Fiona noticed his hesitation and made the decision for him.

"Go. I'm sure you've plenty to do to. But –" she rummaged in her handbag, pulling out an old receipt and a pencil. She scrawled a number on the back. "That's the home phone number. Mammy or Daddy'll probably answer it but just ask for me. If you want."

His face split into a beautiful, wide grin. "I will," he promised before bending down to peck her on the cheek. "See you."

"You too." She waved him goodbye as he made his way along the riverbank with Lucy.

Just out of earshot, his cousin turned to him. "Oooo! *Someone's got an admirer!*" she sang.

He gave her a playful push. She pushed back. "I thought I had many admirers, you being one of them." He threw his arm around her shoulders.

"Don't flatter yourself," she tutted, poking him in the ribs.

"Don't need to. Got plenty of people to do it for me."

Lucy snorted. He reached up and mushed her hair with irritating but brotherly love. She squawked in protest and disentangled herself from his grasp, running ahead to where her brother and sister were waiting with the car.

Iain was draped over the driver's door, the picture of absolute boredom but he perked up on seeing them and stood to his full height.

"*Git yer tardy arses moving, ye lavvy heided clots,*" he called in an expert imitation of his father. "*A've git worrrk tea do.*"

They all piled into the car and, dropping back into his normal voice (though it was a little hoarse from the night's festivities), "Mam said she'd have a fry on for all of us for brekkie when we get home."

"That include me?" Bernie asked.

They all turned and stared at him.

"Why wouldn't it?" Iain asked. "You're part of the family."

Breakfast with the family. But not before milking. And, of course there were all the other jobs to do on the farm that day. And maybe, just maybe, he'd make a certain phone call later in the evening. Breakfast with the family and a chat with a nice girl: happy thoughts to sustain him throughout the day and perhaps have a little daydream about. His life was not an easy one but, at the very least, it was a happy one.

He smiled the entire way home.

THE END